KU-103-017

DIE WITH ME

DIE WITH ME

Elena Forbes

ISIS
LARGE PRINT
Oxford

Copyright © Elena Forbes, 2007

First published in Great Britain 2007
by
Quercus

Published in Large Print 2007 by ISIS Publishing Ltd.,
7 Centremead, Osney Mead, Oxford OX2 0ES
by arrangement with
Quercus

All rights reserved

The moral right of the author has been asserted

British Library Cataloguing in Publication Data
Forbes, Elena
    Die with me. – Large print ed.
    1. Teenage girls – Crimes against – Fiction
    2. Detective and mystery stories
    3. Large type books
    I. Title
    823.9'2 [F]

MORAY COUNCIL
DEPARTMENT OF TECHNICAL
& LEISURE SERVICES
F

ISBN 978–0–7531–7918–5 (hb)
ISBN 978–0–7531–7919–2 (pb)

Printed and bound in Great Britain by
T. J. International Ltd., Padstow, Cornwall

20223981

For Clio and Louis

ACKNOWLEDGEMENTS

Thanks are due to a number of people for their expert advice, as well as apologies for my having ignored it on occasion in the interest of fiction. Any errors are entirely mine. From the Metropolitan Police, Consultant Senior Investigating Officer David Niccol and Tracy Alexander of the Forensic Directorate deserve a particular mention for their invaluable assistance and good humour. I also would like to thank Detective Chief Superintendent Andy Murphy, Detective Chief Inspector David Little and Detective Superintendent Jill McTigue for their help. Thanks go to Jeremy Silewicz, Wayne Kenward and George Andraos for enlightening me on the subjects of Polish vodka, Italian motorbikes and Wi-Fi hotspots, and to my friends and fellow crime writers at Criminal Classes: Margaret Kinsman, Gerry O'Donovan, Richard Holt, Keith Mullins, Cass Bonner, Nicola Williams, and particularly Kathryn Skoyles. Special thanks are due to my agent Sarah Lutyens, to my editor Sue Freestone, and to everyone at Quercus, as well as to Lisanne Radice for words of wisdom. Lastly, I am indebted to Stephen Georgiadis and Jeanne Scott-Forbes for their support and input along the way.

CHAPTER
ONE

The tombstone was nearly six feet tall, weathered and mottled with lichen. A pair of fat-cheeked cherubs framed the inscription: "How short is life, how soon comes death." Soon comes death. So very true. She was late, his bride, his partner 'til death do us part. More than ten bloody minutes late, he noticed, checking his watch yet again. Had she no sense of occasion? Didn't she care that he was standing there in the cold, waiting for her? Soon it would be dark. People would start leaving work to go home and they would miss their chance.

He glanced towards the entrance to the churchyard, his breath a pale cloud blown away by the wind. Still nothing. Stamping his feet hard on a horizontal grave slab for warmth, hands jammed deep in the pockets of his overcoat, he backed into the recess of the church porch. For ceremony's sake he had thought of pinning a flower in his buttonhole but had decided against it. Too noticeable. Besides, he hated flowers.

Where the hell was she? Maybe she had never meant to come. Maybe she had just been stringing him along all the time. Digging his nails into his palms at the thought, he jerked his head over his shoulder and spat on the ground, imagining what he would do to her if she stood him up. Telling himself not to worry, he examined the thick skeins of cobwebs that stretched like gauze between the pillars of the porch, focusing on a fat, dead fly imprisoned in the sticky mesh. She'd be here. She had to come. She wouldn't dare let him down.

He caught a movement out of the corner of his eye and swung round to face the road. Framed by the wrought iron archway at the end of the path, she stood at the top of the steps looking up towards him, eyes startled. Her white face, curtained by long waves of hair, seemed like a full moon, featureless. Sweat pricked his palms and a swell of excitement swept over him, tingling down his back, making the hairs on his neck stand on end. He exhaled sharply. Moistening his lips with his tongue, he smoothed down his hair with his fingers, watching as she came through the gate and walked towards him up the path. Her movements were jerky, like a little bird, nervous, hesitating, never taking her eyes off him. She was younger than he had imagined, no more than fourteen or fifteen. His maiden, his bride. She was perfect. The breath caught in his throat and he was unable to speak.

Dressed in nothing but black, as he had insisted, she was wearing an old raincoat, several sizes too large, that looked as though it had been borrowed or bought in a second-hand shop. Beneath it peeped the uneven fringe of a long skirt and heavy boots with a strap and silver buckle at the ankle. He noticed all the details, pleased that she had done as she was told.

2

She stopped a few feet away as if unsure, peering short-sightedly at him. "Are you Tom?"

Her voice was pitched high, her enunciation childlike. He detected a slight accent but couldn't place it. Trying to contain his excitement, he stepped out of the shadows and smiled, reaching out his arm to welcome her.

"Gemma."

Trembling, tentative, she offered him a small hand from beneath the rolled-up coat sleeve. Her fingers were icy and limp as he pressed them briefly to his lips. As he touched her skin, he caught the faint smell of Pears soap, kindling old, unpleasant memories. He let her hand drop a little too quickly and she looked away, embarrassed, folding her arms tightly and hugging herself. Gently, he took her by the elbow and pulled her towards him.

"Dear Gemma. You're so beautiful, you know. Much more than I'd imagined. Much, much more. So very beautiful."

Still gazing at her feet, she flushed, giving a shy wriggle of pleasure. No doubt it was the first time anyone had ever said those words to her.

"You're sure you want to do this?" he said.

She glanced up at him, her pale-lashed eyes searching his face, looking for reassurance, maybe, or something else. Did she like what she saw? Did she find him handsome? Of course she did. He could see it in her eyes. He was everything she had hoped for, and more. He had filled her dreams for so long and now here he was, Prince Charming, standing in front of her, flesh and blood.

On a hot summer's night, would you offer your throat to the wolf with the red roses? Why did that bloody song keep popping up in his mind? *Will he offer me his mouth? Yes. Will he offer me his teeth? Yes. Will he offer me his jaws? Yes. Will he offer me his hunger? Yes. And will he starve without me? Yes.* The hunger. The yearning. So difficult to control. *And does he love me? Yes.* He had said that he loved her.

He bent down to kiss her properly. Again that foul whiff of Pears. Had she scrubbed herself all over with it? He tried to block it out, watching as she gave a little sigh, screwing her eyelids tight shut as she yielded, her lips in a tight moue, like a child's kiss. He was surprised at her inexperience. Most girls her age were little better than whores.

He kissed her again, allowing his lips to linger for a moment, touching her mouth ever so lightly with his tongue, feeling her soften beneath his grasp as he observed her, the un-plucked eyebrows, the fine golden down on her cheeks, the faded dusting of freckles on her nose. The winter light bleached the colour from her face, giving her a deathly pallor. He was sure she was a virgin, although that had no special appeal for him.

After what he considered to be long enough, he stepped back and she opened her eyes. They were a clear blue, without doubt her best feature. Trusting eyes, soft and innocent. She really was perfect. He smiled at his good fortune, showing her his beautiful white teeth.

"You're really sure? You're not just wasting my time?"

She looked away as if his gaze burnt her, fingers fiddling with a thread hanging from the end of her coat sleeve.

"I'm serious about this, you know," he said, watching her closely. "You're not going to let me down?"

She shook her head slowly but he was unconvinced. He touched her lightly under the chin, making her look up at him again.

"Come on. We're in this together. *Together, forever, you and I.*"

The words came from another song but it was the sort of trite thing she liked. Easily pleased, she had lapped up the poetry he had sent her, all about love and about death. It seemed to touch a chord, opening a floodgate of confession and neediness. The pain, the loneliness, the sad catalogue of neglect and unhappiness. He understood her so well. He was her soul mate, her first and only love.

"Us. Together. Never parted. It's what you wanted, isn't it? It's what you said." He stared at her, trying to inject warmth into his expression, trying to tamp down his impatience. "We don't belong in this world. You know it's the only way."

Gulping, she nodded slowly, tears welling.

"Good. I've got everything we need in here." He patted his rucksack and swung it over his shoulder. Bending forward, he kissed her quickly again. "Come, my darling. It's time." Clamping an arm around her, he marched her into the dimly-lit interior of the church.

The air was stale; damp mingling with the stench of rotting flowers from various stands of wilted white roses and chrysanthemums placed at intervals along the aisle. He couldn't imagine why anyone would choose this church to be married in. There was no atmosphere, nothing remarkable about the bare, cavernous interior with its marble plaques, war memorials and anonymous rows of brown pews, nothing to attract tourists or other casual visitors. It was a neglected place, unloved and unfrequented. Security was also extraordinarily absent, although there was nothing worth taking. He had done his research and chosen it carefully. Weekday mid-afternoons were a void time, perfect for what lay ahead.

Gemma stood transfixed, gazing up at the round stained-glass window at the end of the nave above the altar, its jewel colours illuminated by the dim light from outside. The martyrdom of St Sebastian, early nineteenth century, he remembered reading in the church pamphlet. St Catherine or St Joan would have been a more appropriate backdrop but female martyrs were thin on the ground in London.

He jerked her by the elbow. "Come on. Someone could come along any minute and we can't risk being disturbed."

She allowed herself to be propelled towards the heavy-curtained archway near the pulpit. Behind was a long flight of stairs leading to the organ and the empty gallery high above the nave. As he pulled back the curtain, she stopped and peered up into the dark area above.

"It's so high," she said, drawing out the word "high" as if it were something shocking.

He knew he was going to have trouble. He wanted to say that "high" was the whole point, as she damn well knew. "High" was what it was all about. They'd discussed everything at length. Now was not the time for doubts. For a moment, he pictured her wheeling above him, spinning through the air, her black raincoat fanning out behind her like the wings of a huge crow. He could hear the sound of it flapping and he felt almost feverish.

"Come on, I'm with you. Just a little further now." He took hold of her wrist and started to drag her up the first flight of stairs.

She tried to pull her arm away. "You're hurting me."

He caught the puzzled look in her eyes and let go. "Sorry, my darling. I'm just feeling nervous, that's all. I've waited so long for this. For you. I'll follow you, shall I?"

He watched as she stumbled up the stairs. At the top, she wavered, then collapsed in a heap on the landing. Putting her head in her hands, she bent over double, her hair falling over her face and down her legs like a sleek, brown cloak. Half choking, she started to sob.

Shit. This was all he needed. Even though the sound was muffled, somebody might hear. He wanted to jam his hand over her mouth but he mustn't alarm her. He knelt down on the stair below her, holding her knees, which were clamped tightly together. He would do anything if it would only make her shut up. Slowly, he started to massage her thighs through the thick woollen layers of her skirt.

"It's going to be OK. If you don't want to do it, we don't have to." He cupped his hands around her head and kissed her hair over and over again, feeling almost high with worry. "Please stop crying. Really, it's OK. I'm just so glad I met you." If only she would look at him, he was sure he could win her around. "We don't have to do it. We don't have to, you know." He took her tiny hands in his and peeled them away from her face, forcing her to raise her head, eyes still tight shut. "Look at me, Gemma. We'll do whatever you want. Really . . . I mean that. I love you."

Slowly she opened her eyes and he rewarded her with one of his softest smiles, brushing her wet, sticky hair off her face, using the edge of her coat sleeve to wipe away the slime around her nose and lips.

"I don't want to," she whispered, trembling as she gazed at him. "I don't want to . . ." She couldn't finish the sentence. Die. Die with me. Be mine forever. That's what he had said.

He rose, went over to her and sat down on the step beside her. Wrapping his arm tightly around her, he pulled her into him, cradling her head against his shoulder.

"Nor do I, my darling, nor do I." Stroking her soft hair, he kissed the top of her head. "Not now I've met you, anyway. Do you feel that too?"

She nodded, pressing her head hard into his coat sleeve.

"You've saved me, you know. You're so very special. My little Gemma. Shall we do the ceremony anyway? I have everything ready. Shall we exchange rings as we planned?" She gave a squeak of assent, burying deep into him, nuzzling his shoulder like a kitten. "Very special," he said, still stroking her hair, trying to soothe her. "So very special."

She started as if stung by something, her hand flying to her mouth as she looked up at him.

"What's the matter?"

"The note. I left a note like you told me. What happens when Mum finds it?"

Was that all? He smiled with relief. "Don't worry. We can either get it back or . . ." he let the sentence hang before continuing, "you can come and stay with me. Then it won't matter. You don't have to go home, if you don't want to. There's no way they'll find us. No way at all."

She blushed, glancing at him out of the corner of her eye as she returned the smile. For a moment, in spite of her swollen eyes and blotchy face, she looked almost pretty.

"Come on then. I think you'll like the gallery. It's very private, a really special place. Nobody will bother us there."

He stood up and helped her to her feet, patting down the folds of her coat and brushing away the dust and fluff from the floor. Barely able to contain himself, he took her by the hand and kissed it one last time, closing his eyes briefly as he pictured again what was to come. She was his. All his. He was sure.

CHAPTER
TWO

There was no justice in life. DI Mark Tartaglia gazed
through the glass porthole of the door to the intensive
care room where his boss, DCI Trevor Clarke, was
stretched out in bed, at the centre of a spaghetti
junction of wires and tubes. Apart from the dark strip
of moustache visible beneath the oxygen mask, Clarke
was unrecognisable. He'd been in a coma ever since the
accident, his head held fast in a clamp to protect his
injured spine, with his shattered pelvis and legs
surrounded by a metal cage. Thank God he'd been
wearing a helmet and proper clothing when he came off
his motorbike. But the prognosis wasn't good.

Sally-Anne, Clarke's fiancée, sat by the bed, head
bowed, one of Clarke's huge hands cupped in hers. She
was dressed in a bright pink and white checked suit, her
long, blonde hair pulled back in a ponytail tied with a
gold ribbon. Tartaglia had just missed her the day
before when he had called by and he didn't relish
seeing her now. For a moment he thought about
coming back later. But sod it, Clarke was one of his
best mates; he had every right to be there too. He
rapped on the glass panel, opened the door and went
in.

Sally-Anne looked round briefly. Her eyes were red, rimmed with mascara. He wasn't sure if she was crying for Clarke or for herself. Any woman who could up sticks and leave two small kids and a husband for another man, even if it was someone as nice as Clarke, had to be selfish beyond belief. And it had all happened so fast. Impulsive as always, Clarke never did things by halves. One minute she was just the new bit of squeeze, brought along for the occasional drink or bite to eat. Next thing, she was living in his flat in Clapham, he'd put her name on his mortgage and bank account and now that her divorce had come through, they were talking about getting hitched. But that was before the accident. Maybe Tartaglia was being harsh, but he couldn't imagine Sally-Anne looking after a paraplegic for the rest of her life.

"Any progress?" Tartaglia asked, walking over to the foot of the bed. He'd already heard from Clarke's nurse that there was none but he didn't know what else to say. The longer Clarke stayed in a coma, the worse the likely outcome.

Sally-Anne shook her head, stroking the top of Clarke's hand with her long pink nails, gazing fixedly at what could be seen of his face as if she were willing him to open his eyes or speak. Tartaglia wondered how long she had been there and what was going through her mind. Conversation seemed pointless and he stood behind her, feeling awkward, the silence punctuated by the bleeping of the monitors around the bed and the episodic shushing of the ventilator.

After a moment, Sally-Anne muttered something to Clarke that sounded like "see you later", carefully placed his hand back on top of the sheet, patted it and stood up. Straightening her short skirt, she picked up her handbag and turned to Tartaglia, tears in her eyes.

"I hate hospitals. I hate the smell. It reminds me of having my appendix out when I was a kid and I feel so bloody useless. What's the point of coming? What good can I do? I mean, he doesn't even know I'm here."

Avoiding her gaze, Tartaglia shrugged and stuffed his hands in his pockets. He was there because he cared about Clarke, because he wanted to see him, poor bastard. Of course it wouldn't do Clarke any good, in the state he was in. But that wasn't the point. Even if it was a pretty empty gesture, it was a mark of their friendship, of respect.

She took a tissue out of her bag and blew her nose. Her eyes fastened onto the motorbike helmet under Tartaglia's arm. "Stupid prat. Why did Trevor have to go and buy that wretched bike? He hasn't ridden one in years."

Her tone was bitter and Tartaglia wondered if somehow she held him personally to blame, as he was close to Clarke and the only other member of the murder team to ride a motorbike. For a moment he thought of the gleaming red Ducati 999 in the hospital car park and felt almost guilty. But if Sally-Anne thought he'd led Clarke astray, she was wrong. Mid-life crisis was the phrase that came to mind. At least, that was the joke around the office. Six months, almost to the day, after Clarke's wife left him for her yoga teacher, he'd started WeightWatchers and joined the local gym. Next came the motorbike, the contact lenses, the garish shirts and the leather jacket. What with the seventies-style moustache he refused to shave off, he was starting to look like one of the Village People. Just when they were all wondering if Clarke was going to come out of the closet, along came Sally-Anne, almost young enough to be his daughter, and his brief second stint as a single man was over. Clarke was well aware of what his work mates thought but he didn't seem to mind. He was just happy and at peace with the world. That should have been all that mattered but Tartaglia couldn't help worrying that Clarke would end up getting hurt.

Sally-Anne was still staring at Tartaglia, arms clasped tightly around her handbag. "You know, I just keep hoping he's going to open his eyes. That's all I want. Just to know that he's still all there, up top, I mean. Anything else, we can learn to cope with together."

The way she spoke sounded genuine and he felt a little surprised. Had he been wrong about her? Did she really love Clarke after all?

"Have you thought about playing him some music?" he said, feeling embarrassed, wanting to appear helpful if nothing else. "You know, something he'll recognise. They say it sometimes works."

"That's not a bad idea. I suppose anything's worth a try, given the state he's in. But a Walkman's definitely out." Gulping, she gave a wry smile in Clarke's direction. "I mean, where would you put the headphones?"

She had a point. You could barely make out Clarke's eyes, let alone his ears. "What about one of those portable machines with speakers?"

She nodded slowly, as if he had said something important. "We've got one in the kitchen at home. I'll bring it in this evening with some CDs. Trev really loves Celine Dion, for some weird reason. Maybe the sound of her voice will wake him up, even if mine won't."

Tartaglia grimaced. "God, I'd forgotten he has such crap taste in music. If I were you, I'd try and find something he really hates, like Eminem or 50 Cent. He's such an ornery bastard, you should play it really loud right next to him and see what happens. That'll do the trick, if anything will."

She gave him a wistful smile. "I can just imagine him shouting at me to turn it off. That would be good, wouldn't it?"

She looked up into his eyes for reassurance. Although her face had brightened momentarily, tears were still not far away. In spite of the make-up and sophisticated clothes, she looked like a young girl. She hesitated, head slightly to one side as if there was something else she wanted to say. But after a second she just touched his arm and walked past him, her impossibly high heels squeaking on the linoleum.

Opening the door, she glanced back at him. "Maybe see you tomorrow. If there's any change before then, I'll let you know."

As the door closed behind her, Tartaglia's mobile rang. In spite of the hundreds of notices plastered around the hospital, he had forgotten to switch it off.

14

He flipped it open and heard the smooth tones of Detective Superintendent Clive Cornish, at the other end.

"Are you with Trevor?"

"Yes, but I'm about to leave."

"Any progress?"

"None, I'm afraid," Tartaglia said, turning away and whispering into the mouthpiece, as if Clarke might somehow be able to hear him. "But at least he's still alive."

Cornish gave a heavy sigh. Clarke was well liked and respected by everybody, even Cornish, a man not normally known for warmth or feelings of compassion towards anyone. "That's something, I suppose. Anyway, I need you over in Ealing right away, at a church called St Sebastian's. It's on South Street, just off the main drag. I've told Donovan to meet you there. There's been a suspicious death. With Trevor out of action for the foreseeable future, you're now the acting SIO."

St Sebastian's was set back a little above the road in a leafy residential area, a high wall with iron railings forming the boundary. Bathed in bright winter sunshine, the church was plain, with simple, graceful lines and tall stone pillars flanking the entrance. Georgian, Tartaglia thought, from the little he knew of architecture. It seemed at odds with the endless criss-cross streets of ornate Edwardian redbrick terraced houses that surrounded it, as if it had been taken from somewhere else and plonked down in the middle of Ealing by mistake.

DS Sam Donovan stood huddled by the main gate, hands jammed in her coat pockets, eyes watering and nose red from the cold.

"You took your time," she said, shivering. "It's bloody freezing out here and I'll probably catch my death now."

Tiny and slim, with brutally short, spiky brown hair that framed an otherwise pretty, regular-featured face, she was wearing a purple coat, baggy trousers and Doc Martens, her chin tucked into the thick folds of a long, woolly, lime green scarf, wrapped several times around her neck.

"Sorry. The traffic was bad. I've been over at St Mary's, seeing Trevor."

"How is he?" she asked, ducking under the crime scene tape and leading the way up the steps to the churchyard.

"Unfortunately, no change. But I'll fill you in later." They started to walk together slowly up the long path that curved towards the church door. "Cornish said we've got an unexplained death."

She nodded, taking a crumpled paper tissue from her pocket and blowing her nose loudly, as if she was trying to make a point. "I've had a full briefing with DI Duffey from the on-call MIT. The victim's a fourteen-year-old girl called Gemma Kramer. She fell from the organ gallery inside the church two days ago. Ealing CID initially assumed it was an accident or suicide."

"Was there a note?"

"No. But they didn't find anything suspicious about her death and, after what sounds a pretty cursory forensic exam of the ground floor, the crime scene was released."

"Released?" he said, pausing in the middle of the path and turning to her.

"Afraid so. Apparently there'd been some pressure from the vicar and some locals to reopen the church for a christening."

Shaking his head, he moved on again, Donovan at his side. Manning a cordon around a crime scene twenty-four hours a day was an expensive business and with resources stretched, as always, it wouldn't be the first time such a thing had happened.

"So what changed their minds?"

"Just after the church was cleaned up and re-opened for business, a witness materialises out of the woodwork saying she saw the girl going into the church with a man a couple of hours before her body was found. Somebody then has the sense to ask for a full tox analysis and when the report comes back, it's panic stations. The girl had traces of alcohol and GHB in her system."

"GHB? Was she sexually assaulted?"

"Not according to DI Duffey. The crime scene was re-sealed immediately and a thorough forensic investigation was carried out of the whole church. It was only a cursory clean, hopefully not much damage was done."

"We should be thankful for small mercies, I suppose," he said, stopping again for a moment and glancing around the churchyard, wanting to get his bearings.

The graves were so crowded together that the whole area was almost entirely paved, with hardly a blade of grass to be seen. The stones were deeply weathered and most of the inscriptions barely readable. It seemed that nobody had been buried there for many years. He pulled out a Marlboro red from a pack in his pocket and turned his back to the wind to light it, letting the sun warm his face for a moment.

"Is the girl local?" he asked, taking a long, deep drag and watching the smoke gust away on the cold air.

"No. She's from Streatham. Nobody has a clue what she was doing around here."

"Tell me about the witness."

"I've just been to see her. She's called Mrs Brooke. She's in her late sixties or early seventies and lives a couple of streets away. Don't be put off by her age," she added, no doubt seeing the sceptical look on his face. "She used to be a ladies fashion buyer for Selfridges and has quite an eye for detail. She seemed pretty reliable to me."

He smiled. "OK. I'll take your word for it. What time was all this?"

"Just after four in the afternoon. She was going out to tea with a friend and was sitting in the shelter across the road, waiting for a bus."

Turning, he saw an old-fashioned bus shelter about twenty yards away, partially obscured by a tight row of tombstones and an ancient yew tree.

"According to Mrs Brooke, Gemma came from that direction," Donovan continued, pointing across him to the left. "The Tube's that way, so we assume that's how she got to Ealing. Gemma crossed the road and went up the steps into the churchyard. The next time Mrs Brooke looked over, she was kissing some bloke just over there, in front of the porch. She said she felt a bit shocked as Gemma looked very young and the man was quite a bit older. Then they went into the church together."

"Mrs Brooke saw all of this from where she was sitting?"

"So she says."

Tartaglia strode up the path to the porch and wheeled round. "According to her, they were standing here?"

"That's right."

He looked back across the churchyard to the road in front. At four in the afternoon it would have been getting dark but the line of sight to the bus stop was relatively clear and he felt reassured that Mrs Brooke would have had a good view.

"How old did she say the man was?" Tartaglia asked, taking another pull on his cigarette as Donovan caught him up.

"She thought he was in his thirties or possibly early forties, but she couldn't be sure. He was a lot taller than Gemma, as he had to bend right down when he kissed her. Although, given that Gemma was apparently about my height, that's not saying much." Donovan smiled. She was not much over five foot and proud of it.

He glanced back again at the shelter. Even at this time of day, the interior was shadowed. From where he was standing, it was almost impossible to see if anyone was inside. Maybe Gemma and her friend had been unaware that they were being observed, or maybe they didn't care.

"Do we have a description of the man?"

"White, with dark hair, wearing a dark coat or jacket. He must have been waiting in the churchyard for Gemma, as Mrs Brooke didn't see him arrive."

"Did she see him leave?"

Donovan shook her head. "After a few minutes, the bus came along and she got on. She didn't think anything more about it until she saw the CID boards appealing for witnesses. So far, she's the only person to come forward."

"What have forensics turned up?"

"Just the usual condoms, sweet papers and cigarette butts in the churchyard. But don't get too excited. None of it's recent."

"With the weather we've been having, I'm not surprised."

"I didn't know cold weather was ever a deterrent," she said with a wry grin. "Anyway, I'm going to catch my death out here. Can we go inside?"

He nodded, stubbed out his cigarette and pushed open one half of the heavy panelled door, Donovan slipping under his outstretched arm.

The interior of the church was barn-like, with a high, vaulted ceiling. Light flooded in through various ornate stained glass windows, casting a kaleidoscope of colours and patterns on the walls and the black and white marble floor. The temperature was almost as cold as outside, and an unpleasant musty smell hung in the damp air, coupled with a strange sourness. Decay, he thought. Things rotting away. The smell of neglect and penny pinching. Like so many English churches, the place was redolent of the past, a past with little relevance or connection to the present, the brass work tarnished, the embroidered kneelers threadbare and disintegrating, the memorial plaques that plastered the walls commemorating people long since dead and forgotten.

Although born and brought up a Catholic in Edinburgh, his Catholicism was well lapsed and not a matter that caused him any loss of sleep. But the churches of his youth were places of warmth, much frequented and loved, an integral part of family life and the community, very different to St Sebastian's. The last time he'd set foot inside a church had been at least a year before, when his sister, Nicoletta, had dragged him along to Sunday mass at St Peter's, the Italian church in Clerkenwell, before one of her marathon family-and-friends lunches. The atmosphere in the church had hummed: the air thick with the smell of incense; the rows of crystal chandeliers shimmering; every surface waxed and gleaming; and the metalwork polished within an inch of its life. The pews had been packed, with everyone in their Sunday best. It was a riot of colour and richness. Afterwards, hundreds of people thronged the pavement outside, gossiping and stopping at one of the many local bars and cafés for an espresso or grappa. Looking around the drab interior of St Sebastian's, he couldn't imagine such a scene. It felt unused and uncared for. A sad and lonely place for a young girl to die.

He followed Donovan down the nave, stopping in front of a large dark green stain that spread messily outwards across the marble floor.

"This is apparently where the girl fell."

In order to pinpoint the spot where Gemma Kramer had died, the forensic team had used the chemical LMG to reveal the original blood traces. Around the outside, spatters and tracks from a mop and some sort of brush used to scrub the floor were easily visible, the wash of green fading into a pale verdigris at the edges, shot with bright blue and yellow light from one of the huge, arched windows. Tartaglia gazed up at the wide gallery that spanned the full width of the nave high above, an ornately carved balustrade running along the edge. The thought of the girl plummeting down from such a height made him shiver. Short of a miracle, no one could survive that fall.

"What time was the body found?" he asked, still staring up into the dark space of the gallery, the tall gilt pipes of the organ just visible at the back.

"Just after six, when someone came to tidy up for the evening service. They have Holy Communion at seven-fifteen on a Wednesday."

"So nobody came in here between four and six?"

She shook her head. "According to Duffey, the vicar leaves the main church unlocked for prayer but it's usually empty in the afternoon. I don't think they get many worshippers or visitors."

Finding it extraordinary that it was left unsecured, particularly given its apparent state of disuse, Tartaglia wondered what had brought the girl to such a place. Was it by chance? Or had she and the man known that the church was left unlocked?

"How do we get up to the gallery?" he said.

"Follow me." She walked over to a narrow archway to one side of the pulpit. As she pulled back the heavy red velvet curtain that hung across it, a cloud of dust flew up into the air, the particles dancing in a shaft of sunshine from above. She fumbled around behind the curtain, switching on a series of lights and illuminating the staircase and gallery.

Tartaglia started up the long, steep flight of stairs, Donovan making heavy weather just behind him.

"You know, you really should give up the fags," he said to her when she finally reached the top.

She smiled, still out of breath. "You're hardly one to talk. Anyway, I've been trying the patches but I think I've become addicted to them too."

"They didn't work for me either." Instinctively he felt in his pocket for his cigarettes.

She gave him a withering look.

He turned away, glancing around the gallery. Apart from the organ and the rows of stalls for the choir, it was empty. He walked over to the balustrade and gripped the heavy wooden rail with his hands, trying to see if there was any give. But the whole thing felt solid as stone. It was also a good four feet high. There was no way the girl could have fallen over it by accident. He stared down at the wide green stain way below. The area was now streaked with deep red and gold light and for a moment he pictured her lying there, a small, dark form, broken on the marble paving. Whatever had happened, it was a violent and horrible death.

He turned back to Donovan. "Are there any signs of a struggle?"

She nodded. "They found several clumps of long hair near the edge of the balcony which may belong to Gemma. The hair was pulled out at the root, so they'll be able to compare the DNA. They also found traces of candle wax and incense and what looks like red wine spilt on the floor."

He shrugged. "We are in a church, after all. Are they sure it's recent?"

"There was choir practice on Monday night but the floor was apparently cleaned on Tuesday morning. The vicar says nobody's been in the gallery since. Samples have gone off for analysis and we should get the results back soon."

The combination of incense, candle wax and wine instantly conjured up the idea of a mass or some other sort of ritual. Maybe it was black magic or a form of New Age ceremony, he thought. A young girl and an older man. Even though there appeared to be no evidence of sexual assault, the presence of the GHB in Gemma's system rang alarm bells. The drug, like Rohypnol, was becoming increasingly common in date rape cases. He wondered if the choice of a church as the location was significant in some way. Had Gemma been a willing participant in whatever had gone on, or had she been forced? Had the man dragged her or held her down by her hair for some reason? Had she struggled? Hopefully the post mortem results would reveal more. The main question now was what had become of the man?

"If you've seen enough, we ought to be going," Donovan said, checking her watch. "We've got a meeting with the pathologist in just over half an hour, in Victoria."

"Who did the PM?" he asked, as they started to walk back together towards the stairs.

"Dr Blake."

Tartaglia tensed, glancing quickly over at Donovan. But there wasn't a glimmer of anything untoward in her expression. Being realistic, there was no way she could know what had been going on. No way any of them could. At least he hoped so. He sighed. Shit. Shit. Why did it have to be Fiona Blake?

CHAPTER
THREE

The last time Tartaglia had seen Fiona Blake, she'd been lying naked next to him in his bed. That had been about a month ago and he'd barely spoken to her since.

Today she was dressed in a prim grey suit, auburn hair scraped back tightly in a bun, white blouse buttoned up tight to the collar, as if she was trying to hide any hint of femininity or softness.

"There's no sign of sexual assault," she said in her usual precise tone. "In fact, Gemma Kramer was a virgin."

She stared at him across her desk as if they were total strangers and for a moment he had to remind himself of the intensity he had so recently felt. She had kept him and Donovan waiting outside in the corridor for nearly half an hour. He was sure it was deliberate and it made him feel even more awkward and nervous of seeing her in an official capacity, particularly with Donovan there too. But he felt grateful that Donovan was sitting beside him now, a protective shield, her presence inhibiting any possibility of a more personal conversation.

"I understand you found traces of GHB in her system," Donovan said.

"Yes, and alcohol. There was a small amount of red wine in her stomach. Both were ingested shortly before death."

"GHB's not known as Easy Lay for nothing," Tartaglia said. "Are you sure she wasn't assaulted in some way?"

Blake gave him a piercing look. "As I said, Inspector, I found no evidence of any form of sexual activity."

The use of his title felt like a slap in the face. Although why she should be feeling angry was beyond him. It had been good, better than good, if he was honest, for the short while it had lasted. It had only come to a sudden halt when he had found out accidentally from someone else that she had a long-term boyfriend called Murray, a fact that she had never bothered to mention. He remembered the last terse phone call when, ignoring the subject of Murray, as if it made no difference to anything, she'd suggested that they meet up as usual. He'd shouted at her, told her to leave him alone, to stop calling. Angry with himself as much as with her, he'd slammed the phone down before she could say anything else. Finally he had understood why she could only see him at odd hours, why they only ever met at his flat and why her mobile was invariably switched off late at night and at weekends.

"I suppose there's no way of telling if it was mixed with the wine and then drunk, or if they were taken separately?"

She shifted in her chair, and looked away towards the window. "I can see what you're thinking, but I can't help you. Maybe the wine was spiked, but it's impossible to tell. People do take GHB recreationally, you know."

He shook his head. "The girl was barely fourteen, and a church seems a pretty strange place to choose, if all you want to do is get high." As he spoke, he noticed a large, single diamond on Blake's ring finger. It looked like an engagement ring. Perhaps conscious of his gaze, she slid her hands off the table and folded them in her lap behind the desk.

"Would she have been aware of what was going on around her?" Donovan asked.

Blake gave her a tight smile. "Like someone a little drunk."

"No more than that?"

"With the right dose, the effects are placidity, sensuality and mild euphoria. Anxieties dissolve into a feeling of emotional warmth, well-being and pleasant drowsiness."

"You mean she would lose her inhibitions," Donovan said, glancing at Tartaglia for confirmation. They were obviously thinking along the same lines.

He nodded. "And fear."

"It produces a heightening of the sense of touch, increased sexual enjoyment and performance for both men and women," Blake continued, ignoring where they were going with this.

"Which is why I keep coming back to a sexual motive," Tartaglia said, rapping his fingers lightly on the edge of the desk. "Picture this. Gemma was with a much older man. She met him outside the church —

clearly they had arranged to meet there. They kiss, so we know he's not a stranger, then they go inside together. The church is empty, nobody about at that time of day, and it's more than likely they knew it would be. This all smells to me of careful preparation. They go upstairs to the gallery and sit or lie on the floor. They light candles, burn incense and drink wine, all of which they would have had to bring with them. Then the girl falls to her death and the man disappears."

"What do you want me to say, Inspector?" Blake asked, her face expressionless.

She was still missing the obvious, as far as he was concerned. Pathologists were so literal, so clinical. Just deal with the bald facts, never try to interpret them, let alone use your imagination.

"Look, we're talking about a fourteen-year-old girl," he insisted, holding her gaze. "A virgin, according to you. This was all premeditated, not something that just happened by chance. Why go to all this trouble, unless there's something specific you want to get out of it? The girl's the follower in all of this, the innocent victim. And now she's dead, with GHB in her system. Don't tell me there was no sexual purpose."

Blake shook her head slowly. "This is pure speculation. There is absolutely no physical evidence to suggest a sexual encounter."

Exasperated with not getting the answer he wanted, he exhaled, leaning back in the chair so violently that it made a loud crack beneath him. "You looked for signs of a struggle? Grazing, bruising, scratches? You checked her fingernails?"

Blake looked affronted. "Of course. I did the PM myself but I found nothing suspicious. The details are all in my report, which you'll have in the morning."

She cleared her throat and folded her arms as if that was the end of the matter. For a moment he pictured her, white-skinned, full-breasted and bleary eyed, her hair fanned out on the pillow. But that was history and he felt furious with himself again for allowing his thoughts to wander in that direction.

"OK, going back to the GHB," he said, forcing himself back into the present. "What sort of quantities are we dealing with here?"

"Nothing especially high, nothing more than a couple of grams. Although even a small amount of alcohol would intensify the sedative effect. Gemma would have been in quite a happy and relaxed state, but she may have had trouble staying awake."

"How quickly would it have taken effect?" Donovan asked.

"It depends on the dosage and the purity of the drug. But for someone Gemma's size, on an empty stomach, I'd say fairly quickly, particularly with the alcohol. Probably no more than ten to fifteen minutes at most."

"Might she have wanted to jump off the balcony? You know, like someone on a bad trip?"

Blake shook her head. "GHB doesn't make you hallucinate."

30

"Would she have been capable of climbing over the balcony on her own in that state?"

"Remind me how high the balcony is?"

"About four feet," Tartaglia said. "And very solid."

Blake seemed thoughtful, running a finger over her lips for a moment before folding her hands tidily in front of her. "In my opinion, it's highly unlikely. She wasn't much over five feet tall and she would be feeling very dizzy standing up, maybe even a little nauseous because of the combined effect of the drug and the alcohol. She would increasingly have lost control over her movements. I don't think she would have had the coordination to climb over anything that high, either aided or unaided."

For a moment, his thoughts turned back again to the church and the dark balcony high above the nave where something very strange had gone on. What was the point of the drug if there was no sexual motive? None of it made any sense. The only certainty was that Gemma's death had been no accident.

He stood up to go and Donovan followed suit. As he picked up his jacket, he noticed a couple of framed photographs sitting on top of the filing cabinet. One showed a broad-shouldered man with a deeply tanned face, wearing sunglasses and ski gear, grinning broadly against a snowy mountain backdrop. He was in his late thirties or early forties, with the thick, white-blond hair of a Scandinavian. The one next to it was of the same man, his face paler this time, in one of those stupid wigs and gowns barristers wore. Fucking Murray, he thought. Christ, she'd made such a fool of him.

He glanced over at her and caught her eye. He knew she had seen him looking at the photographs and he forced a smile and leaned over the desk towards her.

"Is there anything else you think I should be aware of, Dr Blake? Something important that I may have missed or maybe forgot to ask you? Every little detail's important. That's where the devil is, as they say."

She coloured, a flicker of emotion crossing her face. Surprised but gratified that he had got some sort of a reaction, he was suddenly aware of Donovan's presence in the room and cursed himself for having said anything.

"I understand what you're getting at," Blake said quietly. "Everything's in my report. But there is something that perhaps I should draw to your attention, in the light of the scene you describe, it may or may not be significant. A lock of the girl's hair had been cut off."

"Lengths of hair were found at the crime scene, but according to the crime scene manager, it was pulled out at the root," Donovan said.

Blake shook her head. "This is different. I've no idea when it was done, although it must have happened very recently. It was sliced off right at the scalp. The section was about two inches wide and whoever did it used a sharp blade."

"Where was this?" Tartaglia asked.

"Just at the base of her neck. We only noticed it by accident when we were turning her over."

★　★　★

Outside, Tartaglia turned to Donovan. "I'll head straight back to Barnes and brief the team. You go and see Gemma's parents. The man's clearly someone she knew and we've got to find him."

Before Donovan could reply, he turned on his heel and strode off towards his motorbike, which was parked further down the road.

Bristling with pent-up curiosity, Donovan unlocked her car and climbed in. Mark Tartaglia and Dr Fiona Blake. She was amazed. Tartaglia always played his cards close to his chest but she usually managed to find out eventually if he was seeing someone. She would never have guessed in a million years that he would have gone for Blake. Blake wasn't bad looking, she had to admit grudgingly. But she was one of those irritating women who thought themselves above everyone else, just because they held a clutch of degrees. Men were unfathomable. They defied all common sense, suckers for any pretty face, never mind the person inside.

She pulled out her A-Z from the glove compartment and looked up Gemma's parents' address. It would take her no more than half an hour to get to Streatham, she reckoned. Switching on the ignition, she let the car idle for a minute, waiting for the heater to kick in. Her thoughts drifted back to Tartaglia and Blake. Their affair had to be recent, as she was pretty sure from conversations she had had with Tartaglia that there'd been no woman in his life a couple of months before. Of course, however much she instinctively disliked Blake, she couldn't blame her for going for Tartaglia. He was bloody gorgeous. It was unfair that any man should be made like that, with those brooding, dark looks and that lovely generous mouth. At times, he could look so serious, so intense. But when he smiled, his whole face lit up. The only consolation was that he seemed generally unaware of the effect he had on others. Thank God he'd never realised what she thought. In the early days, she had taken great pains not to let her feelings show and now that they'd got to know each other much better, she'd stopped hankering after him. They were mates. Good mates. Not a relationship she wanted to put at risk for something she knew couldn't last. Anyway, he was impossible, too independent and single-minded, which would make her feel insecure. Also, who in their right mind would want to have a relationship with a detective on a murder team, on call all hours, having to drop everything when a new case came along, working all day and night and weekends? No sane person would bother for long.

But what had happened between Tartaglia and Blake? There'd definitely been a row of some sort; you could have cut the atmosphere in the room with a knife. At first she'd assumed that they'd had some sort of professional spat, pathologists being bloody awkward creatures at the best of times. But then it had all got very tense just as they were leaving and it was clear that there was something else going on, something personal. Tartaglia had leant over towards Blake and said something. Although she couldn't quite remember what it was, it had sounded pretty innocuous. But the reaction on Blake's face was instantaneous and she looked as though she had been hit.

Trying to replay the conversation in her mind, so as to pin down the exact words, Donovan slipped Maroon 5's *Songs About Jane* into the CD player, tabbing to her favourite song, "She Will Be Loved". She let the music and lyrics wash over her for a moment. Of course Tartaglia could trust her. She wouldn't tell anyone, if that's what he was worried about. But she was buggered if she was going to let him think he could pull the wool over her eyes, try and pretend that there was nothing going on. Not after what she'd witnessed.

CHAPTER
FOUR

Getting to Streatham took longer than Donovan had imagined but she found the Kramers' address without trouble and pulled up on a yellow line outside. The house was modern, semi-detached with a neat strip of lawn to one side and a straight, paved path leading between two tidy flowerbeds to the front door. A black taxicab, which she assumed belonged to Gemma's father, was parked in the driveway in front of the garage, and she could see lights on behind the drawn curtains.

Thank goodness she wasn't there to break the news to the family. That was the part of the job she'd always hated most, particularly when a child was concerned. But it was bad enough having to talk to the parents now, knowing that Gemma's death hadn't been either a suicide or a simple accident. Unlike several of her colleagues, she found it difficult to cut herself off, found it impossible not to empathise with those affected by the death of a loved one. She had often asked herself why she had ever joined Clarke's murder team, and could only suppose that it was for the satisfaction of catching the person responsible, justice and retribution the only compensation for all the pain.

She took a deep breath and pressed the doorbell. The man who answered the chimes was wearing combats, trainers and a T-shirt, with a gold Star of David hanging from a heavy chain around his neck. His head was shaved, which emphasised the roundness of his face, and he looked to be in his early forties. Short, squat and barrel-chested, with the beginnings of a beer gut, he reminded her of a bulldog as he stood planted in the middle of the doorway as if he were guarding it.

"Mr Kramer? I'm DS Donovan." She held out her ID. "I'm with the team looking into Gemma's death."

He stuffed his hands into his pockets as if he didn't know what to do with them and gazed vaguely at the warrant card before moving aside, almost grudgingly, to let her pass.

"I'm Dennis Kramer, her stepdad. You'd better come in." His voice was a deep, throaty growl, his accent instantly recognisable as south London.

The DI at Ealing had said nothing about a stepfather. Stepfathers were prime suspect material in such a case. But whatever the relationship, if Mrs Brooke's description was accurate, Kramer could be ruled out immediately on physical grounds. Although he could have shaved off his hair in the last couple of days, he was still nothing like the man the old lady had described.

"Is Gemma's mother at home?"

"Mary's lying down upstairs. Seeing Gemma's body at the . . ." he struggled for the word then grunted. "I said I'd do it but she insisted on going. It more or less finished her off."

"I hope you don't mind, but I've some questions I need to ask. Is the family liaison officer here?"

He shook his head. "She was getting on my nerves so I sent her off. No point in her hanging around all day and night like a spare penny. The doctor's pumped Mary full of stuff and she's out for the count now so she can't talk to anyone. If you want to ask questions, you'll have to make do with me. I've just put the kettle on. Fancy a cup of tea?"

"Please. White, no sugar," she said, suddenly aware of the familiar ache in the pit of her stomach. What with being tied up with Ealing CID all morning and then with Tartaglia, she had completely forgotten about lunch. Thank goodness she'd managed a proper breakfast, although it was now a distant memory. It was always like this with a new investigation. Adrenalin and coffee were the main things keeping you going and you had to make a conscious effort to remember to eat, grab a sandwich or a takeaway somewhere on the run if you were lucky. It was going to be a battle keeping off the fags.

"The lounge is just there, on your left," Kramer said, waving his hand vaguely towards the door. "Make yourself comfortable and I'll be with you in a sec."

She pushed open the door and walked into a small, cream-coloured room, with thick wall-to-wall carpet and a dark leather three-piece suite. She assumed that Gemma's mother had chosen the decor, as she couldn't picture Kramer selecting the fawn and maroon striped curtains with their neat tiebacks, let alone the line of reproduction botanical prints, which hung on one of the walls. An expensive-looking TV on a glass and chrome stand took pride of place opposite the sofa, next to it a tall shelf unit with a couple of limp-looking pot plants, a collection of DVDs and a series of gilt-framed photographs.

She walked over, her eye drawn by a photo of a pretty young girl with long, glossy brown hair. It was a school photograph, the girl dressed in a navy blue cardigan over a blue and white checked blouse, her hair held back by an Alice band. The photo bore the title "Convent of the Sacred Heart" at the bottom with the previous year's date. Gemma, she assumed. She looked no more than twelve, her smile innocent and open like a child's, with nothing of the self-consciousness of a teenager. Donovan remembered how she herself had hidden from the camera from puberty onwards, pulling faces to disguise her embarrassment whenever she was caught, knowing that she would hate the end result.

She had just turned her attention to a photo of a pair of cheeky-looking little boys, when Kramer came into the room with a mug of tea in each hand.

"That's Patrick and Liam," he said, passing her a mug and taking his own over to the sofa, where he sank down heavily, crossing his feet under the small glass coffee table. "They're my kids, Gemma's half-brothers. I've had to ship them off to their nan's until Mary's better. She can't cope with anything at the moment."

Donovan settled herself in one of the comfortable-looking armchairs and took a notebook and pen out of her bag. "Just for formality's sake, could you tell me where you were on Wednesday afternoon?"

He looked instantly affronted. "What, me? What's it got to do with me?"

"Just a routine question, Mr Kramer. You know how it is. We have to dot the 'i's and cross the 't's." She took a sip of tea. It was good, strong stuff and she instantly felt better.

He nodded slowly, grudgingly appearing to accept the explanation. "I was at Gatwick till about five. Had to pick up a regular, but his flight was delayed coming in."

He gave her the client's name and phone number, which she noted down.

"Perhaps you can start by giving me a little background info. You said you're Gemma's stepfather."

"That's right."

"Are you Irish?" she asked, hoping to ease him into things.

"Do I bloody sound it?"

"It's just that Patrick and Liam . . ." she said, wondering why he was being so prickly.

He shook his head, interrupting. "That's down to Mary. She's from Cork but she come to London when she was ten. I was born and brought up in Elephant and Castle."

"What about Gemma's father? Her biological father, I mean."

"Mick? Yeah, he's bloody Irish. Him and Mary were childhood sweethearts but he didn't stop long once she got pregnant. Mary was just eighteen and he run off a couple of months before Gemma was born."

"Do you know how we can contact him?"

40

He shrugged. "No idea where the bugger is. Turns up like a bad penny from time to time when he wants money, when he knows I'm out at work. Mary's always a soft touch where he's concerned. Caught him nosing round here about a year ago. I'd come home early and we had a right punch-up. He'll think twice about stopping by again, I can tell you."

The bitterness was unmistakable and Donovan suspected that behind the protectiveness for his wife, he was jealous. She wondered how Gemma fitted into the triangle. "What about Gemma? Did she have any contact with him?"

He shook his head. "Wasn't interested. From what I hear, he's fathered a whole litter of kids with various women, in between being in and out of the nick, that is."

"He's in prison?"

"Well, we haven't heard from him in a while. It's either that, or the chinning I give him last time he come round." A flicker of pleasure crossed his face. "His full name's Mick Byrne, if you want to check him out. That's B-Y-R-N-E. He's bound to be on one of your computers, given his record."

Donovan made a note. It would be easy to find out if the father was in prison. "What's his form?"

"Got sticky fingers. Can't keep his hands off other people's things. He's a bit of a conman, but nothing violent, if you know what I mean."

"Is it possible that Gemma might have seen him secretly, given how you felt about him?"

Kramer's eyes bulged angrily and he clenched his lips. "No way. She never kept anything from us. Gemma was a good girl. I've brought her up from the age of five." He paused, swallowing hard. "I was her dad, as far as she was concerned. Her only dad. Why are you interested in Mick?"

"Gemma was seen with a man shortly before she died. He looked to be in his thirties or forties, tall with dark hair. We need to find him."

He grimaced. "Well, that can't be Mick. Last time I saw him, he was nearly as bald as me and not 'coz of a Number One. All his hair dropped out last time he was inside. Alopecia, I think they call it. Serves him bloody right for all the trouble he's caused."

"Gemma was with some man. As I said, we need to find out who it is. That's the main reason I'm here."

He stared at her for a moment, looking puzzled. "What do you mean 'with some man'?"

Donovan took a deep breath. "Gemma was seen kissing this man outside the church where she died. She must have known him pretty well."

"Kissing?" The word shot out of his mouth like a bullet. "You've got it wrong. Gemma wasn't interested in boys."

"This was a man, not a boy, Mr Kramer."

"Gemma didn't know any men," he said emphatically. He bit his lip and looked away, his eyes fixing on one of the flower prints that hung over the TV. 'Course, she was pretty. Takes after her mum. But she wasn't a slag, like a lot of girls her age." For a moment, his thoughts seemed to drift elsewhere.

"I'm only telling you what the witness saw. It's very important that we find this man. He may be able to shed some light on how Gemma died."

He put his mug down and leaned forwards towards her, hands flat on his knees. "Gemma couldn't have been with a man. She was a good girl, Sergeant. A really good girl." He jerked a stubby finger at the photo on the shelf. "See that? It was only taken last autumn. You wouldn't know she was fourteen, would you? She looks so young."

Wondering why he was trying so hard to convince her, she wanted to say that youth had never stopped a young girl from pursuing her dreams or doing something stupid. And parents, however good and caring, were often the last to know. If he wanted to ignore reality, that was his business but she needed to confront him with the facts. It was easily possible that he knew the man in some capacity.

"Mr Kramer, Gemma was seen by a witness kissing a man much older than herself. We're talking proper kissing, not a peck on the cheek. They then went into the church together."

He was shaking his head. "Not Gemma. Like I said, you got it wrong."

"The pathologist found traces of the drug GHB in her system. We come across it sometimes in cases of date-rape."

He frowned. "She wasn't . . ." his voice trailed off.

"No. She wasn't sexually assaulted. But it's pretty clear that she knew the man she was with. Maybe she got the drug from him. We've got to find him and I was hoping maybe you could help."

The words seemed to wash over him and he bent forward and put his face in his hands, closing his eyes and rubbing his temples. He seemed more shocked by the presence of the man than by the fact that Gemma had been drugged, still failing to understand or acknowledge Gemma's death as suspicious. But if he didn't want to join up the dots, it wasn't for her to do it for him. "What about relatives or family friends?"

He looked up and slammed his fist on the table, making the mugs rattle. "What are you saying? You think one of my friends has been messing around with Gemma behind my back?"

"She must have met the man somewhere, Mr Kramer. I'm going to need a list of everyone you know who Gemma's been in contact with recently."

He sighed and sank back in the sofa, staring hard up at the ceiling, shaking his head slowly. "I don't believe what I'm hearing. You didn't know Gemma. She wasn't that way." His scalp was shiny with sweat, small beads starting to run down his cheeks. "She should've been at school," he said, closing his eyes again and pinching the bridge of his thick nose with his fingers, his face red.

"I'll need that list as soon as possible. In the meantime, who are her close friends? Maybe they would know who she was seeing."

He took a crumpled handkerchief out of the pocket of his combats, dabbed at his head and face and blew his nose. "She didn't have any close friends. She's only been at the convent since last Easter. Before that, she was at the local comprehensive."

"There must be someone she's close to, someone her own age who she would confide in."

He shook his head and blew his nose again.

"Why did she change schools?"

"They was bullying Gemma. She was a bright girl, really sensitive. Had a heart of gold, used to work at the local animal shelter in the holidays."

"What happened?"

He gave her a weary look. "The usual stuff. The school wasn't on top of things. They give the kids a good talking-to a few times but it didn't change nothing. They just went out and picked on her again. We had to get her out of there. It's lucky I earn a decent living and we could do something about it. I pity the poor kids who are stuck in a place like that."

"Why did you choose the convent?"

"Mary's Catholic. As I said, Gemma was a bright girl and we thought she'd do well there. Also, we didn't want her growing up too fast."

That was the real reason, Donovan thought, wondering why they were so protective of Gemma. Had she given them cause for concern before? The innocent picture he presented didn't square with what had happened at St Sebastian's, or what she knew of other young girls of Gemma's age. Either he was hiding something, or Gemma had led a secret life.

"Had she made any friends since moving schools?"

"She's come home a few times with a girl called Rosie. Spent the night at her place once or twice, I think."

"Do you have her number?"

"It'll be in her diary."

"May I see it?"

He shrugged and got slowly to his feet. "It's one of them electronic things. It's upstairs in her desk."

"What about a phone?" she said, following him out the door, interested to see Gemma's room. A search team would have to go over it properly but she wanted to take a look for herself.

Kramer shook his head. "No point. Mary walked her to and from school and she didn't have many friends to call."

Most girls Gemma's age were allowed to walk to school on their own. They also had cell phones; it was odd that her parents hadn't given her one and Donovan wondered if Gemma had minded, if she had felt the odd one out in her peer group.

"What about a computer? Did Gemma have access to the internet?"

He nodded. "Used it for her schoolwork. It's all in her room upstairs."

"You'd better show me."

The stairs were narrow and Kramer seemed out of scale as he lumbered up them, holding on so tight to the thin banister that it creaked and wobbled beneath his grasp. Following behind, Donovan passed a half-open door on the first floor landing, glimpsing through it the dark shape of Gemma's mother in bed, deeply asleep judging by the sound of heavy breathing coming from the room. Thank God she didn't have to go through all this with her.

Gemma's bedroom was on the top floor at the front of the house. Kramer hesitated on the landing, staring down at the floor as if he couldn't bring himself even to look at the door.

"Do you mind going in by yourself? I can't bear seeing her things."

"Of course, Mr Kramer," she said. "I'll come and find you downstairs, shall I? I won't be long."

She waited until he disappeared from view then she pushed open the door and walked in.

Light streamed in from the street outside, casting long shadows across the floor. Thinking that someone in one of the houses opposite might be looking out, she moved to close the curtains before switching on the light at the wall. The bed was made, not even a wrinkle in the duvet or pillows, which were patterned with tiny rosebuds and bows. A purple cardigan hung over the back of a chair and a pair of flat black shoes peeped out from under the bed next to a pair of pink slippers. It was as if she had walked into a bubble, separate from the real world, and it brought a knot to her throat. The room was frozen in time, the clock stopped on the day Gemma died, the child never coming home. Having your child die before you must be one of the most terrible things in the world, she had often thought, a scar that would never heal which tainted everything and poisoned the future. She wondered what Kramer and his wife would do with Gemma's room. Would they leave it just as it was or would they change it? Perhaps they would find it impossible to continue living in the house with all its memories.

Looking around, almost everything in the room was pink: walls, curtains, carpet, bed covers, even the string of fairy lights in the shape of little angels hanging in an arc over the bed. It was a little girl's bedroom. Donovan wouldn't have been caught dead with a room like that at the age of fourteen. Six, maybe, when you had no choice in the matter, but never fourteen. Her walls had been papered with posters and photos, but apart from a giltframed print of a girl jumping a fence on a pony, Gemma's were totally blank.

Although Gemma's development seemed to be arrested, no expense had been spared in kitting out the room. Along with a new-looking laptop, Gemma had her own TV and mini hi-fi system. The small collection of CDs, mainly boy bands and similar, were anodyne, nothing to give her parents cause for worry. She remembered Kramer's words: "We didn't want her growing up too fast", wondering what it was that they were trying to protect her from. On the surface at least, the poor kid had had no choice but to remain a child, wrapped in this pastel-pink cocoon. She wondered how Gemma had felt about it, whether she had resented it at all. Maybe what she had been doing in that church had been an attempt to escape.

A small desk stood in a corner of the room, inside the single drawer a collection of coloured pens and pencils, stationery, a mini iPod and a PDA, with a Barbie logo on the front. But there were no letters or cards, no journal or any other personal items of interest. Putting the iPod and PDA in her bag to examine later, she tried the chest of drawers, feeling around amongst the neat piles of clothing. But there was nothing hidden there.

The bookshelf above the desk was packed with a mixture of children's classics, what looked like a full set of Harry Potters and Georgette Heyers, as well as *The Hobbit*, a gift set of the Narnia books and *Artemis Fowl*. Apart from a child's encyclopaedia and a few factual books on horses and riding, fantasy seemed to be the predominant theme. Donovan was surprised to see that Gemma was a reader, given the lack of books in her parents' sitting room downstairs.

A copy of *Wuthering Heights* lay on the low table next to the bed. The paperback was well thumbed and fell open as she picked it up. Flicking through, she noticed several passages heavily underlined in purple, some with a star inscribed in the margin. Wondering if perhaps Gemma was studying it at school, she skimmed through some of the highlighted chunks. They all seemed to be about Heathcliff, a physical description of him on one page accompanied by several exclamation marks and a small inked heart. It instantly struck a chord. For a moment Donovan remembered the acute feeling of teenage longing, the wanting to belong to another world, far removed from family and friends. Heathcliff, the dark and dangerous lover who had filled her dreams too. He had seemed so real for a while. How could the smelly, spotty, greasy-haired youths she had known at school ever measure up? Heathcliff had blighted any opportunities for adolescent romance and she was forced to admit that a part of her still hankered after him even now.

Glancing at her watch, she realised that it was past seven o'clock. She went over to the desk, unplugged the laptop and tucked it under her arm. Checking the room one last time to make sure she hadn't missed anything obvious, she switched off the light and went downstairs. She would send a team over in the morning to go through the rest of Gemma's things more thoroughly.

Downstairs, Kramer walked her to her car, putting the laptop onto the back seat while she wrote out a receipt for the items she was taking. He held the door open for her as she climbed behind the wheel, then handed her a folded piece of paper.

"That's the list you wanted," he said. "I've written down a couple of names but I can't believe any of them would . . ." He shook his head, clenching his lips, unable to finish the sentence.

She gave him a reassuring smile. "Thank you, Mr Kramer. We just have to check every angle you know. We wouldn't be doing our job properly otherwise."

He nodded slowly as if he accepted this, resting his arm heavily on the edge of the door as if he wanted to keep her there. "So, Sergeant. What do you think happened to our Gemma? It was an accident, right?"

"It's too early to tell, Mr Kramer," she said, noncommittally, hoping he'd let her leave without probing any further. Kramer was still a suspect, even though in her heart she didn't believe he had had

50

anything to do with it. She started the engine but he was still holding on to the door as if he wasn't finished.

"You know, they thought it was suicide," he said leaning towards her and speaking in a whisper, as if he was worried that someone might overhear. "But I told them it can't be. Gemma would never do that. It would break her mum's heart, it would."

"It's not suicide, Mr Kramer. You can be sure of that," she replied, surprised again that he seemed unable to understand that Gemma's death was suspicious.

He nodded once more, looking strangely relieved, and stepped back from the car. Something about his reaction didn't feel right and she was aware of him watching her as she closed the door. Turning to reach for her seatbelt, she glanced over at him again and caught a glimmer of something on his face that puzzled her. He looked like someone who had just pulled off a trick, although for the life of her, she couldn't figure out what it was.

CHAPTER
FIVE

It was evening and the investigation into Gemma Kramer's death was well under way. Tartaglia yawned and locked his fingers in front of him, cracking his knuckles and stretching his neck forward to ease the tiredness that had suddenly overwhelmed him. There had been the team to assemble from various other on-going cases, actions to be assigned and a further debriefing and file handover with the DI at Ealing CID. Until he heard back from Donovan, the priority was St Sebastian's. Everyone who was available had gone over to Ealing to conduct interviews, starting with the vicar and the people who used the church regularly, and going on to knock on doors in the area. Local CCTV footage was being checked, although in such a residential district, cameras were few and far between, and the tube station was their main hope. Somehow, they had to try and come up with more witnesses and get a better description of the man seen with Gemma.

As acting SIO, Tartaglia had decided to move out of the cramped quarters he normally shared with Gary Jones, the other DI on Clarke's team. It wasn't an issue of his new seniority. He needed a quiet place where he could gather his thoughts and think through things clearly without interruption.

Standing in the doorway of Clarke's office, he wondered how long it would take him to sort out the mess of papers, files and miscellaneous possessions Clarke had left behind. He felt a pang of sadness as he thought about Clarke lying motionless in his hospital bed but he couldn't work in such chaos. How Clarke had ever managed so effortlessly was beyond him.

The room was little more than a shoebox at the front of the building, the single grimy window facing onto the road that led from Barnes Pond to the common, opposite the backs of a row of expensive period houses, with neat gardens; suburban Barnes in all its glory. Judging by the icy temperature, the heating was on the blink again. Nothing in the bloody building ever worked properly. But at least he didn't have to put up with Jones's BO any longer, the lovey-dovey phone calls to the wife and the smell of the home-made tuna and onion sandwiches which Jones seemed to eat at all hours of the day.

Barnes Green wasn't supposed to be a permanent location for the two murder squads it currently housed. When Tartaglia had joined Team Five of Homicide West, Clarke had jokingly told him not to bother unpacking his things. The low-built early seventies block was past its sell-by date and they'd all be relocating soon. But nearly three years on, there was no sign of a move and they had learned to live with the cramped and shabby working conditions, sandwiched on the first floor between part of the Flying Squad above and a child protection unit on the ground floor below. It was a far cry from the offices up in Hendon, at the Peel Centre, where five of the other murder teams worked in relative luxury.

Feeling hungry, he decided to make some coffee to fill the gap while he sorted out somewhere to put his things in Clarke's office. There was no canteen in the building and he'd have to go out later for something to eat. He walked down the corridor to a tiny internal room, once used for storage, which served as the kitchen for the entire first floor. Functional was the only positive word to describe it; a health hazard was probably more accurate and he used it as little as possible, preferring to get his coffee and food from one of the many fancy delis that peppered the area. He opened the door of the fridge but couldn't see any milk, just an ancient looking tub of margarine and an already opened tin of tomato soup. However, he didn't have time to go out so he boiled the kettle and made a strong brew of instant black coffee. Disgusted at the predictable state of things, he carried the mug back into Clarke's office where he struggled to find a safe place to put it down. He swept a variety of papers and files into a couple of rough piles and helped himself to an unopened Kit-Kat which he found marking a place inside a folder.

He pulled up the saggy brown corduroy chair that Clarke had brought in from somewhere and sat down at the desk to go through the papers. As he stretched out his legs, he kicked against something hard at the back. Digging around underneath, he pulled out a large cardboard box containing two pairs of ancient, mud-encrusted trainers, a humane mousetrap and a blow heater. Wedged behind the box was a rolled-up sleeping bag, which he remembered Clarke using for all-night sessions. At least Tartaglia wouldn't be needing that. His flat in Shepherd's Bush was only a fifteen-minute motorbike ride away. After trying the blow heater, which seemed to be broken, he put everything back in the box, stuffing the sleeping bag on top and dumped it all in the corridor to take away later.

He was about to sit down again at the desk when his mobile rang: it was Donovan.

"I'm on my way back. I've just seen Gemma's stepdad, Dennis Kramer."

"Stepfather?"

"Don't get excited. He doesn't fit the witness description and if his alibi checks out, he's in the clear. I've got Gemma's computer with me. Is Dave around?"

DC Dave Wightman had a degree in something to do with computers and was regarded as the in-house expert on most things technical.

"He's just come back from Ealing."

"Tell him I'll drop it off in about ten minutes. It needs to go over to Newlands Park for analysis but he's so good with computers. I was hoping he could have a quick look at it first. There was nothing else in her room of any interest. In the meantime, a couple of friends of Kramer's want checking out." She gave him the names and addresses, which he noted down. "I'm going to see a girl called Rosie Chapple later on. She seems to be Gemma's only friend."

"Did you see Gemma's mother?"

She gave a long, wheezy sigh. "No. She was out for the count in bed. Can I tell you the rest once I get a bite to eat? I missed lunch and I'll pass out if I don't get something now."

He looked at his watch, realising that he had also had little to eat that day. It would be a while before everyone was back from Ealing and there should be time to nip out for a quick bite. It would probably be the only break he'd get for a while. "I'll see you in the Bull's Head in twenty minutes. I'll order for you. What do you fancy?"

"Don't mind. Just make it large."

Stopping off in the main office outside to tell DC Dave Wightman about the computer, Tartaglia grabbed his jacket from his old office and went downstairs. He walked through the car park at the back of the building and out of the main gate onto the street. It was close to freezing and a mist was rolling up in thick drifts from the Thames. The air was wet on his face and smelled of rotting leaves mixed with wood smoke, someone burning a proper fire nearby. As he turned down Station Road, he could just make out the black wilderness of Barnes Common in the distance, a long string of orange streetlights marking the perimeter.

When he'd first come down to London from Edinburgh shortly after graduating from university, he had felt swamped by its size, lack of cohesion and frenetic pace of life. He remembered having an argument in a pub with some jolly Londoner who had tried to persuade him that the city was really only a friendly series of villages joined together. Having lived in Edinburgh all his life, it was something he failed to see, there being no village-like qualities about Hendon, where he'd done his training as a police cadet, or Oxford Street and its environs, where he had walked his first beat. London seemed just a grey, filthy, sprawling, unfriendly mass and he wondered whether he had made a mistake leaving home. Gradually, as he got to know the city better, he started to realise that most areas had their own distinct personality and community, which made life more tolerable. Nowhere was this more true than in Barnes, picture-postcard pretty and so rural that it could almost be in the country, even though it was only a few miles from the centre of town.

He passed the village green with its pond, barely visible in the mist, a couple of ducks quacking from somewhere near the edge of the water, and followed the road around into the narrow, brightly-lit high street. Unusually for London, it was free of chain stores and retained an old-fashioned feel, offering instead an exotic range of small shops, expensive boutiques and restaurants, along with the myriad of estate agents, reflecting the fact that it was a popular, if expensive, place to live. Cut off from central London by the river Thames, Barnes seemed to be in a world of its own. If the wealthy local clientele, which included several well-known faces from theatre and television, wanted something functional like a pair of socks or underpants, they had to make the trip over Hammersmith Bridge into the smoke.

Approaching the river, the fog bacame dense and he could barely see in front of him. Swathed in a veil of white, The Bull's Head sat at the end of the High Street, overlooking the river embankment, next door to what had once been Barnes Police Station, the old building now converted into expensive flats.

Walking into the large, open-plan bar, Tartaglia was greeted as usual by loud music coming from the back room. The pub was famous for its daily sessions of live jazz, occasionally boasting musicians even he had heard of, such as Humphrey Lyttelton and George Melly. Jazz wasn't his cup of tea in any shape or form and often the music was so loud it was difficult to hold a conversation. But tonight the sounds drifting into the bar were half decent, someone with a voice like John Lee Hooker singing the blues, accompanied by a guitar. There were worse places to drink and it was certainly a lot better than the watering holes around Hendon.

He bought a pint of Youngs Special for himself and a half of their ordinary bitter for Donovan, who tended to prefer something a little less strong. They might still be officially on duty but he didn't give a damn. It had been a long day and he had the feeling that it wasn't anywhere near over yet. He was supposed to have been seeing his cousin Gianni for beer and pizza in front of the TV with the DVD of *Downfall*, but that plan had had to be shelved and, as far as the weekend was concerned, he could kiss goodbye to that too. He ordered two large helpings of lasagne and salad and settled himself at a table in the far corner by one of the windows. He had just started on his pint when

58

Donovan appeared through the main door, pink-faced and out of breath, her hair damp from the air outside. She swung her satchel onto the floor and stripped off several layers of clothing, down to a pair of baggy black trousers, held up with braces, and a red and black striped T-shirt that reminded him amusingly of Dennis the Menace. He liked the way she dressed; it suited her, even if it was rarely ever feminine. She could usually pass for a pretty young boy.

Donovan quickly rubbed her hair with the edge of her scarf, making it stand up in short tufts, then flopped down in the chair opposite him. "That's better. Cheers," she said, taking a gulp of bitter and wiping her top lip with the back of her hand. "God, I needed that."

"We're checking on Kramer's two mates. They both live close together, which makes it easy." He glanced at his watch. "Should hear back soon. What time are you seeing the girl?"

"Not for a while. Her mother said she wouldn't be home before ten at the earliest, as it's Friday night." She took another large sip, then leaned back in her chair, legs stretched out in front of her. "This isn't going to be easy," she said, thoughtfully. "I think Gemma was leading a secret life and I don't think her parents had a clue." She told him about her conversation with Kramer and her initial impressions of Gemma.

He listened carefully, asking the odd question here and there. When she'd finished, he sipped his pint in silence for a moment. Although there had been a few famous cases over the years, stranger killings were rare in London. Usually the killer was to be found within the victim's close circle of family, friends and colleagues and the majority of murders were relatively straightforward to solve, with the main challenge being to get sufficient proof for a conviction. From what Mrs Brooke had said, Gemma had seemed to know the man she met outside the church, so hopefully it was only a matter of time before they'd find out who he was.

"What do you make of Kramer?" he asked, after a minute. "I know you say he doesn't fit the description but . . ."

"He's an odd bloke and really overprotective. But unless he's a brilliant actor, I think he genuinely cared about Gemma. What's strange is that he seemed unable to grasp the fact that her death is suspicious. It's as if he'd already made up his mind about what had happened."

"Or knew what had happened?"

"No. I don't think he would have harmed her, or knowingly let any of his friends mess about with her."

He gave her a searching look. He could tell from her expression that there was something else. "What is it?"

She cradled her nearly empty glass in her hands, swilling the brown liquid around the sides before taking a last gulp of bitter. "I'm pretty sure he's holding something back. I just don't have a clue what it is. I've been over and over in my mind what we talked about but there's nothing I can pin it on, nothing in particular that he said or did that struck a wrong note. Until, that is, just after we'd said goodbye. I was about to drive off and he'd relaxed, thinking I was going. I saw something, just a glimmer in his expression, nothing more than that. He looked as though he'd gotten away with something." She drained her glass and grimaced. "Maybe I'm reading too much into it."

He shook his head. Her instincts were usually spot on. "I doubt it. Let's get him in. Make it formal and turn up the temperature."

"He sees himself as a tough guy, real hardboiled on the surface. Maybe he thought, because I'm a woman, he could pull the wool over my eyes. I just don't see why, if he loved Gemma, he would want to protect someone who had harmed her." She gave a weary sigh and stood up. "Another pint?"

Tartaglia shook his head and watched her move towards the bar. Kramer wouldn't have been the first to underestimate her. Her physical size and looks gave a misleading impression of innocence and fragility. But what was she to do? High heels and red lipstick were hardly the answer. He respected her for getting on with things as if none of it mattered, even though he knew she found it irritating at times. Apart from what had happened with Kramer, she seemed a little on edge, although he couldn't pinpoint why. He wondered if she had picked up the vibes between him and Blake earlier on. The last thing he needed was to be the centre of office gossip, particularly when there was nothing going on anyway. At least Donovan wasn't one to gossip, unlike some. He knew little about her personal life other than that there'd been some man called Richard around for a while. But she had stopped mentioning him and Tartaglia hadn't wanted to appear nosey by asking. Perhaps giving up smoking was making her feel on edge.

Donovan returned after a moment and sat down, a glass with ice and lemon and a slimline tonic in her hand. "Thought I'd better go for something soft. Otherwise I'll be under the table, given the little I've had to eat today." She poured the tonic into the glass and took a large gulp.

"What's bothering you?"

She smiled. "According to Kramer, Gemma had no private life. He said she wasn't interested in boys. I got the impression he really believed what he was telling me, that he wasn't spinning me a yarn."

"Your point is?"

"I was just thinking back to what Mrs Brooke said. She's absolutely positive about what she described. As I told you, she seemed pretty sharp for someone her age. I also checked her out with the vicar, as apparently she's a regular at St Sebastian's. He says she's reliable."

"So, Gemma met the guy in secret. She wouldn't be the first, particularly given how you describe Kramer."

She nodded. "Maybe Gemma's friend Rosie knows something. The man has to be somebody Gemma trusted. She kissed him, after all, and, from what I can tell about her, I don't see her picking up just anybody in the street or in some internet chat room. This girl was a real romantic, I tell you."

As she finished speaking, their food arrived. Tartaglia had just picked up his knife and fork when his phone rang. He answered it, listened for a moment, then snapped it shut.

"Damn," he said, getting to his feet, staring down for a second at the untouched plate of lasagne, the smell unbearably good. "That was Dave. He's found something on her computer. Says it's really weird. We'd better go back to the office right away." He saw the look of desperation on Donovan's face. "Look, you have yours. Then catch me up. Perhaps you can get them to put mine in a doggy bag."

CHAPTER
SIX

Twenty minutes later, Donovan rushed into the main open-plan office. At that hour, the long, low-ceilinged room, which housed the majority of the thirty-odd detectives who made up Clarke's team, was uncharacteristically empty and quiet. Crammed with desks, phones and computers, it buzzed during the day with noise and activity and closely resembled a battery-hen shed. But with less pressing cases in hand, those not in Tartaglia's immediate team had gone home for the night.

Tartaglia was perched on a desk at the front, next to the white board, chewing on a pen, reading some papers. He had taken off his jacket and tie, unbuttoned the top few buttons of his shirt and rolled up his sleeves as if he was settling in for the night. He looked troubled and Donovan wondered what exactly Wightman had discovered on Gemma's laptop. Wightman stood beside him, methodically sorting a thick wedge of papers into several separate piles and stapling them together. Short, fresh-faced and thickset, Wightman was in his late twenties, although he looked barely eighteen and was the newest recruit to the team.

DCs Nick Minderedes and Karen Feeney came into the room immediately behind Donovan, having just got back from knocking on doors in Ealing.

"Sit down, everybody," Tartaglia said, looking up. "We'll be ready in a minute."

Donovan deposited the bag containing Tartaglia's takeaway on a filing cabinet behind him and pulled up a chair between Minderedes and Feeney. Feeney sneezed three times in succession, took a tissue out of her pocket and blew her nose loudly. Her eyes were watering and she looked bedraggled, sitting there wrapped up in her limp mackintosh.

"You OK?" Donovan asked.

"Just tired," Feeney said. "Nothing knackers you like tramping the streets for hours at this time of year. And one of my shoes has sprung a leak." Her voice was thick and nasal and it sounded to Donovan as though she was getting a cold. Feeney took a small mirror out of her bag and peered into it, dabbing her pale cheeks and wiping away the shadow of mascara from under her eyes. "Will you look at my hair," she said, turning her attention to her frizz of bright red curls. "Just takes a drop of rain to ruin a good blow-dry. Thank Christ I wasn't planning on doing anything exciting later."

"That makes two of us," Donovan replied. "I had a hot date lined up with Jonathan Ross but I'm sure he'll understand."

"Sorry you ladies lead such dull lives, but I really did have something on for tonight," Minderedes muttered gloomily. "And it's the third bloody time I've had to cancel this chick because of work. She's going to give up on me at this rate."

Hunched in his overcoat, he took a stick of gum out of the pocket, peeled off the wrapper and put it into his mouth, chewing vigorously as if to compensate for what he was missing. Small and wiry, with thinning dark hair, his eyes were an unusual shade of green, almost yellow, and he had a permanently hungry, restless look, as if never satisfied with anything for long.

"Anyone I know?" Donovan asked, unravelling her scarf and unbuttoning her coat, feeling hot and a little sweaty from her brisk walk back to the office.

"The new barmaid at the Bull's Head. You know, the one with short dark hair. Polish, with big . . ." He gestured, cupping his hands in front of his chest.

"But she barely speaks English," Feeney said, raising her eyebrows.

He grinned, still chewing hard. "What's that got to do with anything?"

Donovan shook her head wearily. Minderedes's success with women was beyond her. He had the emotional maturity of a teenager, although he knew how to turn on the charm in a crude sort of way when it suited him. She prided herself on being one of the few single women in the office who had never succumbed. She wasn't quite sure where Feeney stood in that respect.

As Wightman started to pass around a set of papers to each of the assembled group, DC Yvette Dickenson came into the room, carrying a mug of something hot.

Tartaglia looked round at Dickenson. "Anyone else coming?"

"No, sir," she said. "They're out checking the names Mr Kramer gave us." She walked over to where Donovan, Feeney and Minderedes were sitting, pulled out a chair from a nearby desk and eased herself down onto it carefully. Yawning, she took off her glasses, rubbed her eyes and started to polish the thick lenses on the edge of her shirt. Nearly eight months pregnant, she seemed to be finding most things at work a strain, although she wasn't due to go on maternity leave for another few weeks. Donovan wondered if she would last the course.

"Right," Tartaglia said, clapping his hands to get everyone's attention. "Let's get started now. Dave's found gold on Gemma Kramer's computer. There'll be a full briefing in the morning but I want your views straight away." He turned to Wightman.

Wightman cleared his throat. "The copies I've just given you are from Gemma Kramer's email store. I've only had time for a quick look, as the laptop's going off shortly to Newlands Park for full analysis. But I think I've picked up most, if not all, of the interesting stuff. As you'll see, there are nearly fifty messages going back over the last three months between Gemma and a man called Tom."

"The last email in the sequence from Tom was sent the day before Gemma died," Tartaglia added. "Judging from what's in it, he's the man she was seen with at the church."

As the group started to read through the sheets, the coughs, sniffs and rustling of paper turned to a hushed silence, leaving behind only the sound of underwater gurgling coming from Gemma's laptop, which lay open on one of the desks with a screensaver of brightly coloured tropical fish swimming up and down a reef.

"Turn the bloody sound off, will you?" Tartaglia said, after several minutes, glancing up at Wightman. "Can't hear myself think."

Wightman reached over, fiddled with something on the keyboard and the screensaver disappeared, leaving behind a visual of one of the emails.

For a moment, Donovan gazed blankly at the screen, the words she had just been reading swilling like smoke in her mind. Hearing Gemma Kramer's voice coming off the printed page, she felt sick. Gemma talked of her sense of isolation, how she was being bullied at school, how nobody seemed to understand her, how her mother and stepfather didn't care about her. The language was childish, the tone pathetic and moving. By contrast, the responses from the man called Tom were chilling.

The wooing, the grooming, was subtle and progressive, with layer upon layer of delicate persuasion. Donovan looked back at one of the sheets in her hand, eyes focusing on some lines from one of Tom's emails to Gemma that sounded as if they came from some rubbish pop song. Even if it was cringe-makingly awful, it was exactly the sort of thing calculated to appeal to a naïve young girl. Tom seemed to use anything to touch Gemma and worm his way deeper into her psyche. He orchestrated everything carefully, always in control. Like a piece of music, the emotional intensity of his emails rose and fell, sometimes powerful and dramatic, sometimes quiet, restrained and almost courtly, the concept of love and death and suicide running through them all as a leitmotif. They were two star-crossed lovers, like Romeo and Juliet, with the cruel world set against them. He understood Gemma's psychology perfectly and played her like a master.

Many teenagers had a fascination with death. But what had started out as an abstract idea on Gemma's part, the wish to kill herself little more than a child's cry from the heart, had been inexorably turned into a reality by Tom. It was evil in its purest form.

Although just the wrong side of thirty, Donovan could still recall the sense of alienation and despair of being a teenager, although in her case it had been nowhere as strongly felt as Gemma's. She remembered a girl called Annette who had lived next door to her in Twickenham, where she had grown up. One day, without warning, Annette had gone into her bedroom, closed the door and hanged herself. The shockwaves reverberated around the immediate community but nobody seemed to have any explanation for why Annette had done it. One minute she appeared to be a perfectly normal, happy fourteen-year-old, with everything to look forward to; the next, she was gone. And Donovan, then aged twelve, couldn't make sense of it either. But for months afterwards, the image of Annette haunted her, with her long, fair hair and heavy fringe, hanging dead in her room like some bizarre rag-doll.

Skimming through the last few pages of Gemma's emails, Donovan came to the final one in the sequence, sent by Tom the day before Gemma died.

Darling Gemma
Everything is ready and love is impatient. I thought of phoning you at home, even knowing how risky it is and how I could blow everything. I wanted to reassure you, to tell you how much I want you. Just don't worry. It will all be fine, you'll see. Trust me. I'll be waiting for you by the door of the church at four o'clock. Don't be late and don't forget to bring the ring — I have a beautiful one to give you in return. It was my mother's. We will exchange them when we say our vows. Also, don't forget the note for your mother — you have the wording I sent you. Just copy it out in your best handwriting but don't leave it anywhere too obvious. We don't want her finding it before we're done.

Trust me, there is no other way, not if you want me. When we meet, I'm sure I can make your fears melt away. Until then, remember one thing. This isn't a world worth living in. There can be no future for us here. Think what would happen to you (and me) if they found out. They would never allow us to be together. Just focus on that and I will take care of the rest. As Shakespeare wrote: "If I must die, I will encounter darkness as a bride" and you will be the most beautiful bride. I hardly deserve you.

Die with me, my darling, and we will never be parted.
Your loving bridegroom,
Tomxx

As she read it, she shivered, imagining the high, dark gallery of the church, Gemma and the man called Tom, going through some sort of mock wedding ceremony, incense and candles burning. Poor Gemma. She hadn't stood a chance.

Donovan didn't know much about computers, but for Tom to have been so explicit in writing about his intentions, he must believe that he could never be traced. She had friends in the police who had worked on breaking paedophile rings and she knew that it was easily possible for someone to disappear into thin air if they knew what they were doing.

Feeney and Dickenson were still reading but Minderedes turned to Donovan, having finished.

"I thought I'd seen everything," he whispered, shaking his head. "It makes me sick to read this shit. It's unbelievable."

She nodded in reply, just as Tartaglia got to his feet.

"Hendon are checking out the email addresses that Tom used," he said. "Although I'm sure none of them will be traceable. I'm also bloody sure that the fucker's name isn't Tom."

He walked over to the window, smacking the side of a filing cabinet hard with the palm of his hand as he passed, and stared out for a moment. Then he turned round, frowning, stuffing his hands in his pockets. In the overhead strip-light, his eyes were in deep shadow but he looked as though he wanted to hit someone, lay them out cold.

"We've got to find out how he came across Gemma," he said quietly.

"What about chat rooms?" Feeney asked, looking up from her papers.

"And suicide websites," Dickenson added, with a half-stifled yawn. "I saw a programme on telly recently about strangers meeting up on the internet to commit suicide together. Apart from the odd phone call, the people had never spoken or met before."

"I saw that programme too," Minderedes said.

The whole thing was sick, Donovan thought, remembering the programme, which had been on only a few weeks before. But there was fuck-all the police could do about it. The Suicide Act, which dated back over forty years, hadn't envisaged the opportunities of the internet. For the moment, most of what the sites were doing and the information they were providing to assist would-be suicides was not illegal. Calls to strengthen the law and ban suicide sites had so far fallen on deaf ears, which she found extraordinary. Total strangers meeting to jump off a bridge holding hands, or dying together in a car filled with carbon monoxide was bad enough. But at least there was no compulsion or coercion involved. They were adults and could make up their own minds, although to Donovan, the idea of wanting company when you were going to kill yourself seemed bizarre. But children and teenagers, with over-fertile imaginations, were so vulnerable and easily influenced. They needed protecting from such concepts and material, let alone being exposed to somebody who might use it to do them harm.

"I haven't found any trace of her visiting any chat rooms, let alone suicide websites," Wightman said. "All the places she logged onto were educational or the usual kids' games and stuff."

Donovan flipped through the sheets to the beginning. "However Gemma and Tom met, I don't think they were strangers at the time the emails started."

"How do you work that one out?" Dickenson said, pushing her heavy-rimmed glasses up her nose and peering at Donovan bleary-eyed. "They could have just been chatting on the net. No matter what Dave says, I still fancy that theory until we hear back from Newlands Park."

Donovan held up the copy of the first email in the sequence. "Here, take a look at Tom's first email. He asks her how she is, if she's feeling any better. He asks her if what he said, referring to sometime before, made sense. The tone is intimate, as if he's talking to a lover or a close friend. He certainly doesn't sound like a complete stranger to me."

"That's right," Feeney said, scanning the sheets and nodding slowly. "She also says in one of the emails right at the beginning that she found his voice reassuring."

"And she asks him if she can call him again," Donovan replied. "According to her stepfather, Gemma didn't have a mobile, so maybe she spoke to Tom from home."

"We're checking the phone records now," Tartaglia said quietly, as if he was only half-listening. He turned away towards the window and stared out, his thoughts clearly somewhere else.

"He's got to be someone she knows well," Feeney said. "Gemma seems so comfortable pouring out her feelings to him."

Donovan shook her head. "I'm not sure. All that comes across is that she thinks he understands her better than anyone else. That's intoxicating for any young girl and he bloody knows it. But if he is someone she knew, someone in her close circle of family or friends, or perhaps someone she knew from school or her neighbourhood, surely there would be references in the emails. But there aren't any. He talks about her family but only in general terms. I don't get the impression of familiarity from anything he says."

"Maybe he's someone she knows but she doesn't realise it," Wightman said. "Maybe his email identity is a cover."

"Then why doesn't she recognise his voice?" Feeney asked. "Surely if she knew him, he wouldn't be able to disguise himself for long."

Donovan was on the point of agreeing when Tartaglia wheeled around.

"Karen," he said, clicking his fingers and striding back to the front of the room, a sudden urgency in his voice. "Can you go and get the exhibits book? He talks about this sham ceremony in the email and giving her a ring. Run through the list of personal effects and see if a ring was found on her body." As Feeney got up and went out of the room to find the file, he turned to Minderedes. "Nick, I want you and Dave to start checking the Coroners' records for suicides of young women in London over the last couple of years."

Minderedes looked aghast. "But sir . . ." He stopped short when he saw Tartaglia's expression.

Wightman coloured, raising his pale eyebrows. "All suicides, sir?"

"All suicides," Tartaglia said emphatically.

A half-stifled groan went up from Minderedes and Wightman simultaneously. Donovan sympathised. There was no central record of suicides, each case being dealt with and recorded at a local level by the Coroner for that district. The only way of searching was to go to each office and examine the registers individually by hand. Also, as the business of the Coroner was only to establish the victim's identity, where and when they died and the cause of death, the records were not at all comprehensive. It was going to be a Herculean task and she couldn't see the point of it. There were no grounds so far to think Gemma's death was anything other than a one-off.

"Look," Tartaglia said, staring hard at Minderedes. "I know this is going to involve a lot of work and I'll speak to Superintendent Cornish immediately and see if we can get some extra help. But we must check everything thoroughly."

"But why, sir?" Minderedes said, still looking sceptical. "Surely you don't think he's done it before?"

Before Tartaglia had a chance to reply, Feeney came back into the room with the file.

"A gold ring is listed amongst the effects," she said. "The girl was wearing it on her third finger, left hand."

"I want it fingerprinted immediately," Tartaglia said. "And the hallmark and manufacturer checked. According to the emails, they exchanged rings. I presume the other ring wasn't found at the crime scene?"

Feeney studied the list of exhibits and shook her head. "There's no mention of it."

"Then we must assume Tom has it." He paused, catching Donovan's eye. "Along with the lock of hair he cut from Gemma's head. Sam, you remember what Dr Blake said, don't you?"

Puzzled, she gazed at him for a moment. "God, you're right," she said, thinking back to what Blake had said. She had been so wrapped up in what had been going on at the time between Tartaglia and Blake that she had forgotten all about it.

Tartaglia turned to Minderedes. "Think about this, Nick. It appears that Tom took a ring from Gemma. It also appears, from what the pathologist told us, that he cut off a lock of her hair from the back of the head, where it would least likely be spotted. Unless you have a better idea, they sound like souvenirs to me, which has bad connotations. It's possible he's done this thing before and nobody's picked it up because the death was wrongly recorded as a suicide."

"Which is what almost happened with Gemma," Donovan added, almost shouting. "CID had more or less closed the case."

"Just one thing, sir," Wightman said, looking down at one of the sheets. "In the last email, where Tom talks about the rings, he tells Gemma to leave a note for her mother. But there wasn't one, was there?"

"There's definitely no mention of a note anywhere in the files, sir," Feeney said.

As Feeney spoke, something clicked into place and Donovan jumped to her feet. "I've got it. Now I know what Kramer was holding back. He was so bloody relieved when I said that Gemma's death wasn't a suicide. I bet there was a note and he's either destroyed it or hidden it. It also explains why he wasn't remotely curious about what I was doing there and the fact that Gemma's death was suspicious. He thought he knew for sure what had really happened. He thought Gemma had killed herself and he didn't want that stigma attached to his daughter."

Tartaglia's face creased into a broad smile. "Well done, Sam. Let's pull Kramer in and see what he's got to say." He turned to Feeney. "Call his local nick and get them to send a car to pick him up. Tell them we'll be over shortly. Also, we'd better see if he recognises the ring, although I think we know what the answer will be." He looked at Donovan. "Do you want to come?"

With a quick glance at her watch, she shook her head and stood up. "I've got to go and see Rosie Chapple, Gemma's school friend. I'm already late."

Poor Kramer. She actually felt sorry for him and was glad to have an excuse not to be there. She had seen the wording in one of the emails that Tom had told Gemma to copy. Although the text was brief and quite innocuous, not laying the blame at any particular door, she thought of Kramer's pain, what he must have felt on finding the note, believing that Gemma had killed herself. From the little she knew of Kramer, her gut instinct told her that he had taken it to protect his wife, Mary. Better for a mother to think that her daughter had died in an accident or even in suspicious circumstances than to learn that she had chosen to take her own life, abandoning those who loved her. Donovan wondered how the Kramers would cope once they learned the truth about what had happened. For a moment she pictured Kramer's face earlier that evening as he fought back the tears and the inert shape of Gemma's mother lying in her bed. The loss of their daughter would be something they would never get over, something they would carry with them for the rest of their life.

Kramer would have to be hauled over the coals for what he had done but really they should be thanking him. If he hadn't appropriated the note, nobody would have bothered to request a special post mortem and there would have been no toxicology report revealing the presence of GHB in Gemma's system. Apart from the witness, who easily might have been disregarded, there would have been nothing to arouse suspicion. Gemma Kramer's death would have been recorded as a suicide and Tom would have been home and dry. Case closed.

CHAPTER
SEVEN

Tom unlocked the faded navy-blue front door of the small terraced house and went inside. There was a chill in the air, coupled with an unpleasant, mouldy odour. But he was in a hurry and there was no time to turn on the heating and air the rooms. He switched on the lights, ran up the two short flights of stairs to his grandfather's dressing room on the first floor and pushed open the door.

Even though his grandfather had been dead for over three years, the room still held the familiar medicinal smell mixed with stale tobacco that he'd associated with him since childhood. He went over to the tall mahogany chest of drawers, turned on the lamp and helped himself to the bottle of Trumper's Limes, which stood on the small tray, along with the hair pomade, mouthwash and wooden-backed brushes. As he rubbed some of the cologne on his fingers and patted it on his face, his eye ran along the row of brown-tinted army photographs that hung above on the wall. The old bugger. What glory now? It amused him to use his grandfather's aftershave, to think how angry he would be if he were still alive. Personally, Tom preferred something more modern and musky, a bit more exotic and provocative. But Limes went perfectly with the role he was playing. Tonight he was the dapper young ex-major, and old-fashioned restraint was the keyword. The woman he had met at the bridge club was taking him to the theatre, followed by dinner. It was a nice treat and she was tolerable company. But he hoped she wasn't expecting a fuck at the end of it. If so, she'd be disappointed.

He brushed his hair until it gleamed, then exchanged his cheap cufflinks for a pair of old gold monogrammed ones from the small brown leather box on a tray that contained a variety of ancient studs and collar stiffeners. Almost done, he did up his top button and opened the small wardrobe door, selecting a sober regimental tie from the rack. The tie reeked of mothballs and he sprinkled several drops of Limes on it before knotting it carefully and washing his hands at the small basin under the window.

On his way downstairs he passed his grandmother's room. Automatically, he paused outside the closed door, careful where he put his feet for fear of making one of the floorboards creak. It had been a while since he had lived in the house but he still felt nervous, like a small boy caught out of bed, creeping along the landing to listen to the grown-up conversation going on below. He almost expected to hear the peremptory tinkle of the little bell she used to summon him when she wanted something. But there was nothing this time, not even the tap-tap of her cane as she crept around inside the room. Even so, the silence failed to reassure him. She was still there. He had seen her many times, sometimes no more than a shadow, semi-transparent and rippling like mist in the air, sometimes more tangible so that he could see every wrinkle and age spot that marked her withered skin. She liked to surprise him, catch him unawares. But he was past being frightened of her.

For a moment, his hand lingered near the door handle. He wondered whether, if he opened it quickly, he might catch a fleeting glimpse of her inside. Maybe she would be tucked up in bed listening to the radio — the wireless, as she insisted on calling it — or sitting at her dressing-table in her voluminous nightgown, studying her reflection in the mirror as she smoothed down her long white hair with one of her silver brushes. Ghosts weren't supposed to have a reflection, but she had one and the room still stank of her, no matter how often he cleaned and scrubbed it. It emanated partly from the rows of ancient clothes that hung like discarded skins in her wardrobe. But it also clung to the air she had once breathed. The cloying smell, a mixture of sweet, gardenia perfume, face powder and sour old woman, had worked itself into every corner and crevice, impregnating the very walls. It made him sick every time he went inside. He had thought about selling the house after she died, thinking that perhaps then she would leave him alone. He could do with the cash, but he knew he couldn't rid himself of her that easily. What's more, he didn't want people asking questions, poking around and nosing into their things; his things. Above all, the house was his secret place.

He waited a couple more moments, listening for some sort of sound from inside the room. But there was nothing and he carried on down the stairs. The portrait of his grandfather in the hall, dressed in full military regalia, glowered at him and he gave it a mock salute. The old fucker looked as humourless as ever, with his eye-patch and moustache. Puffed up like a peacock and arrogant as always, so bloody sure of himself, with so little right to be. But that was then. Tom was the master now.

Tom. He'd have to stop thinking of himself as Tom, although he saw himself more as Tom than any of the others. He was currently Matt or George or Colin, depending on who was at the receiving end. The names were ordinary but it was easier that way. Before Tom, he'd been Alain, after watching Alain Delon in some old film. But the stupid girl couldn't spell and kept calling him Alan, a name he loathed, reminding him of a nasty, fat-faced bully of a boy he'd once known at school. Yes, plain and simple was best. Besides, he couldn't see himself as a Brad or Russell or Jude. It just wasn't him and every detail was important. Any false note and they'd smell a rat.

He opened the door to the small sitting room, turned on the overhead light and went over to the small display cabinet by the French windows that housed his grandmother's collection of snuffboxes and tea caddies. They were her little treasures and she had shared them with no one, taking them out lovingly each week and dusting them, allowing him only to look through the glass but never to touch.

He found the small silver key in its hiding place on the ledge at the back, unlocked the glass door and took out a caddy made in the shape of a pear. It was his favourite. As a child, it had particularly fascinated him, so life-like, carved from a single piece of wood. He had liked stroking its smooth, yellow-brown curves when his grandmother had gone out to play cards. Once, when she came home early, she caught him at the cabinet and beat him hard, sending him to bed without his tea. After that, she had hidden the key but he had always found it. Didn't matter where she put it, he was always one step ahead of the old bag. Always. He glanced at the pair of matching black urns on the mantel-piece. It was strange to think of all that energy and loathing reduced to nothing but a few handfuls of grey dust. There were times when he wanted to pour them both down the toilet. But it was better to have them there where he could see them, where he could reassure himself with the tangible evidence that they were both really dead.

He opened the lid of the caddy and took out the signet ring Gemma had given him. Made of old pink gold, it was engraved with someone's initials, the edges smooth from years of wear. Perhaps she had bought it from an antique market stall or maybe it belonged to a relative. Not bad, he thought, given that she was only fourteen. The little bitch had had taste. He slipped it on his finger and took out the long lock of hair he had cut from her head as she lay on the floor of the gallery, semi-comatose. Stupidly, he'd overdone the dose, which had quite spoiled things, and the silly cow hadn't been aware of anything by that point. He twined the long silky strands of brown hair around his finger and closed his eyes, catching its delicate scent and stroking it rhythmically against his cheek as he replayed in his mind what had happened.

She was surprisingly heavy, for such a slip of a girl. A real dead weight, he remembered thinking with a smile, as he lifted her up and carried her to the edge of the balcony. As he looked at her for the last time, her eyes had rolled back in their sockets and for a moment he thought she was going to be sick. At least she was past struggling. Holding her in his arms, he peered down into the dim area below. He savoured that knife-edge moment. It made him high. If only he could prolong it, make it last forever. But the rushing urgency overcame him as before and he couldn't stop himself. With an almighty heave, he had hurled her high into the air, for a second a flapping bundle of black. He thought she gave a little gasp as she fell. Maybe she realised what was happening. But it was all over too quickly and he was left with the aching emptiness again.

He opened his eyes, twisted the hair into a coil and returned it with the ring to the caddy, locking it away in the cabinet, making sure to hide the key. If the shade of his grandmother came rummaging around for it, she'd be out of luck, he thought with satisfaction, as he walked over to the large gilt mirror that hung above the fireplace. Taking a silk handkerchief from his jacket pocket, he wiped the fine layer of dust from the centre and studied his reflection. He flicked a speck from his shoulder, made a final adjustment to his tie and, moistening a finger with his tongue, smoothed down each of his fine brows as he checked his shining white teeth. Perfect. He was ready.

CHAPTER
EIGHT

Rosie Chapple lived not far from Gemma in a two-storey Victorian cottage set back behind a small, untidy front garden. Donovan rang the bell and, after a moment, a tall, gangly woman with wild, frizzy, greying hair answered the door. Her eyes were kohl-rimmed and she looked like a gypsy, with dangly earrings, coloured bangles and a long, flowing patchwork dress.

"Detective Sergeant Donovan," Donovan said, showing her ID. "I phoned earlier. Is Rosie back?"

"I'm Sarah Chapple, her mother," the woman said, with a jingle of bangles as she held out her hand. "She's just got in. You'd better come with me."

Donovan caught a waft of sandalwood as she followed Sarah inside, down a narrow corridor into an open-plan kitchen at the back. A pale-faced girl with a halo of black, curly hair sat at the small scrubbed pine table, shovelling rice crispies into her mouth. She looked up and gave Donovan a weary look, before continuing to eat.

The room was painted a dark rust and had a homely feel, with an old dresser on one side, every shelf heaving with china and books, the walls crammed with photographs and colourful pictures.

"This is Rosie," Sarah said, patting her daughter's hand as she sat down next to her and gestured Donovan to the scuffed wooden chair opposite. "I know you've come about Gemma's death. How can we help?"

"We're trying to piece together what happened. Gemma . . ."

"It was at a church, wasn't it?" Sarah interrupted.

"Yes. Gemma was seen outside with a man before she died. We're trying to find out who he is."

Sarah looked surprised. "Do you mean a boyfriend?"

Donovan nodded. "Although he was considerably older than Gemma."

"Gemma never mentioned anyone," Sarah said, with a quick glance towards Rosie, who was noisily scraping up the last few mouthfuls of cereal and milk, apparently oblivious to what was being discussed around her.

"It's very important we find him," Donovan said, as Rosie clanked her spoon down in the empty bowl, pushed it away and stared down at the table, shoulders hunched.

"What's the man got to do with it?" Sarah asked. "The school said Gemma had a fall. I thought it was an accident."

"It's not as simple as that," Donovan said, looking at Rosie, who was picking at a patch of candle wax stuck on the table. Was she feeling uncomfortable because of her mother being there, or because Donovan was a policewoman? Or was there another reason? "Do you know anything about this man?" she said, trying to catch Rosie's eye.

Sarah shook her head. "I told you, I haven't heard anything about Gemma having a boyfriend."

Donovan tried to contain her irritation. "Thank you, Mrs Chapple. But I need to ask Rosie." She wanted to ask Sarah Chapple to leave, but as Rosie was a minor, that was out of the question. She stared hard at Rosie, willing her to look up. "Did Gemma tell you about a man? I really need to know."

Rosie sniffed and looked away, focusing on a distant point on the far wall.

"Please, Rosie," Donovan said. "He may have had something to do with Gemma's death."

Sarah gasped. "Oh my God! Are you saying she was murdered?"

At the word "murdered", Rosie looked round, and Donovan saw tears in her eyes.

"We're treating her death as suspicious, Mrs Chapple. Which is why I need Rosie to tell me if she knows anything."

Sarah turned to Rosie, clamped an arm around her shoulder and leaned towards her. "Come on, sweetheart. If you know something, you'd better tell the sergeant. There's no point in keeping secrets if Gemma was murdered."

Rosie bowed her head, pulled down the sleeves of her baggy black jumper over a set of bitten fingernails, and hugged herself. "She didn't talk about him much," she said, in a small, high-pitched voice, which Donovan could barely hear. "I thought he was just one of her fantasies."

A look of horror crossed Sarah's face. "Is he a paedophile? Was Gemma assaulted?"

Exasperated, Donovan glared at her. If only the woman would shut up and let her daughter speak. "No, Mrs Chapple. She wasn't assaulted. Please let Rosie continue." She turned back to Rosie. "Do you have any idea where she met him?"

Rosie shook her head. "She never said."

"Please think, Rosie. There must be something else. Every little detail is important. We must find him."

Rosie appeared confused, looking first at her mother, then back at Donovan. "Talked about him like he was real special, like some sort of pop star or actor or something. We all thought she was telling porkies and we teased her." Tears were streaming down her cheeks. "I feel so bad now," she said, burying her face in her arms.

Sarah rubbed her shoulders and stroked her head. "It's all right, sweetheart. You mustn't feel guilty about it." Putting her arm protectively around Rosie, she turned to Donovan. "Gemma was an odd girl, Sergeant. The sort who invited teasing, if you know what I mean. I teach art at the school and I've got three daughters, so I know what girls can be like. Gemma was good at heart but she was full of stories. It was difficult to know what to believe, sometimes. I put it down to a lack of confidence and the fact that her mum should have spent more time with her." She gave Rosie a little squeeze and kissed the top of her head. "Girls need their mums, even at this age. But Gemma's brothers were a handful and they took up all Mary's energy, from what I could see."

"I'm sorry if this is distressing for you," Donovan said, peering down at Rosie. "Nobody's going to blame you for anything. It would just help if you could tell me what you know."

Rosie looked up, gulped, wiped her nose with the back of her hand. "She said she was going to run away with him."

"Did she ever mention suicide?" Donovan asked.

Sarah put her hands to her mouth. "Suicide? Goodness, I thought you said her death was suspicious?"

"Please answer the question, Rosie," Donovan said, ignoring Sarah. "Did Gemma ever talk about suicide?"

Rosie nodded. "Everyone thought she was just trying to get attention for herself, just trying to be different. That's why nobody liked her."

"But you did?"

Rosie sniffed and nodded. "When she wasn't making up stuff, she could be really nice and I felt sorry for her."

"Did she have any interests outside school that you know of? Any clubs or societies?"

"She belonged to a swimming club, I think," she said, rubbing her eyes with her fingers and pushing her springy dark curls off her face.

"Surely you can get all that from her parents?" Sarah asked.

"Gemma kept a lot hidden from them, Mrs Chapple. She met this man somehow and we must find the connection. Is there anything else you can tell me, Rosie?"

Rosie sighed and looked at her for a moment before speaking. "So, he is real?" she said doubtfully, as if she was still trying to take it all in. "You mean she wasn't lying about him?"

"He's real enough," Donovan said. It was almost as if the news was a relief to Rosie and she had the feeling that there was more to come. "Please tell me what you know."

Rosie paused for a moment before replying. "She called me on Wednesday."

Sarah gave her a sharp look. "What, the day she died? You didn't tell me."

"My phone was out of juice and I only picked up the message yesterday. When I listened to it, they'd already told us at school that she was dead. It was really weird, hearing her voice."

"What did she say?" Donovan asked.

Rosie shrugged. "I thought it was just another one of her silly stories. She said she was meeting this bloke Tom at a church and that they were going to be married. She said it would be the last time I'd hear from her, but that I should be happy for her."

"What else?"

Rosie wiped away another tear with the back of her hand. "She said she was late and had seen him standing by the church door, waiting for her. But he hadn't seen her. She sounded really excited. She said she just had to call me quickly to tell me and to say goodbye."

"Where was she calling from?" Donovan asked.

"Must have been a call box," Rosie replied. "Her stupid parents wouldn't allow her a mobile and I could hear traffic in the background."

They would have to check the caller number on Rosie's phone but it sounded plausible. "Is there anything else?"

Rosie hesitated and looked at Donovan uncertainly.

"Go on," Sarah said, firmly. "What else did she say?"

Rosie sighed. "It seemed sort of weird. But she said he looked just like Tom Cruise in *Interview with the Vampire*."

After checking in with Tartaglia and telling him about her conversation with Rosie, Donovan wearily drove the short distance home to the small house she shared with her sister, Claire, in Hammersmith. There was nothing more to be done that night and Tartaglia had told her to go home and get some sleep, ready for the next day. A big glass of wine and a hot, deep bath would sort her out, she thought, letting herself in quietly through the front door. Claire was in, her bag and keys dumped on the hall table, next to a pile of half-opened mail, her briefcase and shoes discarded at the bottom of the narrow flight of stairs. As a solicitor in one of the City law firms, she worked long hours and would have been tucked up in bed hours ago.

Donovan went into the kitchen and checked the answer machine but there were no message and no note either from Claire to say that anyone had called. Disappointed, although not surprised, she dropped her keys onto the table and poured herself a glass of white wine from an open bottle in the fridge. It wasn't very nice but it was all there was and at least it was cold. She and Claire never had time to do any shopping. Resisting the urge to light a cigarette, she took her wine upstairs and tiptoed past Claire's bedroom door into the bathroom where she turned on the taps and helped herself to a large dollop of Claire's Body Shop Orange Blossom Bath Essence. She undressed quickly and sank back into the bath, feet up on either side of the taps, letting the rising water wash over her shoulders and neck as she sipped her wine.

Logic told her that she shouldn't expect to hear from Richard again. Newly promoted to DI, Richard had recently joined one of the murder teams in south London and was working all hours. It had got to the point where they rarely ever saw each other. He had half-suggested she put in for a transfer to somewhere closer to where he worked. But why should she move? She hadn't known him that long and she was enjoying working on Clarke's team. There had never been much of a sparkle about Richard. A small part of her hoped he might get over his pride or inertia and call her. But what then? She needed something different. Someone different. More than anything she wanted some fun for a change and perhaps some excitement.

It was past midnight by the time Tartaglia got home — a ground floor flat in a terraced house off Shepherd's Bush Road. He pushed his motorbike up the short tiled path that led from the street to the front door, parking it out of sight behind the high hedge, by the dustbins.

He'd bought the flat with some money left to him by his grandfather a few years before. The place had been a tip, with wiring, plumbing and fixtures dating back to the seventies. It had taken him, his cousin Gianni, and a couple of the lads from Gianni's building firm several weekends to transform it, painting the walls white, sanding the floorboards and putting in a modern kitchen and bathroom. The flat was the first place he had ever owned and it would take a lot to get him to move again.

As he put his key in the lock, Henry, the Siamese cat belonging to his upstairs neighbour Jenny, twisted around his legs, meowing to be brought in. Judging by the dark windows and drawn curtains on the floor above, Jenny had gone to bed. As he opened the front door and let himself into his flat, Henry slipped through his legs, weaving his way into the sitting room. He wasn't keen on cats, generally; their hair made him sneeze. But Henry had become a frequent visitor, thick-skinned to all efforts to exclude him, and Tartaglia had grown fond of him, often leaving the kitchen window at the side of the house ajar so that Henry could come and go.

He went into the sitting room, switched on the light and drew the shutters across the window, blocking out the orange glare of the streetlamp just outside. He flung his jacket onto the sofa and checked the answer machine. Apart from a bleep where somebody had hung up, there were two messages, one from Sally-Anne saying that there was no change in Clarke's condition and one from his sister, Nicoletta, asking him over for Sunday lunch. She said there was someone she wanted him to meet, no doubt another of her hopeless, single female friends. For once, he was relieved to be working all weekend, with an excuse that even Nicoletta would be forced to accept.

He knew he should try and get some sleep. There was the briefing at seven that morning and it was going to be another long day. But he felt wired, thoughts buzzing in his head. He undid his tie and top button and went into the kitchen for a drink. What was it with women? Not content just to get married themselves, once they'd done that, they spent their whole time matchmaking everybody else. Nicoletta seemed obsessed with getting him hitched and his cousin Elisa, Gianni's sister, was almost as bad. They kept reminding him that he was only a few years away from being forty, a point they viewed as some sort of a watershed, although it meant nothing to him. Why couldn't they understand that he was happy as he was and leave him alone?

Happy? Well, not unhappy, he thought, opening the bottle of Sicilian Nero d'Avola that Gianni had given him for his birthday, and pouring himself a large glass. Seeing Fiona Blake that morning had caused all sorts of uncomfortable feelings to surface. Why was he attracted to complicated women, women he couldn't quite pin down? Why was he never interested in nice, straight-forward women like Donovan?

The wine was a deep, black purple and smelled heady and full of spice. He took a large draught, letting it swill around his mouth, enjoying the pungent flavour. Christ, it was good, he thought, taking another long swig. Gianni really knew a thing or two about wine. Perhaps he had been a bit hard on Fiona but he'd been angry. Screw Murray. Even though it was late, he felt like calling her. Maybe he'd apologise for what had happened earlier. It would be nice to hear her voice. Then he remembered the ring on her finger. No point. She had made her choice and he had to put her out of his mind.

He went into the sitting room, put REM's *Around the Sun* on the CD player and dimmed the lights. He sank down into the middle of the large, comfortable sofa, shoes off, feet up on the glass coffee table, and closed his eyes momentarily. Henry appeared from nowhere and jumped onto his lap, purring loudly, settling himself down into a tight pale beige coil. Tartaglia took another slug of wine and lit a cigarette, trying to lose himself in the music, watching the smoke snake up towards the ceiling. The sound was good. Like his motorbike, the player had been an extravagance, but well worth it. Thank God, he had nobody to dictate how he spent his money.

Donovan had called to tell him about her meeting with Rosie Chapple and he had spoken to Superintendent Cornish to brief him about what they had discovered. Not a man to show emotion easily, Cornish had sounded a little rattled as Tartaglia outlined his theory that Gemma's death might be part of a series. Cornish had refused to give him extra resources to help search the records for matching suicides, saying that he couldn't justify such a thing on the basis of a "pure hunch". But he had promised to come down to Barnes for the next day's morning meeting, clearly wanting to keep closer tabs on things, considering what Tartaglia had said. Tartaglia hoped that that was going to be the limit of his hands-on input. Unlike Clarke, Cornish had almost no murder experience, having risen through the ranks in other departments, almost entirely on the uniform side. Cornish could handle the media, for all he cared, and he would keep him fully briefed, but he wanted to be left in overall day-to-day charge of the case.

He could still feel the reheated lasagne from the pub sitting in his stomach, and wondered whether he'd be able to sleep. He shouldn't have had it, but he was so hungry after seeing Kramer that he would have eaten almost anything. Kramer, the hard man, had gone to pieces once he discovered that they knew about the suicide note. Tartaglia felt deeply sorry for the man. Kramer had handed over the note, written on flowery paper in Gemma's childish handwriting, folded neatly in a pink envelope with her mother's name on the front. But it had revealed nothing new, the wording being identical to what Tom had ordered Gemma to write. Kramer and his two friends' alibis had checked out and they had let him go with a severe bollocking for withholding evidence. Kramer was a dead end. They would have to look for Gemma's killer elsewhere.

CHAPTER
NINE

Monday, six thirty a.m., and Tartaglia sat at Clarke's desk in his large, comfortable corduroy chair, struggling to focus on the file in front of him, a half-drunk mug of lukewarm black coffee at his side. He had had no sleep in the previous twenty-four hours and was finding staying awake a challenge. Contrary to Tartaglia's initial hopes, Cornish had continued to refuse to give him any additional resources to scour the registers at the coroners' offices in the various London districts. It wasn't clear whether this was because he doubted Tartaglia's instincts or whether he feared what might be found, although Tartaglia suspected it was a combination of both. In the end, Tartaglia's team had spent the last couple of days painstakingly going through the books page-by-page, clocking up hundreds of man-hours, complaining vociferously that it was all a complete waste of time. Eventually, they had turned up two suicides that appeared to fit the pattern. The case files had been retrieved from central records and, after Tartaglia had read through the documents in detail, Donovan and Dickenson had been immediately dispatched to interview the families.

Laura Benedetti, aged fifteen, had fallen to her death eight months before in a church in Richmond, her body found by a local woman coming in to change the flowers. Laura lived in a council flat in Islington, several miles away, very close to Tartaglia's sister, Nicoletta's house. According to Donovan, Laura was the only child of a couple from Sardinia who seemed to work all hours of the day and night, the mother cleaning houses in the smarter streets of the area, the father a head waiter in the restaurant of a West End hotel. The photo Tartaglia had seen of Laura reminded him instantly of Nicoletta at the same age, oval face, soft brown eyes and long, dark hair, although there was something dreamy about Laura's expression which was very different to Nicoletta's. Donovan had told Tartaglia how Laura's father had wanted to return home to Sardinia immediately after the tragedy but her mother had so far refused. She was unable to leave the country where her daughter had died, making a shrine of Laura's tiny bedroom and visiting her grave almost daily. Donovan seemed more than usually affected by what she had heard, stating with glistening eyes how some people found it impossible to move on in any way from such a tragedy.

The other girl, Elinor Best, known as Ellie, had died four months after Laura in similar circumstances in a church in Chiswick, her body discovered by a tramp taking refuge inside during a storm. Ellie had lived several miles away in a prosperous residential part of Wandsworth with a younger brother and sister. Her father was a solicitor, her mother a journalist, and her

100

background couldn't have been more different to Gemma and Laura's. Aged sixteen, with reddish-brown hair, a rash of freckles and a pert, turned-up nose, she had been a budding violinist, chosen a few weeks before her death to play in one of the London youth orchestras. Her parents had recently separated and Donovan and Dickenson had only been able to see the mother so far, who was living alone with her two remaining children in the house in Wandsworth, apparently blaming the father for what had happened to Ellie.

But most striking of all had been the fact that both girls had left brief suicide notes and the wording was almost identical to the note left by Gemma Kramer. No doubt they too had been dictated by Tom. There were no witnesses to either Laura or Ellie's death and with nothing to arouse suspicion, no further investigation had seemed necessary. The local coroners had duly recorded verdicts of suicide. With the deaths happening in two different areas, there had been no chance of anyone spotting the similarities and linking the two cases.

At the time the parents of both girls had adamantly refused to believe that their daughters had any reason to kill themselves. However, the local CID investigation had revealed that both Laura and Ellie had been badly bullied at school, echoing what Tartaglia's team already knew about Gemma. Like her, the two girls seemed to be misfits. Laura, small for her age, uncommunicative and sensitive, had been teased about her poor English, whilst Ellie had been overweight and lacking in self-confidence. Struggling academically, music had been her only area of achievement. According to the case notes, Ellie had been prescribed anti-depressants by her GP. Whilst a visit from the police several months later must have been intensely painful for the families, Tartaglia took some comfort from the fact that both Laura's parents and Ellie's mother seemed relieved to learn that their daughters' deaths were being looked into again.

Ellie Best had been cremated. But Laura Benedetti had been buried. Her exhumation had taken place a little after three a.m. that day in an anonymous North London cemetery. Tartaglia and Feeney had attended, together with Alex James, the crime scene manager, Dr Blake, and an annoying middle-aged man from the Coroner's Office who had a streaming head cold and seemed purely concerned with the inconvenience of missing a night's sleep. None of them wanted to be standing there in the middle of the night huddled together around the grave, listening to the rain drumming on the sides and roof of the forensic tent while the undertakers did their work. But the cover of darkness was necessary in order to reduce the chance of anyone finding out what they were doing. The last thing they needed were the prying eyes of local residents, let alone the press. Laura's remains had been taken away to the mortuary for a post mortem and Tartaglia was due there in a couple of hours to see what Blake had found.

He got up from the desk, about to head for the kitchen to make some fresh coffee, when his mobile rang. As he answered it, he caught sight of himself in the small round mirror on the wall, which Clarke used for the occasional morning shave. He looked like shit, with a day's growth of beard and deep, dark circles under his eyes. He ran his fingers quickly through his hair in an attempt to smooth it down, and heard Superintendent Cornish's voice muffled at the other end.

"Has the exhumation taken place?"

"Yes, and the post mortem's being done as we speak." Tartgalia cradled the phone under his ear as he pushed aside a packing case full of Clarke's things, which Sally-Ann was due to collect at some point. He closed the door firmly against the background noise coming from the main office opposite and tried to focus on what Cornish was saying.

"When do you expect to get the results?" Cornish said.

"They're rushing them through, so hopefully within the next twenty-four hours. I'm on my way over shortly to see the pathologist."

The pathologist. The words had a nice, detached ring to them, the opposite of what he really felt, if he was honest. Glancing again in the mirror, he rubbed the thick black stubble on his chin with his fingers. With the morning meeting due to start shortly, there'd be no time to go back home for a shower, a shave and a change of clothes before meeting Fiona Blake later at the mortuary. Clarke's electric razor was in one of the many boxes in the hall but it looked like a health hazard and he preferred a wet shave anyway. Sod it, he thought, smiling at his own vanity. Why should he care about pleasing Fiona? She would just have to take him as she found him. He turned away and sank down in the chair, putting his feet up heavily on the desk.

"The press haven't got wind of anything, I hope?" Cornish said, chewing something loudly as he spoke.

Tartaglia heard the clatter of china and the sound of a woman's voice in the background. Cornish must be at home having breakfast. Knowing Cornish, it would be muesli, granary toast with a low-fat spread and a pot of a particular brand of Earl Grey tea. According to Clarke, the muesli and tea travelled with Cornish everywhere, even when he went away for a work conference. He was a creature of habit in everything he did, imagination not being his strong point.

"Not as far as I know," Tartaglia replied, aware that he didn't have Cornish's full attention.

"Did you find the rings?" Cornish's mouth was still full, the final word sounding like "wings".

There were few things Tartaglia found more irritating than trying to have a conversation with someone who was eating, particularly when he'd been up all the night and had had no breakfast. Trying to stifle his annoyance, he replied: "Laura Benedetti's mother thinks she was wearing one but she's not a hundred per cent certain. If there was a ring, nobody knows where it is."

Cornish made a dissatisfied grunt at the other end. "What a pity."

"But Ellie Best was wearing one when she died and her mother kept it. It's identical to Gemma Kramer's, plain gold, eighteen carat, same hallmark. It looks like Tom bought a job lot. We're still trying to trace the manufacturer."

"When do we hear back about the girls' computers?"

"Again, it's being treated as a priority," Tartaglia said. "But they couldn't give me a precise time."

The computers had been retrieved from other family members, who had been using them, and sent off for analysis. But even if the emails could be recovered, they were unlikely to be much help in finding the killer. According to the experts at Newlands Park, it had proved impossible to trace Tom from Gemma's computer.

"You're sure there are only two deaths that fit the pattern?" Cornish asked, taking a slurp of what Tartaglia assumed was tea.

"As I told you last night, there's one other death we're looking into. But it's not an instant fit. Marion Spear was single, just turned thirty, so she's quite a bit older than the others. She fell from the top storey of a car park nearly two years ago, just within the time frame we've been searching. There was an investigation at the time as there were no witnesses and no suicide note. But in the end, short of any conclusive evidence to the contrary, the coroner recorded an open verdict."

"Why are you bothering with her?"

"Purely on the basis of location. The car park was just down the road from where Gemma died."

Cornish coughed as if something had gone down the wrong way. Tartaglia heard the sound of a chair being scraped back, followed by running water. Growing increasingly impatient as Cornish spluttered and cleared his throat, he stood up and started to pace around the small room.

"What about a ring?" Cornish gasped, after a moment.

"We're checking to see if she was wearing one. If not, I think there's no reason to get an exhumation order at this point."

"So, apart from her, you think we have three victims?"

"Subject to confirmation from the pathologist on Laura, yes. First Laura, then Ellie and then Gemma."

"Just the three?"

"As far as we can tell." Of course, there was no way to be a hundred per cent certain but they'd trawled the records as thoroughly as possible, given limited time and resources. The phrase needles and haystacks came to mind. "Would you like me to widen the search, maybe start looking outside the London area?" As he said this, he knew what the answer would be.

Cornish took another noisy gulp of something and cleared his throat again. "It's too much of a long shot and we haven't got the manpower. Also, I don't want to risk a leak and have the press crawling all over us before we're ready. Call me when you've seen the pathologist."

Holding a handkerchief over his nose to dampen the overpowering stench of decay, Tartaglia stared down at the shrivelled, greenish-black remains of Laura Benedetti stretched out before him on the steel gurney.

Eight months in a London cemetery had reduced her to something barely recognisable as human and with a momentary pang he remembered the photo of her he had seen.

Thanks to the ring, they were sure about Ellie Best. But he needed some sort of confirmation from Fiona Blake that Laura Benedetti was also part of the series. However, Blake was taking her time. He had only just arrived at the mortuary when she had rushed out of the room to the corridor outside to take a call on her mobile. Judging from the peal of what sounded like flirtatious laughter that echoed through the doors, it was personal and he'd put money on it being a man at the other end.

He was on the point of going out to insist that she come back and talk to him, when the double doors swung open and she strode briskly back into the room as if nothing had happened, shoes squeaking on the lino, her white coat hugging her hips as she walked towards him.

"We should get the tox results back by tomorrow," she said matter-of-factly, coming over to where he was standing, hands in the pockets of her coat. "But they're unlikely to tell us much, as you know."

He hadn't expected anything else, given the state of decomposition of Laura's body and the time it had spent in the ground.

"Are you telling me then that there's nothing suspicious about her death?" he said levelly, removing the handkerchief temporarily and trying not to inhale.

His stomach churned and he hoped this wasn't going to take long.

"The girl died from a fall onto a hard surface, just as it says in the coroner's report. Nothing wrong there. But there is one thing," she said, catching his eye. "It's useful that I saw the last victim. I knew what I was looking for."

As she brushed past him and went over to the gurney, putting on a fresh pair of surgical gloves, he caught a faint, fleeting whiff of her perfume and found himself momentarily wanting to reach out and touch her hair, stroke the soft skin of her neck.

Using both hands, she gently shifted the remains of the head to one side, then looked round at him. "Look. Here, by the base of her scalp." She pointed with a finger.

Clamping the handkerchief back over his mouth and nose, he stepped forward and peered down at the blackened mess of flesh, trying to see what she was indicating. It was almost impossible to make out anything meaningful. Then, peering even closer, he saw the razor-sharp line, dark against an even darker mass.

"He's taken a lock of hair?" he guessed, excitement starting to bubble up.

"Yes," she said, with a satisfied smile, as if she had just given him a wonderful present. "It's easy to miss because of the decomposition and the colour of her hair. But do you see here?" As she ran her finger over the spot she met his eye again. For a second, he wondered again who she had been speaking to on the phone.

"A chunk of hair has been removed," she said, still holding his gaze. "It's been cut off cleanly with a sharp blade, exactly like the other girl."

CHAPTER
TEN

"Islington, Wandsworth, Streatham, Richmond, Chiswick and Ealing." Tartaglia pointed with a pen at the large map of Greater London that Wightman had fixed to the white board in the main office, the locations marked with drawing pins. "That's where Laura, Ellie and Gemma lived and died. Marion Spear also lived and died in Ealing. Is there any connection we can make at this point?"

There was a long pause before Wightman replied: "The scale of the map makes the locations look quite close together but it's actually an enormous area. Doesn't make much sense to me."

"Me neither," Donovan added. "Laura from Islington ends up dead in Richmond; Ellie, from Wandsworth, in Chiswick; and Gemma, from Streatham, in Ealing. Apart from the fact that he's killing the girls a good few miles from where they each live, I can't see any pattern either."

The only response from Dickenson was a loud, throaty sigh. It was late afternoon and Donovan and Wightman were perched on a bank of empty desks near the board. Dickenson sat to one side on a chair, feet stretched out in front of her, toes resting on the rail of another chair. Her hands were clasped awkwardly over her stomach and she looked as if she had only had a few hours of sleep, eyes struggling to focus, yawning intermittently. Tartaglia wondered whether it wouldn't be better to send her home, although he knew she'd bite his head off if he suggested any such thing.

All his team's efforts so far had concentrated on researching the victimology of the three girls, trying to find a link between them, be it their schools, clubs, doctors, dentists, and suchlike. It was early days, but so far they had uncovered nothing to suggest that the three girls' paths had crossed during the previous two years. There had to be a link but they were missing it.

"Have any of you come across geographical profiling?" Tartagalia asked.

"We used a profiler once for a rape case when I was in Lewisham," Dickenson said, stifling another yawn. "He had some really interesting things to say."

"You mean, like Cracker, sir?" Wightman asked.

Tartaglia shook his head. "You're talking about psychological profiling. Geographical profiling is totally different." He tapped the map with his pen. "This isn't anything like the real thing. Nowadays it's all done on a computer and you need a minimum of five locations for proper analysis. But it's still worth visualising where the victims lived and where they died, in case something leaps out. Also, the location of a crime's a hard fact. It's not open to interpretation and it tells us a lot about the criminal."

"You mean why Tom chose the places he killed the three girls?" Donovan asked. "Local knowledge, that sort of thing?"

"Exactly. All three murders took place in the general west London area. The churches were all pretty disused and perfect for his purpose. Given what we know of him from the emails, the places weren't chosen at random. Which means he either knows them or spent time finding them."

"For what it's worth, the churches are all close to tube stations on the District Line," Dickenson said. "Perhaps that's how he's getting around."

Tartaglia nodded. "Maybe. Another thing that's interesting is that all three killings happened during the week, in the mid to late afternoon. This also applies to Marion Spear's death. Our killer must be somebody who is either unemployed or who has a relatively flexible working arrangement. He can take time off without it being noticed. It's possible he avoids the weekend because he himself has commitments, a family maybe."

"Or else, because there are fewer people around on weekday afternoons," Wightman said.

Donovan nodded. "And the girls are less likely to be missed by their families. They were all supposed to be at school when they went to the churches."

"What about the fact that all three crime scenes are churches?" Wightman asked. "Maybe the whole church thing turns him on."

Tartaglia shrugged. "The church is certainly part of the whole theatrical ritual which he used to lure the girls to him. But at this stage, I'm not reading anything more into it."

"You don't think the churches mean something special to him?" Dickenson asked, looking surprised.

"Anything's possible," he replied, with a shrug. "But sitting here, how can we possibly tell? If we start wondering about his psychological motivation, we get into the realms of fairytales. Anyway, even if churches have some sort of special significance for him, how does it help us find him?"

"You don't have much time for psychological profiling, then?" Dickenson asked, looking sceptical.

"As far as I'm concerned it's an arcane art and its predictions are about as scientific as a tabloid horoscope." He gazed at her tired face for a moment, feeling a combination of frustration and sympathy for her. "We'd all like to have a magic bullet and I wish I could tell you that it worked. But you only have to look at the screw-ups that have taken place in some well-known cases to see that it can be very misleading."

"Won't you be consulting a psychological profiler?" Donovan asked, with a wry glance in Dickenson's direction.

"At some point, maybe," he said, noncommittally. He knew he would probably be forced to bring one on board eventually, if only to satisfy his superiors that he'd ticked all the right boxes. But as far as he was concerned, any decent, experienced detective could add as much value as a psychological profiler, although it wasn't fashionable to say so.

"But surely they can help in narrowing the field of focus," Dickenson said, irritably, refusing to give up.

"That's the theory. But like everything, it depends on the quality of the input. Garbage in, garbage out."

Tartaglia sighed, wishing that Dickenson hadn't pushed him. But he might as well be honest, even if word of his heresy somehow filtered back to Cornish, who was a staunch believer. "Look, I'll give you a perfect example. The bloke we used on the North London Strangler case was worse than useless, even though he's got a list of degrees the length of your arm and is reckoned to be one of the top profilers in this country. He . . ."

"But there've been some fantastic books on profiling," Dickenson interrupted. "Surely, they can't all be rubbish."

"I'm not saying they are, although many of the case studies have been rewritten with the benefit of hindsight. My point is that we don't need the distraction. Going back to the North London Strangler case, the profiler, or Behavioural Investigative Analyst, as we're supposed to call them now, as if it makes them sound more scientific, was way off the mark. He wasted a lot of our time. He told us that the man we were looking for — a violent rapist-turned-murderer — was in his early to mid-twenties, sexually dysfunctional, lived alone and had difficulty making friends. In fact, Michael Barton was in his late thirties, popular with his mates and a right Jack-the-Lad with the ladies. His wife was so happy with his performance in the sack that she didn't question what he got up to late at night, when he supposedly took the dog out for a walk."

"But you caught him," Donovan said.

"No thanks to the profiler. If we'd followed his advice, we'd still be looking for the murderer and, no doubt, there would have been further victims."

"How did you get him, then?" Wightman asked.

"The area of the attacks was very small, which was striking. Most murderers don't have unlimited time. They need to feel comfortable with the territory, know where's safe, where they're unlikely to be disturbed and how to make a quick getaway. With Barton, we drew our own conclusions, based on common sense. We focused on all locals, irrespective of age and background, with previous convictions for assault, particularly of a sexual nature. Barton popped up on the radar screen as he had been arrested several years before on two separate charges of attempted rape, although both victims refused to go to court and the charges were dropped, which was why there was no record of his DNA. It was before the change in the law."

Dickenson still looked doubtful. "But Gemma Kramer, Ellie Best and Laura Benedetti are all under twenty. Surely, that tells us something about the killer?"

Tartaglia shook his head. "Not necessarily. Tom may be targeting all sorts of women. But the only ones he's successful in luring to their deaths happen to be in that age group. Perhaps they're self-selecting."

"You mean because they're young, naïve and easily suggestible," Donovan added, appearing to agree with what he had said. "They were also in a vulnerable state of mind. We know that all three were being bullied at school and one was on Prozac. People like that aren't thinking straight. How else can he con them into believing that they should go and top themselves with him?"

Tartaglia nodded. "Maybe we're just seeing the tip of the iceberg. For every victim, how many failures, and what's the profile of each of the failures? Maybe he goes after older women too but they don't buy his story. It's too early to jump to conclusions, we don't have enough information yet, which is why I'm keeping an open mind on Marion Spear."

"A woman in her late twenties or early thirties, like Marion Spear, wouldn't fall for his crap. And she'd be more likely to report him," Dickenson said emphatically, shifting in her chair and folding her arms tightly across her chest. "Why would he take the risk?"

Donovan shook her head. "We know nothing about her yet. Maybe there's a reason."

"But the way Marion Spear died is different to the other three," Dickenson said sharply. "And there was no suicide note. The verdict was accidental death."

"I agree," Tartaglia said. "But she fell to her death from a high place and lived and died in Ealing, only a few blocks away from where Gemma was killed. Personally, I find that interesting. Certainly worth a closer look."

As he spoke, he knew it sounded flimsy. But it was impossible to explain gut feeling to most people. All he had to pin it on were a couple of lines in one of the

116

emails to Gemma that kept niggling at him. Tom had asked Gemma if she found high places exciting, if she got a thrill looking down from a tall building or a cliff. Still trying to justify to himself why he felt Marion Spear's death worth looking into, Tartaglia had re-read the email earlier that morning after coming back from the cemetery.

Do you feel the attraction of the void? Do you feel the pull as you look over the edge of a high place, knowing that you're only a second away from death if you choose?

"Are you going to exhume Marion Spear?" Wightman asked, interrupting Tartaglia's train of thought.

He shook his head. "We need to find out a lot more about her background. For now, let's concentrate on the three confirmed victims. What about where the girls lived?" He glanced over at Donovan. "Sam, any thoughts?"

She stared at the board for a moment, ruffling her hair with her fingers. "Well, Gemma only lived a couple of miles away from Ellie, which is a coincidence. But I can't see any link with Islington."

"Maybe he has a job where he travels around London," Wightman said.

"Or maybe he met them over the internet and where they live is irrelevant," Dickenson added, still sticking doggedly to her original theory.

"But I told you, he didn't meet Gemma over the internet," Donovan replied, with an exasperated look in Dickenson's direction. "At least not according to what was on her computer. There was some other connection, wasn't there? I mean, what holds true for her, may also hold true for the others."

"We'll know for sure once we get the results back from the analysis of Laura and Ellie's computers," Tartaglia said, just as Cornish's tall, slim figure appeared in the doorway. He was carrying a shiny black leather briefcase, which Tartaglia had never seen before, and looked sleek as a Savile Row tailor's dummy in a well-cut, silver-grey suit.

"Mark, sorry to interrupt. I need a word."

Cornish's manner was tense. He rarely made the trip from Hendon down to Barnes and Tartaglia felt instantly wary. Leaving the group still speculating about possible interpretations of the locations, Tartaglia followed Cornish out of the room and down the corridor to Clarke's office.

Cornish shut the door behind them and gestured towards Clarke's chair. "Have a seat."

"I'm fine here," Tartaglia replied, feeling even more suspicious. "You take the chair. They're like gold-dust in this office."

He rolled the chair over towards Cornish and perched himself on the edge of the desk. Cornish studied it with distaste before brushing the seat with his hand and sitting down gingerly. He opened the briefcase and thrust a folded copy of the *Evening Standard* at Tartaglia. "You'd better read that."

As Tartaglia unfolded it and saw the front-page headline, he felt his stomach knot. "Metropolitan Police Hunt Serial Killer". How on earth had they found out so quickly? It was incredible how journalists managed to worm their foul tentacles into the most unlikely places. Spite and jealousy often played a part and some people would do anything for a bung or a free lunch. But it would be almost impossible to trace the source. Wherever the truth lay, for the press to have discovered what was going on at such an early stage was very bad news.

"I'm sure the leak's not from here," he said, quickly scanning the first few paragraphs. "None of the team would . . ."

"Of course not," Cornish snapped, although his expression was less than convincing. "But it's definitely someone on the inside. They've got all the bloody details."

Tartaglia searched down the page again. "Except for the lock of hair and the GHB."

"That's something, I suppose," Cornish said bitterly. He snatched back the paper, shoved it in his briefcase and flipped the locks several times, as though he was securing a top-secret document. Dumping the case down on the floor, he stood up and started to pace the small room, hands stuffed in his trouser pockets. "But they know about the rings and the fake marriage ceremony. That's far too much, in my book." He turned back momentarily to Tartaglia with a pained look. "And they've given him a bloody moniker. 'The Bridegroom', I ask you."

"That's how the killer signed himself in the final email."

"Exactly. Which means they've talked to someone who's seen the emails. We're leaking like a bloody sieve." Cornish paused in front of Clarke's mirror and made a minute adjustment to the knot of his pale blue silk tie.

The gesture almost made Tartaglia smile. Trust Cornish to be worrying about his appearance at such a time. "You know how difficult it is keeping such things out of the press, sir. It's not the first time . . ."

"They're even speculating about the number of victims," Cornish continued, as if he hadn't heard. "They're wondering how many suicides have been misdiagnosed, wondering if we have another Shipman on our hands." Cornish stared into the mirror, smoothing his sleek, silver hair with a palm, as if to calm himself.

"That's ludicrous."

"Of course it is." Cornish suddenly swung around, expression startled. "We are sure about the third, aren't we?"

Tartaglia nodded. "Dr Blake confirmed it. The tox results are unlikely to tell us anything, but a lock of hair is definitely missing, same as with Gemma Kramer."

"But how the hell do they know about number three? You only dug her up this morning."

"As I said, sir, this is not the first time there's been a leak." He had to make the point even though he knew that Cornish wasn't listening.

120

Cornish shook his head slowly. "This is exactly what I didn't want to happen. How do they expect us to do our jobs with this sort of pressure, under a bloody microscope, all the details out there for any Tom, Dick or Harry to pick over?"

"You've spoken to the press office?"

"Of course, but there's nothing they can do now. The genie's out of the bottle and there's no putting it back. Damage limitation's our main objective. I'm doing a briefing in time for the evening news." He paused, deep in thought for a moment, then turned to Tartaglia, rocking back on his heels, hands back in his pockets, looking uncomfortable. "Look, Mark. This has forced my hand, I hope you understand."

"Meaning?"

"Well, I'm going to have to ask you to step down as SIO."

"What? You can't blame me for this?"

Cornish pursed his lips. "Of course I don't. But this is all getting out of control. With Trevor in hospital, I have no choice."

"So you're taking over?"

Cornish shook his head and folded his arms defensively. "Can't do that. Haven't got the time. I'm bringing someone experienced in."

Tartaglia felt a jolt of anger and the blood rise to his face. He stared hard at Cornish who looked suddenly embarrassed. "But I'm experienced, sir. You could come in as SIO and handle the press. I could still report directly to you."

"Can't do, Mark. We have a linked series on our hands. It's big news and I must make sure everything's properly handled."

"But I've worked two serial cases in the last two years, both with a successful conviction."

"I know. But Clarke headed up the team."

Fists clenched behind his back, nails digging deep into his palms, Tartaglia shook his head, still not quite believing what was happening. "We worked together. He'd tell you the same if he were here."

Cornish forced a smile. "Look, Mark, I'm not doubting that. You're bloody good at what you do. That's why I asked you to step up as SIO in the first place."

"Yes, and I'm the one who's found out that there's a serial killer at work. I can handle the investigation. You don't need to bring in someone from outside."

"I must, given what's happened, given that things are now a lot more . . ." Cornish paused, searching for the word then shrugged his shoulders apologetically. "Well, complicated, shall we say, and high profile. It's very delicate, don't you see? I need someone very experienced on the ground in Barnes to take overall charge."

"I could carry on reporting to you," Tartaglia continued, almost shouting. "It's been done before."

Cornish blinked, speaking slowly between clenched his teeth. "I told you, I haven't got the time."

Or the experience, Tartaglia thought, bitterly. That's what was at the root of it all. The other superintendents and chief superintendents up in Hendon wouldn't think twice about stepping in and taking charge, leaving Tartaglia as SIO. But not Cornish. He didn't feel secure enough, just in case he screwed up. It was fucking unfair. This should have been Tartaglia's big break, an important stepping-stone in the path to becoming a DCI himself. He had done all the spadework. He had found out about the other girls. Now, just because Cornish wasn't up to it, someone else was going to come in, steal his thunder and take over.

"So, who is it?" Tartaglia said, trying to contain his desire to punch Cornish.

Cornish spoke quietly. "DCI Carolyn Steele. Maybe you've come across her."

Carolyn Steele. Although Tartaglia had never had any direct dealings with her, he knew who she was by sight. There weren't that many female DCIs heading up murder teams, certainly not half-decent looking ones. In her early forties, he guessed, Steele was short and shapely in an athletic sort of way, with dark hair, almost luminously pale skin and a pair of striking green eyes. She'd been working up in Hendon for a while and had a good enough reputation, although that didn't make it any better. Before that, he thought she'd been running one of the murder teams based in East London.

Another thought occurred to Tartaglia and made him even more furious. "When did you decide this? It wasn't today, was it? You're not just doing this because of the leak?"

Cornish shook his head, avoiding his eyes as he picked at a tiny thread from his jacket sleeve. "Once it was clear that we were looking at a series, I had to do something. As I said, I'm very busy. It's just a shame it couldn't be managed in a more gradual way."

Before Tartaglia had a chance to reply, there was a knock and Carolyn Steele put her head around the door.

"They told me you were in here, sir," she said to Cornish. "Are you ready for me?"

Cornish nodded. "Come in Carolyn. This is Mark Tartaglia."

Steele closed the door behind her and turned abruptly to Tartaglia. She held out a small, firm hand that was cold to the touch, studying him in a way that instantly irritated him.

"Hello, Mark. I'm looking forward to working with you. It's an interesting case we've got here."

CHAPTER
ELEVEN

Carolyn Steele sat in Clarke's office, reading through the files. Tartaglia had given her a full debriefing and, so far, she couldn't fault anything that he had done in the investigation or the conclusions that he had drawn. Before coming, she had checked him out with various people up in Hendon. He was generally well thought of, although very much Clarke's man, with a reputation for being a little headstrong. But stepping into that small, claustrophobic office and meeting him for the first time, arrogant and cock-sure were the words that came to mind. The air almost hummed with it, the antagonism in his eyes blinding. She was taken aback by the strength of his reaction. After all, she was just following orders. It wasn't her fault she had been parachuted in over his head.

Was it because she was a woman, perhaps? Anyone who thought sexism in the Met was a thing of the past had his or her head in the sand. Perhaps Cornish had prepared the ground badly or, worse still, had deliberately said something to undermine her. It wouldn't be the first time, she thought, remembering a previous investigation where, for reasons of his own, the waters had been poisoned by her superior. Cornish had seemed even more awkward than usual and he had scuttled out of the room and back to Hendon almost immediately as if he seemed embarrassed or had something to hide. She had never worked directly for him before and found his behaviour hard to read. Perhaps he was the kind who liked to light the touch paper, step back and watch what happened.

It had been particularly awkward asking Tartaglia to vacate Clarke's office; yet another slap in the face. But there was no available alternative, the facilities at Barnes being even more cramped and dilapidated than she had been led to believe, with barely room to swing a mouse, let alone a cat. She had made the mistake of parking her car in the building's small underground car park, only to be told that it was for the exclusive use of the robbery squad on the second floor. She had to take her chances with the rest of them, fighting for a free space in the open back yard, in the end blocking someone in and having to leave a note. For the first time, she actually thought with some fondness of her glass box of an office up in Hendon. Hopefully she wouldn't have to be away for long, although with a case like this, anything was possible.

She had left Tartaglia and his team in charge of the Gemma Kramer investigation, continuing to research the girl's background, checking phone records, the places she visited every day, the people she saw, trying to find a link with the other victims. The other DI, Gary Jones, and his team were doing the same for Laura Benedetti and Ellie Best. Unfortunately, Clarke's team was even more stretched than Cornish had led her to believe, with only two DIs rather than the usual three, and even lighter in the lower ranks. The issue was common throughout the Met. Of course, there were the usual explanations; several members of the team had moved on elsewhere, yet to be replaced, one was off on long-term sick leave, one on maternity leave, and another about to join her shortly. But with a high profile case like this one, it didn't help. Not for the first time, she wondered if she had been handed a poisoned chalice.

She glanced at her watch. Cornish would have just finished the media briefing. Following on from that, the press office had managed to get her a last-minute slot on *Crimewatch* the next day. She knew they were likely to be inundated with calls, all of which would have to be followed up whether helpful or not, taking up valuable time and manpower. But there was no alternative. With little to go on, they urgently needed more information. Once the calls started coming in, it would be vital to narrow the field of focus as far as possible. The next step was to call in a profiler.

As usual, neither of the Met's two in-house profilers was available. Looking down the handful of other names on the National Crime Faculty approved register, a few were familiar. However, she was unlikely to have the luxury of choice. Although she wanted input right away, it was going to be difficult finding anybody immediately who had time to spare. Scattered all over the country, they were usually tied up with academic or clinical matters and she knew from experience that you could wait weeks, or even months, before getting an opinion, by which time it was often of no use.

A particular name kept leaping out at her from the list. Although she tried to avoid looking at it, her eyes couldn't help returning to it. He was the obvious solution. He was based in London and, if anyone was likely to do her a favour and drop everything, he would. But should she ask him? Was it wise? Probably not. Shoes off, stockinged feet up on the edge of the desk drawer, she swivelled slowly from side to side, weighing up the pros and cons, Clarke's ancient chair squeaking worryingly beneath her. No, it wasn't wise but who else was there? Besides, it was the right thing for the case. She would worry about the consequences later. She swung her feet onto the floor, feeling for her shoes with her toes as she stretched for the phone and dialled his number. It was disturbing that she could still remember it by heart.

"It's an unusual case, don't you think?" Steele said, pretending to focus on her bitter lemon, swirling the ice around in the glass, as she studied Dr Patrick Kennedy's reaction out of the corner of her eye. Although he was doing his best to appear only casually interested in what she had told him, she could tell he was intrigued. It amused her that with all his knowledge of psychology he could sometimes be so transparent, as well as unaware of the fact. She looked up at him and smiled sweetly. "Naturally, your name came to mind because of the book you're writing on serial killers. I thought you'd find the case particularly interesting so I haven't spoken to anyone else about it yet."

"I appreciate that," he said, after taking a swig of sauvignon blanc, a broad grin on his boyish face. "You've only given me a brief outline, but I can see all sorts of fascinating aspects about the case already."

They were sitting at the back of a half-empty wine bar in South Kensington, around the corner from where Kennedy worked in the Unit for Forensic Psychology, part of London University. Kennedy was well known within the Met and she had suggested somewhere near him, rather than Barnes, as she didn't want any of her new team seeing them together until he was officially on board. She was now regretting leaving the choice to him. Although it was late afternoon, the air was still thick with the smell of fried food and cigarette smoke, left over from the lunchtime crowd. Her hair and clothes would reek of it afterwards and she hoped she wouldn't have to stay long.

As usual, Kennedy was looking good. Dressed casually for a change in a leather jacket, shirt and jeans, his broad face was almost unlined and his thick, wavy brown hair devoid of any grey. Although just over forty, according to the brief biographical information on his website that she had re-checked earlier, he could easily be taken for one of his postgraduate students. It had been a stroke of luck bumping into him the previous week at the Peel Centre in Hendon, where she normally worked. Kennedy had just given a lecture on Behavioural Investigative Analysis, the new buzzword for profiling, at the Met's Crime Academy. He was trying to find his way around the huge, sprawling complex to one of the canteens but had lost his way. It had been a while since they had last seen each other and he seemed uncharacteristically hesitant, almost embarrassed, as he asked her to join him for a coffee. But she was late for a meeting and they agreed to catch up sometime soon for a drink. He had left a couple of messages on her answer machine a few days later, suggesting a couple of dates, but feeling suddenly wary, she had failed to return the calls. At least he didn't seem to be holding it against her now.

"So, Patrick, what do you think? Do you have time to look at it?" She caught his eye, trying to gauge his reaction. He pursed his lips and took a large mouthful of wine, spinning it out. He knew he was her best option at such short notice, that nobody else would be likely to make space for her immediately. Calling in personal favours was not something she liked to do, as a rule, but what other choice did she have? She needed input right away. And from his perspective, it wasn't often that such a case came along. Surely, he wouldn't say no.

He put his glass down with a shrug. "I'm very busy at the moment, but what's new."

"So, can you help?" she said, wanting to hurry things along, desperate to get his agreement and get out of that foul-smelling, airless place.

"From the little you've told me, it's certainly intriguing. I'd need to juggle a few things." He let the sentence hang, studying her carefully in a way that was suddenly intimate and made her feel uncomfortable.

She had the impression that there was something he wanted to say and she hoped he wasn't going to allude to what had happened between them before. Then he nodded slowly and smiled. "It's good of you to ask me, Carolyn. And I'm very pleased to see you again, even if you don't return my calls."

"Well?" she asked, ignoring the comment. "Will you help?"

He nodded slowly. "Yes, I think I can. It's a shame the press have got involved quite so early and that the source seems to be so accurate. But, in a funny way, that may be to our advantage."

"How?"

"Because it buys us some time. The reptile will have to go to ground for a while. No blushing young virgin's going to march up the aisle with him now, are they? When can I see the files?"

"I'll get copies sent over to you straight away." She scribbled down the Barnes address on the back of a business card and passed it to him. "This is where I'm based for the moment."

As she stood up to go, he put his hand on her arm. "Surely you don't have to rush off? Stay and finish your drink."

She smiled, shaking her head. "Gotta go. They'll be wondering where I am. I'll see you tomorrow morning, my office at eight a.m. OK?"

He returned her smile, although he looked disappointed, and gave her a mock salute.

"Ay, ay, ma'am. Anything you say. As always."

★　★　★

Early the next morning, Tartaglia headed down the corridor towards the office he was once again sharing with DI Gary Jones. On his way in, he had picked up a bacon sarni and a cup of good, strong cappuccino from the local deli, looking forward to tucking into both of them at his desk undisturbed before the morning briefing. Jones was out until lunchtime and he would have the room to himself, for a change. Approaching Clarke's office, he heard voices and laughter coming from inside. The door was half-open door and he saw Steele sitting behind the desk, talking to someone hidden from view. As he passed by, Steele turned and caught his eye.

"Mark, there you are. Can you come in here for a minute?"

Tartaglia pushed back the door and saw a familiar figure in an expensive-looking suit lounging casually against the windowsill next to Steele. The man gave him a wide grin.

"Hi there, Mark. How are you these days?"

Fuck. Dr Patrick Kennedy. The profiler who had nearly screwed up the Barton case. Feeling instantly suspicious, Tartaglia waited in the doorway for Steele to say something.

"Patrick's just been telling me that you've worked together before on another case."

Kennedy was still grinning. "Yes, Mark and I are old friends."

"Patrick's going to assist us with this one," Steele said, seemingly unaware that anything was wrong.

132

Unable to trust himself to reply, Tartaglia said nothing, staring hard at Kennedy. He hadn't changed at all. Glossy and smug, with his thick mane of hair — an indecent amount of hair for a real man, according to Clarke, who was thinning on top — Kennedy looked more like a game show host than a university professor, particularly inappropriate in the context of Clarke's dingy, threadbare office. Had Steele brought Kennedy in herself? Or was the decision down to Cornish, something that wouldn't surprise him at all?

"Patrick needs to see the places where the girls died," she continued. "Can you give him the guided tour?"

"I was supposed to be trying to track down Marion Spear's family this morning," he said as levelly as possible.

"Get someone else to do it. Patrick's part of the team now and you're the best person to bring him up-to-date."

"I don't have a car." It was a lame excuse but he couldn't think of anything better.

Kennedy pulled out a set of keys from his jacket pocket and jangled them at Tartaglia. "Let's take mine. I'll drive; you navigate. you can fill me in on the way."

Increasingly impatient and angry, Tartaglia sat in the passenger seat of Kennedy's old, dark green Morgan, which was parked in front of St Sebastian's, the scene of Gemma Kramer's murder. Kennedy had been gone for almost three quarters of an hour. There was little to see inside the church and Tartaglia was sure he must be deliberately spinning it all out in some pathetic show of

133

power. The car radio was out of commission, the aerial snapped off, and the only cassettes Tartaglia could find were the sound-tracks to *Phantom of the Opera* and *Les Misérables*, both of which would be torture. Short of making pointless calls or playing games on his mobile, he had nothing to do. Perhaps he should have gone with Kennedy into the church but he had already had more than enough of Kennedy's company and comments on the case.

Everything about Kennedy grated. He was so self-seeking, so arrogant, so unashamedly sure of himself. Earlier, a small posse of photographers and reporters had been hanging around outside the gates of the car park in Barnes. Instead of ignoring them and driving away like any sensible person, Kennedy had stopped and rolled down the window to talk to them, also waving cheerily at a well-known actor who lived next door who had come out to walk his dog. Whether or not the actor had a clue who Kennedy was, the reporters lapped it up. When asked by one of them if he was now engaged on profiling "The Bridegroom" case, Kennedy winked and smiled enigmatically, with a "no comment" that any decent reporter would take as absolute confirmation. Remembering how Kennedy had courted publicity in the Barton case, Tartaglia wondered if Kennedy had actually tipped them off. Whether true or not, photos of Kennedy's mug would be plastered all over the evening papers. It was amusing to think what Cornish, who hated any form of publicity, would make of that.

Outside, the temperature was only a few degrees above freezing and Tartaglia had been forced to switch on the engine to keep warm and to stop the windows from misting up completely. The car idled noisily, white smoke gusting from the exhaust. In spite of the gleaming paintwork and chrome trimmings, it felt as though it was on its last legs. Clunking and jerking, it had gasped its way around the tour of the two other London churches where the other girls had died. Every time Kennedy changed gear, it made alarming grinding sounds and it had nearly expired behind the car park where Marion Spear had fallen to her death. No doubt it spent a lot of time in an expensive repair shop, as Tartaglia couldn't see Kennedy getting his manicured hands dirty under the bonnet.

Above the noise of the engine, Tartaglia heard the sound of someone singing. He looked up to see Kennedy sauntering down the church path towards him, swinging his briefcase back and forth like a child with a new toy.

"Let's grab a bite to eat. I'm absolutely famished," Kennedy said cheerfully, levering himself in through the driver's door and automatically passing his briefcase to Tartaglia to hold. He slid down into the leather bucket seat and slammed the gear into first. As he tried to pull away, the car lurched forward and stalled.

He grunted. "Like all women, she's a trifle temperamental."

Tartaglia stared at him aghast. "She?"

Kennedy patted the steering wheel and grinned as he tried the ignition again. "Daisy, my motor. Mark, this is Daisy," he said, waving his hand expansively towards the rattling bonnet of the car as if he were making a formal introduction.

Tartaglia closed his eyes momentarily, stifling a groan. "We ought to head back to Barnes," he said, trying to ignore the pangs of hunger in his stomach. Even though it was almost two o'clock and he'd had nothing to eat since early that morning, starvation was preferable to another hour in Kennedy's company.

"I've got to eat," Kennedy replied emphatically, in the manner of someone not used to skipping a meal. "I'm sure Carolyn will understand if we're not back pronto. I know a decent little tapas bar just around the corner. I'll put it on expenses," he added, as if that was all that was needed. He clunked the car into gear again and they juddered away from the pavement.

Carolyn. It wasn't the first time Kennedy had dropped her Christian name into the conversation and it felt as though he was trying to make a point. Steele had also used Kennedy's Christian name and it appeared that she and Kennedy were already on pretty friendly terms, something that Tartaglia had been feeling increasingly annoyed about all morning.

The tapas bar was in a small parade of shops facing Ealing Green. Kennedy seemed to be a valued customer, the Spanish manager greeting him like a long-lost friend and offering them drinks on the house. Feeling churlish, Tartaglia insisted on a glass of tap water while Kennedy accepted a jumbo glass of house

Rioja. Tartaglia wasn't averse to the odd drink at lunchtime but he was buggered if he was going to relax and make merry with Kennedy. While they waited for two portions of mixed tapas, Tartaglia reached into his jacket pocket for a cigarette to calm himself and fill the silence. As he pulled out his lighter and packet of Marlboro reds, Kennedy shook his head, smiling and pointing at the small "No Smoking" sign immediately behind Tartaglia on the wall. Inwardly seething, Tartaglia zipped away the pack and took a long sip of water. Such a stance was surprising, given most Spaniards' love of good, strong, tobacco anywhere and at any time of day. But there were puritans in every race. This was what it would soon be like, once the smoking ban came into force. Sanctimonious pricks like Kennedy would have a field day.

"Aren't you interested to know what I think?" Kennedy asked.

"Of course," Tartaglia said, as politely as possible. He might as well listen. Steele would be getting the full story when they got back to Barnes and it would be important to be prepared. "I just know how you experts like to take your time, consider everything carefully, before you give us an opinion."

Kennedy relaxed back in his chair. "Sure. I've only got the barest of details at the moment. But I can give you some off-the-cuff comments . . . which might help you. I've been up all night reading the files and it's pretty fascinating stuff." He raised his eyebrows meaningfully, as if waiting for some sort of encouragement.

Tartaglia steeled himself. "So, what have you found out?"

Kennedy sucked in his breath and was silent for a moment as if he was considering the question carefully. The mannerism was something Tartaglia remembered from the past. It had seemed a put-on then and it still seemed fake, but he said nothing. After a moment, Kennedy leaned forwards, planted his elbows on the table and clasped his hands in front of him. "Well, the locations, the churches are particularly interesting."

"What about the car park?"

Kennedy shook his head. "I think we can forget that one. It doesn't fit in any respect."

"But Marion Spear fell to her death like the others and it's just around the corner from where Gemma Kramer died. Surely that warrants closer investigation?"

"What's the point?" Kennedy shrugged.

"I was hoping you'd tell me, Dr Kennedy. You're the one with the imagination."

Kennedy smiled. "Psychological insight, you mean. Think of Cinderella. If the shoe don't fit, no amount of trying it on will change things."

Tartaglia looked away for a moment, resisting the impulse to smack him. The fact that Kennedy was prepared to dismiss Marion Spear's death so categorically was enough to give him fresh hope. Kennedy had been wrong in the past and there was a good chance he was wrong now. Even before hearing his view, Tartaglia had been determined to carry on looking into what had happened to her, at least until they had strong evidence to rule her out. He had managed to get hold of her mother's phone number and, whatever Kennedy said, he was going to call her as soon as he got back to the office. He just hoped Kennedy wouldn't try and queer the pitch with Steele.

"I just think it's worth following up," he said quietly, meeting Kennedy's gaze. "That's all."

Kennedy shook his head. "Square pegs and round holes. Don't waste your time on it."

Tartaglia glanced away again, watching the manager unload what looked like their food from the dumb waiter behind the bar. Just sit back and listen, don't argue, Tartaglia told himself, as the manager came bustling over with the assorted plates of tapas. It wasn't worth risking World War Three at this point.

"Let's go back to the three confirmed victims," Kennedy said, loading his plate with slices of ham and more than his fair share of hot squid in tomato sauce without waiting for Tartaglia. Taking a large bite, Kennedy pronounced the squid delicious. "The fact that they all died in churches has a particular significance for our killer. Let's call him Tom, although of course that's not his real name." He shovelled more squid into his mouth.

"You don't think it's just part of the act, the way he attracts the girls, making them think they're going through some sort of religious ceremony?"

Kennedy shook his head, struggling to speak, mouth still full. "No. I think . . . actually . . . it means something particular to him . . . maybe some sort of 'V' sign at the church and the establishment. I'm sure he had a religious upbringing and I think the profanity appeals to him. It's a sort of personal joke."

Tartaglia's personal theory was that Tom had chosen churches because they were places that would lull the girls into a false sense of security, but Kennedy's idea was interesting and not implausible. He spooned some prawns in garlic sauce onto his plate and waited for Kennedy to continue.

"Look, we have three girls, all roughly the same age," Kennedy said, between mouthfuls. "We have to ask ourselves, why does he choose *them*? What makes them vulnerable? Why are they falling prey?"

Tartaglia shrugged, helping himself to a few small slices of cured ham and olives. "You tell me."

Kennedy was silent for a moment as if he was formulating the theory. "It's sexual, of course. All about control and dominance. These poor little darlings are easy pickings. No doubt he believes they deserve their fate. Although he doesn't sexually assault them per se, killing them, watching them die, is his equivalent. He may even achieve orgasm when he does it, although my guess is that he's impotent."

"No trace of semen was found at the crime scene."

"It doesn't matter. Whether he has a wank or not, it's still sexual. He's like those perverts who watch snuff movies. Only, he wants it live. And now he's got a taste for it, he's going to keep going back for more, possibly developing his little fantasy as he perfects his skills. I'm sure he thinks he's so clever that he won't be caught."

"Really?" Tartaglia said flatly, trying what little Kennedy had left of the ham. Kennedy was spouting the usual serial killer stuff that you could find in any station bookshop.

"He's also bloody ballsy," Kennedy said, stabbing the air with his knife. "I'll give him that. He's taking a big risk that he won't be disturbed, although that possibly adds to the excitement. This is a highly organised individual, someone calm and methodical in everything he does. He plans the killings down to the last detail. He's also a good communicator and highly literate, judging from the emails. He pitches them just right for each girl."

Annoyingly, Tartaglia found himself agreeing with Kennedy again, although he would rather be punched in the face than say so. "Maybe he has had a good education. But how does that help us find him? What about his age, background, formative life experiences, shoe size and inside leg measurement? That's what you profilers are so good at working out. What do you see in your crystal ball?"

"No need to be facetious, Mark. You and I are old friends. We can both take credit for catching Michael Barton."

Tartaglia shook his head in disbelief. "You really think you can take credit for Barton?"

"Naturally," Kennedy replied, with a disingenuous smile, using his napkin to wipe a trace of tomato sauce from his lips. "I know we've had our little disagreements but we were all part of the winning team that caught the reptile." Noting Tartaglia's expression, he added: "Anyway, let's not waste energy raking over history. Regarding this case, I'll need some time to put together a full profile on Tom. But you're looking at a very different type of individual to Barton. Our Tom's a classic psychopath."

Tartaglia sighed. "Yes, yes. He feels no remorse or empathy with the victim. They are just a means to an end and he has no conscience. Tell me something I don't know."

Kennedy forced an indulgent smile, looking like a teacher trying to deal with a difficult pupil. "Well, judging from the emails, I'd say this one was a grammar school boy or possibly privately educated. That should help you narrow the search when you eventually find some suspects."

"That's an interesting theory," Tartaglia said flatly. He finished what was left of the ham and added some butter bean salad to his plate, trying to block out Kennedy from his consciousness, wishing he had allowed himself a glass of wine to go with it and dull the pain.

"Look, it's always about resources, isn't it?" Kennedy continued, oblivious. "Once Carolyn does *Crimewatch* tonight, you're going to be inundated. You know what it's like? Too much information, most of it useless, and not enough manpower or hours in the day. You're going to have to focus. I'm telling you, don't waste your time on the car park girl." He wagged his finger at Tartaglia, with a knowing grin. "I know you. You haven't given up on her, have you? Just stick with the three girls and find out what they have in common, how it was Tom came across them."

142

"That's what we're already doing," Tartaglia said, scraping up some beans from his plate, trying not to let Kennedy rile him further.

"There have got to be similarities," Kennedy said emphatically. He tossed back his wine and waved his empty glass in the air until he caught the manager's attention. "Sure you won't join me?" he asked Tartaglia, as the manager came over with the bottle.

Tartaglia shook his head. "You shouldn't either. You're driving."

"Lighten up, Mark. One more won't hurt. I'm a big guy and I can take it." Kennedy patted his chest with satisfaction as he watched the manager fill the glass to the brim.

As the manager moved away, Tartaglia could hold back no longer. "You know Tom's going to try and do it again, don't you? I'm sure he's got several prospects lined up."

"Hang on a minute," Kennedy said, tipping the remains of the little bowls of tapas onto his plate. "With all the publicity, what girl in her right mind is going to go along with him now?"

Tartaglia slapped down his knife and fork on his plate. "But they're NOT in their right mind, are they? That's why they're such easy prey."

"He's been outed. Nobody's going to fall for the suicide pact rubbish now."

"What do you think he's going to do? Give up and go back to the day job? He's a chameleon. He'll adapt. Tom's got a taste for killing. He's going to have to satisfy the craving again somehow, even if he has to change the game."

"But as we know, most serial killers are creatures of habit."

"This man's cleverer than most. Think about it. These young girls are just a piece of piss for him; they're too easy. He'll soon want something more challenging. The press hype may be the catalyst."

"If you're right, that gives us an opportunity. He may screw up."

"Let's hope so. I'm afraid I don't think you're going to have long to wait."

CHAPTER
TWELVE

Tom stared at the TV screen, smiling. Detective Chief Inspector Carolyn Steele was doing well, her husky voice hitting just the right note of gravity mixed with emotion, as she appealed for witnesses. Shame though about the boxy jacket and plain white blouse. They weren't flattering. Maybe she thought it made her look business-like, but a uniform would have been better, if that was the image she wanted. There was also something about a woman in uniform that was a real turn-on. For a moment he pictured Carolyn slowly undoing the buttons and peeling off the layers to music, down to stockings and suspenders and a skimpy black bra and thong.

It reminded him of a stag night he'd been to a few years before. There had been three strippers dressed up as WPCs with handcuffs and truncheons, two bottle-blondes and a brunette, all clapped-out slags, well past their sell-by date. Having taken off their clothes to indiscriminate drunken applause, the brunette had made a beeline for him, slithering her stinking, sweat-slippery body down onto his lap, asking if he wanted extras. She tried to cuff him to a chair but he smacked her hard and shoved her off him, throwing

145

her onto the floor. She hit her face on something, drawing blood, and started screaming hysterically, threatening to call the cops. Everyone was roaring with laughter, even the other whores joined in. But in the end, he'd been forced to give the slag a whacking great tip to shut her up and leave him alone. The reek of her cheap perfume had stayed in his nose for days.

But there was nothing cheap about Carolyn Steele. She was a class act, just the sort of woman he liked. Her sleek black hair framed her broad face nicely and the make-up artist had dolled her up to look as good as Fiona Bruce. Better, in fact.

The camera cut to a crime scene reconstruction. A young girl, posing as Gemma Kramer, stood outside St Sebastian's talking to a man dressed in a dark overcoat. It took him a few seconds to realise that the man was supposed to be him. What a joke. While the girl bore a passing resemblance to Gemma, the man was nothing like him. Wrong hair, wrong clothes, wrong build. Even his body language was wrong as he talked to Gemma, bending forwards to kiss her as if he actually enjoyed it. The fucking plods were way off the mark there. Couldn't they get anything right? Details were so important. Details were what mattered.

The camera retreated, showing a panoramic view of the church. It was just as he recalled it, although he had never bothered to admire it from that angle. A head and shoulders photograph of Gemma appeared on the screen. She was wearing school uniform and looked even younger than he remembered. The sight of her sent a shiver of pleasure through him, taking him straight back. He closed his eyes, struggling to block out the droning commentary, trying to focus. What he would give to live each exquisite moment again. He could picture the real flesh and blood Gemma so clearly, he could almost touch her, smell her. The long brown hair, the fine down on her cheeks, the creamy skin with its sprinkling of freckles. Soon she would fade, details blurring, then bleaching into nothingness, like an old photograph, until she was of no use to him. As with the others, he would have to replace her. But for the moment, she was still fresh enough. In his mind, she looked at him with her clear blue eyes and held out her hand, enticing him forward. He smiled, and this time she smiled back. She wanted it as much as he did, the little bitch. He took her hand, feeling it cold in his, but she was still smiling, egging him on. As he drew her slowly into the dark interior of the church, he felt the rush of blood once again.

CHAPTER
THIRTEEN

Donovan pulled up outside Tartaglia's flat in Shepherd's Bush and killed the engine. She had been busy all day and had hardly set foot in the office. The only time she had caught sight of Tartaglia was on his way up the stairs, coming in from the trip with Kennedy as she made her way out of the building to follow up on what had proved to be another dead end. Pausing briefly on the half-landing, he had hurriedly sketched out what happened with Kennedy and they arranged to meet after work at his flat for a late drink, when they would have time to talk uninterrupted.

Although she was not on Clarke's team at the time of the Barton investigation, she couldn't help agreeing with Tartaglia: Kennedy seemed very pleased with himself. Somehow, he made them all feel as though they had a celebrity in their midst and Yvette Dickenson seemed particularly impressed, asking Kennedy to sign her copy of his latest book on profiling. He lapped it up as if it were his due, flashing his mouthful of brilliant white teeth and scribbling down a dedication in huge, loopy handwriting, with Yvette gazing at him like a teenage girl, even in her state. It was sick-making. However, Kennedy seemed to be oblivious to the stir he was causing, Steele being the prime focus of his attentions. Donovan couldn't fathom the precise nature of their relationship but had decided that it definitely went beyond the purely professional, although Steele treated Kennedy more like an old friend than a lover. Perhaps she hadn't noticed the way Kennedy looked at her. Maybe she wasn't interested. It was going to be worth keeping a close watch on the pair.

Lights glimmered through the crack at the top of the shutters in Tartaglia's sitting room but there was no response when she rang the bell. When she dialled his home number from her mobile, the answer machine clicked on. Maybe he'd given up on her or nipped out for a pint of milk or a quick drink on his own. But she was sure he'd be back. He wasn't the type to forget an arrangement. A fine drizzle had set in and she climbed back into her car and turned on the engine to keep warm, eyes scanning the road in front while she waited.

Tartaglia had seemed more than usually on edge when she had seen him earlier. No doubt the hours spent with Kennedy had had something to do with it. But she sensed there was more to it than that. The tension between him and Steele was obvious to everyone, the atmosphere unpleasant and heavy like before a storm. Although they both went out of their way to be polite, each deferring almost unnecessarily to the other, they reminded her of a pair of dogs, hackles up, skirting warily around each other, spoiling for a fight. She just hoped for Tartaglia's sake that he would be able to keep his temper under control and not do anything stupid.

Everything was Cornish's fault and she didn't blame Tartaglia for a second for feeling so bitter — no one did, certainly not those in Tartaglia's immediate team. There had been no need to bring in Steele. But Cornish hadn't the balls to oversee things himself and to let Tartaglia carry on running things. Self-preservation was Cornish's motto and he had made sure that Steele's neck was on the line, not his. If she succeeded in finding the killer, he would take ultimate credit for it. If she failed, he would step back and she would be the one blamed. Donovan wondered if Steele knew this, if she had had any choice in the matter.

She waited a few more minutes and was on the point of leaving a note and driving off when she caught sight of Tartaglia briefly illuminated under a street lamp, jogging around the corner at the far end of the road. Climbing out of the car, she popped the locks and sheltered under her umbrella as she watched him slog along the pavement towards her. As he spotted her, he waved.

"Good thing I was late," she said, when he came up to her, panting. Hair soaked, water running down his face, he was wearing running shorts, trainers and a white T-shirt that stuck to his skin. Bloody hell, he looked great, even like that, she thought, hoping he couldn't read her mind.

"Sorry," he said, in between deep breaths, plastering his hair back off his face with his hand and stretching

150

his legs. "Thought you'd been held up, so I went out for a run. Helps clear the mind."

She followed him up the path to the front door. "Wouldn't it be better if you gave up the fags?"

He turned round and grinned, still out of breath. "What, like you, you mean? I saw you having a quick one in the car park this morning. Thought you'd stopped?"

"Don't give me a hard time. I need it at the moment. Look, I've brought you a present."

"What is it?" he said, eyeing the plastic bag in her hand as he fumbled in his pocket for his keys.

"A tape of this evening's appeal on *Crimewatch*. I went by my flat to collect it. In spite of what you said earlier, I thought you might like to see it."

He gave her a withering look as they went inside. "Just what I've always wanted." He unlocked the door to his flat and held the door open for her.

"Steele did a good job. Came across really well."

"I just hope it shakes out some new information," he said, closing the door behind them. "I'm going to take a shower. If the phone rings, can you answer it? It may be Sally-Anne."

"Any news?"

"Sorry, I should have told you. She called earlier to say that Trevor came round a couple of hours ago."

"Thank God," she said, feeling an instant surge of relief. "That's fantastic news."

He was grinning at her. "And guess what, Sally-Anne played Eminem really loudly in his ear and after ten minutes he opened his eyes."

She laughed, trying to picture the scene. "Typical Trevor. Did he yell at her to turn it off?"

"Probably. It's about the only fucking chink of light in the last twenty-four shitty hours. Sally-Anne said she'll call back once she's found out when I can visit." He waved vaguely in the direction of the sofa as he walked towards the door to the inner hall. "Put on some music and make yourself at home. I think there's a bottle of decent white open in the fridge, or some red in the rack next to the sink. I won't be long. Then maybe we can get something to eat. I'm starving."

She put the package down on the glass and chrome coffee table, took off her coat and went into the kitchen, where she found an open bottle of Italian Gavi in the fridge. Pouring herself a glass, she took it back into the sitting room where she examined Tartaglia's extraordinary music collection, which ranged from obscure Italian opera to hip-hop, finally selecting an old Moby CD. She slid it into the player and sat down on the comfortable leather chair by the window.

Gradually starting to unwind, she gazed around the room, searching for the slightest trace of female occupation. She hadn't forgotten the scene in Dr Blake's office. But there were no telltale signs. No signs of anything interesting at all. As usual, the flat was absurdly tidy, with none of the usual haphazardness, unconscious or deliberate, which she associated with other male colleagues and friends. Everything had a place and a function, from the long lines of DVDs, CDs and books grouped alphabetically on the shelves, to the neat rows of glasses, crockery, drinks and cooking ingredients in the kitchen cupboards. Compared to the over-flowing, cosy house she shared with her sister, Tartaglia's flat was clinical. No family photos, personal knick-knacks, objects of a sentimental nature brought home from a holiday or marking a particular relationship. Knowing him, it wasn't that he couldn't be bothered to make a home. It was a matter of deliberate choice.

Although the lack of clutter was alien to her, she liked the bare, white walls and the large black and white photograph over the fireplace. It was the only picture in the entire room. She got up, glass in hand, to take a closer look. It was simple but evocative. A young woman strolled down a sun-drenched, cobbled street, sweeping a lock of dark hair off her face. She seemed preoccupied by something, unaware of the photographer. Behind her was a high arched doorway, the name "Bar Toto" hanging in large neon letters above it, some words in what looked like Latin carved deep into the stone to one side. Judging from the woman's clothing and shoes, it had been taken sometime in the late fifties or early sixties. It reminded her of *La Dolce Vita*, the only Italian film she had ever seen. Apart from the fact that the picture was of somewhere in Italy, she had no idea why Tartaglia had chosen it, although the image was very striking.

As she continued to stare at it, losing herself in the scene, imagining a story behind it, the phone rang. She picked it up, hoping to hear Sally-Anne's voice at the other end.

"Is Mark there?" a woman asked, in a light Scottish accent.

"He's taking a shower," she replied, instantly curious. Definitely not Fiona Blake.

There was a pause. "Will he be long?"

"I don't know. He's just come back from a run. I'm Sam Donovan. I work with him," Donovan said, something in the woman's tone compelling her to explain.

"Ah." The woman sounded a little disappointed. "I'm Nicoletta, his sister. Could you please just let him know that I called and that we're expecting him for lunch this Sunday. Tell him, no arguments. John and the kids want to see him and Elisa and Gianni and some friends are coming over. It's all arranged."

Wondering what Tartaglia's reaction would be to such an order, Donovan put down the phone just as Tartaglia reappeared, bare-foot, wearing jeans and a loose, open-necked shirt, vigorously rubbing his hair dry with a towel. Donovan relayed the message.

"Shit," he said, lobbing the towel into the small hall, which led to the rest of the flat. "I've been with the murder squad for nearly three years and, whatever I say, Nicoletta still doesn't get it. As far as she's concerned, the case can get fucked. Sunday is sacrosanct and nothing stops a family get-together, not even somebody lying dead in a mortuary. I need a bloody drink."

He went into the kitchen, returning with the bottle of wine and a large, full glass. He sank down in the middle of the sofa, exhaling loudly as he put his bare feet up

154

heavily on the coffee table. "God, it's been a bugger of a day. It's only a matter of time before I'll be having to take orders from that prick, Kennedy."

He looked rougher than she had seen him for a while, with dark shadows under his eyes, almost like bruises. Judging by the thick stubble on his chin, he hadn't shaved since early morning. Perhaps all he needed was a few good nights of sleep, although there was little chance of that in the foreseeable future. She hoped that was all that was wrong with him.

She sat down again, kicking off her shoes and leaning forward to massage her tired feet. "You said Kennedy wanted to stop you looking into Marion Spear's death."

He nodded. "According to the expert, she doesn't fit his victim profile. But I don't give a flying fuck what he thinks. I still think it's worth pursuing."

"How can you be so sure?"

"In here and here," he said, pounding his heart and stomach with his fist. "Something a spineless idiot like Kennedy wouldn't have a clue about."

She was taken aback by the strength of the emotion in his dark eyes. She had never seen him like this before and she wasn't sure why he cared so much. Tartaglia's instincts were usually good but the policeman who solved a case on gut feel was a cliché reserved for detective novels. Maybe he was letting his hatred of Kennedy cloud his judgment. "Have you found out anything more?"

"I've finally tracked down Marion's mum. She's still living up in Leicester, where Marion came from. She gave me some stuff on Marion's background, although most of it I already knew from the file. Apparently, Marion had come down south to work as an estate agent, first in Acton and then in Ealing. On the day she died, she had taken a client to visit a flat. After that, nobody saw her again. The flat was quite close to the car park where she fell."

"Don't tell me it's another Mr Kipper."

Tartaglia shook his head. "The bloke was traced at the time and crossed off the list. But I'd still like to talk to him again and to the people in the estate agent's. Reading through the file, the investigation seems pretty cursory to me. According to Marion's mum, Marion didn't know many people and had been feeling lonely living in London. When she died, she was thinking of going back home to Leicester."

"You really think she's worth looking into?"

He nodded. "We're grubbing around in the dark. Ellie Best's computer was wiped clean and the only way to link her to the other deaths is the ring. Copies of the emails recovered from Laura Benedetti's computer came in this afternoon but they tell us nothing. Surprise, surprise, they are almost identical to what we found on Gemma Kramer's computer, although the killer called himself Sean instead of Tom. We have no clue how he got to the girls or who he is. We have fucking nada."

"Maybe *Crimewatch* will do the trick."

He shrugged. "The response is usually great but with a complicated case like this it isn't always straightforward. Take the Barton case. Loads of calls came in after Trevor appeared on TV and we spent a huge amount of time sifting through all the information and following it up. But in the end, none of it helped catch Barton."

She started to feel a little depressed. "I still don't see why you think it's worth considering Marion Spear?"

He took a large gulp of wine, put the glass down on the table and folded his arms wearily. "It's simple. Laura Benedetti wasn't necessarily Tom's first attempt at killing."

"She was the first that fits the pattern that we know of."

"Tom didn't spring from nowhere as a fully-fledged psychopath. He must have killed, or tried to, before. There's usually an escalation in what happens."

"But we've searched the records."

"We don't know what we're searching for. Take Michael Barton. He started off as a petty burglar who turned to rape."

"Are you saying Barton killed a woman by mistake?"

"Although Barton's attacks were becoming increasingly violent, when he set out that night I personally doubt he had murder in mind. He didn't mean to strangle Jane Withers but she wouldn't do what he wanted. Unlike the others, she kept screaming and struggling. We know from her autopsy that she fought hard. He had to subdue her and silence her, otherwise he risked being caught. In the process, he got carried away and what was supposed to be rape, turned into murder."

"But I understand he killed four more women. They can't all have been accidents."

"We don't know what went on in his mind — the bastard won't talk. But probably somewhere in the middle of throttling the life out of poor Jane, he discovered that killing turned him on in a whole new way. A lot of what he did to her was post mortem. Perhaps he wasn't aware at that point if she was alive or dead."

Donovan was silent for a moment as she finished her wine. "Why are you so anti Dr Kennedy? I agree he's a prick but there are enough of those around and we all make mistakes. Also, he has had some successes."

Tartaglia shook his head. "Maybe. But to Kennedy, the Barton case was just another academic puzzle. He forgot he was dealing with real people, flesh and blood, who had families, husbands, children . . ." His voice tailed off for a moment before he continued. "It was all a game to him," he said bitterly. "His refusal to believe that he might be wrong wasted valuable time and, in my view, cost the last two victims their lives."

"You didn't have to listen to him."

"No. But it's difficult to filter out the noise, particularly when it's coming from a so-called expert. It makes you doubt your own instincts. Also, what if we'd been wrong? We'd have had a job explaining to the powers-that-be why we ignored him."

"Everything's easy to see with the benefit of hindsight."

"Of course, but Trevor and I blame ourselves. If we hadn't paid so much attention to Kennedy, I'm sure we would have found Barton sooner. That's why I intend to follow my nose this time. If Trevor were here, he'd back me up, I know."

"You really think Marion Spear could be an early victim?"

"To be honest, I've no idea. But at the moment, she's all we've got. We must find the early victims, the botched attempts before Tom perfected his act. Unless something lands in our lap, it's our best chance of catching him."

"We've only been looking in London. Maybe Tom started killing somewhere else."

"It's possible. But you know how difficult it's been to search thoroughly without a central log. As it is, I'm not convinced we've found all the victims. But extending the search outside London is impossible. We haven't got the resources nor is there any reason to justify doing it at the moment. Perhaps *Crimewatch* will do the job for us. We'll soon hear if there's been anything similar going on in other parts of the country."

"Do you think he's killing them in different parts of London to make it difficult for someone to spot?"

"The thought had occurred to me. At least now, with all the publicity, he won't get away with it again so easily."

She sank back in her chair and closed her eyes, rubbing her temples with her fingers, feeling suddenly out of her depth. In the short space of time she'd been on Clarke's team, she'd had to deal with a number of murders. Although grisly and upsetting, they had usually been cases of domestic violence gone wrong, or someone with a grievance against a member of their family, friend or work colleague. Nothing she had seen so far had prepared her for something like this.

"He's not going to stop, is he?" she said, softly, after a moment.

Tartaglia shook his head. "The clock's ticking. Unless we can establish the connection between Laura, Ellie and Gemma, our only other means of catching him is to wait for him to do it again. If so, let's just hope with all the media pressure, he fucks up."

As he reached for his glass, the phone rang and he got up to answer it. Donovan realised almost immediately from Tartaglia's tone of voice that it wasn't Sally-Anne at the other end. After a brief exchange, he grabbed a pencil and a piece of paper from the table, jotted something down, then slammed the phone into its cradle.

Stretching his arms in the air, he yawned and came back to the sofa. "That was the blessed Carolyn. Sounded pretty chuffed with her performance on TV."

"Was that all she wanted?"

"Some bloke's phoned in to say that he thinks he saw Gemma's killer steaming out of the church late that afternoon. The timing checks out, so hopefully we may get a better description of the man."

"You're going round to see him now?"

He shook his head. "Thank God, no. It's been fixed for tomorrow morning, eight a.m. at Ealing nick. Apparently, the caller lives nearby. I'd like you to be there too."

She nodded, grateful that it wasn't six or seven a.m. The description of Gemma's killer released on

Crimewatch had been kept deliberately vague and it would be interesting to see if what the caller had seen tallied with Mrs Brooke's statement.

"That should tie in nicely with following up on Marion's Mr Kipper and the local estate agent," he said, rubbing his hands together, smiling. "Meantime, I *have* to eat something. Let's order a takeaway and watch effing Carolyn on film. Maybe she'll be nominated for an Oscar."

He was about to reach for the phone when the doorbell rang.

Donovan gave him an enquiring look. "Expecting someone?"

"I'm not expecting anyone."

As surprised as Donovan, he went out of the flat and opened the front door to find a woman standing at the bottom of the steps in the middle of the path, sheltering from the rain under a large umbrella. It took him a moment to realise that it was Fiona Blake. He stared at her, not knowing what to say.

"I was just passing and saw your light on," she said. There was a moment's hesitation before she added: "May I come in?"

Her speech was a touch slurred. Although she said she was passing, she lived on the other side of town. Even though her face was in shadow, he could see that she was dressed up, lips shiny, just catching the light, hair sleek around her shoulders. He wondered what she was doing at that hour in his neighbourhood. Part of him would have given a great deal to invite her inside but he knew he shouldn't. He still felt bruised after everything that had happened, remembering the photographs in her office, the ring on her finger. Anyway, with Donovan just on the other side of the wall, the choice was made for him. Thank God, temptation was put out of his way.

"It's not a good time," he said, instantly gauging from the tightening of her expression that he'd said the wrong thing. He saw her eyes focusing on his bare feet then moving to the half-drunk glass of wine in his hand. He was suddenly aware of the music drifting softly out the door behind him and realised how it all must look.

"I can see you're busy," she said frostily.

"Work, I'm afraid."

"Work? Of course. You're always working. Perhaps another time."

She slipped her handbag over her shoulder and started to walk back down the path towards the street.

"Fiona, wait. It's not like that." He felt stupid as soon as he'd said it.

She stopped by the front gate and turned, teetering a little on her very high heels as she stared hard at him. "Not like what?"

"I've got a colleague with me. We're discussing the case." He didn't see why he should have to explain himself to her but he found himself doing it anyway.

"I just thought we should talk, that's all," she said, clearly not believing him. "But as you say, it's not a good time. I'm sorry, I shouldn't have come."

"I'd like to talk. Honestly, I would. But not now."

She hesitated, shifting her weight awkwardly from one foot to another as if her shoes were uncomfortable. "When?"

"I'll call you," he said, hoping to placate her, although he wasn't sure if he would.

She shook her head slowly as if she didn't believe him and turned away without a word, walking off down the road.

Thoughts racing, feeling stupid and inept, he watched her go, listening to the clip of her heels on the wet pavement. He waited for a moment then went back inside, slamming the front door behind him, and then the door to the flat, as he tried to stifle the yearning to go after her.

Donovan was still sitting in the chair by the window, feet tucked up under her, a huge grin on her face. The walls in the house weren't thick and she must have heard part, if not all, of what had been said.

"Would you like me to go?" she asked, taking a sip of wine as if she had no intention of doing any such thing. "I really don't want to be in the way . . ."

"You're not," he said firmly, walking over to the table and topping up his glass. He felt suddenly relieved that Donovan was there and grateful for her company.

"Was it Dr Blake?" she asked after a moment.

He nodded.

She put down her glass, unfolded her legs and got to her feet. "Really, I'm very happy to leave, if you want me to. Why don't you call her back?"

"Not a good idea."

She sighed, shaking her head slowly as if she understood everything. "Ah, Mark. Life's never simple, is it?"

He could tell what was going through her mind: he was thinking with his dick, and she was probably right. "I don't want to talk about it," he said firmly. "Now let's order that sodding curry."

A bitter wind gusted across Hammersmith Bridge, blowing with it a mist of icy rain. Kelly Goodhart stopped and closed her eyes for a moment listening to the sound as it whistled around the tall gothic towers, rushing through the ironwork structure high above. The air was so cold, she could barely feel her toes in her sodden boots, let alone her fingers. But none of that would matter soon. It was nearly midnight and she wouldn't have much longer to wait.

The last time she had stood there, almost on that very spot, had been with Michael. They had been for a long walk along the towpath, stopping on the bridge to watch the sun set. Afterwards, they had gone to The Dove in Hammersmith for a couple of drinks before returning home for supper. It was Sunday evening, late autumn and unusually warm for that time of year. They had sat out on the little terrace at the back overlooking the river, watching the rowing boats plough up and down, gazing contentedly at the darkening outline and playing fields of St Paul's school opposite, where Michael had studied as a boy.

Hearing the perennial drone of an aeroplane somewhere above, she opened her eyes and leaned back against the wrought iron balustrade, peering across the water. She could just make out the pub amongst the stretch of old houses on the opposite shore, its lights still shining even at that hour. The memory of happier times brought tears to her eyes, which mingled with the rain. It all seemed so distant now.

Not wanting to think about it anymore, she turned away into the wind and looked down-river, holding tight onto the wooden handrail as she gazed at the glittering modern office buildings and warehouse conversions further along, silhouetted against the cloudy night sky. The river ran high up against the wall, the sodium lights along the bank reflecting in the rippling black water, which looked deceptively calm from a distance. The river curved sharply away to the right, towards Fulham and Chelsea and the next string of bridges, which were hidden from view. The opposite bank was dark and it was almost impossible to make out where the river ended and land began, the only light glinting through the thick, swaying trees coming from the terrace of houses that backed onto the towpath.

The line of old-fashioned lamps along the bridge cast intermittent pools of pinkish-yellow light on the churning water immediately below, the current moving furiously along, carrying with it all manner of detritus. Gazing down, she spotted a small, uprooted tree or branch, reaching up like a bony outstretched hand, momentarily caught in an arc of light before being swept away beneath the bridge. It was as if it was beckoning to her and she felt the invisible pull of the water, inviting her, drawing her down towards it. Thank God the darkness that had enveloped her for so long would soon be over.

She heard the rattle of wheels on the bridge as a car sped towards her, the headlamps momentarily blinding, and she turned away, retreating into the shadow of one of the huge buttresses, stuffing her hands in her pockets for warmth. At that hour there was hardly any traffic and it was only the fourth car she had counted in the past ten minutes, along with a single pedestrian, an elderly man out walking a Labrador, who was so bundled up in hat and coat against the weather that he didn't even look at her as he went past.

Finding it impossible to stand still, as much from nerves as the cold, she started to walk back across the bridge, listening to the hollow thud of her footsteps on the path. She went over her checklist again in her mind: the note and money for her cleaner, ready on the kitchen table along with the keys to her car and the letter for her brother, containing details of her bank accounts and other assets, her will with its short list of bequests and the instructions for her burial. So many loose ends that needed to be carefully tied up. But everything was in order, she reassured herself. She had forgotten nothing.

Drowning was supposed to be a pleasant way to go, according to what she had read. As your lungs filled with water, you experienced a high, a feeling of euphoria and floatiness. On a night like this, if you didn't drown instantly, you would die of hypothermia, the effects of which weren't very different. She wasn't a good swimmer so she would probably drown, although she had no strong feelings either way. All that mattered was that it happened tonight.

She looked at her watch. It was now just past midnight. He said he would be coming by tube and she stopped and scanned the length of the bridge towards Hammersmith, eyes straining to catch any movement. But there was none. He was only a few minutes late but every minute counted and already she started to feel anxious. When they had spoken that morning, he had given her his word that he would be there, that he wouldn't fail her. She rubbed her wedding ring with her thumb, turning it round and round her finger in her pocket as she worried about what she would do if he didn't come. She knew she couldn't go through with it on her own but the thought of living another day was unbearable. Surely he wouldn't let her down.

Trying to calm herself, she started to walk again, stamping hard on the path to keep warm. She was almost on the other side when her eyes caught a movement in the distance and she noticed the small, dark, bobbing shape of someone coming along the pavement below towards her, just before the foot of the bridge. Hesitant, she stopped again and squinted into the distance, her breath catching in her throat. It looked like a man. It could be him. As he slowly approached, she struggled to make out his features in the orange streetlight but she was sure she recognised the tall, broad-shouldered outline and the long, loping gait that was so distinctive. Tears in her eyes, she exhaled sharply, gasping from sheer relief, and hugging herself tightly. She had been foolish to worry. He had come as he had promised and with a surge of elation, she watched him draw near.

CHAPTER
FOURTEEN

Tartaglia strode into room three at Ealing Police Station, where a youngish-looking man and Donovan were seated opposite each other at the table, engrossed in conversation.

"Sorry to keep you waiting," Tartaglia said, banging the door closed with his heel.

Donovan gave Tartaglia an enquiring look but the man smiled and shrugged good-humouredly as if he had all the time in the world.

"Not a problem," the man said. "Sergeant Donovan has been taking good care of me. I was in the middle of explaining what happened."

"This is Adam Zaleski," Donovan said. "He's just been telling me about the man he saw running away from the church where Gemma Kramer died."

Zaleski gave Donovan another easy smile and leant back in his chair, pushing his small, steel-rimmed glasses up his nose. Young, slim, with very short dark hair, wet from the rain outside, he was dressed in a sober grey suit and plain, navy tie, clearly on his way in to the office.

Tartaglia dumped his helmet and gloves on the floor in the corner and fumbled to unzip his soaking jacket.

It was a relief to take it off for a while and he shook it energetically a few times to get rid of the water clinging to the surface, before hanging it on the coat rack behind the door. In spite of the waterproofs, he felt as though the freezing rain outside had penetrated right through to his skin. His cheeks smarted in the stuffy warmth of the small room, his hands still like blocks of ice.

The day had started badly. For some reason he had overslept, waking with a churning stomach and a thick head. No doubt the greasy takeaway he had shared with Donovan the previous evening was something to do with it, as well as the half bottle of Barolo he had polished off on his own after she had gone, trying to obliterate Fiona Blake from his thoughts. To make matters worse, it had been raining heavily when he left the flat this morning. Still dark outside, the roads were slick as a skidpan, and the traffic was much heavier than normal.

He hated being late; hated others being late too. It was unforgivable. But as he came back to the table, he saw from the clock by the door that it was worse than he had imagined. He should have been there nearly three-quarters of an hour ago. He sighed and shook his head, angry with himself, as he sat down next to Donovan opposite Zaleski. He felt unfocused and out of control, desperate now for a large cup of strong, black coffee, a cigarette or three and something to eat. But that would have to wait until they finished with Zaleski. Hopefully the interview wouldn't take long.

170

He took out a notebook and pen from his pocket, more for formality's sake than anything else, as he could see that Donovan had been taking copious notes. As he did so, Zaleski stood up.

"I hope you don't mind if I remove my jacket. It's like the Sahara in here." His voice was flat and accentless, the tone a little husky, as if he was getting over a cold.

Draping the jacket carefully over the back of his chair, Zaleski sat down again and folded his hands in front of him on the table, ready for business. He looked more muscular without the jacket, a pristine white shirt taut across his chest and upper arms.

Zaleski might be dying of heat but Tartaglia was still freezing. Rubbing his hands together to get his circulation going, Tartaglia leaned across the table. "Please can you take me through what you've already told Sergeant Donovan?"

"Sure. It's pretty simple, really," Zaleski said, shrugging again, giving Tartaglia a pleasant smile. "I was walking along Kenilworth Avenue. Just as I was passing St Sebastian's, this bloke comes down the steps and out of the gate. He wasn't looking where he was going and he nearly walked straight into me."

"You say 'nearly'. Did he touch you at all?"

Zaleski looked puzzled. "Touch me?"

"If this man proves to be the person we're looking for and he had physical contact with you, we'll need the clothes you were wearing for forensic examination."

Zaleski nodded. "Oh, I see. No, he didn't touch me. He just glared at me for a second, almost angry, as if it

171

was my fault. Then he turned and walked off. After a moment, I heard a car engine start up further along the road and it drove away. I didn't see anyone else around, so I presume it was his car."

Zaleski spoke in a quiet, considered manner as if aware of the importance of each detail. He would come across well in court, if it ever came to that.

"Did you see the car?"

"Only its taillights disappearing. It was too dark."

"You said you thought it was a car, not a van," Donovan said.

"That's right. At least it didn't sound like a van, if you know what I mean."

"But you got a good look at the man?" Donovan prompted.

Zaleski nodded. "I'd say so. He was very close and there's a streetlamp right by the entrance to the church. He's white, clean-shaven, round about my age."

"Which is?"

"Thirty-six."

Tartaglia studied Zaleski. He was usually good at judging someone's age but Zaleski looked barely thirty.

"What about height?"

Zaleski paused for a moment, rubbing his chin thoughtfully. "I don't know. I'm about five ten. I'd say he was possibly a bit taller but I really can't be sure. You see, it all happened so quickly."

"What about hair colour?"

"Brown. Thick, I think, and longish."

"Brown?"

"Well, certainly lighter than mine, although the streetlamp was one of those orange ones so it's difficult to be precise."

Tartaglia nodded. Although Zaleski seemed to have good recall of what had happened, orange street lighting made it almost impossible to read colours accurately. Mrs Brooke had described the man as having dark hair but then she had seen him from a distance in fading daylight. Some sort of mid-to-dark-brown was probably the best they could do for the moment.

"You said you saw his face clearly. I don't suppose you have any idea about eye colour?"

Zaleski considered for a moment, picking at a loose thread attached to his cuff button.

"I'd say they were pale."

"Pale?" Donovan said, checking her notes and scribbling something down.

"Well, I think if he had dark eyes they would have stood out, even under the streetlamp. But now you ask, I'm not so sure."

"Of course, you only saw him briefly," Tartaglia said, aware that he'd pushed Zaleski too far. Sometimes, in a misguided effort to be helpful, witnesses remembered things that they hadn't actually seen. Zaleski seemed eager to please and he realised he would have to tread more carefully.

"Do you happen to remember what he was wearing?"

Zaleski grimaced. "It's funny, but I really only remember his face, the way he looked at me. That's what sticks in my mind. The rest is a bit of a blur, although I think he was dressed in a coat, the way you had him in the reconstruction, with his hands in the pockets. I haven't a clue about the trousers or shoes. It all happened so quickly, you see. One minute he's there, the next he's gone."

Although Zaleski seemed to feel that he should have remembered things more clearly, they were making progress. Mrs Brooke hadn't been able to see the man's features from where she was standing, whereas Zaleski had seen him up close, albeit for only a few seconds.

"That's perfectly understandable. Do you think you saw him well enough to help us put together an e-fit?"

"I could certainly try."

"Assuming the car you heard was his, which way did he go?"

"South."

Donovan checked her notes. "You said, towards Popes Lane."

"That's right."

"What time was this?" Tartaglia asked.

"Definitely after five. Maybe about five-fifteen. I was on my way over to pick up my car from the garage. It was there for a service and an MOT. They shut at half past and I was in a bit of a rush to get there in time, as I needed it that evening. I've given Sergeant Donovan the details, if you want to check it out. They may be able to remember exactly what time I arrived."

They would check as a matter of course but the time fitted perfectly. Without doubt, Zaleski had seen Tom.

174

Hopefully, he would be able to pick him out of a line-up if they ever found him.

"Why didn't you come forward sooner?" Donovan asked. "Didn't you see the witness appeal boards? They were dotted all around the streets close to the church."

Zaleski shook his head. "I don't normally go that way. I live right on the other side of Ealing and I work in South Ken. I only found out about what had happened when I watched *Crimewatch* last night."

Tartaglia closed his notebook and slipped it into his pocket. "What do you do for a living, Mr Zaleski?"

"I'm a hypnotist."

"Stage shows, you mean?" Tartaglia barely stifled his surprise. There was nothing showy or theatrical about Zaleski, qualities he imagined were par for the course for a hypnotist, which, in his view, was tantamount to being a fairground conjurer. If anything, Zaleski looked like a drone accountant or lawyer in one of the big City firms.

Zaleski grinned, clearly having come across such a reaction before. "Nothing glamorous like that. I'm not Paul McKenna. I just have a small practice. Perhaps I should be more ambitious, but I enjoy what I do and it pays the bills, so my bank manager's happy."

Trataglia struggled to imagine how anybody could earn a living from such a profession. "What sort of things do you do?"

"My main area of interest is in treating people with phobias and addictions. Claustrophobia, fear of flying, things like that. Most of the people who come to see me simply want to lose weight or stop smoking." He glanced at Donovan and smiled as if they shared some secret. "That's my bread and butter. Luckily, there's a lot of demand and I usually get good results. It normally only takes a few sessions."

"It's that easy?" Tartaglia said sceptically, acutely aware of the half-empty packet of cigarettes in his pocket and suddenly craving a smoke again.

"It certainly works for some people," Donovan said, a little defensively, he thought, as she tucked away her notebook and pen in her bag. "A friend of mine's company paid for all the smokers in the office to be hypnotised in order to get them to give up. She used to smoke twenty a day and she hasn't touched one since."

Tartaglia looked back at Zaleski, still unconvinced. "You really could make me give up smoking or drinking?"

Zaleski was smiling. "You'd have to want to give up. Real-life hypnosis is nothing like you see in films. I can't make you do anything you don't want to do. I can't take control of your mind."

"Then how does it work?"

"Through suggestion. I just help you along the path you've already chosen." Zaleski reached behind into his jacket pocket for his wallet, plucked out a business card and handed it to Tartaglia. "Why don't you try it some time?"

"Maybe. If ever I find there's something I can't deal with myself. In the meantime, I think we've covered everything for now." He stood up, Zaleski and Donovan following suit. "I'll get someone from my team to contact you later this morning about the e-fit. We'll also

176

need you to make a formal statement. Nowadays, we have to record these things both on video and audio."

He walked Zaleski to the door and pointed him in the direction of the front desk and the way out. Once he was out of sight, Tartaglia crumpled up Zaleski's business card and aimed it at the bin in the corner. Annoyingly, it landed just short.

"You're just like my father," Donovan said, walking over and scooping it up to drop it in the bin. "He never picks up anything."

From what he remembered, Donovan's father was an overweight, grey-bearded former English teacher in his early sixties. Only a few years older than Donovan, Tartaglia felt stung by the remark. "I can't believe I'm anything like your father." He unhooked his jacket from the rack, where it had been dripping onto the lino, creating a small pool, and gave it a vigorous shake to get rid of the last few drops of water. "And you're hardly Miss Tidy. Your house looked like a gypsy encampment last time I saw it."

"Well, I do try, but Claire totally defeats me. Don't worry. You're not really like Dad," she said, patting his arm and smiling as if she knew what he had been thinking.

He walked to the door and held it open for her impatiently. "There's a Starbucks on the High Street just down the road from the estate agents where Marion Spear worked. If we get a move on, we've time for a quick breakfast before the estate agent opens."

CHAPTER
FIFTEEN

After several strong coffees and a plate of stodgy croissants, Tartaglia left Donovan to interview the owner of Grafton Estate Agents while he went to find Harry Angel, the man to whom Marion Spear had been showing a flat and the last person known to have seen her alive. The driving rain had slowed to a drizzle and the cold, wet air felt pleasantly fresh on his face after the fug of the café, helping to clear his head as he walked the few blocks to the bookshop where Angel worked.

From what he could tell from the slim case file, the local CID investigation into Marion Spear's death had been cursory. Given the usual issues of finite resources and heavy workload, it wasn't surprising. Harry Angel had been interviewed several times. But he had stuck to his story about leaving Marion Spear outside a flat in Carlton Road, Ealing. With no witnesses to contradict him, no apparent motive and nothing to link him to the crime scene, they had eventually given up on him.

No evidence of foul play had emerged. Marion had either fallen to her death by accident, which seemed unlikely owing to the height of the car park walls, or she had committed suicide. Although no note had been found, he could see why suicide had seemed the most plausible conclusion, with significant weight being attached to statements from both Spear's mother and a flatmate, who said that Marion was unhappy and was finding it difficult to make friends in London. Nobody had looked beyond this fact, to consider how a lonely young woman like Marion might easily fall prey to something sinister.

Thinking of the photograph of Marion in the file, he wondered if he was right. She was attractive, in an unthreatening, girl-next-door way, young-looking for her thirty years, with shoulder-length, dark blonde hair and a wistful, sweet expression in her eyes. Perhaps he was reading too much into it, but she looked sad. She must have had admirers; someone would have taken an interest, surely. But according to the statements, Marion kept herself to herself and rarely went out. Kennedy was wrong about her not fitting the victim profile. Even if Marion Spear was a lot older than Gemma, Ellie and Laura, even if she had died in a different way, there was a common strand. They were all lonely, all isolated, all vulnerable in their different ways. Had Marion somehow caught Tom's attention?

The bookshop where Angel worked was in the middle of the parade facing onto Ealing Green, a few doors along from the tapas bar where Tartaglia and Kennedy had lunched the day before. Sandwiched between a bright, organic food shop and a fancy French coffee bar, the bookshop seemed out of place, the front painted with several uneven layers of ancient-looking black gloss, the name "Soane Antiquarian Books" written in faded gold lettering across the top.

He peered briefly through the partially misted-up window at the display of second-hand books on architecture and history of art, then tried pushing the door. It was locked and he noticed from the sign on the door that the shop wasn't due to open for another half hour. But he could see a light on towards the back of the dim interior and somebody moving around inside. After trying the bell a few times, he gave up and rapped loudly on the door. A minute later, a tall, rangy man appeared out of the gloom. Studying Tartaglia suspiciously, he pointed at the sign, mouthing in slow motion, as if for an idiot, the words, "We're closed." Tartaglia mouthed back the word "Police", holding up his warrant card to the glass. The man hesitated, deciding what to do, then slowly unlocked the door, opening it a few inches and scanning the warrant card through the crack.

"What do you want?" he said.

"Are you Harry Angel?"

The man hesitated again then nodded.

"I'm Detective Inspector Mark Tartaglia. May I come in? I'm sure you wouldn't want me to discuss things with you from the pavement."

With a grudging look, Angel threw open the door and let him pass, a small bell attached to the door jingling violently.

The interior was cramped and barely warmer than outside, the dark red walls lined with shelves of hardbacks, some of them leather-bound. Some sort

180

of strident modern opera was playing in the background and Tartaglia could smell freshly brewed coffee.

"What's this about?" Angel asked, hands on hips. He was a couple of inches taller than Tartaglia, well over six foot, with large feet encased in a pair of ancient velvet slippers with a gold crest on the front. Dressed in faded jeans and a baggy dark green pullover, Angel was older than he had initially appeared, perhaps in his late thirties or early forties, with a pale, bony face and a sweep of floppy, dark reddish-brown hair. Although his height was a possible stumbling point, he just about matched Zaleski's description of the man seen running from St Sebastian's. It was a wild leap of imagination, Tartaglia knew, with nothing whatsoever to link the two, but he couldn't help feeling a twinge of excitement.

"It's about Marion Spear. I understand you were one of the last people to see her alive."

"Marion Spear?" Angel looked doubtful, as if he had never heard the name before, but Tartaglia had noticed a flicker of recognition cross his face.

"Yes, Marion Spear. She fell to her death from a car park quite close to here, shortly after she had taken you to see a flat in Carlton Road. It was barely two years ago. Surely you haven't forgotten?"

"Shit." Angel wheeled around and bounded off out of sight towards the back of the shop.

The smell of something burning suddenly filled the air. Tartaglia followed him through the ranks of shelves to a long, narrow kitchen, built in an extension overlooking a small, overgrown garden. Angel was busy mopping up what appeared to be milk from the top of an old electric cooker, an expression of distaste puckering his thin lips. The lime green units and brown lino looked vintage seventies but the room was tidy and spotlessly clean, surprisingly at odds with Angel's scruffy appearance.

"Come on, Mr Angel. Marion Spear. I'm sure you remember who she is."

Angel turned and glared at him. "Look, of course I remember, Inspector. I just don't know what I can add to what I told you lot last time." He rinsed the cloth under the tap and went back to wiping the surface of the cooker until all traces of milk had disappeared.

"I'd like to hear it for myself, if you don't mind."

Angel slapped the cloth down on the worktop. "Why are you bothering about her now?"

"Because we're looking into her death again."

Angel tossed the milk pan into the sink and filled it with water. "That was the last of the bloody milk," he said, as if Tartaglia were to blame. "If you want to share my coffee, it'll have to be black."

"Thanks, but I can manage without," Tartaglia said, eyeing the small glass cafetiere of muddy-looking brown liquid next to the stove. The stuff at Starbucks had been like dishwater and Angel's looked no better. Angel reached for a mug from the plate rack above the sink and poured a full cup. Taking a large gulp, he smacked his lips, then leaned back against the sink, cradling his mug. "OK. What can I tell you?"

"Let's start with how you knew Marion Spear."

Angel sighed deeply as if it were all a waste of time. "I didn't know her, per se. She just took me around a few flats." He took another mouthful of coffee before adding: "It wasn't my fault that she chose to top herself straight after an appointment with me."

"Top herself? Why do you say that?"

Angel shrugged. "That's what everyone thought at the time, if I remember correctly. Although, as I told your boys in blue, she seemed perfectly normal when I left her. Quite chirpy, actually." Angel scratched his beaky nose. "You think it was an accident?"

"It's possible, although unlikely."

"Yes, it didn't seem right to me," he said, emphatically. "I know that car park. The walls are really high. All these new safety regulations, you know what it's like. They build walls so you can't even bloody see over them, let alone fall over them." He let the sentence hang then turned to Tartaglia with a look of surprise. "You think her death is suspicious?"

"Let's say, for the moment we're keeping an open mind."

"Are you re-opening the case?"

"We're just taking a fresh look."

"You've got new evidence?"

"I didn't say that, Mr Angel. I'm just checking things over, kicking the tyres, that's all."

Angel clearly didn't believe him, raising his eyes to the ceiling and smiling. "Ah, I see where this is going. Muggins here was one of the last people to see her alive so you think I may have had something to do with it. It's just like last time. You lot have no imagination."

"Naturally, I need to talk to you, which is why I'm here."

Angel shook his head reprovingly. "As I said, I've been through those hoops before. Surely you can do better than that? I mean, what's my motive? Or perhaps I'm just a psycho?" He widened his eyes and bared his teeth, in a Norman Bates impersonation. "They couldn't find anything on me last time, so why are you bothering?"

Although Angel seemed to think he'd been given a tough time, from what Tartaglia had seen of the file, there were many unanswered questions. Also, there hadn't been a thorough check on Angel's background or any real attempt to find a link between him and Marion beyond the obvious. No doubt, as the suicide theory gained credence, it hadn't seemed necessary.

For the moment, he wanted to allay Angel's suspicions. "It's early days, Mr Angel. Before we jump to conclusions, perhaps you can tell me what you remember about Marion Spear."

"Look, I made a statement at the time and I've nothing new to add."

"I've read your statement but I'd like to hear what happened myself."

Still grinning, as if it were all a bad joke, Angel took a large gulp of coffee then shrugged. "All right. From what I remember, she was a nice girl, a cheerful sort. I think she was relatively new to the job and eager to please. Not like some of the jaded old trouts in the estate agents around here who can't be bothered to get

184

off their fat arses. She took me to see a lot of flats but none of them was quite right."

"You said she seemed perfectly normal that day?"

He nodded. "She showed me a couple of new things that had just come on the books. That was it. Business as usual. First time I know something's wrong is when one of your lot comes calling a couple of days later."

Angel's casual manner seemed a little forced and Tartaglia was sure he was hiding something. "Didn't she mention where she was going next after seeing you? Didn't she say anything?"

"Why should she? I mean, I was just a client."

"Where did you think she was going?"

Angel gave another deep sigh, as if the whole subject bored him. "Search me. I assumed she was either going back to the office or to meet another client. Surely, you can check her diary."

"There were no further entries until late that afternoon. She should have gone straight back to the office but she didn't." He studied Angel for a moment. "So, you had absolutely no idea where she went?"

Angel drained his mug and banged it down on the counter. "Of course not."

"Your relationship was purely professional?"

"I'd hardly call it a relationship. The lady took me to see some flats, that's all."

"You never saw her socially?"

There was a second's hesitation. "We might have bumped into each other in the street. Maybe she came into the bookshop once or twice. But nothing more than that."

Tartaglia hid the little stab of excitement he felt at hearing this. According to Angel's original statement, Marion Spear had never set foot in the bookshop. They had only ever met at the estate agents where she worked or at a flat that she was showing him. Angel had been adamant on that point but he wasn't going to remind him. "Was she interested in second-hand books on architecture?" he asked, casually.

"Amazing though it may seem, Inspector, a lot of people are. Anyway, we stock a wide variety of books."

"But I'm talking about Marion Spear. Why would she come in here?"

"I seem to remember she liked reading."

"You discussed books together?"

"Maybe."

"So, she came in to buy a book?"

"Probably. It's what people do."

"Or was it to see you, for some reason?"

Angel's expression hardened and he folded his arms defensively. "Look, I really don't remember. Maybe she didn't come here."

Tartaglia was sure he was lying. "But you just said that she did."

"I said that she might have done. I just don't remember her doing so. Clear?" Angel's voice went up a tone.

"It's curious. You remember some things so very clearly, and other things, not at all." Angel puckered his lips but said nothing. Reminding himself that even if Angel had lied, it wasn't evidence of anything, he decided to leave it for the moment. "Do you have a computer, Mr Angel?"

Angel looked surprised. "Yes, why?"

"Is it here or at home?"

"This is my home. I live upstairs."

"Where's your computer?"

"Down in the basement, where we pack up all the books we send out. We do a lot of business over the net."

"May I see it?"

Angel stared at him for a moment, then shrugged. "Be my guest. Although, I can't see why it's of any interest."

Angel seemed almost relieved, which was puzzling. Maybe it was an act or maybe the subject of the computer didn't bother him.

He followed Angel down a narrow flight of stairs to a low-ceilinged, windowless room that ran the full length of the shop. While the ground floor had the air of an old-fashioned library, the basement operation was modern and streamlined. Boxes full of books were neatly stacked and labelled in rows on the floor, with a shelving unit along one wall housing business stationery and thick rolls of bubble wrap and brown paper. Three cheap, pine trestle tables were lined up against the other wall for the actual packing. Judging by the number of books waiting to be wrapped and sent, the internet was an important source of business and the operation looked efficient. A new-looking Apple Mac sat on a small table in a corner, its screen dead. Short of asking Angel to turn it on and let him scan the hard drive, there was little Tartaglia could do without a warrant and there wasn't sufficient grounds for that yet. Angel still seemed curiously relaxed. Maybe he had another computer elsewhere.

"Very impressive," Tartaglia said, turning away and gazing at a tower of full jiffy bags and neatly wrapped parcels waiting to be posted out, the top one addressed to somewhere in Canada. "You send books all over the world?"

Angel nodded. "Thanks to the internet. We wouldn't be able to survive without it."

"You keep saying "we". Do you have a business partner?"

Angel shook his head. "Force of habit. The business used to belong to my grandfather and we worked together. But he's dead now."

"So, you take care of this entirely on your own?" There had been no mention of anyone else in the file but, judging by the scale of the operation, he felt sure that Angel had help of some kind. Angel hesitated. "If you don't want to tell me," Tartaglia continued, "I can find out."

Angel looked annoyed. "Look, I've nothing to hide. A woman comes in to help a couple of days a week. That's all."

"Could you give me her details?"

"What's she got to do with Marion Spear?"

"I'll be the judge of that," Tartaglia said, curious that Angel seemed reluctant to give it to him.

188

Angel sighed. "She's called Annie Klein. She's only been helping me out in the last few months. Surely you don't need to bother her?"

"Probably not, but I'd like her details all the same."

Angel scribbled something down on a piece of paper and thrust it at Tartaglia. "Is there anything else or can we go back upstairs? I should be opening up soon and I haven't even had my breakfast."

"Thank you. I've seen enough for now."

Tartaglia led the way back upstairs. At the top, he turned to face Angel. "Just a couple more things. Could you tell me what you were doing between four and six last Wednesday afternoon?"

"Why on earth do you want to know about that?"

"Please answer the question, Mr Angel."

It took a moment for Angel to answer as if he were debating in his mind whether he needed to. "I was here, of course."

"Can anyone corroborate that?"

"Now what's this about?"

"Please answer the question, Mr Angel."

"Nobody was here apart from me. Annie doesn't usually work Wednesdays."

"What about customers coming into the shop? Might someone have seen you here during that time?"

"Weekday afternoons are usually quiet but I really can't remember."

"Perhaps you can check your records."

"Look, what's all this got to do with Marion Spear?"

"Absolutely nothing at the moment." He let the words sink in before adding: "But we're investigating a murder which took place at St Sebastian's, just around the corner from here."

It took a second for the significance of the words to penetrate. Angel's eyes widened. "What, that young girl? You think . . ." He put his hands on his hips and stared at Tartaglia, his face turning red, his expression a mixture of anger and indignation. He was either a good actor or the reaction was genuine. "Now look here, Inspector. I've tried to be helpful and I've answered all your questions. But if you start trying to join up the dots and make a cat look like a horse, I'm going to have to call a lawyer."

"Calm down, Mr Angel. You're a local. It's just a routine question. I'm sure you'll be able to prove that you were here at that time."

Before Angel could reply, the sound of someone knocking loudly on the shop front door made Tartaglia turn around. Donovan was standing on the step, nose pressed to the glass.

"Can't she bloody see we're closed," Angel muttered, looking round in the direction of the door.

"That's my Sergeant. One last question; do you have a car, Mr Angel?"

Angel turned back and glared at him, arms still folded. "A van. Before you get any ideas, I use it for book-buying trips."

Tartaglia smiled. "What sort of ideas would those be?"

Angel said nothing, biting his lip.

"What sort of a van?"

190

"A VW camper. Now, if that's all, I've got work to do."

"Thank you, Mr Angel," Tartaglia said, unlocking the door and opening it wide, letting a gust of freezing, damp air blow inside. "I'll get someone to call you later about last Wednesday. Perhaps you can give them the licence number of the van at the same time. Just for the record."

Without waiting for a response, Tartaglia went out, slamming the door behind him, the little bell jangling furiously. Aware that Angel was watching from the window, he and Donovan walked down the street until they were out of sight, sheltering under a shop awning from the rain while he gave her the gist of his conversation with Angel.

"I want you to go and see this woman right away." He handed Donovan the paper with Annie Klein's details and explained what Angel had said. "When you've done that, can you check with the shops on either side of Angel's. See if they remember him going out at all last Wednesday afternoon."

"Will do."

"There's also Marion's ex-flatmate, Karen Thomas. She works somewhere near here." He passed her another slip of paper. "Did you get anything interesting from Angela Grafton?"

She was about to reply when her mobile rang. Answering it, she listened for a moment before speaking. "Yes, he's here. I'll tell him. Right away, I understand." She snapped her phone shut and turned to Tartaglia looking excited. "That was Steele. She's been trying to get hold of you but you're not answering your pager and your mobile's apparently switched off."

"Damn." In his hurry to get out the door that morning, he'd left his pager in his other jacket pocket and he had forgotten to turn on his phone after the interview with Zaleski. "What does she want?"

"A woman was seen struggling with a man late last night on Hammersmith Bridge. The woman fell in and the man ran away. They can't find her body but she's probably dead. Local CID called us right away and Yvette's been briefed. She'll meet you at the rendezvous point on the Hammersmith side of the bridge."

CHAPTER
SIXTEEN

"Where did it happen?" Tartaglia asked, ducking under the tape that marked the inner cordon on the north side of Hammersmith Bridge.

"About three quarters of the way along, on the Barnes side, sir," Yvette Dickenson said.

Out of breath, her over-sized, overstuffed handbag constantly slipping off her shoulder, she had been struggling to keep up with him from the rendezvous point. Stifling impatience, he held the tape up high for her to step through. Although the rain had stopped temporarily, the wind had picked up and was whipping her thick brown hair across her face, strands catching on the edges of her glasses, which were spattered with rain. She made a couple of futile attempts to restrain her hair with a gloved hand, then seemed to give in to the forces of nature. Bundled up in a large grey overcoat, which barely met around her stomach, her eyes were red, nose streaming, and she looked miserable. Tartaglia wondered why Steele couldn't have let her stay behind in the warmth of the office and sent someone else to brief him instead. Also, why Dickenson wasn't tucked up at home enjoying the last month or so of her pregnancy in relative tranquillity was beyond him. But he knew it was her choice and not a subject she liked to discuss.

Scanning the length of the bridge, he could just make out the flapping white material of the forensic tent, tucked away behind one of the tall towers that held up the bridge. He crossed the bridge on his motorbike every day on his way to work but he had long since stopped noticing it. With the pressure of daily life, of getting from A to B as quickly as possible, it had faded into the general background, like so much of London. However, on foot it seemed much more substantial and garish. In his view, whoever was responsible for painting it that particular shade of goose-shit green should be taken out and shot. But it was still handsome in a solid, Victorian sort of way, with ornate ironwork picked out in gold and four tall towers, each looking like a mini replica of Big Ben. It formed the gateway between urban Hammersmith and rural Barnes and was a favourite spot for couples watching the sun set over the river, as well as suicides. More extraordinarily, it had survived three separate terrorist attacks, although why anyone should target it was beyond him. There were far more famous and important bridges along the Thames to choose.

Dickenson had fallen behind and he stopped for a moment, turning away from the icy wind, hands stuffed in his pockets. The sky was ominously dark, with only a glimmer of light on the horizon. After the heavy rain, the swollen river below was the colour of milky coffee, awash with debris and flowing particularly fast around the pontoons of the bridge. On the south side, it was so high that it skimmed the bank, almost at the level of the towpath. Anyone going over, particularly at night, would have stood little chance.

"They were standing just over there, sir," Dickenson said, out of breath as she caught up with him, gesturing ahead towards an area at the foot of one of the towers where the footway had been taped off by the forensic team.

Just at that point, the path looped outwards around the tower, forming a balcony overlooking the river. He remembered standing close to the spot with friends a few years before, watching the Oxford and Cambridge boat race. The area was covered with scaffolding and a makeshift tent to protect it from the elements, bright lights shining inside and the shadows of the SOCOs moving around.

He turned to Dickenson. "Where was the witness when she saw the couple?"

"On the other side of the road, sir. She said the man and woman were standing very close together. She first thought they were kissing but when she went past she heard them arguing."

"What time was this?"

"Just after midnight. She lives in Barnes and was on her way home."

"Could she hear what they were they saying?"

"Not the exact words, what with wind and the noise of the river. But she said the woman was crying and seemed to be pleading with the man. She thought the woman sounded American, although she couldn't be sure. The witness was nearly on the other side when she heard the woman scream. She turned around and saw the woman struggling with the man; he then pushed her over the bridge."

"He pushed her? She's sure?"

"That's what she said. She thought she heard a splash and ran to the other side of the bridge but the water was so dark, she couldn't see the woman at all."

"What about the man?"

"He was bending right over the edge looking down. For a moment, she worried that he might fall in too. He seemed to be talking to himself, totally unaware of her presence and she thought maybe he was high on something. After a moment, he ran off towards Hammersmith."

"Do we have a description?" The bridge was quite well lit at night and visibility should have been good.

"Pretty basic, I'm afraid. Tall, slim build, and scruffily dressed. He was wearing a coat or jacket with a hood, which was pulled up over his head so the witness couldn't see his face clearly. The woman was older and quite smartly dressed. She said they looked an odd pair."

He couldn't help feeling a little disappointed that the description of the man was so vague. "What about forensics?"

"The SOCOs have found some scuffmarks on the railings and a whole load of fingerprints, although some are badly smudged."

He nodded. "It's a popular place to stand and admire the view."

196

Although there was a lot of pedestrian traffic on the bridge, if the man had held onto the rail as he looked over, they might get some prints. But if it was Tom, why had he taken the woman there? With the previous three murders, Tom had chosen quiet, private places where there was little risk of interruption and where he could control the environment. The bridge, with cars, cycles and pedestrians going by even late at night, was very public and to kill someone there would require a degree of improvisation. Yet Tom's previous killings seemed to have been so carefully planned and staged, down to the last detail, the ritual seemingly important. In Tartaglia's view, it didn't feel right. Hypersensitive, given all the publicity, Cornish had insisted that they look at any possible crime that could be linked. But Tartaglia cursed the tenseness of a situation which had brought him there simply because a woman had been pushed from a high place.

"I assume there's no sign of the body yet?" he asked, knowing the answer. It could take days, sometimes weeks, for a body to surface from the murky depths of the Thames. Given the current, it was probably half way down the river by now, somewhere near Greenwich.

Dickenson shook her head. "The River Police have been alerted and the local uniforms are searching the banks on either side. Maybe she managed to swim away."

"Unlikely. The current's particularly strong at this time of year. Unless she was a very strong swimmer, she would have been pulled under almost immediately.

Have you checked to see if anyone's reported her missing?"

"Nothing's come in so far. I'm liaising with DS Daley at Hammersmith, who's in charge of the case for the moment."

"What about CCTV footage?"

"DS Daley's dealing with that now. It's lucky the bloke went off Hammersmith way. The area around the Broadway's littered with cameras."

Tartaglia looked over the bridge again at the swirling water below. His instincts told him that they were wasting their time. But one thing held him back from saying so outright. The incident had happened on Hammersmith Bridge, right on the doorstep of the Barnes murder investigation team, almost like a direct challenge. But if Tom was responsible, he had changed his MO. They would have to wait for the body to surface to discover more. In the meantime, the priority was to find the man.

He turned and started to walk back towards Hammersmith, Dickenson stumbling along beside him. "How much longer is the bridge going to stay closed?" he asked, after a moment.

"The crime scene manager thinks it may be another few hours, sir. I just hope it's open before I have to go home." She sighed, every step an effort. He considered offering her his arm but thought better of it. Knowing Dickenson, she would misinterpret the gesture as patronising or a reminder of the fact that she was finding it difficult doing her job in the last few months of her pregnancy. "I had quite a time getting into work this morning," she continued, irritably. "I had to go all the way over to Putney Bridge to get across. The traffic was a ruddy nightmare, I can tell you."

He nodded sympathetically. Despite the fact that the Barnes office was straight over the bridge, only a quarter of a mile away, he was going to have to make a lengthy detour to get there. Thank God he had his bike. "It's a bugger having to go all the way around. Hopefully, it won't be for much longer. I'll bet the worthy burghers of Barnes are up in arms."

She gave him a weak smile. "There've been no end of complaints and it's barely lunchtime. It's as if they think we've done it deliberately to ruin their day."

He shook his head. You couldn't win. When the bridge had been closed for over two years for structural work and refurbishment, the doctors, dentists, writers, musicians, actors and other solidly middle class residents on the Barnes side had campaigned militantly to keep it permanently closed to cars, so as to preserve their nice little village haven from commuter traffic. But close it for a day and everyone was screaming blue murder. It mattered not a jot that some poor woman might have died, let alone been killed.

Donovan slid Coldplay's X & Y into the CD player and shoved the car into gear. According to the A-Z, Annie Klein lived about a ten-minute drive away from Soane Antiquarian Books, close to the M4 motorway. Hopefully, she'd get there before Harry Angel had a chance to call Klein and prime her. Although there was no evidence that Marion Spear had been murdered, let alone anything to link her death with that of the other three girls, she agreed with Tartaglia. Angel definitely merited closer investigation.

Inching along in heavy traffic, she thought back to the conversation earlier that morning with Angela Grafton, Marion Spear's former boss. Grafton, a large-boned, red-faced woman in her late fifties, with a helmet of lacquered, bottle blonde hair, had been forthright and helpful. Chain-smoking, planted behind her large desk, she tipped a long tube of ash into a saucer and said: "Marion may have been nearly thirty but she had as much nous as a sixteen-year-old. Or less so, given what sixteen-year-olds are like these days."

In full flow, hardly needing any prompting from Donovan, she spoke emphatically, her opinions not open to question. "Of course, it's not surprising when you understand Marion's background." She gave Donovan a knowing look as if to say that she'd seen much of the world and understood all its ins and outs. "Only child, with Dad running off at a young age, leaving Mum to cope on her own. I certainly remember the mum, silly goose of a woman; always on the phone, fussing and fretting, never letting Marion be, whining about how lonely she was without her. Passive aggressive, I think they call that type nowadays. She wanted Marion to throw in the towel and go home to Leicester. Poor Marion, I remember thinking on more than one occasion, what a waste it was. She was a decent girl but there was something about her that made you feel sorry for her, and want to take her under your wing. But there's only so much you can do."

Sighing deeply, as if Marion had been an accident waiting to happen, she had added that Marion had been popular with clients but that she didn't remember anyone in particular ringing up or coming around to see her at the office. "I certainly don't recall her talking about a boyfriend or admirer. But then why would she mention it to me?" She shrugged her broad shoulders. "Marion wasn't the type to confide. She was a pretty little thing but she didn't stand a chance, with her god-awful mother. A woman like that would make anyone secretive, don't you think?"

The traffic was still creeping along and Donovan heard a siren in the distance. With the roads still slick from the rain, she wondered if maybe there had been an accident up ahead. Worrying that Angel would be calling Klein any minute now, Donovan took the next turning off the main road and started to cut through the side streets and onto Popes Lane, where things were moving faster. Stopping once outside the gates of Brentford Cemetery to consult the A-Z, five minutes later she turned into the road where Klein lived.

Although not much more than half a mile from Ealing Green, the area had a different feel, paint peeling, front gardens untidy, estate agent boards scattered everywhere, interspersed with the odd sign offering B&B accommodation. Klein's address was in the middle of a long row of tall, ramshackle semi-detached houses. Stepping around a collection of kids' bikes that had been abandoned in a pile in the middle of the path, the owners probably having gone off home for lunch, Donovan walked up to the front door and peered at the intercom. "Klein" was scrawled in biro on a piece of tape stuck against the top bell. She pressed the buzzer several times until a sleepy female voice answered.

"Who is it?"

"I'm looking for Annie Klein. I'm Detective Sergeant Donovan."

"Police?"

Donovan heard the alarm in the woman's voice. Used to the reaction, even from completely innocent members of the public who weren't accustomed to dealing with the police, she tried to sound as friendly as possible. "Nothing to worry about, I assure you. I just need a quick word concerning Harry Angel."

There was silence followed by the screech of a sash window being hauled open somewhere above. Donovan craned her neck upwards and saw a woman with long, bright red hair peering down at her.

"I'm Annie. Is Harry OK?"

"He's absolutely fine. May I come up?"

"Are you really a policewoman?" She sounded a little sceptical.

Donovan held out her warrant card, although at that distance it was just a token gesture.

"It's all right, I believe you," Annie said. "Here, catch this." A couple of Yale keys on a key ring landed at Donovan's feet. "The buzzer's not working. Top floor, just follow the stairs."

Annie appeared to have a trusting, accommodating nature. At least it seemed as though Angel hadn't yet warned her to expect a visit from the police.

The hall floor was awash with unopened post, directories still in their plastic wrappings piled haphazardly in a corner. With its stale smell, threadbare carpet and tatty green paint, the place reminded Donovan of her university digs. Panting, pausing for breath on each narrow landing, she laboured up the steep stairs to the fourth floor. She really must do something about the ciggies. She was only thirty-three and, according to the drivel she read in magazines on the rare occasions she found time to go to the hairdresser, she ought to be in her prime, ought to be able to gallop up the stairs like a thoroughbred and make wild, passionate love to some good-looking bloke waiting for her at the top. Pigs might fly, she thought, as she turned up the final flight of stairs.

Annie Klein stood in the open doorway, barefoot, wearing a frayed, embroidered silk dressing gown and little else. Bleary-eyed, she yawned and folded her arms, pulling the dressing gown tightly around her tall, skinny frame.

"I was right," she said, smiling, staring down at Donovan. "You don't look at all like a policeman. Not that I'd know much about that, apart from watching *The Bill*."

She looked to be in her late twenties or early thirties. Her voice was pleasant, quite deep, with a transatlantic twang that sounded a little fake. The dark, petrol blue of her dressing gown set off her pale skin and long, curly copper-colored hair. Her eyes were a startling dark brown. She was at least six foot tall, Donovan realised, following her inside, wishing that she hadn't chosen to wear flat boots that morning, not that heels would have made much difference. Usually her lack of height didn't bother her but for some reason suddenly she felt at a disadvantage.

"Do you feel like a cup of tea?" Annie asked. "I was just about to make some when you rang the bell."

"Please." Donovan sat down in a deep, saggy armchair covered with a sparkly orange throw. After all the coffee she'd drunk that morning, she was buzzing. Tea would make a welcome change.

The large room was light, with sloping eaves and two windows, the walls painted a bright pink. A mirror hung above the small fireplace, decorated with gold-painted scallop shells, and a large, professional-looking black and white photograph of a young woman covered most of the wall next to it. It took Donovan several seconds to realise that the picture was of Annie, the makeup, clothes and lighting completely transforming her.

Watching her make tea in the tiny kitchen area in the corner of the room, Donovan was intrigued. Annie seemed far too exotic a creature to be working for Angel packing books.

"Do you model?" she asked, as Annie came over with two full mugs.

"I used to. But I'm more interested in acting these days." She grimaced. "Sadly, it's not that interested in me." She sat down on the sofa opposite, gracefully swinging her long legs up underneath her and tucking the folds of her dressing gown tightly around her feet.

"I understand you work part-time at Soane Books."

Annie hesitated, taking a sip of tea. "Well . . . not officially. What I mean is, Harry pays me cash and I don't declare it."

Donovan smiled, hoping to put her at ease. "Don't worry. I'm not interested in that. How long have you worked there?"

"Just a few months. The internet business has really taken off and Harry can't cope on his own."

"Do you know if he had any help in the shop a couple of years ago?"

Annie shook her head. "I don't think so, but you'd better ask him. Anyway, why do you want to know?"

"We're investigating the death of a woman called Marion Spear."

Annie looked doubtful. "What's this got to do with Harry?"

"Mr Angel was one of her clients. I just need to get some basic details so that we can eliminate him from our enquiries."

"Harry knows you're here?"

"Oh, yes. He gave us your name and address." It was stretching the truth but Annie didn't seem the suspicious type. By the time she found out that Angel wasn't at all keen for her to talk to the police, it would be too late.

Annie seemed easily reassured and smiled. "Well then, I suppose there's no harm my talking to you."

"As I said, I just want a bit of background, that's all. Perhaps you can start by telling me how often you work at the shop?"

"It depends. I've got a lot of free time at the moment and Harry's pretty laid-back about when I come and go."

"You're there most days?"

"On and off if it's busy, when I haven't got auditions."

It seemed a cosy arrangement and Donovan got the impression that Harry Angel was more of a friend than a boss. "Have you known each other long?"

Annie smiled and took another sip of tea. "A few years, actually."

"You had a relationship?" Donovan asked, catching a certain look in her eyes and reading between the lines.

"Well, I wouldn't really call it that. We went out a few times but it didn't work out."

"Why was that?"

Annie took refuge in her tea. "Look. I don't want to talk out of school. Harry's a decent guy."

"But it didn't work out."

Annie sighed and shook her head. "No." She took a long sip of tea and, after a moment, added: "Harry's a bit intense. Gets carried away too quickly and I wasn't after anything serious."

"Intense?"

Annie brushed away a long lock of hair that had fallen across her face. "Yeah. You know how guys can be."

Apart from a spotty fifth-form admirer who haunted the school gates waiting for her to come out, Donovan had little personal experience of such things. Somehow, since then, she'd failed to inspire intensity in any man.

But, thinking about it, maybe that was no bad thing. Obsession was unhealthy, particularly when it was one-way. Give her a normal, down-to-earth bloke any day. Although they seemed to be pretty thin on the ground and, thinking of Richard, her ex, "normal" didn't exactly make the earth move.

"Can you be more specific?" Donovan asked.

Annie hesitated. "Well, he used to leave little notes and poems at night under the windscreen wiper of my car. I had a car in those days, you see."

"Anonymous notes, you mean?"

Annie nodded. "I'd come out the next morning and find them waiting for me. Of course, I knew they were from him, even though he wouldn't admit it."

"You think he was checking up on you? Watching you?"

Annie shrugged as if she didn't mind. "Maybe. I hadn't really thought of it like that."

"What did the notes say?"

"Oh, they were just a few lines. Sort of . . . well . . ." she furrowed her brow, searching for the word, ". . . sort of enigmatic."

"They weren't threatening?"

Annie looked surprised at the idea. "No way. I think they were supposed to be kind of romantic."

"Did he do anything else?"

She giggled. "He left a dollar bill under the wiper once but I never worked out what he meant by it."

Any initial disadvantage she had felt when first meeting Annie swiftly evaporated. Annie might have the advantage in terms of height and looks but she seemed out of touch with reality. Even if she hadn't found Angel's behaviour peculiar, let alone threatening, in Donovan's book he had all the makings of a stalker. Also, although she had only glimpsed Angel briefly, she had to agree with Tartaglia. In poor light, Angel might easily fit the description given by Zaleski.

"So, you called a halt to things?"

"Yeah. He kept ringing me for a while but eventually he got the message."

"How did you get back in touch?"

"I was looking for some part-time work and I answered an ad he'd put in the local paper. I thought twice about it when I realised who it was, I can tell you. But I needed the money and he seemed pretty cool about things." She giggled again, looking down at her mug. "Actually, I get the feeling he's still pretty keen on me."

"And that doesn't bother you?" Donovan asked, finding it impossible to fathom Annie's attitude. Her manner was so ridiculously open and easy-going, so trusting. It reminded Donovan of the way Marion Spear had been described and she felt increasingly concerned.

Annie's eyes opened wide. "Why should it? Harry's a sweetie, really, and I can handle it." She uncoiled herself from the sofa and stood up. "Would you like another cup of tea?"

Donovan shook her head and put her mug down on the floor beside her chair. It was still almost full, the tea so weak it was little more than water mixed with milk

208

and now lukewarm. "What about family and friends? Who does Mr Angel see regularly?"

"I honestly don't know," Annie said, walking over to the kitchen area and switching on the kettle. "He never talks about his family or anyone in particular. He's real private."

"But surely he gets phone calls at work."

"I'm stuck down in the basement most of the time and I can't hear anything. There's an answer-machine upstairs, so there's no need to take messages."

"So, you don't know if he's got a girlfriend?"

Annie turned back to Donovan with a smile. "If he has, it sure isn't anything serious. Anyway, he wouldn't tell me. I mean, it'd spoil his chances, wouldn't it?"

Donovan waited while Annie finished making her tea and came back to the sofa. "Just to recap; you've never heard him mention Marion Spear."

Annie shook her head, sitting down again. "You said this woman died. What happened?"

Donovan decided to give her the bare facts. It might give Annie a much-needed jolt and help her to remember things more clearly. If nothing else, it was worth putting her on her guard about Harry Angel.

"She fell to her death from the top storey of a car park near where she worked. It's quite close to the bookshop. The coroner recorded an open verdict but we're now looking into it again."

Annie looked blank. "You haven't told me what Harry's got to do with any of this."

"We're trying to trace Marion Spear's final movements. He was one of the last people to see her on the day she died. She showed him a flat in Carlton Road in Ealing but we don't know where she went after that."

Annie looked puzzled. "Harry looking at flats? Are you sure?"

"Why does that surprise you?"

Annie seemed embarrassed, as if she had said the wrong thing, coiling a long strand of hair around her finger. "Well, when his granddad died, he left Harry the shop. The upstairs rooms had been used for storage and were in quite a state. But Harry cleaned the place out, gave it all a lick of paint and moved in."

"When was this?"

"I'm not sure, but Harry was already living there when I first met him. I think he had moved in quite recently, as I remember the smell of the paint. It was overwhelming."

According to the file, Harry had given the shop address when Marion Spear died. "Maybe he decided he wanted a change."

Annie shook her head. "He's never talked about wanting to move. I mean, why would he? The space over the shop is enormous and all he has to do is roll downstairs to work in the morning. I wish I had it that easy."

Feeling increasingly impatient, Donovan realised she was going to have to spell it out for Annie. "An hour after the appointment with Mr Angel, Marion Spear was dead."

Annie stared at her. "Surely you can't think Harry had anything to do with it? I know he's a bit eccentric

210

but he means well." She started to chew one of her long fingernails, shaking her head slowly as she mulled it over. "I don't know what he was doing, going to see a flat with that woman, but I know he wouldn't harm a fly."

"I'm sure you're right," Donovan said. She'd done her best and there was no point in pushing Annie further, as she clearly refused to entertain any suspicions about Angel. She stood up to go. "Just one more question. Were you working at the shop last Wednesday afternoon?"

Annie paused for a moment, thinking back, then shook her head. "Not Wednesday. I had an audition in Hammersmith."

"So, you didn't see Mr Angel at all on Wednesday?"

"No."

"If you're not there, what does he do if he has to go out?"

"He normally puts a note up on the door saying 'Back in five minutes'. It's a bit of a con because he's usually gone longer than that, but it means that people tend to come back."

Donovan picked up her bag, took out a card and handed it to Annie. "Thanks for being so helpful. If you remember anything else, would you give me a call?"

Annie took the card with the delight of a child being handed a sweet. Clearly fond of Angel, she appeared to be unaware of the implications of some of the things she had said. Still wondering how a woman of roughly her own age could be such an ingénue, Donovan hoped Annie wouldn't be foolish enough to repeat the conversation verbatim to Angel and put him on his guard. Simple Annie might be, but she was right about one thing, Donovan was sure; Angel wasn't interested in looking at flats. He was personally interested in Marion Spear, something he'd successfully hidden from the previous investigation.

CHAPTER
SEVENTEEN

To: Carolyn.Steele@met.police.uk
From: Tom659873362@greenmail.com

Dear Carolyn,

I hope you don't mind first names but I hate formalities, don't you? Also, I feel I already know you, even though we haven't yet met — I certainly look forward to that pleasure one day very soon. For the moment, though, let me congratulate you on your performance last night on *Crimewatch*. You looked good and you struck just the right note, I thought. Well done for keeping just a few interesting details back from the public. We wouldn't want them knowing all our little secrets, would we? Just so you know it's me writing this and not some cheap imitation trying to get your attention, you could have mentioned Gemma's long, silky brown hair. I think of her every time I stroke that lovely lock. She's very dear to me, you know. But hey, I'm a fickle sort of guy. You know that already, don't you? I think you understand me. Perhaps to you, I'd be true. Perhaps. But we can talk about that another time — when we meet.

I'm straying from the point. Getting back to the show last night, people should be praised when they do something well. You deserve to be kissed for it, by a man who knows how. I, too, deserve praise, don't you think? I'm very good at what I do; I'm getting away with murder!

With fondest wishes

Yours (dare I say, your?)

Tom

Steele swivelled round in her chair to face Tartaglia, expressionless. "So, what do you make of it?" Her tone was business-like, without any trace of emotion, as if she were asking his opinion about a run-of-the-mill communiqué.

It was early evening and she had called him into her office, taking care to shut the door behind them, which was unusual. She had never had anything private to discuss with him until now, never solicited his opinion about anything major so far and he felt surprised and a little bewildered that she had sought him out now. The email left him momentarily speechless, not sure what to say, other than the obvious platitudes. Angry on her behalf, feeling a spark of unaccustomed concern for her, he was amazed at the barefaced cheek of it. The cocky, sexual overtones were particularly revolting. He had no idea if Steele lived alone or if she had a partner. Notwithstanding the general resentment he felt for her, he was instantly worried, wondering how, as a woman, she was affected by it, whether or not she felt intimidated.

Even with all her years of experience with the Met, seeing the darker side of humanity on a daily basis, emails from a serial killer were not run of the mill. It had to touch her in some manner. She had to feel something. But she was giving nothing away, matter-of-factly treating what had happened as if it were all part of the normal workday routine. Although perhaps it was all an act for his benefit, trying to show how tough she could be.

She sat very upright, mouth taut, face a pale, blank canvas, looking at him, waiting for his response. He struggled to find the right words and failed. "Did you mention in *Crimewatch* that he calls himself Tom?"

She nodded. "I decided to do so, just in case either it really is his name or nickname, or might ring a bell with someone."

"When did you receive the email?"

"About an hour ago. Of course it's untraceable."

He put his hands in his pockets and leaned back against the wall, studying her closely. But there was still no sign of emotion in her eyes. An hour ago? She had been dealing with it on her own for a full hour, without saying anything to the members of her team in the room outside? How could she keep it all to herself? She was extraordinary. Clarke would have been out of his office like a rocket, hopping mad or excited, or both, wanting to share it, wanting to get everyone's view.

"I've spoken to the lads at Newlands Park. According to them, sending emails like this is a piece of piss. All Tom has to do is drive around with a laptop in his car and tap into any unsecured network. Apparently, there are thousands and thousands of official and unofficial wi-fi hotspots all over London."

"What about the email address?"

"He's probably set up a sack-load of them especially for the purpose. There's no way of tracing him at all."

He shook his head in disbelief. "Are they sure?"

"That's what they said. Of course they'll have a go, but they told me not to expect anything."

She sighed, stifling a yawn, again as if they were talking about something trivial. "Apparently, if we knew where he was when he was online, we might be able to trace the signal back to the modem, then trace the modem back to the place where the computer was purchased. But even if the computer's not stolen, knowing our Tom, he's unlikely to have given his real details to the shop, don't you think? Anyway, if he's moving around, as they suspect, it won't work."

"Have you told Cornish?"

She nodded. "And I'm telling you and Gary, when he gets back. But nobody else needs to know. I can't risk another leak to the press."

As if stiff from sitting at the desk too long, she bowed her head, leaning forward in her chair, locking her fingers and stretching her arms out in front of her. Slim and lithe, with her sleek dark hair and green eyes, she reminded him of a cat. Like all cats, she was inscrutable. She did her duty as a boss but kept him at arm's length wherever possible, as if she was wary of him.

He wasn't expecting her to treat him the way Clarke had done — that easy, mutually rewarding relationship had been built up over several years. But he had expected something more of her. He'd heard good reports of her from people who had worked for her in the past, but as far as he could see, they were talking about a different person.

"Now, tell me about what happened on the bridge," she said, tilting her chair back and putting her feet up on the bottom drawer of her desk, which was slightly open.

As he started to explain what had happened, he pictured the bridge in his mind, with the brown swelling water below, trying yet again to make sense of what had gone on. Was it really connected to the other girls? It was like trying to find your way in thick, drifting fog, he thought. Just when you managed to make out something familiar and got your bearings, another wave of fog would roll in and the landscape would become unrecognisable again. He wasn't sure what he thought about any of it anymore.

"So, there's nothing yet to link what happened to the killings?" she said once he had finished.

He shook his head. "Not until we find the body."

"Why did CID call us?"

"Some bright spark had been reading the papers and thought it wasn't worth taking any chances. If it turns out to be Tom, they'll deserve a medal."

"But we only have the witness's word for what happened."

"CCTV footage from the bridge confirms what she saw. Some sort of incident definitely took place, although we have no clear visual of the man's face. But

I spoke to forensics and it seems as though they've retrieved some decent prints. Let's hope that at least one will belong to him."

Steele looked thoughtful. "The MO's very different. But I suppose we must keep an open mind. Tom's a clever sod and he's hardly going to get away with the same routine after all the stuff in the media."

"But if Tom is responsible, why didn't he refer to it in the email to you? You'd think he'd be bragging about it."

She shrugged, her eyes flicking back to the screen. "The thought occurred to me, too, when I first read this shit," she said, distractedly. He caught a slight tensing in her face, as if it pained her to look at it. Perhaps it had affected her in some way after all. "But maybe he thinks we don't yet know about what happened on the bridge."

She had a point. In normal circumstances, the local CID would handle the investigation until it was clear that the death was suspicious. Given their heavy workload and the lack of a body, it was unlikely the bridge would have been closed down so quickly, if at all. Perhaps Tom had been counting on that.

"But if it is him, why choose Hammersmith Bridge?" he said. "Unless he *wants* us to find out about it?"

For a moment she said nothing, still staring at the screen, fingers steepled under her chin as if she was thinking it all through. Then she reached for the mouse, closed down the email and turned to face him. "I'm going to get Patrick's opinion on it. Maybe he can shed some light on all this. Now, tell me about Ealing, this morning," she said briskly, as if wanting to get off the subject of Kennedy. "I hear the witness had some useful information."

"Yes. He seems to have had a good look at the man and the e-fit should come out well."

"I also hear you've been stirring things up with a man called Harry Angel. He's made a complaint to the Borough Commander. He claims you were harassing him."

Surprised that Angel had taken things so far, so quickly, Tartaglia shrugged. "He didn't like my line of questioning."

"Is this to do with the Marion Spear case?"

He nodded.

"Why are you chasing after that, when we've so much on our plate already?"

"I've told you, I think she could be an early victim."

"But Marion Spear doesn't fit the victim profile."

It was as if Kennedy himself was talking. "I haven't seen Dr Kennedy's written report yet," he said, trying to contain his resentment.

"Don't be pedantic, Mark. You know what he thinks."

"Yes, and he's jumping to the wrong conclusion."

She tensed as if he had criticised her personally. "Tom goes for young girls. Marion Spear was thirty. She doesn't fit."

"Maybe it's just a coincidence that the three victims we know about were all in their teens. Maybe there are others we don't yet know about who weren't so young."

"There's no time to speculate about what he might have done. We've got to stick to what we know."

"If he only goes for young girls, why did he write you that email?" He was clutching at straws but somehow he had to convince her.

She coloured and her expression hardened as if somehow he had touched a nerve. "That's different. The email is just a windup, to prove how clever he is."

"Let's hope so."

"It doesn't change the profile."

He sighed with frustration. "OK. For argument's sake, let's take the three girls. I agree their age is a common factor. But there's another one, which the profile ignores: personality type. They were all loners, all apparently depressed. All three had a history of being bullied at school and it was so bad that Ellie Best was on anti-depressants. With that background, they were all vulnerable and open to the idea of suicide. We know Marion Spear was depressed and lonely too. Yes, she's older, but maybe her age is irrelevant or maybe he was less fussy before."

"We're overloaded as it is, not even counting what's just happened on the bridge. We haven't got the resources to chase up every long shot."

"How else are we going to find him? Unless any new leads come in from *Crimewatch*, we've got nowhere with the three girls. He's covered his tracks too well and we can't find the link. If Marion Spear is an early victim, maybe he made mistakes."

"But you've got nothing, have you? Nothing concrete."

"Not yet. But I want to keep trying. I have a hunch." The minute the words were out of his mouth, he knew he'd made a mistake.

She shook her head. "That's not enough. Look, Mark. If you insist on following this up, it will have to be in your own time."

He was about to reply that he would do just that when there was a knock and the door swung open to reveal Kennedy.

"Sorry I'm late," he said, grinning broadly. "With the bridge closed off, I had to go all around the houses via Putney to get here. Hope I'm not interrupting."

"Of course not, Patrick," Steele said, getting to her feet. "Mark and I had just finished."

After the talk with Steele, Tartaglia had retreated to his office to try and finish the day's paperwork. But he was soon forced to give up. It was useless. The heating was working overtime for a change and the room was like on oven. He couldn't concentrate, as he thought about their conversation. To make matters worse, Gary Jones had just got back from following up a fruitless set of calls that had come in from *Crimewatch*. Several new "witnesses" had come forward, claiming to have seen Gemma with Tom, not just at the church in Ealing but at various locations dotted all over the city. Some of them were cranks and time-wasters, some just wishful-thinkers, wanting to appear helpful. But none of the reports held water even at the most basic of levels. In addition, half of London, with a teenage daughter who used the internet, now seemed convinced that they might have come across Tom in a chat room somewhere. However loony some of the callers appeared, each call had to be properly investigated. But so far there were no genuine fresh leads. At least none of the calls had thrown up any evidence that Tom had been active outside the London area.

Sweating, feet up on the desk, shoes off, Jones was on the phone to what sounded like his brother, letting off steam at top volume about some rugby match or other. Built like a prop-forward gone to seed, with a thinning thatch of short fair hair, Jones dominated the cramped space with his sheer physical presence. Tartaglia felt hemmed in, almost claustrophobic, and he couldn't hear himself think over the rich, booming voice. He got up from his desk and started to change into waterproofs, thinking of going to see Clarke on his way home, although he had no idea yet about whether Clarke would be fit to see him. As he picked up his keys and helmet, Donovan appeared in the doorway.

"I've just got in. Fancy a drink? It's on me, this time."

Ten minutes later, they were sitting in a corner of The Bull's Head, each with a pint of Young's Special, trying to ignore the buzz of speculation around them about what had happened on the bridge the night before.

"Fucking Rasputin. I'll bet he's giving her more than just professional advice." Tartaglia gave Donovan a meaningful look and took a large swig of bitter.

"Ignore him."

"Easier said than done."

222

She watched him light a cigarette.

As the smoke coiled in her direction, she was amazed to find she had no desire to follow suit. On a moment's impulse, she had retrieved Adam Zaleski's card from the bin that morning, making an excuse to Tartaglia, as they left to go to the café, that she had left something behind in the meeting room. Zaleski had managed to fit her in for a quick half-hour session of hypnosis before she was due back in Barnes. Knowing Tartaglia's views on such things, she thought it best not to mention it. Zaleski was a witness and, strictly speaking, she shouldn't have sought him out. But she admitted to herself that she found him quite attractive. He had told her that she would only need another couple of sessions and she felt calm, almost serene, and in control. Perhaps that was what meditation was all about.

Drawing hard on his cigarette, Tartaglia leaned towards her. "Am I mad to think that the Marion Spear case could be related?"

She smiled, unused to seeing him so full of self-doubt. "Listen. From what I've heard today, it's well worth pursuing. That's what I wanted to talk to you about." She told him about her chat with Annie.

Tartaglia looked a little disappointed. "So, Angel wasn't interested in looking at flats but was after Marion. We can't hang him for that."

"But Annie practically admitted he'd been stalking her. And the fact that he went out of his way to hide his interest in Marion, is suspicious."

He shook his head. "Lying doesn't add up to murder. People lie to us all the time, even innocent ones. You know that."

"I still think it's worth following up. If he's innocent of anything other than fancying Marion, why doesn't he come clean? Knowing we're taking a second look is an ideal opportunity for him to set the record straight, particularly when he also knows that we're investigating the other murders."

She paused, studying him closely as she took a sip of her beer, noting the doubt and strain in his face. If only Clarke was still around, he would know what to do. The news from the hospital had been positive since he had come out of the coma, but it seemed that recovery was going to be slow. Nobody in the office, let alone Tartaglia, had dared yet voice the thought that Clarke might never be coming back. It was as if by not talking about it, and skirting around the subject, there was still a good chance that Clarke might, one day, stride in through the door, sweep Steele aside and take charge again with all of his old good humour and warmth. However, the likelihood was that Clarke would never be able to work again, certainly not take charge of a murder squad, with all the pressures and physical stresses the role entailed. In their hearts, they all knew it. But the moment wasn't right to talk to Tartaglia about it, although she sensed it wasn't far from his thoughts. Not for the first time, she felt how much he was in need of his mentor.

"This isn't like you, Mark," she said, touching his hand gently. "Don't listen to Steele and Kennedy. Just think what Trevor would say if he were here. He'd tell you to follow your instincts, wouldn't he? He always trusted your judgement and backed you up. You've got to remember that, keep hold of it, and trust yourself. I certainly do."

His face creased into a tired smile. "Thanks."

"Don't look so depressed. I may have something else. After I saw Annie, I went to see Marion Spear's flatmate, Karen."

"The one who made the statement when she died?"

"Yes. She gave me the same spiel about Marion being lonely and wanting to go back up north to be with her Mum. She said she tried many times to get her to go out with her and the gang but apparently Marion preferred to stay in and watch TV. To be honest, given what I know about Marion and having met Karen, it doesn't surprise me. I think I'd prefer to stay in and watch *Big Brother* too."

"What about Angel? Does Karen remember him?"

"No. Doesn't remember any particular bloke hanging around Marion. But Karen said that she was often out, staying over at her then boyfriend's flat. However, when I pressed her, she mentioned another girl, called Nicola, who had been living in the flat temporarily. Karen said that although Nicola wasn't there for long, she and Marion became quite chummy. Apparently they occasionally used to go out to the pub or to see a film together."

"There's no mention of this Nicola woman in the file."

225

"What's new? Nicola was only there for a month or so and she moved on before Marion died. Karen has no idea if she and Marion even stayed in touch after Nicola left. Maybe CID thought that Karen's statement was enough to determine Marion's state of mind or maybe they didn't bother to find out if there'd been anybody else living in the flat."

"We must find her."

"Don't worry, I'm onto it and I won't say anything to Steele. Karen isn't sure where Nicola's gone but she's given me the landlord's number. Maybe Nicola left a forwarding address. I'll check it out first thing in the morning."

Somebody passed behind her carrying drinks to one of the tables and Donovan caught the words "fucking marvellous" and "about bloody time" accompanied by a round of raucous cheers and applause. Listening for a moment, she gathered that the bridge had reopened.

"That's a relief," she said, turning back to Tartaglia. "I thought it was going to take me several hours to get home."

Tartaglia downed the remainder of his pint. "Going back to Angel, what about last Wednesday afternoon? Do any of his neighbours remember what he was up to?"

She shook her head. "I checked with several of the shops on either side of him and nobody noticed whether he was in or out. However, they told me that he tends to keep odd hours. Reading between the lines, they think he's a bit eccentric. I've left my card in case somebody remembers something."

He sighed, running his fingers through his hair. "Angel's a bloody long shot but we've got to keep checking. Maybe Nicola will remember him, if only you can find her. At the moment, she's our best bet."

"Our only bet, you mean."

CHAPTER
EIGHTEEN

"Well, he's playing with you, isn't he?" Kennedy said, helping himself to the mound of gnocchi alla gorgonzola which Steele had left almost untouched on her plate. "Cat and mouse. Showing you who's in control, who's boss. Thinks he's so bloody clever. He's deliberately belittling you, of course, treating you as a sex object. But then he sees all women as objects. Some just suit his purposes better than others." He scooped up another large forkful of gnocchi.

Steele watched him silently, amazed that he kept so svelte, given how much he seemed to eat. She had no appetite, the words in the email still swimming around in her mind. They had been to Hammersmith Bridge for a cursory look and she had waited patiently for nearly half an hour in the warmth of Kennedy's car while he paced up and down, talking into a dictaphone as he examined every detail of the bridge and the immediate surrounding area. When he was done, he had confirmed that it was far too early to make any pronouncements as to whether what had happened might possibly fit the pattern. On the one hand, the MO had changed. On the other, he agreed that the proximity to the murder team's office was striking, almost like a direct challenge. Hungry and irritated at being kept waiting for so long for so little result, she bit back the desire to tell him that Tartaglia had already arrived at the same conclusions.

Kennedy seemed to be taking it all blithely in his stride, back in the car talking nineteen to the dozen, in a state of professional elation about the email. She found it impossible to be so detached. She felt shaken, somehow dirtied by having received it and she wanted to punch fucking Tom, get him on the ground and take a pair of heavy boots to his head. How dare he. How fucking dare he. She knew she was an obvious target but it still got to her, eating away at her in every quiet moment. The thought that he knew, or had somehow guessed, that she lived on her own was particularly unnerving.

Kennedy stretched his arm across the table and patted her hand. "Carolyn, you're not upset, are you?" Wary of giving him any encouragement, she slid her hand away and reached for her glass, taking a sip of wine to hide her confusion.

"You mustn't let it get to you," he continued, thick-skinned as ever, ignoring the small rejection.

"I'm not," she said firmly.

"It's what he wants. He's trying to get under your skin. He has a very high opinion of himself and it's a game to him, nothing more. You've got to try and remember that."

She took another sip of wine. "Thanks. I'll bear it in mind."

Was there any point in keeping up the pretence? Part of her wanted to tell him how she really felt, get it off her chest. Maybe she'd feel better. But if she opened up, she knew he would use it to his advantage, draw closer to her, and it would be impossible to push him away again. She had to keep a distance between them. The easiest policy was to let him talk, not interrupt the flow, and try and let it wash over her, as if none of it mattered.

He gave her his usual warm smile. "You know, it might have been better if you'd got one of the blokes to do *Crimewatch*. On the other hand, maybe it's good to get a dialogue going."

"Dialogue? Is that what you call it? I hardly have the right of reply, do I? The bastard's untraceable."

"Of course. He's calling the shots and that's how he likes it," he said, eyeing her kindly, if a little questioningly, as he drained his glass. He grabbed the half-empty bottle, poured himself some more wine and topped up hers at the same time. "He conforms perfectly to type, you know. Organised, with a grandiose sense of self-worth, as well as being manipulative and devious. He's incapable of feeling empathy, guilt or remorse. Other people are only objects to serve his purpose. Although labels aren't really helpful to you, he's your classic charismatic psychopath."

"Charismatic? You're joking."

"It's a clinical sub-group. He has the ability to be engaging, charming, slick and verbally facile, as we've seen in his emails to the girls, as well as this one to you.

He also needs excitement, likes taking risks and living dangerously, which is why he emailed you. He's upped the temperature and thinks he's invincible."

She took a gulp of wine and smacked the glass down hard on the table. "He's bloody evil, that's what he is."

"Maybe, but the more risks he takes, the more chance we have of catching him." He put on a pair of half-moon reading glasses and unfolded the copy of the email, studying it again carefully. She had never seen him in glasses before and he looked different, suddenly older and more scholarly. She found it strangely endearing, as if it made him more approachable and human.

"It's interesting how he's changed his style," he said, still scanning the page. "He was much more flowery when he was writing to the girls. But with you, of course, he's pitching to a different audience. He's quite a chameleon, don't you think?"

"What the hell does it matter?"

Wishing that she could be as logical and dispassionate, she stared down at the table, trying to clear her mind and press down on the anger she felt. But it was impossible. She didn't usually drink much and her head was spinning, thoughts whirling uncontrollably, unable to obliterate the email from her mind. She felt out of control and feared that she might burst into tears at any minute.

Misinterpreting what she was thinking, he added: "You're not his type. So I shouldn't worry."

She looked up at him, not sure whether to laugh or cry. "Yes. He likes young flesh, doesn't he?"

"It's not just that. Of course, you're very attractive. But you're far too strong and together for him. He picks weak victims because underneath it all, in spite of his bravura, he's not up to a real challenge. He can manipulate these poor little girls and do what he wants with them, although he despises them all the more for it. In sending you that email, he's trying to make you one of them. But he can't. He knows you're not like that. It's interesting that his seeing you on the TV is the trigger for the email. He probably hates strong women even more than weak ones. Probably had a domineering, bullying mother at home, bossing him, controlling him, smothering him, forcing him to escape into the fantasy world in his head. It was the only place where he was in control, where he could be himself and play out his games without interference."

"Lots of people were fucked up as children. But they don't turn into murderers."

He smiled serenely, ignoring her. "I'll put my money on his being an only child, or the youngest child, with a big gap between him and the next sibling. I also expect he was a real weed and bullied at school. But I'll give you chapter and verse on all of that when I finish my report."

She folded her arms, leaning back in her chair until she felt the edge touch the wall behind her. "I don't give a stuff about what happened in his childhood. All that matters is that he's evil."

He shrugged. "Maybe. Whatever the reality, the simple fact is that he's angry. He's been made to feel inadequate all his life and, as I think I told you, I'm pretty sure he's impotent. That only adds to the anger and violence he feels inside. In killing, he's taking back the power. It's all about control. You may think his background is only of academic interest to people like me, but he's targeting you specifically because you're a woman. A man in charge of the case wouldn't have got the same reaction, I'm positive. Like it or not, you may have to deal with him in the near future, so you need to bear in mind his psychology."

She looked at him aghast. "Deal with him? What do you mean?"

He looked surprised. "He's going to contact you again, of course. Maybe he'll try and get you to respond." Perhaps sensing her revulsion, he added: "I wouldn't worry. I don't think he actually wants to see you face to face. It's just a little fantasy of his, all part of the game, kidding himself that he has the ability to form a relationship with you, if he so chooses."

"It's a fucking sick fantasy," she said, as the waiter took away the plates and left them with dessert menus.

Kennedy gave his a cursory look and slapped it down on the table. "Panna cotta for me. What about you?"

She shook her head. "Nothing, thanks. I'm just not hungry."

He took off his glasses and tucked them away in his breast pocket. A moment passed before he said: "You are going to tell your whole team what's happened, aren't you?"

"Only Mark and Gary. I don't think it's a good idea for the rest of them to know."

"What are you worried about? The email's an important piece of the puzzle."

"What if the press get to hear of it?"

"I still think it's a risk worth taking. Why don't you break the news at the morning meeting tomorrow and I'll come and give them a profile update?" Sensing her hesitation, he added: "You're ashamed of the way he's written to you, aren't you? You find all the personal stuff an affront."

"Damn right I do," she said bitterly, suddenly finding it a relief that Kennedy seemed to understand.

"But it's not about you, it's about him. Put yourself in his shoes. By treating you like all the others he's actually de-personalising you."

"Well, it doesn't come across that way."

"I understand why you feel that but . . ."

"Don't give me all that psychologist crap, Patrick. You have no idea what it feels like."

He nodded sympathetically, as though he was dealing with a fractious child, which made her feel even angrier. "Naturally, you're upset . . ." he said, looking concerned.

"Upset? Of course I'm bloody upset. But this is all just a job to you, isn't it?"

The room suddenly felt very hot. She stood up, wanting to dash to the ladies to get away from his gaze, splash some water on her face. But he caught hold of her hands and forced her back down in her chair.

"Please listen to me, Carolyn. Of course the case fascinates me. I'd be an out and out liar to say otherwise. But I only took it on because you asked me

234

to. I'm not you, I don't know exactly what you're feeling but I can imagine. Bloody furious, I expect. Absolutely livid. You also feel vulnerable, don't you? And that's not a comfortable feeling for someone like you, is it?"

Embarrassed by the warmth in his eyes, she tugged her hands away and folded her arms tightly across her chest again. "I don't need analysing, thanks."

"It doesn't help that you feel isolated within your own team. I can see what's happening with Tartaglia. He's an arrogant, headstrong sod and he hates the fact that you've been brought in over his head. I'll bet he's trying to undermine you at every possible opportunity, maybe even turn the whole team against you. It's all that latin machismo stuff coursing in his veins. Probably doesn't like taking orders from a woman. You need support at a time like this, not gang warfare." He paused, rubbing his lips thoughtfully with a finger before adding: "I don't know how it works, but maybe if you have a word with Cornish, you can get him taken off the case or even transferred elsewhere. There must be some disciplinary issue you could get him on."

She shook her head, not wishing to discuss the situation any further. It pained her to think about it. Like it or not, what Kennedy said about Tartaglia rang uncomfortably true and she felt threatened. But she knew she would get no sympathy from Cornish. Attitude and arrogance were not hanging offences and Tartaglia had a good stock of credit with the people who mattered up in Hendon. If she couldn't handle him, it would only reflect badly on her. With no solution to the case in sight, she was already on rocky ground.

She felt a headache coming on and closed her eyes, putting her hands to her face and massaging her temples and the bridge of her nose with her fingers, trying to fight back the tears. He was right about everything, of course. Too bloody right for comfort and she hated him seeing her that way. She must seem so pathetic and weak. The fact that he appeared to understand her, that he saw what was inside so clearly, made her feel ten times more vulnerable, drawing her towards him in spite of herself. There was nobody else she could talk to who understood and he seemed genuinely to care about her. But she wondered why he did, why he bothered. She felt all the old wariness surfacing again, suspicious of his motives for wanting to get close, questioning what it was that really interested him. Could she trust him?

"Going back to the email, you feel despoiled by it, don't you?" he said.

She nodded slowly, not able to meet his eye, focusing on the flickering flame of the candle in front of them.

"But that's exactly what Tom wants," he continued. "He wants to get to you, pollute your thoughts and dreams, play mind games with you. If you let him, he will be winning. Take a deep breath, clear your head and try and think straight."

He reached over and took her hand again in his. His grasp felt cool and strong, his fingers gently stroking her skin. It felt so reassuring and this time she didn't pull away immediately, although she still found it impossible to look him in the eye.

"I'm with you on this, Carolyn. Trust me. I'll look after you and together we'll nail the bastard, I promise."

Tartaglia said goodbye to Donovan and headed out to his motorbike, which was parked outside the pub by the embankment. A light wind was blowing and the night air was cold and damp, the sky almost cloudless with the moon rising just above the river. He put on his helmet and drove off down the High Street.

Nearing the intersection with Castelnau, he spotted what looked like Kennedy's Morgan, parked on a double yellow line on the wrong side of the road, in front of the parade of shops just before the crossroads. As he slowed to check, he saw Kennedy and Steele come out of one of the restaurants. They were walking close together, almost arm in arm, and appeared to be deep in conversation. He passed them and pulled up just around the corner, watching behind in his mirror. Kennedy escorted Steele over to the passenger side and unlocked the door, giving her his hand to help her into the low seat. Kennedy said something to her then, before closing the door, he tucked the trailing folds of her coat around her. The gesture struck Tartaglia as intimate and inappropriate. Fearing that his worst suspicions were being confirmed, he watched Kennedy walk around to the other side and climb in.

Even in the mirror, Tartaglia could see the smile on Kennedy's face. Like the cat with the proverbial cream,

237

he thought. If they were having an affair, he'd go straight to Cornish. Cornish was notoriously intolerant of such things and in the current tense climate, fearful of the press getting wind of anything negative, he'd have Kennedy, and possibly Steele too, off the case in a flash. Determined to find out for sure what was going on, Tartaglia decided to follow them.

Kennedy drove along Castelnau, over the bridge and headed for Kensington, then Hyde Park and north up the Edgware Road. Although Tartaglia had no idea where either of them lived, they were going in the general direction of Hendon, probably making for Steele's place. Keeping a safe distance behind, each time they stopped at a set of lights he could see Kennedy through the small back window, gesticulating and nodding, as if engaged in a lively conversation. Kennedy was driving conspicuously slowly, possibly worried about being stopped and breathalysed and Tartaglia was tempted to call in his licence number. But with Steele in the car, he had to leave it. After another ten minutes, they turned off Kilburn High Road, past West Hampstead tube and forked right down a series of wide, residential side streets, eventually pulling over and double-parking in front of a large, semi-detached house set back from the street behind a low wall and a hedge.

Tartaglia stopped behind a small van under some trees on the opposite side of the road and killed the engine, waiting. After a moment, Kennedy got out, walked round to Steele's side and opened the door for her, again offering her his hand to help her out. They exchanged a few words on the pavement and pecked each other briefly on the cheek. As Steele turned to go, Kennedy seemed to catch hold of her hand again but she pulled away and walked up the path. Kennedy stood by the gate, watching as she put her key in the door and she gave him a brief wave before turning and going inside. Shortly after, lights came on at garden level and someone Tartaglia assumed was Steele drew the curtains across the large bay window at the front. Kennedy waited for a moment, staring at the front of the house, then got back in the car and started the engine, turning on the headlamps.

That appeared to be it. Tartaglia didn't know whether to feel disappointed or relieved. It certainly didn't look like an affair to him. From what he had seen, Kennedy was interested but Steele seemed to be treating him merely as a friend. The thought of Kennedy's ego receiving a bruising gave him a brief flicker of satisfaction. He waited in the shadows, not wanting to start up the bike until Kennedy had gone. But five minutes later, Kennedy was still sitting there in his car, engine idling. Perhaps Steele was coming out again after all. Perhaps he had misread the situation and she was getting some things and they were going to Kennedy's place for the night. Suddenly Kennedy's headlamps went out again and the engine stopped running.

A few seconds later, Kennedy got out of the car and walked up to Steele's front door, lingering by the steps for a moment as if wondering whether or not to ring the bell. Then he walked around to the front window where he stood, his head just visible over the top of the hedge, shifting from one foot to the other, as though he was trying to peer though a crack in the curtains. His movements were furtive. After a moment, he walked back to the front gate, peered up and down the street, then went down into the garden, disappearing around the side, presumably towards the rear of the house.

Kennedy was peeping. Almost unable to believe what he was seeing, Tartaglia's first instinct was to follow him and catch him red-handed. It would be a very sweet moment. But even as he thought about doing it, he stopped himself, knowing just what Kennedy would say, how he would lie through his teeth. Tartaglia could just imagine his tone of outrage: "I was just making sure Carolyn's safe, that there's nobody lurking in her back garden." The email she had received was ample justification for concern and Steele would believe Kennedy. Also, how on earth could Tartaglia explain his own presence there? As he wondered what to do, his mobile rang. He bent down, cradling it into his chest to dampen the noise, and saw Fiona Blake's name flash on the screen. After a second's hesitation, he flipped it open.

"Mark. It's me. Can we talk?" Her voice sounded husky and thick.

"When did you have in mind?" he whispered, his eyes on Steele's front garden, watching for any sign of movement.

"Is there something wrong with the line? I can barely hear you. I know it's late but what about now? Can I come and see you?"

240

"I'm not at home. I'm in the middle of something."

"Oh." She sounded disappointed. "Tomorrow, then?"

"Maybe. I'll call you when I finish work. Got to go." Seeing Kennedy re-emerging down the path, he hit the red button before she could reply.

With a last, lingering look over his shoulder in the direction of Steele's front window, Kennedy climbed back into his car and drove off. Tartagalia waited a few more minutes to make sure that Kennedy was not going to return, and then he switched on his engine. It was definitely going to be worth keeping a closer eye on Kennedy.

Carolyn Steele kicked off her shoes, tossed her coat over the back of the sofa in the sitting room and went from room to room closing the curtains and blinds, checking that all the windows and both the front door and the French windows at the back were securely locked. It was all because of that stupid email. Irrational fears were one of the penalties of choosing to live on your own, she told herself, but she was prone to them. "Night fears" was what her dad used to call them when, as a child, she'd been unable to go to sleep or would wake up crying in the middle of the night. All to do with chemicals in the brain, she'd read in some magazine. But it didn't put a stop to them. Would the comfort of having somebody sleeping next to her drive them away? She doubted it.

She had lived in this flat for over ten years, spending time and money getting it exactly the way she wanted.

Although the ceilings were low, it had large windows front and back, almost to ground level, and was light and airy during the day. She had gone to a lot of trouble to make it comfortable and welcoming, buying a colourful rug to brighten up the dull beige carpet and putting a gas log fire in the old marble fireplace, hanging an antique mirror above. She had built cupboards on either side, with a few rows of shelving above for her books, CDs and the few things which held any sentimental value, like the photos of her nephew and niece and the Victorian sewing box, inlaid with small diamonds of ivory, which used to belong to her grandmother.

She felt more at ease here than anywhere else. Even so, dark corners could open up and take her by surprise and occasionally she was forced to sleep with the light on. Perhaps she should have allowed Patrick to come in for coffee, just tonight. But he'd been quite pushy about it in the car, which she had found annoying. He was so bloody presumptuous and sure of himself and she resented feeling as though she was being manoeuvred into a corner. Maybe it would have been good to carry on talking, but she was worried that things wouldn't stop there. Better to seem rude than to do anything impulsive that she might regret later.

Her head was starting to throb and she grabbed a couple of Hedex from the cabinet in the bathroom and went into the galley kitchen. Searching in a cupboard for a tin of cocoa, she caught sight of a bottle of single malt whisky that an admirer had given her the Christmas before last. Designed to impress, it had a

242

fancy label and looked expensive. She rarely drank spirits and it had stayed lurking at the back of the cupboard behind the baked beans ever since, untouched. Knowing that it was unlikely to make her feel any better, she cracked open the seal and poured herself a small measure, just for the hell of it. It tasted sharp and smoky in an unpleasant way but she was determined to drink it. Maybe if she got properly pissed she'd be able to forget about everything and sleep. She took the glass into the sitting room and sat for a moment in one of the large, deep chairs, flicking through the TV channels before switching off in disgust. As usual, there was nothing worth watching.

Gulping down the remainder of the whisky, she went into the bedroom and got undressed. She turned on the shower, stepped in and closed her eyes, letting the hot water wash over her. Patrick. Had she made a mistake in involving him in the case? Or was she silly to be so wary? Perhaps she should just stop worrying and let herself go. She had to admit that she still found him superficially attractive and the attention was flattering. It wasn't as if she was spoilt for choice. Beneath the bravado, he had a more serious side, almost steely at times, and he was rarely boring. But something kept holding her back, although she wasn't exactly sure what it was.

She knew little about his background, other than that he was a Catholic and had never been married. For a man the wrong side of forty, that was telling you something. Once he had said jokingly that he'd never married because he hadn't found the right woman. But she knew it was a load of rubbish. He was so self-absorbed, she couldn't imagine him caring deeply about anyone else, let alone ever really letting go and falling in love. Her good friend Lottie always seemed to pick men like that. She'd often watched the trajectory of Lottie's relationships, wondering why Lottie, who in other respects was a relatively sensible person, couldn't see what was in front of her nose. Some men were walking disasters and any woman who allowed herself to get involved with someone like that was just asking to get hurt. She was determined that it wouldn't happen to her. Although knowing it with one's head was one thing; physical attraction made even the sanest people do the silliest of things.

She thought back to that one drunken night they had spent together nearly a year before. The sex had been fine, at a basic functional level. But somehow she had been expecting more of a connection, more electricity. Something. The whole thing felt impersonal, disappointing and flat like a glass of champagne that had lost its fizz. It was as though she didn't matter; she could have been anybody. It was all about him and she realised she had made a mistake to let things go so far. Kennedy seemed blithely unaware of her reaction and had asked her to go away with him the following weekend. When she had refused, he had seemed very surprised, as if nobody ever turned him down, and had pestered her to have dinner with him again. But the more he persisted, the more her instincts told her to back off and she had avoided all contact with him on the work front until the phone calls finally stopped.

One thing that puzzled her was why, after everything that had happened, he still seemed drawn to her. Was it her independence, perhaps, and the fact that she hadn't succumbed easily to him? It was all about conquest, surely. She was unfinished business as far as he was concerned, a challenge. With all his psychological insight about others, had he any inkling of his own motivation? Had he any self-awareness at all? She doubted it. A relationship with such a man would be doomed. Every time she felt herself weaken, she must remember that and not allow sheer physical attraction and flattery to lead her astray. Even so, she felt as though she was struggling to keep her balance at the top of a slippery slope. A slope that probably had all sorts of unpleasant and potentially damaging things waiting at the bottom.

CHAPTER
NINETEEN

Café Montmartre was new and gleaming with fresh paint, fixtures and fittings. An attempt had been made to recreate the feel of the genuine French article. But with its lilac walls, dinky gilt mirrors and brass lights, it was a cheap parody, totally lacking in any kind of atmosphere. They had got all sorts of other details wrong too, Tom thought, spreading a large dollop of marmalade on his croissant. For starters, the French didn't eat marmalade, from what he could remember. Instead they made something unpleasantly sweet and gloopy out of oranges that had none of the tangy bitterness and bite of a decent English marmalade. At least this one came in its own small pot, safe from contamination by someone else's buttery knife or, worse still, toast crumbs. Grudgingly, he was forced to admit that it didn't taste too bad, although it couldn't hold a candle to his grandmother's. She cut her peel nice and thick and sometimes put brandy in it. Hers was the best he had ever tasted, made with Seville oranges when they came into season once a year just before Christmas. He remembered the pleasure of being allowed to lick the pan and spoon, if he had been good. Luckily, the old bat had made a new batch just before he'd throttled the life out of her and he had enough to last him a long while.

He took a bite of croissant. The butter was salted, of course, unlike real French butter, but although a bit chewy, the croissant was acceptable. Which was more than could be said for the coffee, which he'd had to send back twice. The waitress looked pretty pissed off, failing totally to understand what he was talking about and, when he'd insisted on hot milk, instead of cold, she seemed to think he was being difficult. From what he could tell, she was Russian or from some unsophisticated, Central European shithole. It wasn't surprising she hadn't a clue. But her attitude left a lot to be desired. She wouldn't be getting a tip from him and if she had the gall to try and add service to his bill, he'd strike it off.

Something about her, smilingly oblivious each time she spoke to the way she murdered the English language, made him think of Yolanda. She was another of these stupid cunts who came over here and made no proper effort to get to grips with the native tongue. They were just there for a good time; slags, all of them. All thanks to the EU and the stupid British taxpayer. But in a way, that played nicely into his hands. The papers had tried to spoil things for him and the old routine wouldn't work any longer. But it was time for a change anyway and it would be fun to try something new. There was little Yolanda, totally unaware of what was going on in the big world around her, just ripe for the picking. He was amazed that anybody had employed her to look after their kids. Didn't parents have more care these days? Or were they so engrossed in their own work and lives that they didn't give a stuff? His talents were wasted on her but he wasn't going to pass up the opportunity. She was asking for it, stupid little bitch.

He glanced at the headlines in the café's newspaper, skim-reading the first few pages, then laid it down beside him on the red leatherette bench. There was nothing in it about him today, which was a little disappointing. Perhaps it was a deliberate ploy to try and make him feel unimportant. He didn't like the moniker they had given him. "The Bridegroom". It sounded rather limp, unless perhaps they were thinking of Death as a bridegroom. It certainly didn't have the same oomph as "The Yorkshire Ripper" or "The Night Stalker". But maybe they'd come up with something more imaginative once they got to appreciate his talents a little better. So far, they didn't know the half of it.

The waitress slapped what looked like a cappuccino down in front of him. He took a sip through the nasty sprinkling of cocoa on the surface and pushed it away. It was an empty gesture, as the slag was already busy with another customer, taking down his order and giving him a cheap, flirty smile. Watching her, hating her, with her greasy, pudding-face and bleach-streaked hair, he felt on edge. Nasty, low-cut T-shirt and tight, short denim skirt which revealed an unappetising amount of shapeless leg — piano legs, as his grandmother would have called them. Nothing left to the imagination.

248

Seeing her stirred him up, rekindling the familiar desire. He closed his eyes and pictured taking her somewhere quiet, slamming her up against a wall, pressing hard against her, her hands forced behind her back, his hand tight like a clamp over her mouth and nose. He was so much stronger. He could see the panic in her eyes, kicking, thrashing, trying to bite him, her face turning pink and then purple as she struggled to breathe. Like a butterfly stuck with a pin, he would hold her there for as long as it took, waiting for her to finally weaken and go limp. That exquisite moment as the light was snuffed out. Then the look of surprise permanently frozen on her face as he slowly removed his hand. Just like that old witch, his grandmother. How he treasured that memory.

He'd been to confession that morning, the first time in weeks, and he'd seen her in one of the pews dressed in her black widows' weeds, like so many of the foul old women who infested the place as if they had nothing better to do with their day. She didn't look at him — as if she didn't care that he was there or what he might tell the priest. He ignored her in return, walking to the front to wait his turn by the confessional without giving her the satisfaction of looking back. When he came out later, she was gone. But back at the house, he found her sitting in her favourite red velvet armchair by the fireplace, arrogantly oblivious to the fact that the grate was empty and cold. Her image flickered, translucent like a candle flame and she turned her sour, yellow face slowly towards him, malice in her eyes as she mouthed something. Bastard. That was the word, he was sure.

He'd gone out of the room and slammed the door on her. She could just fuck off. Bastard. The little bastard. That was what she had always called him. How he hated her. He would squeeze the life out of her again and again, if only he could.

The longing was back much sooner than before, aching, gnawing at him, pulsing like a heartbeat. The hunger, the deep gut-twisting desire. It was getting stronger. There was only one way to deal with it. He would have to change the setting, alter the script a little, but it was good to improvise and he was sure it would be just as satisfying. As he sketched out in his mind a scenario for little Yolanda, the policewoman's face rose inexplicably in his mind.

CHAPTER
TWENTY

It was late afternoon when Tartaglia took the call from DI Mike Fullerton of Hammersmith CID.

"We know who the woman on the bridge was," said Fullerton. "Her name's Kelly Goodhart. She's an American lawyer living in London. She was in her early forties and lived alone in Kensington. Her boss reported her missing and when someone from her local station went over to her flat, they found a suicide note."

"Have you checked her emails?"

"That's why I'm calling you. She made an agreement to top herself with some bloke. But there's more and it doesn't smell right. You'd better come and take a look."

An hour later, Tartaglia sat opposite Fullerton in his small office, just off Hammersmith Broadway, pouring over copies of Kelly Goodhart's recent email correspondence. With a spreading gut and thinning sandy hair, Fullerton was due to retire at the end of the month and he seemed less than delighted to have such a case land in his lap.

His team had made a start by analysing the email traffic over the past three months, although there were several years' worth that might have to be gone through if Kelly's death turned out to be suspicious. Apart from the odd item of shopping on the net, or theatre ticket bookings, the majority of her emails were to family and friends in the US. But in the last month Kelly had exchanged over a dozen emails with someone calling himself Chris, culminating in an agreement to meet on Hammersmith Bridge to commit suicide together.

Tartaglia was struck by the difference in tone and style of Chris's emails to the ones Tom had exchanged with the three girls. Chris's emails to Kelly were short, almost businesslike. As they discussed the concept of suicide and arranged when and where to meet and how to go about killing themselves, they sounded like two people deciding on the best way of getting to the airport. There was no evidence of coercion on Chris's part and at face value, Chris sounded nothing like Tom. But maybe Tom was smart enough to change his modus operandi with someone like Kelly, who was clearly intent on killing herself without anyone's persuasion.

"Do you have any idea how they met?" Tartaglia asked.

Fullerton shook his head. "It's not clear from what we have so far. But I assume it's down to one of these effing suicide websites. It's a bit like lonely hearts, putting total strangers together to top themselves. There are hundreds of the bloody things all over the world. They should all be closed down, in my opinion. They're evil, encouraging the poor, desperate sods, telling them how to do it and the like."

Flicking through the emails, Tartaglia nodded agreement. Chris had pasted a DIY guide to suicide from one of the websites in an email, asking Kelly which method appealed to her. A rapid series of brief, matter-of-fact emails ensued.

Do you have any preference? At least sleeping pills are easy to get hold of.
I personally don't like the idea of hanging . . .

The barbecue tray in the car seems a pretty painless way to go. I suppose we would just drift off after a short while . . .

Perhaps we could put on some nice music, although we would have to decide what and I suspect we have different tastes. But if that idea appeals, I'm sure we could work it out . . .

Do you have a car? I sold mine a couple of months back . . .

Any ideas where we could go? I like the South Downs or maybe somewhere else by the sea. Or would you rather stay in London?

Honestly, I'm easy. Like you, I just want to get on with it.

It looked as though Hammersmith Bridge had been Kelly's idea, for "sentimental reasons", which she didn't seem prepared to elaborate.

Fullerton took a pipe and pouch of tobacco from his jacket breast pocket. "It's bloody weird, all this, don't you think?" he said, after adding a pinch of fresh tobacco to the bowl and lighting it. He blew several puffs of pungent smoke into the room.

The smell instantly reminded Tartaglia of his grandfather and namesake, who had smoked a pipe all his life, even on his deathbed. All the smoking paraphernalia that went with the habit, the racks, the collection of worn pipes and cleaners and the old-fashioned turned-wood jars where the pouches of tobacco were kept, was now cluttering up the mantelpiece of his father's small study in Edinburgh. Nobody had the heart to get rid of them.

"How's that?" Tartaglia asked.

"Well, I can understand someone getting so depressed that all they want to do is kill themselves. In my view, that's a person's right. But it beggars belief that they'd want company, particularly with someone they'd never met."

"Perhaps they're worried that they'll bottle out if they try on their own. Perhaps they want moral support."

"That's a bit weedy, don't you think? Imagine this," Fullerton poked the air with the chewed tip of his pipe, "I don't know if you've ever been on a blind date but it can be bloody awkward. You turn up at the place as arranged, then along comes the other person and they're not at all how they described themselves. You feel let down and maybe you take an instant dislike to

254

them too. What do you do then? Tell them it's all a big mistake and go home?"

"Worse still, what if the other person turns out not to be interested in killing themselves but just wants to watch you die?"

Fullerton, who was trying to relight his pipe, stopped, holding it in mid-air. "That's sick, that is," he said, shaking his head in disgust.

"I agree. But that's what we could be dealing with here," Tartaglia said, studying Kelly's most recent emails to Chris, written a couple of days before the incident on the bridge. He read out a few of the sentences.

Can I really trust you? How do I know that you are who you say you are, and that you're not lying to me? Forgive me for being blunt. I don't want to put you off if you're genuine.

I told you what happened before and you can understand why I'm wary. There are some very strange people out there. I just pray you're not one of them.

Is Chris your real name? Or are you Tony, trying to fool me again? Please call me and put my mind at rest. I really want to do this and I don't want to wait much longer.

"Chris, Tony, it's all a bit confusing, isn't it?" Fullerton said.

"Our guy uses many different names. It's too early to tell what's going on. I'm going to need to see some more of her emails."

255

Fullerton sighed, and made a chuffing sound as he sucked on the pipe and puffed out some plumes of smoke. "I was afraid you were going to say that. How much do you want?"

"Say, for the last year to start with. When do you think you can get it done?"

"We'll deal with it straight away, but we're short-staffed at the moment and I've only got a couple of people available. Can you spare us anyone?"

"We're very stretched too but I'll talk to DCI Steele and see if we can find someone to send over here. At least there's now a stronger case for our involvement," Tartaglia said, looking at his watch. He would have to call Steele right away. He was due at the hospital in half an hour to see Trevor and there was no time to go back to Barnes. After that, he had reluctantly arranged to meet Fiona Blake for a drink. "Any news from forensics?"

Fullerton shook his head. "I'll give them another call to chase them. They know it's top priority but then so is everything these days."

Tartaglia stood up and Fullerton followed suit, walking him to the door.

"What's Kelly Goodhart's background?"

"I spoke to her boss," Fullerton said. "He was the one who reported her missing. He sounded pretty upset, although he said he wasn't entirely surprised. According to him, Kelly had been depressed for quite a while and he thought she'd been receiving counselling. You see, she married another lawyer in her office. They went out to Sri Lanka for their honeymoon and got caught up in the Boxing Day tsunami. The husband was killed and his body was never found. Apparently, she couldn't get over it."

It had taken Donovan most of the day to locate Nicola Slade. She had moved several times in the previous two years and was now settled in a flat-share on the ground floor of a wide terraced house in Cricklewood. She had just come in after finishing for the day at the local primary school, where she worked as a supply teacher. Plump and nearly as short as Donovan, she had thin, shoulder-length mid-brown hair and glasses, and looked to be in her late twenties or early thirties. She was dressed in a baggy purple jumper and a flared grey corduroy skirt that just skimmed the top of her thick-soled boots.

She offered Donovan tea and ginger biscuits and they sat down together in the shabby sitting room that overlooked the concrete patch of front garden, Donovan choosing the sofa, Nicola a large floor cushion, where she sat cross-legged, skirt draped over her lap like a rug. Festooned with a forest of pot plants in macramé containers, the room was gloomy, the only light coming from a single bulb hanging in the centre of the ceiling hidden by a Japanese paper lantern.

Nicola's manner was brisk and efficient once Donovan had explained the situation. "Of course I remember Marion," she said, offering Donovan the plate of biscuits before helping herself to one and taking a large bite. "We were cooped up together in that tiny flat for weeks, neither of us knowing anyone in London. It's lucky we hit it off."

"But you didn't know she was dead?"

Nicola shook her head. "My fault as usual. I'm hopeless at keeping in touch. We saw each other a couple of times after I left Ealing but I'd moved down to Dulwich to be close to what I thought was a permanent job and it was quite a trek meeting up. You know what it's like, I'm sure. It's very easy to lose touch in this city, even with people you like. After that, we exchanged the odd phone call and Christmas cards, but that was about it. I feel guilty now, knowing she's dead." Nicola shivered and pulled her knees tightly into her chest, hugging them and taking a sip of tea. "Perhaps I should have made more of an effort to see her," she added, after a moment.

"If it makes you feel any better, I don't think it would have made any difference to what happened."

"You said at first everyone thought she had committed suicide."

"Yes. We're still not sure what happened."

"Well, she would never have killed herself. That much I know."

"Really? Both Karen and Marion's mother made statements saying that she was very depressed."

Nicola shook her head dismissively. "You would be, too, if you had to live with that dreadful Karen. As for Marion's mother, I don't think she knew if it was morning or night half the time. She was a real basket case, from what I could gather. I had to speak to her on the phone many times when Marion was out and I was very pleased she wasn't my mum."

"You're saying Marion wasn't depressed?"

"Look, everyone's lonely when they first come to London. Or at least most people are," she said, nibbling the last chunk of her biscuit. "What I'm saying is that it wouldn't matter how depressed Marion was, she wouldn't kill herself. Marion was into religion, big time. Went to the Catholic church around the corner at least twice a week. Along with sex before marriage, contraception and abortion, suicide's a mortal sin, according to them, isn't it?"

Donovan shrugged. She'd been brought up by atheist parents and had nothing more than a vague idea about Catholicism.

"Shame priests don't take the same view about paedophilia," Nicola continued, helping herself to another biscuit and dunking it deep in her tea. "They're such bloody hypocrites."

Donovan finished her mug and put it down on the floor, there being no other obvious place. "When did you last hear from Marion?"

"God. It's ages ago, I suppose. Well over two years. I've moved around a lot and changed my mobile a zillion times too. She probably had no idea where I'd gone. Even my mum has a job keeping up with me."

"Going back to Ealing, did you and Marion go out a lot together?"

"Occasionally we went to the pub round the corner for a drink or to see a film. But usually we stayed in and watched the telly or read a book. Neither of us had much money, you see. Karen was rarely in, thank God, and we had great fun cooking, although Marion did most of the work. We'd watch one of those chef programmes like *Ready Steady Cook* and try out some of the recipes. Unlike me, Marion was a right little domestic goddess when she put her mind to it."

"Do you remember Marion having any boyfriends?"

"Well, no one who turned up at the breakfast table, if that's what you mean. Although I doubt whether Marion would be on for that. But there was definitely the odd admirer. Marion was a pretty girl. Whenever we went out together, there was always some bloke coming over, trying to chat her up. I think some of her clients tried it on, but that's just an impression."

"Was there anybody in particular?" Donovan said, wondering if she meant Angel.

Nicola thought hard. "There was some bloke but it was all a bit strange. He made a real fuss over her, gave her some flowers and chocolates. She said he was really charming and different from the others."

"Different?" Donovan gave her a questioning look.

Nicola grinned. "Wasn't trying to get into her knickers on the first date."

"When was this?"

"Just before I moved out."

"This was a client?"

"Could be. But I'm not sure. Although how else was she likely to meet anyone?"

Donovan made a note. She didn't want to give Nicola the impression that they already had a suspect within their sights. For the sake of being thorough, it

260

would also be worth checking with Grafton's to see who else, apart from Angel, they had on their books at the time.

"She went out with this man?" Donovan asked.

"At least twice, if not more. Of course, she was flattered by all the attention but I remember her saying he was out of her league."

"What did she mean by that?"

"I don't know. For someone so pretty, Marion really lacked confidence. She wasn't at all full of herself, which is probably why she was so likeable."

"Did you meet him?"

"No. He didn't come to the flat. They always met somewhere else, somewhere public like a pub or a bar. I thought it was really odd and it made me wonder if he had something to hide, like he was married or in a relationship, or something. Marion insisted he wasn't but she could be unbelievably naïve, particularly where men were concerned. Although she wasn't the sort to tell lies, I did wonder at first if maybe he was a figment of her imagination. You know, like the pretend boyfriends some girls had in school. That was until I saw him, of course."

"You saw him?" Donovan said, matter-of-factly, not wanting to appear too excited.

"Once, by accident. I was on my way home and I spotted them standing together on the opposite side of the road. I think they were outside the cinema. They were facing each other and he was holding her hands, gazing into her eyes, saying something. It looked pretty romantic to me."

"Did he see you?"

"Oh, no. He was very intent on Marion and she didn't see me either. They were so engrossed, I thought it best to leave them to it. Then they got into a car and drove off somewhere."

"Can you describe him?"

"Good-looking. Quite flashy, I thought. Not at all Marion's type really. I sort of understood what she meant by out of her league, although she was lovely enough for any man."

"What about height, hair colour, you know?"

"I'd say tall, but don't forget I was on the other side of the road. Dark hair, sort of longish but well cut, I think. God, it's all coming back to me now. I can just picture him standing there looking at her. He was smiling. He had a really cheesy smile. You know, gleaming and perfect like in a toothpaste ad."

Although the description was quite general, it could easily fit Angel and Donovan felt very pleased with herself. It also tallied with the description given by the witnesses of the man seen at St Sebastian's. Hopefully, she had found the link between Marion and the other girls. If she was right, it would be one in the eye for Steele and Kennedy. Tartaglia would be over the moon.

"You're sure it's the same man Marion talked about?"

"Oh, yes. She came home about half an hour later and I made a point of asking her. She said it was him."

"Do you know if she carried on seeing him after you moved out of the flat?"

Nicola took off her glasses, breathed on them and started to polish them with the hem of her skirt. "She didn't seem to want to talk about him and I got the impression it had fizzled out for some reason, but she didn't say why."

"Did he have a name?"

She put her glasses back on and shook her head slowly. "David? Simon? Peter? I'm hopeless, aren't I? Memory like a sieve. I know she told me. It was something simple like that, nothing fancy like kids get called these days. Hopefully, it'll come back to me."

"Do you have any idea where they met?"

"No. Marion was a bit coy about that, I seem to remember, as if she was embarrassed for some reason. That's one of the reasons why I first wondered if he really existed."

"Do you know what sort of car it was?"

Nicola laughed. "You're asking the wrong person. I can't tell one make from another. Anyway, I was far too busy looking at him."

"Was it a saloon or a sports car?"

"No idea whatsoever, I'm afraid."

"Could it have been a van?"

"Definitely not a van. That much I can tell you."

Donovan wondered how long Angel had owned his camper van and if he also had had access to a car two years before. "But you could identify him?"

Nicola hesitated then nodded. "If I saw him again, I'm pretty sure I'd recognise him."

CHAPTER
TWENTY-ONE

Tartaglia returned from the bar with two glasses of wine and sat down at the small table opposite Fiona Blake. She was wearing a simple cream blouse and navy blue suit that set off her pale skin and hair, which she wore down, the way he liked it, full, just skimming her shoulders. She had got to the bar first. When he had kissed her lightly on the cheek before sitting down, he had smelt alcohol on her breath and assumed she had had a quick drink on her own before he arrived, although there was no glass in front of her. Perhaps she was feeling as nervous as he was. He still wasn't convinced that it was a good idea to meet, and he had thought about calling her and making an excuse. But in the end he couldn't help himself. He had to know why she wanted to see him.

They were in a basement wine bar close to where Blake worked. The long, narrow room was filling up quickly with people from the offices around and the buzz of conversation mingled with the background thud of music. The bar was Blake's regular haunt, where they had first met for a drink a couple of months before when it had all started. He wondered if she had suggested the place deliberately or had simply forgotten. Perhaps it wasn't important to her. By coincidence, they were even sitting at the same table. But he wasn't sentimental about such things, although it felt strange to be there with her again, after everything that had happened.

He lit a cigarette, watching as she picked up her full glass. She took a sip then put the glass down, folding her small hands neatly on the table in front of her, as though she had something important to say. He noticed instantly that she wasn't wearing her engagement ring. Maybe she and Murray had split up and that was what she wanted to tell him. But he checked himself, doubting that things could be so simple.

She took a deep breath. "Look, Mark. I'm really very sorry about what happened."

"What do you mean?"

"In my office and at the mortuary the other day. I just felt so awkward seeing you again and I handled myself badly. It was childish and I shouldn't have behaved like that. That's why I came round the other night. I wanted to apologise."

"I felt awkward too," he said. Still do, he wanted to say, although he had no wish to show her how much she affected him.

She gave him a nervous smile, flicking a long strand of copper hair away from her face. "I'm sorry about everything really. I wanted to explain but you wouldn't see me. I know you think I haven't been straight with you . . ."

She looked at him intently, as if waiting for him to say something. The colour had come to her cheeks and her eyes were a fierce blue. He took a mouthful of wine, a pinot grigio and the best on offer. But it was thin and sharp and he put the glass down, taking another draw on his cigarette instead. What was he supposed to say? That she'd lied to him, deliberately led him up the garden path and humiliated him? He'd said it all before on the phone and there was no point in having another row face to face. Surely that wasn't why she'd asked him to come.

She sighed heavily. "This is very difficult for me, Mark. I thought you knew how things stood."

"How things stood?"

She shrugged. "With Murray, I mean."

He could feel the blood rise. "How was I supposed to know? I'm not telepathic. I only found out by mistake, from someone else."

She waved her hand vaguely in the air as if it was all something trivial. "It's a complicated situation; you know how these things are. You and I barely knew one another and I didn't know how to explain."

"It's pretty simple, Fiona. You just tell me you have a partner. End of story."

She nodded slowly. "Of course, I should have done. I see that now. Again, I'm sorry. Do you forgive me?" She was looking at him questioningly. However sweet her expression, he still couldn't help feeling bitter and he looked away, taking another deep pull on his cigarette. If she had told him about Murray, he would never have allowed things to go so far. And she knew it too, which was why she had said nothing. She still wasn't being honest either, with herself or with him.

266

"Can't we be friends again?" she said quietly.

Friends. She made it sound so simple but it felt like a slap in the face. "Sure. I've no problem with that," he said, biting his lip. The word was hollow, yet another lie. They had never been friends. Their brief relationship, such as it was, had been entirely sexual; the word "friend" had never once entered his thoughts in those few heady weeks. Did "friends" now mean that they were to act as if nothing had ever happened, that it could all be switched off at a touch, like a light? He certainly had never had that sort of control over his emotions, once they were engaged. Perhaps what had happened between them meant little or nothing to her after all. If so, why come round to his flat, why the late night call, why bother to see him now? It didn't make sense. But he'd never been very good at understanding women.

She smiled. "Good. I'm glad you're OK about it. Now we've cleared the air, tell me about the case. Is it going well?"

He took a drag of smoke and shook his head, suddenly relieved that she had moved things onto a less emotional level. "It's not going well at all," he said, and proceeded to tell her about Kelly Goodhart. Blake seemed genuinely interested, listening quietly, asking a few pertinent questions. He gave her the basic run through, finding it good for a change to be able to talk to someone who was only involved on the periphery of the case. "Even if someone else does the autopsy," he added, "I'd like you to examine her, once we find the body. You know exactly what we're looking for."

"Delighted to help in any way I can. You really think she's another in the series?"

"It's too early to tell. But the stuff in the emails rang alarm bells."

"How are you getting on with Carolyn Steele?"

"OK," he said, noncommittally. "Why?"

"Just wondered. I've come across her a few times before. She's quite attractive, don't you think?"

"Not my type," he said, surprised. Women never understood what attracted men to other women, and vice versa. He was still baffled by what Fiona saw in the weak-mouthed, cotton-haired man in the photographs in her office.

"Any news on DCI Clarke?"

"He's making good progress, thank God."

"When will he be able to come back to work?"

He shrugged. "No idea, at the moment. He was very badly injured and it could be several months." That was the official line anyway, although he knew deep down that there was little likelihood of Trevor coming back. Of course, it was still too early to be sure but when he'd spoken to Sally-Anne that morning, she had let slip something about moving to the seaside, once Trevor was out of hospital. It had sounded permanent, not like a holiday for recuperation.

"So, you may find yourself working for Carolyn Steele for a while?"

"I suppose so." He stubbed out his cigarette, suddenly wondering if Cornish would ask Steele to take over permanently. There would be several other candidates for the job and Steele might not want it.

However, the thought of Steele as his boss for the long term was a daunting prospect.

"The papers said you've got some sort of psychological profiler involved."

He looked at her warily, wondering if perhaps office gossip had filtered as far as the pathology lab. "Yes, Dr Patrick Kennedy."

"He's quite well known, isn't he?"

"He's good at self-publicity, if that's what you mean."

"I find the whole idea of psychological profiling very unscientific."

"That depends," he said, moving to light another cigarette. "The FBI do a fantastic job but they have a lot more experience of serial killers than we do. Our approach is pretty ad hoc by comparison and, as you say, unscientific. We do have a few decent profilers in this country but they're like gold dust."

She looked amused, smoothing back her hair from her face and tucking it behind her ears. "Dr Kennedy's not one of them, I take it, judging by your expression."

Tartaglia smiled. "It's not my call, but he doesn't seem to be adding much value so far."

There was another awkward silence and he wondered if he ought to make some sort of excuse and go. But she hadn't finished her glass of wine and he didn't want to appear rude. Again, he had the impression that she was waiting for him to say something. He just didn't know what it was. The whole situation seemed forced. He was suddenly reminded again of how they had never really talked before about anything other than work, never really engaged in normal, everyday conversation and he felt at a loss for words, not having a clue what to say to ease things along. He had no idea what she was interested in, didn't know much about her at all, and there was only one question he wanted to ask: was she still with that fucking barrister? But he couldn't bring himself to say it.

"Have you seen any good films lately?" she asked, after a moment.

He almost laughed, wondering if she was going through the same thought processes as he, struggling to find an area of commonality. "Haven't had time. You know what it's like."

She nodded sympathetically. He noticed a smear of lipstick on the edge of her lovely mouth and was tempted to reach across and wipe it away. But he held back, worried that she might misinterpret the gesture and not sure if he could trust himself to stop there.

"Do you know, Mark, it's really good to see you."

"I'm glad," he said, hiding his surprise at the warmth of her tone by forcing down a gulp of the awful wine. At least she had had the sense to ask for a glass of red.

"Perhaps we can go to a film or something next week. There are several things on I'd like to see."

"A film? Maybe." Without knowing why, he was sure they wouldn't have the same taste in films. "What about Murray? Won't he mind?" He tried to keep the bitterness out of his voice.

She waved her hand dismissively. "Oh, he's away on a case all next week."

Well, that answered the only question he had wanted to ask. She and Murray were still together. "Next week's no good for me," he said, thinking that he really should make his excuses now and go. "We're working all hours at the moment. I shouldn't really even be here now."

She smiled. "Then I appreciate your coming all the more." Without warning, she leaned forward and started to stroke his cheek, running her fingers through his hair. "I've missed you, you know. Can't stop thinking about you."

Confused, he pulled away. He hadn't seen this coming at all. "What are you doing?"

She looked surprised. "What's wrong? I want to kiss you."

"Look, Fiona. I don't think it's a very good idea."

She was still smiling. "Are you worried this is a public place? It didn't stop you before."

"We were talking about friendship only a moment ago."

"Friendship, of course. But I bloody fancy you. That's all. I had this dream about you . . ."

"You're engaged to another bloke, I seem to remember," he said, trying to stifle the urgent desire to grab hold of her.

She took a sip of her wine and glanced away, squeezing her lips together as if she had tasted something sour. He lit another cigarette, hoping that maybe she would say something to contradict him. But she refused to meet his eye.

"You are still engaged to him, aren't you?" he said, when she didn't reply. Still no response. "I'll take that as a 'yes'. So, we're back where we were before which, as far as I'm concerned, is nowhere that interests me. Why can't you just be honest?"

She banged her glass down on the table and stared at him angrily. "You're so bloody puritanical, you know. Life's not black and white, at least mine isn't. Why can't we see each other again? What's wrong with it, if we both want to? And I know you do."

"The way it was before?"

She frowned. "Maybe not exactly like before."

"But close enough, you mean? That doesn't work for me, as you well know. And what about Murray? You're supposed to be marrying the guy, for Christ's sake."

She sighed heavily, looking down at her hands. "If you must know, Murray and I aren't getting on."

"Now, that's a surprise." He reached over and touched her lightly under the chin, forcing her to look up at him. "But you're still engaged to him. Yes? Why don't you just come out and say it?"

She glared at him. "All right, then. For what it's worth, which is not a great fucking deal to me, I'm still officially engaged to Murray."

Seeing tears not far away, he stubbed out his cigarette and reached over and took her hand. "I'm sorry you're not happy, truly I am. But I've made my position clear." He kissed her fingers gently and stood up to go. "You've got to sort out your life, Fiona, and you've got to decide what you want. As that boring old saying goes, you can't have your cake and eat it."

272

CHAPTER
TWENTY-TWO

Tom was late. Deliberately so. Entrances were so important and he'd wanted to keep Yolanda waiting, make her feel insecure. He pushed open the door of the Dog and Bone and went inside. He'd first come there many years ago when it was called something else, when it had been down-at-heel and inhabited mainly by a contingent of smelly old men who had the knack of making a pint last most of the evening. Now it was part of the new wave of pubs sweeping across London, not an ounce of brass or etched glass to be seen anymore, the dark purple walls studded with dreadful modern oils, all for sale, sofas and chairs dotted about everywhere, instead of old-fashioned fixed banquettes, and big, thick candles guttering on every available surface. It looked like a brothel. Already packed, the noise was deafening, music throbbing through ceiling speakers, the air thick with smoke. He had chosen it carefully. Located in a seedy part of town on the Regent's Canal, it had no regular local clientele, the majority of drinkers being tourists from some of the nearby cheap hotels, or transients passing through London for a few months. He was sure he and Yolanda would go unnoticed.

He weaved his way through the dimly-lit interior, checking the faces until he eventually spotted what he assumed was Yolanda, the only girl on her own, occupying the centre of a large, brown leather sofa at the back. Her posture was upright, hands at her sides, legs carefully crossed in front of her as if she'd come for an interview. As he approached, her eyes flitted towards him and she smiled hesitantly. He saw she was smoking; something he couldn't bear. Thank God, if things went to plan, he wouldn't have to kiss her. He forced a broad smile to his face.

"Yolanda?"

She nodded, fumbling with her cigarette and putting it down in the filthy ashtray on the table in front of her. He noticed that her nails were bitten to the quick; something else that revolted him.

"Hi. I'm Matt," he said. She gave him another shy smile in return, moving aside to make space for him next to her.

She had loved the two Jason Bourne films and he thought "Matt" would do well enough for her, although he knew he looked nothing like Matt Damon. However, he could tell from her expression, she was pleased. And so she damn well should be. In the normal course of events she hadn't a hope in hell of having a drink, let alone anything else, with someone like him. Small, sallow-skinned and totally flat-chested, she was as plain as a sheet of cardboard, although her dark hair was nice and shiny — clean, he was pleased to note — and she had large, round brown eyes that looked as though they'd trust the devil. She was dressed demurely in a long-sleeved blue T-shirt that had gone through the wash a few too many times, and a knee-length cotton skirt, with thick black tights and boots beneath. There was nothing improperly tight or revealing, unlike the rest of the tarts in the room who were flaunting their flesh like pros. Yolanda was a mouse by comparison, with next to no make-up and an outbreak of spots on her chin, which she hadn't bothered to disguise. She looked a lot younger than twenty-one and he wondered if she had lied about her age, not that it mattered.

"Would you like another drink?" he said, noticing the half-empty glass of what looked like Coca-Cola. "Maybe something stronger?"

"Please. Thank you." She spoke so quietly, he could barely hear her.

"A glass of wine?"

She nodded, picked up the smouldering stub of her cigarette and started to pull on it again, as if every centimetre counted. Disgusted, he got up and shouldered his way to the bar where he ordered two large glasses of the cheapest plonk. No point wasting good money on her and he wasn't intending to drink much himself. While the barman uncorked a fresh bottle, Tom glanced over his shoulder through the crowd and saw her staring fixedly at him, mouth slightly open. Catching his eye, she ducked away out of sight. Wasn't she just the little blushing bride, although he wasn't bothering with all that crap tonight. She would do very well, he thought, making his way slowly back towards her with the wine, careful not to spill a drop.

Conversation was laboured and almost entirely one-way. He asked her about her work as an au pair, about her family back in Spain, her studies and all sorts of other trivial and tiresome questions. He was having to shout above the noise of the room, repeating himself several times before the stupid girl understood. Clutching her glass tightly as if she was afraid someone was going to take it from her, she nodded like one of those dogs some people have in the back of their car. From what he remembered, her English wasn't bad but she seemed stunned into near silence, her replies monosyllabic. The whole process was exhausting and he wondered how much more he was going to have to endure. At least the wine seemed to be working its magic. For such a whippet of a thing, she was knocking it back in a hearty manner, getting quite giggly and almost flirtatious, like a silly little schoolgirl, her round, cow eyes on him all the time, as if she couldn't believe her luck. If she carried on like this, the whole thing would be a piece of cake. The only difficulty was how to get her from A to B.

"Shall we go somewhere a bit quieter?" he shouted, after a while. "I have a car and I know a really nice little place nearby where we can talk."

"No car, thank you. I like here," she said, frowning, after he had repeated himself three times.

She seemed to particularly disapprove of the mention of a car. He almost laughed. What did she think he was going to do with her in it? He'd rather jump out of a plane without a parachute than screw the pathetic little bitch. The very thought was absurd.

He stretched out his hand. "Come on, Yolanda. It's too noisy."

She shook her head looking mulish. "No. Is OK here."

Perhaps he was pushing too hard. Maybe she needed another injection of alcohol to loosen her up. He might even have to give it a few drops of GHB if she carried on being so fucking tricky. Although that might cock up the timing of what he had planned.

"Another drink? Yes?" he said, forcing a smile.

She nodded slowly, looking quite sulky, which angered him. She should be bloody grateful that he was paying her any attention at all, stupid fucking little bitch. He tipped the remainder of his wine into her glass and got up to buy another round.

Yolanda watched him as he threaded his way through the packed room towards the bar. The noise was so loud, she wanted to clamp her hands over her ears. She felt tired suddenly and very alone. London was a cruel place. Everything pressed in on her and she felt almost suffocated. London sucks the life out of you, her friend Dolores had said, before going back to Spain for good. Nobody cares. Nobody wants to know, everyone so tense, in a hurry, no time for anyone else. They don't even look at you as you pass them in the street, let alone say "hello", as people do where she came from. A wave of homesickness flooded over her and she felt tears prick her eyes. What was she doing here with this man?

When they had spoken on the phone and exchanged all of those emails, she had felt he really understood her, that he felt the same way too. She had gone to the library each day to see if he'd sent her a message, feeling ecstatic when there was one, desperate when there was nothing. She hadn't expected him to be so good-looking or polished. She had pictured someone younger, sensitive, unsure, full of doubt and loneliness, trying to make sense of a difficult life. But this man wasn't like that. He was confident. Assured. In control. It showed in the way he held himself, in his every move and gesture. He couldn't disguise it. Everything about him made her want to retreat back inside herself away from him. Men had always made her feel that way, awkward, unattractive, cheapened by the occasional attention and, whatever they said, unworthy. They told such lies. All they wanted was one thing. That's what her mother had always said, and this one was no different. He'd mentioned his car — she knew what that meant. All the stuff about understanding her had been a sham and, when he wasn't smiling — which he did a lot — the look in his eye frightened her.

She couldn't see him from where she was sitting. Hopefully, he couldn't see her either and it would take him a while to get their drinks. But he would be back. Then, what would she do? How in heaven would she get away? He wouldn't simply let her go. He'd follow her outside and she wouldn't be safe from him there. Wondering if she could attach herself to somebody, she looked around at the tables nearby but everyone was deep in conversation. Nobody looked as if they'd be going home for hours. And what would she say, anyway? Can I come with you? Can you see me home safely? They would probably think she was weird. The room was hot. She wasn't used to drinking — had done it to please him and to give herself courage — and her head was beginning to spin. He'd be back soon with their drinks and a rush of panic swept over her. She had to go now. Before he came back. Spotting an exit at the back of the room, she picked up her bag, slipped her jacket off the nearby rack and dashed outside.

The air was freezing but it was good to breathe after the sweaty smoky atmosphere of the pub. She ducked down as she passed in front of the windows until she was clear, then rushed as fast as she could, slipping, sliding, almost falling, down the short flight of damp steps to the canal. She remembered the way she had come earlier. It was the quickest way back to the tube and anyway there was no time to stop and look at her A-Z. If he found out she'd gone, she was sure he'd come after her. She had to press on. Put some distance between them. Hopefully, he wouldn't know which way she'd gone.

The path was so dark, the few lights widely spaced, casting strange intermittent pools of orange light on the ground. Eyes streaming from the cold, lips dry with fear, she ran on, the sound of her feet echoing on the concrete. The rank smell from the water was overpowering, making her feel sick, but she couldn't stop now. The path curved round to the left, following the course of the canal, tall buildings hugging it close on either side, only a few lights on in the windows, nobody around. As she rounded the bend, a dark shape was silhouetted against the light on the path in front of her. It looked like a man but she couldn't be sure. Was it him? Sweet Mary, mother of Jesus, had he found her? Heart pounding, gasping, she stopped, the scream rising from deep inside. She clamped her hands over her mouth before it could come out. It couldn't be him. She was being silly. Even if he had worked out which way she'd gone, he couldn't be out there in front of her. There hadn't been time. Perhaps this person would help. Take her to the tube and make sure she was safe.

"Please. I need help," she called out. Her eyes adjusting to the half-light, she could see now that it was a man, the outline tall and broad-shouldered, the ragged edge of short hair catching the light. But he didn't move, planted in the middle of the path, legs slightly apart, arms at his side, his face in shadow. He stood so still, he might be a statue. Like the bronze ones of people walking, near the canal by Paddington Station. They had taken her by surprise when she'd first seen them, they were so lifelike. But she didn't remember any statue along this stretch, certainly nothing in the middle of the path. Would he help her? Should she tell him what had happened? As she went hesitantly towards him she heard the sound of running feet accelerating just behind her and she was thrown to the ground.

CHAPTER
TWENTY-THREE

There was a crush of half-drunk Australians at the bar and it took a long while to be served. When Tom got back, he couldn't see Yolanda anywhere.

She must have gone to the loo. Not surprising, after all the drink she had put away. Her bag had gone, but women always took their bags with them when they went to have a pee. It was one of life's many mysteries why the bag had to go with them everywhere, like a security blanket. His grandmother was rarely to be parted from hers and she had been intensely proud of the fact that it was real crocodile skin, although it was so battered, the poor croc must have been slaughtered a good century before. It had a faceted crystal clasp the colour of a tiger's eye and it was rigid and upright in a strangely prim way. When he was naughty as a child, it had often been the first thing that came to hand; she had hit him over the head with it more times than he cared to remember, often drawing blood. The brass edges were like a wide, cruel mouth and he used to have nightmares about it opening its lips and gobbling him up into the red leather interior. He remembered discovering it sitting on the floor like an unwanted guest beside his grandmother when he was trying to work out what to do with her body.

He had been waiting for what seemed like a very long while indeed for Yolanda to return when a thickset man with a shaved head, shiny with sweat, plonked himself down beside him on the sofa.

"Excuse me, someone's sitting there," Tom said.

"Someone's sitting here?" The man mimicked his tone, going through the pretence of examining the seat cushion. "You need glasses, mate. There's nobody here." He threw his head back, opening his mouth wide and roared at his own wit. He was drunk, or certainly on his way there. Tom had learnt how to handle himself with bullies like this and it wouldn't take much to silence the cunt. But he couldn't risk a scene, couldn't risk anyone remembering him there.

"My friend's sitting here," Tom said firmly. "She's just gone to the ladies."

The man laughed again, almost spilling his pint as he eased his bulk down into the seat cushion, trying to get comfortable. "You mean the young bird with the black hair? She skipped out the door over there before you came back." He jerked his head in the direction of the exit on the far side of the room. "She's done a runner on you, mate," he said, looping a muscular arm around a half-naked teenage slapper with a stud in her eyebrow and top lip, who appeared on his lap from nowhere. "Must have rumbled your little game."

Staring hard at the man for a second, Tom realised that there was no reason for him to lie. Yolanda had escaped. Furious, trying to keep tight control of his

282

facial muscles, he got to his feet. Such a thing had never happened to him. No one had ever dared stand him up before.

"Thanks for telling me," he said forcing a smile. "She said she was feeling sick. I'd better make my way home."

The man ignored him and started to bury his face in the slapper's tits, making her shriek with delight. Judging from his demeanour, the man was well pissed already. The night was still young and by the next morning, his memory of what had happened in the pub would be blurred or even totally forgotten.

Tom picked up his coat and disappeared quickly out the door into the cold night air. He had to find Yolanda. He had underestimated the little bitch, he realised. In spite of all her pathetic moaning and whingeing and her apparent air of vulnerability, there was a core of toughness. She wasn't sweet and pliant like the others. They would have done anything for him, but not this one. Her talk of suicide was just a sham to get his attention. She was a cunning, fucking whore and she had deceived him. The thought made him feel violent. He wanted to strangle the life out of her scrawny body, stamp her out then and there, put an end to her, whatever the risk. He couldn't afford to let her live. She mustn't get home.

The pub was perched on the side of a bridge overlooking part of the Grand Union Canal. The quickest way to the nearest tube was along the towpath and he had secretly observed Yolanda coming along that way earlier. It wasn't at all a nice place to walk alone at night, particularly if you were young and female. But half-drunk and new to London, he was sure she would have taken the same route back.

He walked down the steps on the far side of the bridge leading to the canal. The air was cold and damp and a light mist was rising from the water blurring the edge of the towpath. Hemmed in by buildings on either side, the canal curved away like a slick of black oil, reflecting the shimmering light of the moon, which was emerging from behind the office blocks on the horizon. As far as he could see, there was nobody around, the only noise coming from the traffic on the flyover close by.

He was walking fast, almost running. The path was amazingly poorly lit, the lamps casting pools of sickly light, which only seemed to accentuate the deep shadows around. The fishy, stagnant stench from the canal was almost unbearable and he held his coat sleeve to his nose as he went along. Still sure she had come this way — after all, the stupid girl had no imagination — he kept going until he heard a strange, whimpering sound up ahead. It sounded like a dog chained up alone. Wary of what might be in front of him, he slowed his pace, keeping close to the shadow of the high wall that ran alongside the canal. Peering into the gloom beyond, he made out the shape of someone sitting on the ground a little further along. He braced himself for something unpleasant. But as he cautiously drew nearer, he recognised her.

Yolanda. He felt a surge of excitement. Cowering against the wall, her face turning towards him, she stared at him like a small, frightened animal. He walked up to where she sat and looked down at her. She was trembling but he saw the relief on her face as she recognised him. She sat motionless on the bare ground, huddled in her jacket, hugging her knees and clutching her skirt tightly around her. As he looked closer, he noticed that her skirt was practically hanging off her, slit into long tails of fabric. Her tights were also ripped, exposing the pale flesh of her knees and a large part of her thighs. Looking quickly up and down the path to make sure that nobody was around, he knelt down beside her. Something was wrong with her face. As he reached over to touch a dark smear on her cheek, she flinched and cried out. Peering at her in the dim light, he could see what looked like blood running down her forehead and out of her mouth and nose.

"What happened?" he said, softly, although seeing no sign of her bag anywhere, he thought he could guess. Serve her bloody right for running off like that. Teach her a fucking lesson, it would.

For a moment she didn't reply and he repeated the question.

"Man, two man. He . . ." She looked away and started to cry again. "They have . . ." she gasped, struggling for the word, ". . . knife." She gestured as if holding it to her throat.

He wasn't sure from what she was saying what had happened, not that it mattered. But at least he had found her, although the sight of her revolted him. He had to quiet her down so as not to attract any unwanted attention. He had to get her out of there somehow before anyone came along and called the police.

Gritting his teeth, he reached forward and stroked her hand. It felt cold and disgustingly wet to the touch. "Please don't cry, Yolanda. I'm here now and you're going to be OK."

Whether or not she understood him, his tone seemed to calm her and she stopped crying and started to dab her eyes with the sleeve of her jacket. At least he'd found the stupid little bitch. It wasn't the way he'd planned things and he felt furious with her for trying to spoil everything. But at least he had her now. However disgusting she was, there was no way she would get away from him again.

"You were very silly to go off like that," he said softly. "What did you think you were doing?"

She shook her head and immediately vomited on the ground. He looked away until she had finished, wondering how he was going to get her to come with him. If push came to shove, he'd have to pick her up by force, but he didn't relish the thought of touching her again, let alone holding her.

"You have water? Please," she mumbled, after a moment.

What did she think he was, a fucking packhorse? He shook his head. "No water." Then he had an idea. "But I have brandy. You know, cognac." He remembered that the Spanish word was similar to the French. He pulled out the large silver hipflask that had belonged to his grandfather and waved it in front of her, giving her his most warm and gorgeous smile. "You want? Make you feel better."

The smile, or possibly the prospect of more alcohol, seemed to do the trick and she nodded slowly.

"One minute. I can't see. I need some light." Turning his back to her, he got up and walked over to the edge of the canal. Checking to make sure that they were still alone, he unscrewed the cap of the flask, took a little plastic container from his inside coat pocket and poured it into the flask. It was a shame to ruin decent brandy but there was no other way. Luckily, GHB was tasteless. He came back and knelt down beside her again, sliding off the oval cup from the bottom of the flask and pouring out a large measure of brandy. He put the cup to her lips and slowly tipped it towards her. The first sip made her splutter and cough and she cried out. No doubt it burnt like hell. But she seemed to like it and took the cup in her fingers, draining it in a few minutes.

"Want some more?"

She shook her head, still holding onto the cup as if her life depended on it. He prised it out of her fingers and shook any remaining drops on the ground. The cup would have her fingerprints on it and he would have to clean it very carefully when he got home. Drying it temporarily on his handkerchief, he clipped it back onto the bottom of the flask and tucked the flask away in his pocket. He must get a move on. He had done a number of experiments with GHB on himself and, when laced with something strong like brandy, the effect could be very quick, particularly on someone as small and thin as Yolanda.

He bent over her. "We must go."

"You call police, yes?" She had huddled back against the wall and looked as if she was prepared to stay there all night if necessary.

"Yes, but not now. Can't stay here. It's dangerous. Dangerous." He repeated the word, hoping to instil some urgency into her.

"You think they come back?"

Noticing with pleasure the alarm in her eyes, he nodded. He watched as she struggled slowly to her feet, hugging her sides and leaning back heavily against the wall for support. She closed her eyes and groaned. Fearing that she was either going to faint or be sick again, he backed away. But after a moment, she seemed to pull herself together and took a few unsteady steps towards him before her legs crumpled and she fell forward, hitting the ground hard with her knees. He could see he was going to have to help, although the thought of touching her made him want to retch. He took her by the arm and hoisted her up onto her feet again.

"Come on, Yolanda. You can do it."

"Where we go?"

"Back to the pub."

"The pub?"

"Yes. We can get help there."

She nodded as if this was acceptable, leaning her head heavily against him as she allowed him to steer her onto the path. She stank of vomit and brandy but he would have to put up with it for a short while.

It seemed to take an hour to cover a hundred metres. Looking down at her, as they passed under a streetlamp, he noticed with distaste that she had been slobbering all over the sleeve of his coat. No doubt she had got blood on it too. Fucking little bitch. What was she playing at? He tried to pull his arm away but she clung on tight, stumbling into him and giggling now. The GHB was beginning to take effect. He wouldn't be able to let go of her in case she tipped into the water by herself and ruined the whole damn thing. He would have to ditch his clothes in the morning, which was intensely annoying, but it would be worth it, he told himself. It would all be worth it. He'd make bloody sure it was.

As they rounded the bend, he could see the pub in the distance, overlooking the water. It wasn't far from there to his car but he doubted that she would make it. She was muttering something to herself in Spanish, eyes closed, head lolling, as he dragged her along, his arms locked around her to stop her falling. She was a dead weight and he was getting tired of supporting her. He could try picking her up properly and carrying her all the way to the car. If anyone saw them together they would probably assume she was drunk or ill, and he was helping her home. But there were too many bloody police crawling around the streets these days and he couldn't afford to take the risk.

Scanning the horizon, wondering what to do, he noticed the dark outline of a small pedestrian bridge half way along. Although not that high above the water, it would be better than nothing. As he tried to get her to take a step forward, she slipped through his arms and collapsed in an untidy heap on the ground, moaning quietly to herself. She was well gone now. It was all happening too quickly. Furious, he realised that he would have to pick her up and carry her after all. Tucking the remnants of her damp skirt tightly around her thighs, he picked her up in his arms and walked the short distance to the bridge. Why were they always so fucking heavy? God help him if he came across a six-footer.

He was almost half way across when he heard the sound of a bell and looked round to see a cyclist coming fast towards him along the towpath. Fuck. This was all he needed. Hoping that they wouldn't come across the bridge, he put Yolanda down, propping her against the iron rail for support. He wrapped his arms tightly around her, bent forwards and kissed her. He could taste the blood and vomit on her mouth and felt sick. He waited, listening, and after what seemed ages, he heard the wheels whoosh past on the path followed by another tinkle from the bell, now further on, as the cyclist speeded into the distance.

He straightened up, spat into the water and wiped his mouth on his sleeve. Still holding her, he gazed at the sky. Apart from a few wispy clouds, it was clear and full of stars. He felt his skin begin to tingle. He was so close now. He wanted to prolong the moment, capture it in his mind just like before. The moon was high in the sky and, as it came out from behind the veil of a cloud, the light illuminated the bridge like a spotlight. He looked down at Yolanda. Her eyes were tightly closed and her breathing almost imperceptible. She wasn't aware of anything around her now. The moonlight bleached her skin a strange bluey-white and she looked unreal, like a doll.

His blood was humming. He could barely contain himself. He was almost there. Almost. Just one last thing to do. He took his grandmother's old sewing scissors from his pocket. Resting Yolanda's head on his shoulder like a sleeping child, he snipped off a long, thick lock of hair then tucked it away with the scissors in his pocket. He was ready. He lifted her up and sat her on the edge of the bridge facing him, holding her tightly by her upper arms so that she wouldn't tip over just yet. Her head flopped forward and her hair fell over her face, spoiling everything. He had to see her face. Cradling the back of her head in his hand, he swept back her hair and gazed at her, almost unable to contain himself. He needed to freeze this last image in his mind. She was so still. Still as death.

Excitement rising like a tide, he closed his eyes, and breathed deeply for a second. He had the fleeting memory of heat and a garden in full summer. An intense, sweet smell filled his head. The scent of stocks, or was it gardenia? It was intoxicating. Just like the last time. He inhaled deeply again, high with yearning. After a moment, he half-opened his eyes and gazed at her once more. He felt the rush of blood, the wave of heat from deep down and slowly loosened his grip on her arms, watching her topple backwards over the bridge. With a shudder, he gasped, closing his eyes again as he heard the splash.

CHAPTER
TWENTY-FOUR

Tartaglia got out of the car and watched Wightman nudge the Mondeo into an impossibly small parking space up against the railings, above the canal. It was late afternoon and would soon be dark. Mercifully, it had stopped raining, but the air was thick with damp and a wind was getting up. He had last been here in the heat of summer many years before, when he had first arrived in London and had taken a guided walk along the towpath of the Regent's Canal from Little Venice all the way to Camden Lock.

Gazing over the railings, the only thing that had changed was the horizon, now filled with the glittering cluster of office blocks that had sprung up around Paddington Basin. Immediately below, a strip of public gardens stretched down to the towpath and the canal. Beyond was the large triangle of dark water where three canals converged, known as Browning's Pool, after the poet Robert Browning who had once lived opposite. It was bordered by an incongruous mix of seventies housing on one side and rows of cream-coloured neo-classical villas, worth many millions, set back above the canal behind manicured hedges. A body was not what you expected to find on your doorstep in this part of town and he saw several people standing in the windows of the houses, watching the activities down below on the canal.

Wightman joined Tartaglia and they walked along the road to where a section had been cordoned off, just in front of where the mortuary van was parked. They showed their IDs to a uniformed PC from the local station and descended a steep, slippery set of stairs to the towpath and canal below.

At the bottom, Tartaglia stopped and looked across the water again, taking in the scene. Apart from the sound of the wind whipping through the trees and across the water, all he could hear was the squawking of geese from the small island in the middle. Even in summer, the pool had been a disturbing thick, browny-green soup. But close up, under a darkening sky, it looked poisonous and he pitied the divers who had had the task of retrieving the body.

Two large narrow boats were moored along that side of the bank, one a floating puppet theatre, the other somebody's home. Just beyond, the path was screened off and a small forensic tent was pitched on the paving next to an empty tourist boat. Gathered beside it, chatting, with takeaway cups of tea or coffee in their hands, were what he assumed were a couple of officers from the local CID, along with the mortuary van driver and his assistant. As they approached, a young man in a short, dark overcoat stepped forward from the group and introduced himself as DS Grant.

294

"We fished the body out a few hours ago from under the water bus, sir," he said to Tartaglia, pointing at the tourist boat.

"I hear it's a young girl," Tartaglia said.

Grant nodded. "She got caught up on the propeller." He pointed to the far end of the tourist boat. "She's in a right state. Dr Blake's in the tent with her now."

It was lucky that Blake had been on call when the body was found and he was grateful that she had made sure that he was called to the scene. He ducked in through the flap, leaving Wightman and Grant outside.

The body lay on the ground, already sheeted up, ready for removal to the mortuary. Blake was kneeling beside it, dictating something into a recorder. She looked up and gave him a fleeting smile.

"Oh, good. I'm glad you've got here. I was just finishing up."

"I got your message. I hear there's a lock of hair missing."

She nodded and got to her feet slowly, as if she was stiff from kneeling for a while. "Just like the last two. That's why I insisted they call you right away. But there's one big difference. This girl's been beaten up and, from what I can see without examining her properly, she's also been sexually assaulted. Quite brutally, in fact."

"Assaulted? He's never done that before." Tartaglia rubbed his chin, surprised. Some killers stuck more or less to the same pattern. With others, like Michael Barton, there was a gradual progression of violence, as if they needed more and more to satisfy them, often leading them to make mistakes. It was usually what led to their being caught. But he had never heard of a change in MO as sudden or extreme as this. There hadn't been even a whiff of that kind of violence used against any of the other girls, let alone any form of sexual assault. He felt baffled.

She was looking at him inquiringly. "Do you think it could be a copycat?"

He shook his head. "Nobody knows about the locks of hair. It's one of the few details that wasn't leaked. Do you have any idea how long she's been in the water?"

"She's not in bad condition, so I'd say not long. Certainly less than twenty-four hours and probably closer to twelve."

"That's very helpful. Was she already dead when she went in, or did she drown?"

"I'm not sure at the moment. I'll have to get her back to the lab and see how much water's in her lungs. However, she put up quite a fight and I'm hopeful, given the extent of her injuries, that we may get a DNA profile of your man."

"What about a ring?" he said, thinking back to the other girls.

"Apart from a gold cross around her neck, she isn't wearing any jewellery."

He stared down at the body, wishing, not for the first time, that the dead could speak. Maybe the ring had come off in the struggle or afterwards in the water. Or maybe there was no ring, in which case, was Tom the killer? It still didn't feel right. "You're sure the hair's been deliberately cut off? Couldn't it have been caught up somehow in the propeller?"

Blake shook her head. "Some of the injuries to the torso are definitely post mortem and caused by the propeller. But the head is undamaged, apart from some bruising to her face, which happened shortly before death, presumably when she was attacked."

Still trying to puzzle it out, he said nothing for a moment. Seeing he was unconvinced, she added: "If her hair had been caught up on something, it would have been pulled out at the root. However, this was done with a sharp blade, just like the other two I examined. I really wouldn't have troubled you otherwise. Do you want to see for yourself?"

He shook his head. "I'll take your word for it. I suppose it has to be him then. But it's bizarre. He didn't assault the others in any way whatsoever. Why would he go and do this now? It makes no sense from a psychological point of view."

She shrugged. "That's for you to work out. I can only tell you what I find. I'll call you once I get her back to the lab and take a proper look. Maybe something else will turn up."

He nodded and was about to go when she touched his arm.

"Mark, wait," she said, peeling off her gloves. "I just wanted to say you were right about what you said last night. About me, I mean. I know I need to sort things out. I just need a good kick up the arse." She hesitated, then added: "Thanks for being honest. That's all."

He smiled, relieved that she wasn't angry. "I didn't mean to be harsh."

She shook her head with a rueful smile. "I deserved it. Are we still friends?"

He nodded, although the word "friends" again struck a false note. Perhaps it was a euphemism for something he didn't quite understand. Whatever she meant by it, he decided not to hold it against her. Before he said something he knew he would regret, he ducked out of the tent and walked over to where Wightman and Grant were standing together on the towpath talking.

"Do we know who she is?" Tartaglia asked Grant.

"It's possible she's a Spanish girl called Yolanda Garcia. She works as an au pair for a family called Everett in Paddington. They reported her missing when she didn't come home last night and the physical description fits."

"Last night? That ties in nicely with what Dr Blake has just told me about timing," Tartaglia said. He turned to Wightman. "Call Sam and ask her to go and see the family right away and get some background on the girl and a firm ID. If she lived in Paddington, she didn't have far to come. Also, ask Sam to see if the girl left any form of a suicide note." As Wightman moved away to make the call, he turned to Grant. "Do we have any idea where she went in?" From memory, that stretch of the canal was nearly two miles long. There was no point wasting time and resources knocking on doors and combing the canals for witnesses until they had a better idea of where it had happened.

Grant shook his head. "Apparently, there's almost no current. So, I'm assuming it must be somewhere close by. But you're best off speaking to the skipper of the boat. He seems to be a walking encyclopaedia on these canals."

"What about CCTV footage?"

"I've already spoken to someone at British Waterways and they'll let us have whatever there is. But there aren't many cameras along this part of the canal."

"I don't suppose there were any reports of someone being pushed in last night?"

Grant shook his head. "No such luck. It's been so cold, I guess everyone was inside."

"Where's the skipper?"

"Last time I saw him, he was in the floating café over there, having a cup of tea and a piece of home-made cake." Grant nodded in the direction of a narrowboat moored on the other side of the canal. "He's pretty pissed off that he can't put his boat away and go home until we're done."

Tartaglia grinned. "Life's tough, isn't it. He should try our job for a change."

Tartaglia found Ed Sullivan, the skipper of the tourist boat, huddled in a corner of the café, nursing what looked like a fresh mug of tea. In his late forties, he was thin and wiry, with short, greying dark hair and the permanently tanned skin of somebody who spent most of his life out in the open. After being told again firmly that he wasn't going to be able to take the boat back to

Camden for a while, Sullivan seemed resigned to his fate and relaxed into his seat to tell his story.

"I was just going under that bridge over there, when the engine stopped," he said, taking a gulp of tea and pointing out the window towards the small bridge that spanned the entrance to the Regent's Canal. "I opened the hatch to take a recce at the propeller and when I reached inside, I felt something soft and a bit mushy, sort of like a wet carpet. But I couldn't shift it so I had to let the boat drift to the bank over there. Then I got out and took a look. When I dug around underneath the platform with a boat hook, I found a foot. That's when I called you lot." He took another mouthful of tea. "Had a whole load of Russians on board. They got out and started taking pictures. Can you believe it? The ghouls. I couldn't bloody get rid of them and they had the cheek to demand their money back, even though we were practically home and all they had to do was walk across the ruddy bridge. I suppose we should be thankful nobody's slapped us with a lawsuit for emotional damage."

Tartaglia shook his head in sympathy, although nothing surprised him any longer about human behaviour. "You said that the body was under some sort of a platform?" he asked, knowing nothing about boats.

Sullivan nodded. "See over there, on the left-hand side at the end." He pointed to one end of the tourist boat on the opposite side of the pool. "The platform sits just on the water, in front of the engine room. It's where I stand and steer the boat. The girl was lying crossways, wedged in between the platform and the propeller." Noticing Tartaglia's puzzled expression he added: "Look, I'll show you." Sullivan took out a pen from his pocket and drew a diagram on the back of a paper napkin.

Tartaglia looked at the drawing for a moment. "Thanks. That makes it much clearer." He studied Sullivan's weather-beaten face, surprised at how unaffected he seemed by what had happened. "You seem very calm. Are you all right?"

Sullivan waved his hand in the air nonchalantly. "Oh, don't worry about me. This isn't the first time."

"Really?"

Sullivan nodded matter-of-factly. "I was working on a dredger on one of the Oxford canals and got another body jammed in the propeller. It was some poor student who had fallen off his bike into the water and drowned. He'd only been on the bottom of the canal a short time when the boat snagged him. They offered me counselling and everything but I've been fine about it. Can't let these things get to you, can you? Otherwise we'd all be nervous wrecks."

"Quite," Tartaglia said, glad that in addition to being apparently unaffected by what had happened, Sullivan seemed not in the least bit curious as to how the girl came to be in the water. No doubt he assumed it was another accident. "You say the engine stopped when you went under that bridge over there. Is that where you think the girl fell in?"

Sullivan shrugged. "Not necessarily. She *could* have been caught up on another boat first or maybe we picked her up somewhere else along the way. We were coming back from Camden and were nearly home when the engine stopped so she could have gone in anywhere along that stretch."

Tartaglia shook his head wearily, struggling to understand it all. Blake had said that the body hadn't been in the water long. Decomposition had barely started and it would have been lying at the bottom of the canal, not floating on the surface. "Explain one thing please, Mr Sullivan. How can a body lying at the bottom of a canal get caught up on a boat? Surely there's ample room for a boat to pass over."

Sullivan gave him an indulgent look as if he was used to people unfamiliar with boats and canals. "This is the boat, right?" he said, pointing at the drawing on the napkin. "And here's the waterline." He drew it in. "There's the rudder, see? And the propeller and the platform we were talking about. The canals around here are no more than six feet deep and less than that in some places. Modern boats don't have much draft . . ."

"Draft?" Tartaglia interrupted.

"Depth in the water. The modern ones float over most things without a problem. But an old boat like this one, or the dredger I was working on in Oxford, they sit quite a bit lower in the water. There's not much between the bottom of the boat and the bottom of the canal. As you go along, the water underneath gets quite churned up, particularly if you're passing through somewhere narrow and enclosed, like under a bridge."

"I see. So, you would have disturbed the body as you passed over it?"

Sullivan nodded. "It's easy for all sorts of rubbish and stuff to get picked up and trapped in the propeller. I often have to stop and clear it out. It's bloody lucky we didn't break down in the Maida Tunnel. It's black as pitch and there's no towpath. In the olden days, the bargemen had to send the horses over the top and lie on their backs on the roof of their barge and push themselves along inside with their feet. Then they'd re-hitch the horses on the other side. It's where the expression 'legging it' comes from," he said with a smile. "I wouldn't like to be stuck in there for long, particularly with all those Russian harpies and a dead body, I can tell you."

"You clearly know these boats and canals like the back of your hand, Mr Sullivan. Can't you hazard a guess where she went in?"

Sullivan smiled, as if flattered to be consulted. "My guess, and it's only a guess, mind, is that she fell in close to where we picked her up. It seems the most probable but don't hang me if you find out she fell in at Limehouse."

"Can't you be more precise? I promise I won't hang you if you're wrong. It's very important we find out where she went in."

Sullivan nodded thoughtfully and drained his mug, putting it down with a satisfied sigh. "OK. Allowing time for her to get caught up under the boat and possibly moved along just a little way before she hit the propeller, that would put it on the stretch just before the Maida Tunnel. On the eastern side, around Lisson Grove."

Donovan found the Everett family's address without a problem. They lived in a maisonette in a huge terraced house near Paddington Station, only ten minutes away from Little Venice. The call had been logged just after midnight and Judy Everett didn't seem in the least surprised when Donovan explained that a girl's body had been found, matching the description given of Yolanda.

"Of course it's a shock," Judy Everett said, attempting to spoon the pink, mushy contents of a small jar into the mouth of a toddler, who was sitting in a high chair looking unenthusiastic. Seeing what was inside the jar, Donovan didn't blame him.

Tall and gawky, with a mass of unruly brown hair and a healthy, scrubbed complexion, Judy seemed to be taking things in her stride. Although the large, airy kitchen was in a state of chaos with paper and colouring pens littering the floor, the sink and draining board groaning with unwashed dishes and pans and plates of half-eaten food lying discarded on the counter.

"I knew right away that something had happened when Yolanda didn't come home," Judy said, turning to Donovan hand on hip. "She was always back well before midnight. It's one of our house rules and she'd never broken it before."

"How long had she been living with you, Mrs Everett?"

"Oh, about five months."

"So you know her quite well."

"Not really. In fact, she was a complete mystery to me. I normally have some sort of a rapport going with

304

the girls while they're here. They never stay long but I've become quite fond of many of them. They've really become like members of the family and we keep in touch."

"But not Yolanda?"

Judy shook her head. "I can't pretend, can I?" She sighed heavily. "God, it's awful, if it is Yolanda. I feel really guilty now, not liking her. I mean, there was nothing wrong with her and she actually seemed to be quite bright. I never had to tell her anything twice. But she wasn't the sort of girl you immediately warm to. She was good with my two boys, though, which was all that really mattered." She sighed again, rubbing her face with her hand and frowned. "If it's her, I don't know what I'm going to tell Alex. He's my elder son and he's five. He was really fond of her."

"Was she unhappy, do you think?"

Judy shrugged. "To be honest, I don't know. She was such a serious little thing and she didn't have much of a sense of humour, although her English wasn't fantastic, so perhaps that's unfair. As I said, she did her job OK, so I had no complaints. I just have no idea what went on underneath."

Red-faced, nose streaming, the child spat out the last spoonful of food and banged the side of his chair with a fat, grubby fist. Judy wiped his mouth and the tray in front of him quickly with some kitchen paper and offered him a child's beaker of what looked like juice, which he sucked for a moment then brandished in the air triumphantly as if it was the FA Cup.

"Had she worked somewhere else before coming to you?"

"No. This was her first time in this country and she didn't seem to know anybody. She didn't go out much, apart from her English classes. I felt sorry for her, but what can you do? I'm not her mother. I work four days a week and I haven't got time to look after the girls, as well as everybody else. They have to learn to fend for themselves."

Her tone was a little defensive and Donovan wondered if maybe she was also feeling guilty after all for not having taken more of an interest. For a moment, thinking back to what people had said about Marion Spear, Donovan felt for Yolanda. Donovan had grown up in the leafy suburbs of St Margaret's, Twickenham, on the outskirts of London. She had a sense of belonging, a network of family and close friends, yet even she found London a cold and lonely place at times. How must it be for someone coming to it for the first time, trying to carve out a life for themselves on their own, with little or no support? It would make anyone vulnerable.

"Did Yolanda have access to the internet from here?" she asked.

The child threw the beaker onto the floor and Judy stooped to pick it up, handing it back to him without a glance. "She wasn't allowed on our computer but I remember her going off to the local library sometimes to send emails home."

"When did you last see her?" Donovan said, making a mental note to check the library computers if the body turned out to be Yolanda's.

"She gave the boys their tea yesterday, that would be about five-thirty. Alex is having tea at a friend's at the moment." She glanced at her watch. "Which reminds me, I ought to go and pick him up soon."

"I won't take up much more of your time, Mrs Everett. But I need a rough idea of when Yolanda went out."

Judy thought for a moment. "That's a bit tricky. I came home from work and took over at about six, as it was her evening off. I didn't see her after that. She usually stays in her room and watches TV, even on her evenings off. We put one in the au pair's bedroom to keep them occupied. That way, we don't have them hanging around with us in the evening."

"So, you didn't hear her go out?"

"No. But she creeps around like a mouse. I suppose it might have been when I was giving the boys a bath, but I can't be sure. The walls in these houses are so thick."

"What time was that?"

"About seven. But it could have been any time after that. I didn't notice she'd gone out until Johnny came home, which was just before eight." The toddler had thrown the cup onto the floor again and started to cry. Judy picked him up, balancing him on her hip and wiping his nose with a crumpled tissue, which she retrieved from the sleeve of her cardigan. "So, what happens now?"

"We obviously need to make sure that the girl is Yolanda. Do you know if she has any family in this country?"

Judy shook her head. "They're all in Spain. She came from somewhere in the north by the sea. I don't remember where, I'm afraid, but I can probably dig out an address or phone number somewhere if you want it." Her eyes flitted briefly towards a small desk in the corner of the room, its surface covered in a sea of papers and books.

"I'll need that if it turns out to be her. Do you think your husband would be able to come and identify her?"

Judy gave a rasping laugh. "I'm afraid it will have to be me. Johnny would pass out at the sight of a dead body. But I'm a GP so I'm used to these things. I'll make a phone call so that Alex can stay where he is, then I'll see if my mum can come and mind Toby. I imagine you want it done straight away."

Donovan nodded. "The sooner the better. If it is her, we'll also need to go through her things."

With Toby happily perched on her hip, Judy walked Donovan to the front door of the flat. "Assuming it is Yolanda, can you tell me what happened? Did she fall in?"

"We're not sure yet what happened," Donovan said noncommittally. "I don't suppose you found any sort of note?"

"You mean a suicide note?" Judy looked shocked. "I can check her bedroom again but I didn't see anything when I went in there last night. She didn't even say

308

goodbye when she went out. You really think she might have killed herself?"

"We don't know, Mrs Everett. The first step is to identify her."

CHAPTER
TWENTY-FIVE

Tartaglia left Wightman beside the canal, waiting for backup from Barnes and some local uniforms to arrive in order to start the search for witnesses along the canal. Based on what Sullivan had said, they had decided to work their way east from the Maida Tunnel. He just hoped Sullivan's guess was a good one.

The course of a murder investigation rarely ran straight. Even with what looked superficially to be the simplest of cases, there were always ups and downs, twists and turns and, with the more complicated ones, often long periods when nothing seemed to give. He felt completely baffled by what he had seen at the canal. The missing lock of hair meant that it had to be Tom. But why had he attacked the girl? Why risk leaving his DNA at the scene? The more he thought about it, the less sense he was able to make of it.

He consoled himself with the thought that Steele would do no better. He was sure her first action, on hearing about what he had learned, would be to call in Kennedy. He gave her a minute, or five at the outside, from the moment he had spoken to her on his mobile beside the canal before she would be punching in Kennedy's number. Whatever was going on between them, they seemed to be joined at the hip. Kennedy would have a field day with all of this. Tartaglia could already picture him swaggering up and down her office, spouting his shit as if he were God. Just to save himself from the experience of having to hear it all, Tartaglia was tempted again to tell Steele what he had seen outside her flat. But what was the point? He'd been through all the pros and cons already and he knew she wouldn't believe him.

He found her a little intimidating, he had to admit. She was so bloody cold and unreadable. Cornish wasn't exactly cuddly either, but at least he was transparent and totally predictable, with all his silly little foibles and vanities. By comparison he was almost endearing. Whereas Steele had all the charm of an automaton. Fearing what she would say, Tartaglia still hadn't found the right moment to tell her what Donovan had learned from Nicola Slade about Marion Spear's secret lover. As far as he was concerned, even if there was nothing but a whisper of suspicion to link Harry Angel to any of the others, he was still in the frame for what Tartaglia was sure was Spear's murder. But he wanted Kennedy's cloud of heat and light to pass before he attempted to convince Steele to let him have another go with Angel. And there was no point in even attempting that, until they found out where the forensic trail would lead from the canal body. Hopefully, there would be news from Fiona Blake within the next forty-eight hours.

What worried him most was that he no longer trusted his instincts — almost felt as though he hadn't got any anymore. Everything was obscure and he wished again that Clarke was still around. He would know what to make of it all, if anyone would. St Mary's Hospital wasn't more than a stone's throw from Maida Vale and he decided to chance it and see if Clarke would be up to seeing him. It would also be a good idea to give Barnes a miss, at least until the morning. Hopefully, by then Kennedy would have been and gone.

"I thought if I was hypnotised I'd become a robot or do something stupid or embarrassing, you know, like you see in stage shows," Donovan said.

Adam Zaleski grinned. "That's just theatre. Those people you see taking their clothes off, or pretending to be chickens, do it because they want to. I can't make you do anything you don't want to do."

They were sitting at a table in the ground floor bar of the Polish Club, just up the road from Zaleski's practice in South Kensington. After Donovan's second hypnotherapy session early that evening, he had suggested going for a quick drink afterwards. He intrigued her and she had found it impossible to say no. After all, who could blame her for wanting a life outside work and how else was she ever going to meet anyone new who wasn't in the police?

With a twenty foot ceiling and huge windows overlooking Exhibition Road and part of Imperial College opposite, the room was an extraordinary mix of styles, with bits of sixties and seventies décor, together with chandeliers, large carved mirrors and faded gilt.

The atmosphere evoked an earlier, grander era, somehow not entirely English. There were also elements of seediness, the carpet and curtains reminiscent of a cheap hotel, as if there hadn't been enough money around in recent years to maintain standards. Some sort of elevator jazz was playing in the background and the room was nearly full, everybody talking Polish. If it hadn't been for the view out the front, Donovan could have easily imagined herself in a foreign country.

Zaleski had insisted that they drink vodka and had ordered some special variety flavoured with rowanberries. He had also refused to let her pay for her drink, saying that this was his territory. Although he was not much older than she was, he had an old-fashioned charm that she found very appealing.

"The first time I was very conscious of what you were saying," she said. "But this time I found myself drifting off, as if I was asleep. I feel so incredibly relaxed now, it's amazing."

"It's a bit like being in a trance," he replied, as the waiter brought over two small shot glasses of clear liquid on a silver tray. "But you're actually in a heightened state of awareness. Your conscious mind is suppressed and I'm talking to your inner-conscious mind." He picked up his glass and clinked hers. "*Na zdrowie*. It means cheers."

"Cheers." She had never drunk neat vodka before and she took a sip warily. It was icy cold and viscous. Not unpleasant at all, in fact.

He downed his in one gulp. "That's how you're supposed to drink it," he said, smiling. "But I'll let you off this time, as you're new to it."

She took another sip, swilling it round on her tongue to get the full taste. It had much more flavour than the stuff you bought at the supermarket and she could now understand why it was drunk on its own. "Why do I have to wear those headphones when you're hypnotising me?"

"I use a technique called Neuro-Linguistic Programming, or NLP, as we call it. You don't want all the science stuff, but basically wearing headphones maximises concentration, so all you hear is my voice and what I'm saying."

"I still find it unbelievable that I'm sitting here having a drink and I don't even fancy a cigarette."

"The most important thing is that you really want to make the change. It won't work otherwise."

She took another, larger sip of vodka, feeling pleased with herself. If she finally cracked the smoking thing, it would be one in the eye for that sceptic, Tartaglia. "Tell me about the club," she said after a moment. "Has it been here for long?"

"Donkey's years. It goes back at least to the Second World War, when the Polish government in exile used to meet upstairs. But it was dying on its feet until Poland joined the EU. It's still caught in a bit of a time warp but at least the average age of the members has come down by about four decades. You know, there are now more Poles living in the UK than in Warsaw."

It was amazing how the EU had changed London, with the huge migration of immigrants from Eastern Europe and other countries. The Brits had at last become a bit more diluted, which was so much for the better in her opinion, the huge cultural mix being one of the many reasons she liked living and working in London.

She drained her glass with a final sip. "Do you come here a lot?"

He nodded. "It's a funny old place, but I'm rather fond of it. It's got a terrace out at the back, which is quite nice in summer, and I do like a shot or two of vodka after a hard day at work. Speaking of which, would you like another?" he said, noticing her empty glass. "They're very small, after all, and one barely touches the sides, I find."

"Please." It was already giving her a deliciously warm feeling but she was sure she could handle one more. "Are we supposed to throw our empty glasses into the fireplace?"

He laughed. "Only in the movies or in Russia. I think if you tried it here, you'd give one of the older members a heart attack. It's safer to let the waiter take them." He gestured for the waiter who appeared almost immediately.

"Who are they?" she asked, looking up at the many portraits on the walls, after the waiter had removed the glasses and taken their order.

"They're pretty hideous, aren't they? I suppose they're all Poles. But apart from Rula Lenska, I don't recognise any of them, although the blokes in the berets over the bar must be war heroes. However, I don't think there's much logic to it, as there's a huge picture of the Duke of Kent over the fireplace in the dining room and I doubt whether he even has a Polish maid."

She laughed and, still looking around, said: "It's quite a collection. But I'm not sure if I'd give any of them wall space, myself."

"I imagine somebody bequeathed them to the club — I'd put good money on it being the artist — and I expect the old biddies on the committee were too polite to refuse."

"What about that gold eagle over there, with the crown?"

"It's the national emblem and it's supposed to be a white eagle. The communists removed the crown from the emblem when they came to power. But of course this one here still has his."

Their drinks arrived. "How do you say 'cheers' again in Polish?" she said, raising her glass.

"*Na zdrowie.*"

It sounded so lovely when he said it and she tried to copy him. She had never had much of an ear for languages at school but it seemed to trip off the tongue quite easily. "It sounds so much nicer than cheers."

"Let alone 'down the hatch' or 'bottoms up'," he said, smiling. "English vocabulary can be very functional and un-poetic, particularly when it comes to drinking or romance."

She felt her cheeks turn pink. She wasn't sure if it was the vodka or the way he was looking at her.

"Do you speak Polish fluently?" she asked.

"I was born and brought up over here but we always spoke it at home." He downed his vodka and smiled at her. "Now, it's your turn."

"In one, you mean? OK. Here goes."

He watched as she knocked it back. It was ice cold and made the back of her throat burn. But it tasted even better than the first.

"That one's called Jebrowska," he said. "It means Bison Grass. Are you up for trying another one? They have a lemon vodka which is quite delicious. Or maybe you've had enough. It can be quite powerful when you're not used to it."

She hesitated. She was supposed to be cooking supper for Claire, although she hadn't even got around to buying it yet. Luckily there was a Tesco just round the corner from their house which was open late. It wouldn't do to arrive home pissed. But what the hell. She felt so relaxed, sitting there with him, that she wanted to postpone the inevitable moment of departure. "OK. Just one more and then I really must go."

The waiter was nowhere to be seen and Zaleski went up to the bar to order the final round.

"You know, you're not at all what I imagine a policewoman to be like," he said, sitting down again a few minutes later with their drinks.

She laughed. "Really?"

"I hasten to add that I haven't met any. Not up close, anyway, apart from some bloke who did me for speeding once."

"The murder squad's a bit different to traffic," she said, hoping he wasn't going to ask her about the case.

"I can imagine. What's your background? I mean, why did you join the police in the first place? You don't seem the type."

She shrugged. "There's no type, really, particularly these days. I've got a degree in English but that's not much use for anything, unless you want to teach, like my parents did. My father's a card-carrying *New Statesman* reader and joining the police was probably the only way I could shock him, other than becoming a Young Conservative."

He smiled. "What I really meant when I said you didn't look the type was that you're very feminine and petite."

"Short, you mean?"

"No, petite. I chose the word carefully."

"Don't worry, it doesn't bother me. I'm very happy the way I am and luckily these days there's no minimum height requirement. Anyway, for what I do, I don't need to be physically strong."

"No. I suppose detecting is all about brain power." They clinked glasses. "Here's to you, Sam, and good detecting." He smiled and downed his vodka. Then he said something in Polish.

"What does that mean?"

He grinned. "I said you have beautiful eyes."

She felt herself colour again. Why did such things always sound so much nicer in a foreign language? She thought of Jamie Lee Curtis being turned on by Russian in *A Fish Called Wanda*. But Polish was just as sexy, particularly when spoken by Adam. He had the quiet sort of looks that grew on you. If he took off his nerdy glasses and wore his hair a little longer, he'd almost give Tartaglia a run for his money. He could also do with sharpening up his clothes. But she liked the fact that he didn't bother or didn't seem to be aware that he was attractive.

"Sorry. I should be behaving more professionally," he said, still smiling. "You are my client but at least you've only one more session to go."

"Do you really think I won't ever want a cigarette again?"

"We'll see. But that's usually all that's needed. Your last session's on Friday, isn't it?"

She nodded.

"I'm pretty sure you're my last appointment, like today. Why don't I take you out to dinner afterwards to celebrate?"

She didn't want to appear too keen but there was nothing she wanted to do more. "That would be lovely. Shall we come here again?"

He shook his head with a smile. "All Poles eat is pig, cabbage and potatoes. I think we can do a little better than this funny old place. Leave it to me."

CHAPTER
TWENTY-SIX

To: Carolyn.Steele@met.police.uk
From: Tom837920ixye8785@hotmail.com

My Dear Carolyn,
Have you missed me? I know you've been thinking of me and I've certainly been thinking of you. Loads, and in ways that you can't even begin to picture. What is it about you that draws me to you? Is it your lovely, silky dark hair and your white, white skin? I love your eyes, they're like a cat's and cats are such sensual, playful animals. But it's so much more than that. I'm not superficial, truly I'm not. It's not about looks, is it? You have something really special. Has anyone ever told you? I'm sure they have, I'm not so green that I believe I'm the first. But nobody will appreciate you quite like me. You know that, don't you? Does it excite you to think of me? Does it make you yearn for me? Do I fill your dreams? I'm the lover you've always longed for, the one who'll never leave you. Shall I come and see you? Would you like that? I don't want to be impatient. I don't want to push it until you're ready. But I know it's going to be *so good*,

I can hardly wait. When you're alone in your bed tonight, close your eyes and think of me there with you. I'm very, very good. The best you'll ever have. Just close your eyes and imagine. The reality will be so much better.

Tomxxx

p.s. Have you found little Yolanda yet? She was nothing compared to you.

Steele stared at the screen, the words swimming in front of her. She felt sick, deeply shaken by what she had read. She had tried to get hold of Cornish but he had left the office and hadn't arrived home yet. He also wasn't answering his mobile and she left a message asking him to call her urgently. Tartaglia and Jones were out on the road somewhere but there was no point in speaking to them until they could see what she had in front of her. Besides, she was afraid her voice would give her away. She didn't want either of them to know how she really felt.

The mention of Yolanda's name was yet another pinprick. Her body had been officially identified earlier by her employer and her parents in Spain were being contacted. A search of Yolanda's room had revealed nothing of interest and, unlike the previous girls, no suicide note of any shape or form could be found in the flat. Perhaps the routine had changed or perhaps, thinking about the canal scene Tartaglia had described, something had gone wrong. The two computers in Yolanda's local library had been removed and sent away for analysis but Steele held out little hope of their providing much new information, let alone a link to Tom. He covered his tracks too well. He was untouchable.

She stood up and walked over to the window, gazing for a moment at the street below. It was dark outside and people were hurrying home from Barnes Station up the road, briefcases and shopping bags in hand. Lights were on in most of the houses opposite and where people had forgotten to close their curtains, she could see happy little domestic scenes, children playing or watching television, somebody cooking supper, somebody else arriving back from work. She felt as though she was somewhere remote, looking at another world that had nothing to do with her.

Somehow Tom knew how to press all the right buttons. But how could he? Was she so transparent to him, so typical of a woman of her age and background? Was it perhaps a lucky guess, had he hit the bull's-eye by accident or had he talked to someone who knew her? She shivered. She felt that he was getting closer, moving nearer, in ever decreasing circles. He was toying with her, playing with her, but would he really come? Should she ask Cornish for protection? Or did Tom only want to frighten her? She was sure that he would know that he had got to her, that this is how she would react. Maybe he would be gloating, picturing her state of mind. She felt furious at the thought and impotent. But however much she tried to fight it, stop it getting to her, it was useless. The bastard knew where she was vulnerable.

322

Feeling close to tears, she walked over to the door, made sure it was properly closed, and locked it. She couldn't risk anybody coming in at the moment. Flopping back down in her chair, she squeezed the bridge of her nose with her fingers, squeezed until it hurt and all she could focus on was the pain. She *would not* let herself cry, would not let them all see her like that. But she had to tell someone. She needed to talk and there was only person she could trust. Taking several deep breaths to calm herself, hoping that her voice wouldn't give her away, she picked up the phone and punched in Kennedy's number.

"You're in a right pickle, aren't you, Mark?" Clarke said, his face creasing into an awkward smile, clearly delighted that Tartaglia had come to seek his advice.

"Nice of you to care. But you know me, I never like things easy."

Clarke sighed heavily. "No, you're a demanding bugger . . . even at the best of times."

Tartaglia was perched next to Clarke's bed on a small, hard chair, which he had had to carry in from a nearby waiting room, there being no chairs for visitors in the ward. Clarke lay beside him, flat on his back, attached to a drip, which Tartaglia presumed was to kill the pain, the lower half of his body still imprisoned under the large protective cage. Surrounded by a sea of cards, flowers and untouched baskets of fruit still in their cellophane, Clarke seemed in good spirits, considering everything. But his eyes were bloodshot and his long, boney face looked grey. He had been a big man but he had lost a considerable amount of weight, almost shrivelling overnight, and he had aged at least ten years. Tartaglia hoped that the shock on his face, when he'd first caught sight of Clarke, hadn't shown.

A huge, fluffy pink teddy bear was tucked up under the sheets next to Clarke, a tag with the words: "Darling Trevor, I love you" pinned to a silk bow around its neck. It was such a funny, incongruous sight that, if it wasn't also so incredibly sad, Tartaglia would have been tempted to take a photo with his mobile for the team to see.

Although Clarke didn't have his own room any longer, they had at least put him in a small ward, with only four beds, one of which was empty, and given him the end bay by one of the windows. Tartaglia had thought of pulling the curtains around the bed for privacy, but as the man next door was out for the count and snoring loudly and the one opposite seemed deeply engrossed in listening to something on a set of headphones, there didn't seem much point.

"So Trevor, what do you think?" Tartaglia said, after a moment.

Clarke was silent, staring hard at the ceiling, as he pretended to give the matter further consideration. But Tartaglia wasn't fooled. He had seen Clarke's eyes light up as he recounted, blow by blow, the details of what had happened. Clarke was rarely slow to make up his mind, usually having a flash of insight or inspiration that usually took everybody by surprise and cut straight to the chase. But here he was, lying almost immobile in the bed, just savouring the moment and enjoying keeping Tartaglia dangling. Some things never changed.

"Y'know, I wish they'd put an effing flatscreen up there," Clarke said. "I'm getting fed up with the view." His voice was laboured, words coming out a touch slurred and slower than his usual machine gun fire delivery. Tartaglia wondered if he had been wrong to come, wrong to trouble him with all of this.

"I'm surprised Sally-Anne hasn't rigged one up. She'd do anything for you, wouldn't she?"

Clarke half smiled. "Yeah, I'm a lucky sod, aren't I. Way more than I deserve. You should stop messing about. Get yourself a good woman like that."

"Quit fooling around, Trevor, and tell me what you think?"

Clarke turned his head slowly and glanced over at him. "You mean about Carolyn Steele?"

"Stop teasing, Trevor, and spill the beans. I can see right through you."

"OK. OK. We'll sort out the little matter of Carolyn later. What do I bloody think? Well . . . Other than I'd kill for a fag, and that I miss this flaming lark like nobody's business . . . I think . . . you're not looking in the right place."

"Are you sure you're up to this, Trevor? I can easily come back another time."

"Don't you bloody dare," Clarke growled. "This, and Sally-Anne, is all I got to keep me going." He paused and smacked his lips. "As I said, you've got it wrong somewhere."

"Tell me something I don't know."

"Fucking sod's law I smash m'self up when something interesting like this comes along." He sighed and reached over with his huge hand and patted Tartaglia's knee. "Nice of you to come and see me, though. I was wondering how you were all getting on without me." He shifted his shoulders stiffly in the bed in preparation and pursed his lips. "Well, let's start with Marion Spear. You're dead right to link her to the others."

Hearing Clarke say it brought instant relief. At least Clarke, the wisest of them all, didn't think he was mad. "But there's no real reason."

"Yeah there is, and you know it. If you want reminding or convincing again, she fell from a high spot and she matches the personality type. Just don't give me all that crap that bloody Kennedy said. He talks the talk and walks the walk but you know he don't know his arse from his elbow. What a fucking wanker he is." Clarke paused before going on. "Tell me this: why would a sweet girl like Marion Spear throw herself from a car park? She had her mum. She had a decent job. And she had a lover. Even if he is a fucking psycho, she didn't know that."

"Maybe he dumped her."

"Maybe. Maybe she was so gutted she wanted to top herself. Although from what you say, I think she'd have gone for something that takes less courage . . . like pills or something that makes less of a mess. And good girls like her . . . with a mum like that . . . they would have left a note, see? She was an only child. Stands to reason she's not going to make her final exit without telling her dear old mum why."

"What about the lover?"

Clarke gave a glimmer of a smile. "I'd put good money on him being Tom."

"You make it sound so simple."

Clarke winced and shook his head slowly, taking his time before he replied. "It's not rocket science. I just have a fresh pair of eyes, that's all. It's what Steele should be doing for you. Keeping her distance so she can give you that."

"She's keeping her distance, all right."

Clarke sighed. "Sam's done a good job finding that flatmate. You tell her so from me." He reached over again and squeezed Tartaglia's hand. "I miss you lot, you know."

Tartaglia puckered his lips, fighting hard not to show how sad he felt, wondering if Clarke knew that he would probably never be coming back. He had heard from Sally-Anne that morning that although Clarke wasn't paralysed, thank God, his legs were so damaged that the rest of his life was likely to be spent in a wheelchair or, at best, on crutches, unless the drugs and physio worked a miracle.

"You mentioned any of this to Carolyn?" Clarke said, after a moment.

"No. I haven't found the right moment."

"Yeah, she's not listening is she . . . with that pussy Kennedy buzzing around . . . whispering sweet nothings in her ear. I can just imagine what he's saying 'bout you and me. Won't be pretty."

"You think I should tell her? I'd like to get Angel in and see if either Nicola Slade or Adam Zaleski can identify him."

Clarke was momentarily silent again, rubbing his thick moustache slowly with his fingers as if it was good to still feel it there. "Don't think you need to rush it. Even if she agrees . . . which she may well not, way things are going. Say one of them picks him out of a line up. What's it going to give you? OK, so you now know he's the one . . . and he's effing guilty. What are you going to do about it? You're not going to bang him to rights without proper . . . hard evidence, are you? He's unlikely to go all wimpy and confess. You need something more. But I'm buggered if I know what."

"But if he was IDd, we'd have grounds for a search warrant."

Clarke shook his head and closed his eyes.

"Really, Trevor. I think I should come back another time," Tartaglia said after a moment.

Clarke jerked his head round, looking at Tartaglia out of the corner of his eye. "Fuck off with that, will you? If you bleeding bugger off . . . I'll never speak to you again. I swear."

His tone and expression was so fierce that Tartaglia decided to let it go. He could see that it meant more to Clarke than anything at that moment.

"What were you saying?" Clarke said, a minute later.

"About the search warrant."

Clarke grunted. "So what if you persuade Steele and some frigging judge to let you have a go? You know me, always like to assume the worst and work backwards.

What if you search his flat . . . and shop . . . and find nothing? Where are you then? From what you say, this Tom's a right clever bastard. He's not going to leave stuff lying around willy nilly for you to find. He'll have it stashed away. Safe. Somewhere not at his main address. Nah, I think you're going to have to sit tight . . . bide your time for a little longer. 'Til you see what comes out of this canal business."

Tartaglia stifled a sigh. Clarke was right, of course. To move things forward, they needed some sort of a break but he had no idea where, or in what shape, it was going to come.

"What about Kelly Goodhart, the woman on Hammersmith Bridge?" Tartaglia said.

"Like you . . . I'm pretty sure our Tom was in touch with her at some point. If you're lucky . . . and you've always had the luck of the devil . . . not like me . . . he may even turn out to be the bloke who ran away. Don't suppose the body's turned up?"

"Not yet."

"Typical. Father bloody Thames having fun with us as usual. But see here. You're so wrapped up in all this. You're forgetting about the three girls."

"Hardly."

Clarke shook his head. "Yeah you are. You've gotta go back to square one. Go over your tracks again. See what you've missed."

"We've checked everything, over and over, the schools, the clubs they belonged to, their friends, everything."

"Leave it out Mark, it's not good enough and you know it. You have to keep doing it . . . 'til you find the link . . . deliverymen . . . taxi drivers who may've taken them somewhere . . . dentists . . . doctors . . . all of that. You know the stuff. Even down to what bloody perfume and shampoo they used."

"You really think there's a link?"

"Course there is. Has to be." Clarke closed his eyes, wincing. He was sweating heavily and Tartaglia wondered if he should call a nurse. But he knew what Clarke's response would be. At least Clarke was still alive and his mind was all there. Tartaglia sat back in his chair as far as he could, so that Clarke couldn't see his face.

"He's not picking them at random . . . out of the phone book . . . is he?" Clarke continued, almost in a whisper. "Ask yourself again what they all have in common. Forget age. I agree with you. It's about personality. The sort of girls they were. What put them in his way. They all were depressed, for starters. Weren't they? At least three of them wanted to top themselves with him. If it wasn't on the internet . . . where do people like that meet one another?"

"We've tried the Samaritans but according to the phone records, Kelly Goodhart's the only one who ever called them."

"What about all the public phone boxes round where they lived? They may not have wanted to call from home."

Tartaglia groaned. With everything else on their plate, the job of checking the records going back over the last couple of years was the last thing they needed. They were still grappling with following up all the calls that had come in from *Crimewatch*. "True. But if so, they could have called from anywhere, near their school, near the tube, near a friend's house, et cetera, et cetera."

"C'mon, Mark. I know it's a long shot, but what else you got? Talk to Carolyn at least. See if she can persuade Cornish to give you more manpower."

"She won't pay any attention to me, I know."

Clarke exhaled loudly, his breath rasping. "Listen, mate, what's happened to you? This isn't the old Mark talking. What do you do with a woman? You, of all people, should know that."

Tartaglia smiled. "Try not to lose my temper, with this one at any rate."

"That would be nice for starters. But you've got to work on her . . . charm her . . . haven't you? They've all got their little ways. I know she's your boss and you're pissed off because she came in and stole the bloody case from under you. But that was that prick Cornish's doing. Problem is . . . you don't fancy her . . . so you can't be arsed to make peace. But you've got to swallow your pride 'n' have a go. You know I'm right."

"Easier said than done. She's as warm and approachable as a rattlesnake."

Clarke waved a hand slowly in the air dismissively. "That tough stuff's just an act. Believe me. Women are all the same underneath . . . 'part from the bloody muff divers, of course. Even your charm would be lost on them, I agree. But I'm pretty sure Carolyn doesn't bat for their side."

"Trevor, you're not listening. She's really taken against me, for some reason."

"She told you that, did she? Nah, didn't think so. You just need your heads knocking together, you two. She probably thinks . . . like the rest of us . . . that you're a smartarse . . . arrogant . . . prick . . . who believes he's God's gift. But you do have another side to you. When you can be fucked. That's why we all love you."

"That's nice. I'll try and remember that, when Steele has me out on my ear."

"As I said, you've got to try and charm the lady. Like that wanker Kennedy's been doing. He knows which side his bloody bread is buttered. Carolyn's not a bad sort underneath. You need to try and patch things up. Get her on your side."

"You think I should tell her that I saw Kennedy peeping?"

Clarke thought for a moment before shaking his head slowly. "Don't waste your time. But you ought to be keeping tabs on him. See what *he's* up to. The pansy deserves a good chinning, if you ask me. If he does it again, shop him to Cornish. Just make sure it's not you that sees him doing it. Going back to the case. My gut feel is that it's a botched job so far. There's no case on earth where there aren't clues. Believe me. You're either blind . . . and it's staring you in the bloody face . . . or you've been barking up the wrong tree."

"Thanks, Trevor. You've made my day."

Tartaglia was about to tell Clarke that it was time for him to go when his mobile rang. As usual, he'd forgotten to follow hospital instructions to switch it off. He saw from the screen that it was Steele. He flipped it open and listened to what she had to say. When he had finished he turned back to Trevor.

"Yes!" Tartaglia punched the air.

Clarke craned his head round to look at him. "Fucking cat that's got the cream now, eh? So, what's up?"

"We may have a breakthrough at last. We've got a fingerprint match from Hammersmith Bridge. It's a bloke called Sean Asher and he fits the description of the man seen with Kelly Goodhart. They're taking him in for questioning to his local nick and I've got to get over there right away."

Clarke sighed. "Bugger me. Forget everything I've just said. Lady Luck loves you, mate, even if Carolyn Steele doesn't. Maybe . . . sodding devil that you are . . . you're going to be bailed out. I'll be expecting an instant update, mind."

Tartaglia drew in his breath with a whistle and shook his head. "Sorry, Trevor. Looks like I'm going to be very busy for a while. Don't know when I'll find the time to drop by and see you again."

Clarke narrowed his eyes and gave him a lopsided grin. "You sod. Here's me in my state 'n' you're sat there winding me up. Thought you was interested in *me* and not this friggin' case. Now bugger off. Don't come back until you've made some progress. If not . . . I'll get

Sally-Anne to wheel me in my bed straight down to Barnes. I'll sort you idle plonkers out and there'll be blood on the carpet, I warn you."

CHAPTER
TWENTY-SEVEN

Sitting in meeting room three at Paddington Green Station, half-drunk cups of cold coffee littering the table in front of them, tape and camera still running after nearly two hours, it occurred to Tartaglia that he'd been bowled yet another googly. It was proving to be a long and frustrating night and the pressure of knowing that Steele and Kennedy were watching in another room on the video link, along with Dave Wightman, didn't help.

Sean Asher had been arrested on suspicion of murder but was proving impervious to any of the usual tactics. He seemed quite resigned to sitting there all night, if need be. Whatever Tartaglia and Nick Minderedes threw at him, he refused to admit to having killed Kelly Goodhart. He spoke quietly and emphatically and refused to raise his voice. He had even politely told his brief to shut up when she had tried to intervene at one point. Considering everything, Asher seemed extraordinarily calm and in control of himself. It was as if none of it mattered. He was innocent and he didn't need anybody to look out for him. He had all the self-righteousness of a martyr.

The room was hot and airless and beneath his jacket, Tartaglia could feel his shirt sticking to his skin, the collar uncomfortably tight. He wondered how much longer Asher would hold out. Asher sat calmly opposite, upright in his chair, dressed like a student in torn, faded jeans, trainers and a short-sleeved black T-shirt which showed off a muscular pair of arms. Judging by the smell coming from Asher's corner, he hadn't washed in days. He was in his early thirties, tall and well-built, with very short spiky brown hair that looked recently cut. Apart from the length of his hair, he fitted the general description of the man seen with Gemma Kramer. However, there was something soft, almost girlish about his round face, which was at odds with his muscular physique, and the nails of his nicotine-stained fingers were bitten to the quick, indicating a nervous, self-destructive disposition. He was not how Tartaglia had pictured Tom.

Asher's fingerprint had popped up on the system because he had been arrested for a minor affray during an anti-Iraq war demonstration a few years before. There was nothing else on the system and it was hardly a textbook background for a serial killer. It didn't feel right. Tom didn't seem the type to waste time with ideals. Tartaglia couldn't see him waving the flag for anybody other than himself and if he had, he certainly wouldn't be so stupid as to get arrested for something so trivial.

Before the interview had started, Steele had shown Tartaglia a copy of the most recent email from Tom. She was matter-of-fact about it, but he sensed beneath that cool exterior that it was getting to her and, thinking back again to the lines in the email, he felt full of doubt. He just couldn't square the tone and vocabulary of what he had read with the weak-faced man sitting in front of him.

The brief, Harriet Wilson, was a tired-looking woman in her mid-forties, with a mess of sandy hair threaded heavily with grey. She sat silently beside Asher, fanning her face with a notebook, eyes focused on a far corner of the room while Asher went through the answers for the umpteenth time. Yes, he had gone to Hammersmith Bridge with Kelly Goodhart. Yes, they had made a suicide pact to jump off the bridge together. But no, he hadn't tried to kill her. She had tried to take him with her instead. The witness was either lying or blind. The one thing he wouldn't volunteer was why he had wanted to kill himself in the first place.

"You really expect me to believe that she tried to pull you over with her? What a load of crap," Minderedes said, throwing his eyes up to the ceiling and shaking his head as if he couldn't stomach such a lie.

Asher shrugged. "Why not? It's the truth. She was in a right state, I can tell you. Didn't want to do it on her own." His voice was surprisingly high pitched for a tall man, nasal, almost reedy, and he had a light northern accent.

"But according to you, you let her."

"Couldn't help it. As I said, when I got there, I bottled out. Found I couldn't go through with it."

"You say you changed your mind," Tartaglia said, cutting in. "You still haven't told us why."

Asher raised his thin brows. "Why? I got cold feet, like. It's allowed, isn't it? Hadn't signed a ruddy contract."

Late at night, forty feet up on a freezing, windy bridge, with a total stranger, Tartaglia could almost sympathise. But Tom was a clever bastard and it was the only story that made sense, other than genuine innocence.

Minderedes leaned across the table with his hard man face. He too was sweating heavily, his usually fluffy dark hair plastered back on his skull. With his strange yellow-green eyes and beetley black brows, he actually looked quite menacing.

"Pull the other one, Tom. It's got bells on it," he said.

"Why do you keep calling me Tom? My name's Sean."

"Silly me. I'm the one who's confused again," Minderedes said. "You told her your name was Chris, didn't you?"

"Right. I explained that."

"You said you didn't want her to know who you really were, in case she was some sort of nutter."

"That's right."

"But you're the nutter, aren't you?"

Asher shook his head. "Christ, you people are so cynical. It's sad."

"Goes with the job. If you saw what we see every day . . . but there, I'm forgetting that you do."

Asher's expression hardened. "If I want to do away with myself, that's my business. Nobody else's. And it don't make me a nutter."

"It does, when you try to involve someone else."

"I didn't 'try to involve her', as you say. She was acting under her own free will. That's not against the law, is it, or is Big Brother already onto that little loophole? Fuck free will. Just do what you're told. Is that it?"

"You think it's a loophole, persuading people to kill themselves in front of you, pushing them off when they don't want to do it? In our book, it's murder."

Asher shook his head slowly as if he found the question incredible. "I didn't push her and I didn't have to persuade her. It was what she wanted to do. How many more times do I have to say it?"

Minderedes banged the table with his fist and stood up. "As many as it will take until you tell us the truth, matey."

"I give up. You folk are worse than on the box." Asher folded his arms tightly in front of him, clamping his lips shut as if there was nothing more to be said. He was mistaken if he thought they were going to let it go at that.

"I've had enough of your fucking stories," Minderedes said, and turned his back on Asher, striding over to the tiny barred window in the corner and appearing to look out. It was a good dramatic gesture until you knew that there was only the car park outside.

Tartaglia had so far taken a back seat for most of the proceedings and let Minderedes have his head.

He was an excellent detective and generally good at interviews, usually because he knew how to get up the interviewee's nose to the point where they let something slip out of sheer annoyance. But Asher seemed impervious. It was time for a more subtle approach.

"OK, Sean. Let's say we believe you for a moment. We've read the emails between you and Kelly Goodhart. Why was she so wary of you? What was she scared of?"

"I told you, she thought I was someone else."

"Who?"

"Search me."

"You obviously said something to reassure her when you spoke on the phone, otherwise she would have never agreed to meet you."

"Don't remember."

"That's not good enough, you know. Unless you can convince us otherwise, we're looking at a charge of murder here."

The brief sprang to life. "Hang on a minute. We're going round in circles here. You don't even have a body."

"Come on, Mrs Wilson," Tartaglia said. "Don't get technical. You don't think Kelly Goodhart would have survived, do you?" Wilson stared blankly at him. "It's only a matter of time before her body turns up."

She sighed. "OK, Inspector. Say it does. Even in your wildest dreams, you can't turn this into a charge of murder."

"Can't we? The witness saw him struggle with Mrs Goodhart. She said she thought he pushed her over."

"Inspector, I don't want to teach my grandmother to suck eggs but you know there's all the difference in the world between someone thinking something might have happened and it actually happening. All you have is suspicion."

"Yes, reasonable suspicion in the circumstances."

Wilson shook her head. "As I see it, we have a set of circumstances here which can be interpreted at least two ways."

Tartaglia stifled a sigh, wiping his brow with the back of his hand. Wilson was right, of course. Somehow, just by articulating it, she had managed to deflate even the smallest bubble of hope. They had nothing at that juncture that would even get past the CPS, unless of course Asher confessed, and it looked very unlikely that he was going to oblige.

"My client is trying to be helpful, Inspector," Wilson continued. "But if you insist on pushing this murder lark without any proper evidence, I'm going to have to advise him to stop talking to you."

Tartaglia continued to look at Sean, who was staring down at the table in front of him, expression fixed as if he was no longer engaged in the conversation.

"Help me, Sean, and I'll help you." He waited for a moment, studying Asher's blank moon of a face, wondering what was going on in his mind. "See here, Sean, we're looking for somebody who was in contact with Kelly Goodhart and wanted to watch her die. Sick

341

though that is, he wouldn't just leave it there. If she got cold feet, like you say happened to you, he'd damn well make sure she did it, whether she wanted to or not." There was still no reaction from Asher. "How would you feel if somebody had forced you to go through with it? Not because they wanted company in the last moments of their life, like Mrs Goodhart, but because they're warped and twisted and get turned on by it. This bloke is sick. He gets his kicks from watching innocent people die." Asher looked up, an almost imperceptible softening about the corners of his eyes. "If you're not this man, as you say you're not, we need to find him." Still watching Asher, Tartaglia let the sentence hang before continuing. "We know he's done it before. Not with mature women like Mrs Goodhart, who were sure about what they were doing, but with young, defenceless, depressed little girls."

"Don't start trying to shift the ground, Inspector," Mrs Wilson said. "We're here to talk about only one thing and that's what happened on Hammersmith Bridge."

"This is the bloke in the papers, right?" Asher said, ignoring her, looking puzzled.

"We think so," Tartaglia said. "Please try and remember what Kelly Goodhart told you. It's very important."

Asher scratched his bottom lip. For a moment it looked as if he was about to come out with something meaningful. Then he shook his head. "I don't remember, I'm sorry."

342

Tartaglia sighed. He didn't believe him for a second. "OK. Let's take a break here. Interview suspended at ten fifty p.m."

He wanted to give Asher time to reflect. He had seen the hesitation in his eyes, the slight unbending as though he had finally caught his interest. Hopefully, what he had said had struck a chord. On a more practical note, he also needed a pee, some fresh air and some more coffee to keep him going. And if he was lucky, he'd also be able to nip out back for a quick fag before Steele caught him.

"So, we've got nothing so far," Steele said, in an almost accusatory voice looking from Tartaglia to Minderedes and back again.

"Certainly nothing to hold him on," Minderedes said, shrugging. "Unless we turn up something juicy when we search his flat, that is."

They were in another meeting room along the corridor from where Asher was being held. Steele, Tartaglia, Wightman and Minderedes were grouped around the small table, coffee and a half-eaten plate of stale sandwiches from the canteen in front of them. Kennedy stood behind, as if he wanted to separate himself from proceedings, leaning against the wall, hands in pockets, his expression unreadable.

The room was just as airless and stiflingly hot, thick with the sour smell of stale sweat and tired bodies, the occasional whiff of aftershave coming from Minderedes whenever he leaned across for his coffee or a sandwich. It was enough to give anyone a headache. Still dying for a smoke, Tartaglia wondered how much longer Steele would keep them there, pointlessly going round and round in circles. He wanted to get back to Asher. He knew he had something interesting to say.

The only surprising thing was how silent Kennedy was. Never one normally to hold back with his opinions, it almost seemed as if he wasn't there. Either he was deliberately trying not to intrude, which was uncharacteristic, or he was stumped and didn't want to admit it.

Steele turned to Tartaglia. "Mark?"

Tartaglia was fast coming to the conclusion that Asher wasn't Tom but there was no point in telling them that. Gut feel counted for nothing in that room and he could already hear what Steele would say: "Give me facts, not feelings". Everything was black and white to her.

"I agree with Nick," Tartaglia said, trying to focus on concrete matters, things that could be explained in a few simple words. "We've all seen the emails. Kelly Goodhart wanted to kill herself. Asher just happened to be there for the ride, according to him, and we can't prove otherwise. The witness was quite far away when she saw the struggle. She thought she saw him push Mrs Goodhart over the bridge. But she isn't a hundred per cent sure. It won't stand up to cross-examination, if it ever gets that far, which is unlikely. No, whether Asher really is Tom or not, if he sticks to his story he'll be home and dry."

"Dave? Have you got anything to add?"

Wightman shook his head. It had all been said already.

"What about you, Patrick," Steele asked, looking over her shoulder at Kennedy. "What do you think?"

Kennedy frowned and pursed his lips, running his fingers through his thick hair for a moment, as if giving the matter deep consideration. "Well, it's tricky," he said slowly. "Given what I've just seen, Asher's not the type to respond to pressure. I watched him closely. If anything, strong-arm tactics seemed to reinforce his statement of innocence. Now, you could read that two ways: either he's a tough nut, who's worked out that if he sticks to the story, you have nothing on him; or he's probably telling the truth." It was stating the obvious but somehow Kennedy made it sound as if he had invented it.

"Do you think this is our man?" Steele asked, still looking at Kennedy as if she was hoping for something more.

Again Kennedy paused for thought, then shook his head. "Impossible to tell. It's all academic anyway, if you can't hold him."

Steele sighed, locked her fingers and stretched her arms out in front as if her shoulders were stiff. "We can't let him go yet," she said. "He's all we've got. If he doesn't want to talk, we'd better search his flat and see if we can turn something up. Can you sort it out, Nick?"

Minderedes was about to reply when there was a knock and Harriet Wilson put her head around the door, catching Tartaglia's eye.

"Mr Asher would like to talk to you, Inspector. Off the record."

"Off the record, what does he think this is?" Steele said. "A blooming free session of counselling?"

Wilson shrugged. "Don't shoot the messenger. I don't even know what it is he wants to say. But he's said he will only speak to the Inspector alone."

"Just me?" Tartaglia asked.

"Yes," she said. "Doesn't even want me there. I think he's actually trying to be cooperative," she added, seeing Steele shaking her head. "If you assume innocence for a change rather than instant guilt, why don't you give it a whirl?"

"Why should we?" Steele said flatly. "He's in here on suspicion of murder. We're not at his beck and call."

"I know it's nothing to do with me," Wilson said. "But what have you got to lose? The time's ticking away and you know that you've got nothing to hold him here."

"We haven't searched his flat yet."

"If he's innocent, like he says, you won't find anything and I doubt whether he'll want to speak to you anymore after that." She looked around the room at the watching faces. "Look, what harm can it do, just a few minutes of the Inspector's time. If you don't learn anything, you can always go back to plan A, that is if you have a plan A."

After a bit of bartering they had compromised. No tape and no video, but Tartaglia, now sitting opposite Asher, alone in the room, was allowed to make notes. If, in the end, he was wrong and Asher turned out to be Tom, it would be the strangest of games. He had brought Asher a sandwich and a cup of coffee, both of which sat on the table untouched.

"We spoke on the phone a couple of times," Asher said quietly. "At first she was very wary, kept trying to catch me out. I began to think that it wasn't worth the ticket. But gradually she came round a bit."

"Why do you think that was?"

Asher paused for a moment, as if he was trying to think back. "Well, she said my voice was different, for starters."

"In what way different?"

"Don't know. Different tone maybe. I got the feeling the other bloke spoke posh, like the people who read the news on the telly. She thought I was putting on my accent at first."

"You persuaded her you weren't?"

"Not to start with. Asked me where I come from and all sorts of other things like that, family, school, you know. It was like being interviewed for a bloody job. I had to tell her my name's not Chris. That put her off for a bit. Then she rang me again with some more questions."

"Did she tell you anything about herself?"

"Said she was a lawyer. That didn't surprise me, the way she kept asking the bleeding questions. Really pissed me off, it did. But when she told me her husband had died in the tsunami, I felt sorry for her. Then she told me about the other bloke and I understood why she had to check me out."

"This was all on the phone?"

Asher nodded.

"For someone who was so wary to start off with, it sounds as if she was easily convinced, don't you think? How did she know that you weren't the other man?"

"Gut feel, I suppose," Asher said, almost a little too quickly. "You just make your mind up about someone."

Tartaglia stared hard at him, making Asher look away. "There's more, isn't there, Mr Asher?"

Asher was silent for a moment before replying. "Yeah. It's what I didn't want to say before." He looked up at Tartaglia. "Do you have a fag?"

In spite of the no smoking sign on the wall, Tartaglia offered him one and lit one himself. Asher took the first pull as if it were his last, then leaned back hard against his chair, making it creak. He sighed heavily. "I suppose you'd better know. She wouldn't meet me at all, until I told her why I wanted to top myself."

Again Asher was silent, as if something was weighing heavily on his mind. His face was slack, mouth half open, eyes vacant as if he were somewhere else.

"Well?" Tartaglia said.

Asher looked up. "I used to be a PE teacher, until recently, that is. My last job was at a posh girls' school out in Surrey." He paused, filling his lungs with more smoke. "I made the stupid mistake of falling for one of the girls. It was nothing smutty," he added quickly, catching the look on Tartaglia's face. "Nothing like that, Inspector. I'm not a paedophile. Really I'm not. All we did was a bit of kissing and cuddling, that's all."

"I've heard that before."

348

"I can see what you're thinking but you're wrong. They were all wrong. Her name's Sarah and I loved her, you see. I really loved her and wanted to marry her when she was old enough. She was fifteen going on twenty-five. A beautiful young thing with a wise head on young shoulders. She was a lot wiser than me, I can tell you."

Asher took another deep drag on the cigarette, blowing the smoke into rings, which curled up towards the strip light above. "To cut a long story short, her parents found out, went to see the bloody headmistress and I was sacked. It's not fair, is it?"

"What, being sacked?"

"No. I didn't mind about that so much. What's unfair is you can't choose who you love, can you?"

Tartaglia saw the pain in Asher's eyes and nodded. How right Asher was. The pursuit of love, nothing sensible or reasoned about it, something that, try as you might, was impossible to control: the madness; the highs; the terrible lows. He thought back, remembering all those stupid mistakes and errors of judgement that he'd made, the time and energy wasted, hope burning strong, followed by disillusionment, finding that he'd been chasing after a fantasy. The cold light of day that flooded in afterwards was always so harsh and unforgiving. But he had never been totally desperate and without hope. He had never lost all sense of himself or his trust in the goodness of life and the future. Perhaps he had never let himself go to the brink, never completely put himself on the line. Some people were just more highly tuned than others. Although he wasn't like Sean Asher, he could still feel for him and pity his pain.

"You wanted to kill yourself because of her?" Tartalia asked.

Asher nodded, nibbling hard at a piece of loose skin around one of his nails. His finger was bleeding but he didn't seem to care. "Her parents took her away from school and sent her abroad for the summer. She got over it quickly but I didn't. Still haven't," he added after a moment.

"We'll have to check this out, you know."

Asher shrugged. "Be my guest. I've nothing to hide now. I thought she still loved me, you see, that it was only a matter of time before we could be together. Then . . ."

"Then?"

Asher sighed. "Then she wrote to me. They call it a Dear John letter, don't they? Except mine was addressed to Dear Sean. It was horrible, like another person talking, someone I didn't know. Maybe her mother made her write it but she signed it. And it was her writing. It did me in, I can tell you. When Kelly asked to see proof of why I wanted to top myself, to see that I was genuine, like, I sent her the letter. Then she understood."

"We didn't come across anything like that in her flat when we went through her things."

"She sent it back to me, didn't she. I've still got it and I can show you, if you want."

"Please. Why didn't you tell us this before?"

"None of you were listening, were you? Too busy trying to make me confess to something I hadn't done. I thought you wouldn't understand about Sarah, thought you'd judge me, call me a fucking paedophile and lock me up. Anyway, it's private. It's my business, nobody else's."

Asher was probably right about how they might have reacted earlier. Tartaglia couldn't help respecting his reasons for wanting to keep quiet, relieved that at least he now appeared to be telling the truth. "So, getting back to Kelly Goodhart. You managed to convince her that you were genuine."

Asher nodded.

"Do you remember anything else she may have said about the other man who contacted her?"

"I know she never met him. But she said she thought she could trust him and he proved her wrong."

"Those were her exact words?"

"Maybe I haven't got it quite right but something along those lines. We'd met up, you see. She said she wanted to see me, face to face, like. It was the last hurdle she put me through. We went to a café just off the North End Road. I showed her my passport, just so she'd know I was who I said I was. She said the other bloke had freaked her out. She said he'd been playing with her, egging her on, messing with her head. She could see I wasn't into that sort of thing."

From what Asher had said, it sounded like Tom had tried to get to Kelly Goodhart. "Did she tell you how he was doing this?"

"No."

"Is there anything else you can tell me about him?"

"Sorry, no."

"Was there anything else she said?"

"She told me she'd been born and brought up a Catholic and she asked me if I was religious. When I said I'm not, haven't been to church since I was a kid, she seemed relieved. Said that religion was a disguise for all sorts of evil things. That people use it to get what they want. It was just after we'd been talking about the other bloke but I don't know if it had anything to do with him."

"You're sure there's nothing else?"

Asher took a final drag on his cigarette, which was almost down to the butt, and dropped it into his cup of coffee, where it hissed momentarily. "I've told you everything, I swear. She was a sharp lady, Inspector. Real brainy and nice. I'm sorry she's gone, truly I am."

"Why didn't you try and talk her out of it?"

"Because I understood her. I knew what she were feeling, what she was going through. She wanted to end it and I respected that. I could see that the light had gone out for her and it were how I felt at the time too. She just had a darn sight more courage than me."

They would still have to search Asher's flat just to make sure, but Tartaglia was convinced by now that nothing would come of it. At least in the meantime, whatever Steele and Kennedy thought, he knew somehow he had made progress.

Dave Wightman drew up along the road from the address in West Hampstead that Tartaglia had given him, and killed the engine. They had let Sean Asher go just before midnight and Wightman had driven quickly over from Paddington Green so that he was ready and waiting for Steele when she arrived home. If Kennedy was with her, Tartaglia had told him to keep watch and take notes. If not, he could go home. When Tartaglia had explained the situation and told him what Clarke had said to him earlier in the hospital, Wightman was only too happy to be involved and trusted with the task. If that's what the boss wanted, that's what he would do, no questions asked. He respected both Clarke and Tartaglia more than anybody and he had no liking for Kennedy. He seemed so full of himself and there was also something rather odd about him, although he couldn't put his finger on exactly what it was. However, he wasn't entirely surprised to find that Kennedy was a bloody peeping Tom. In his view, all perverts deserved to be outed. Never mind that Steele would be hopping mad if she found out. She had a real blind spot where Kennedy was concerned and if something peculiar was going on, it needed to be exposed.

Wightman looked at his watch. It was well past midnight. Luckily, he had nobody waiting at home for him, apart from his mum, and she was used to his erratic hours and would have been in bed, asleep, long ago. He listened to Heart FM for about ten minutes, until he saw Steele's car coming down the road and switched off the radio. He ducked down as she passed and waited for her to get out. She was on her own and he watched her park a little further along the road, walk to the front door and go in.

* * *

Tartaglia had left Paddington Green before any of them and in ten minutes he was home. He felt wired, thoughts buzzing in his mind. Even though it would be an early start next morning, there was no point in trying to go to sleep yet. He switched on the music system, not bothering to check what CD was in the machine, opened a bottle of Gavi which had been chilling in the fridge, and poured himself a large glass. It tasted a little sharp but he didn't care. Unbuttoning his shirt, he walked around the room with his glass of wine, thinking about Sean Asher. Something Asher had said kept niggling at him but try as he might, he couldn't think what it was. He tried replaying the interview in his mind, word by word, seeing Asher sitting in front of him, picturing his expressions and reactions. But it still wouldn't come. From experience he knew not to try and winkle it out, no point in trying to force it. It would come when it was ready, if at all.

There was only one message on the answer machine, from Nicoletta, again insisting that he come to lunch. He was positive now that she was hatching a plot and, irritated by her persistence, he deleted the message, went into the bathroom, turned on the shower and got undressed. As soon as the water was hot, he stepped in, turned the tap on full to get maximum pressure and moved the temperature gauge up a little until the heat was almost unbearable. The cubicle filled with steam almost immediately and he took several deep breaths, shutting his eyes, trying to clear his thoughts.

Thinking of the second email that Steele had received that day, he wondered how she was feeling, going back to her flat on her own. He couldn't believe that the words had left her untouched, that she wouldn't be worried. But there was no point in offering help where it wasn't wanted. He grabbed a bottle of shampoo from the rack and massaged a small amount into his scalp. It felt good and he stood rubbing it in, thanking his lucky stars that his thick hair showed no signs of thinning as he got older, unlike his brother-in-law John, Nicoletta's husband, who had lost most of his hair in the space of five years.

When he had finished, he got out and had just started to dry himself when he heard his mobile ringing in the sitting room. He picked it up just before voicemail kicked in and heard Wightman's voice at the other end.

"I did what you said, sir," Wightman said. "She came home on her own and went inside. I waited, like you asked me to, and about ten minutes later, Kennedy showed. He hung around for a bit in the street and then went round the back, just like you said. Her lights were still on and he was gone a good quarter of an hour. Then he came out again and drove off."

"You wrote all of this down?"

"Yeah, with the exact times. I waited a bit, just to make sure he wouldn't come back and, when he didn't, I thought I'd go and take a look round the back. There's a gate halfway down the side passage but the lock's broken, so anyone can go through. Her bathroom and kitchen's down there. She'd left the lights blazing all over the place. The blind was drawn in the bathroom but I could see right into the kitchen."

"What about her bedroom?"

"It's round the back. She had the curtains drawn but they don't quite meet and I could see her quite clearly lying in bed. I think she had the telly on because I could hear the noise in the background. He must have stood there, watching her."

"Good work. I had a feeling he'd go there again, particularly after seeing her this evening. He just can't resist."

"What are you going to do, sir?"

"I'd like you to do the same tomorrow night and I think you should take somebody with you. If Kennedy does it again, I want you to call me and we'll bring him in. No point in messing about any longer."

"No, and he bloody deserves what's coming."

CHAPTER
TWENTY-EIGHT

Tom pushed away the remains of his smoked chicken and avocado salad and sipped his glass of wine, watching the tail-end of the lunchtime crowd from his seat in the far corner of the wine bar. Most of the men were dressed in badly cut suits, with loud ties and gallons of hair gel. The women looked even more ridiculous, perched on stools around the small high tables, their short skirts hugging their fat thighs, tits pushed up and out, the heels of their shoes so high they could barely walk. Faces lathered in slap, they had "fuck me" written all over them. It was all so bloody obvious, so fake and nasty, but the men seemed to be gagging for it like stupid, bouncy little puppies, lapping up every giggle, every cheap sideways glance and calculated flick of the dyed hair. In the normal course of events, he'd have been long gone. But he had more important things to think about.

The fever had passed and he felt calm again, satiated for the moment. He'd been stupid with Yolanda, although he reminded himself how much worse it might have been if the little bitch had lived to tell the tale. Nobody must ever be allowed to get away. No point in beating himself up about it now but he must never do something so risky and badly thought out again. He'd been up for most of the past night, unable to sleep. He'd watched part of a war film on TV and then, when that was over, listened to some music, until the fucking arsehole of an estate agent who lived next door had banged on the wall and shouted so loudly that he was forced finally to turn it off.

He felt tired today but at least he had come to a decision. It was time to go away for a bit, take a long holiday until things quietened down. There were places in the world where you could live cheaply, where life was cheap, where nobody would notice if you were there one day and gone the next. It would be a different game but it might be amusing for a while. Certainly different. Variety was the spice of life, according to someone in the know and it was time for a change. Lots of people took sabbaticals these days, so why shouldn't he? Anyway, he had a fair bit of money put by in the bank and he could afford it. He would find a safe place for his little treasures and then he would be off somewhere exotic and hot. It would be good to lounge around on a beach, drink margaritas and get a tan, somewhere where there were lots of backpackers and tourists coming and going, lots of slags looking for a bit of tawdry romance and a quick shag, where the police were crass amateurs at the game.

Just thinking about it got the old buzz going again. It would be a new beginning and he would reinvent himself. Like a magician, he would disappear in a puff of smoke and leave the London lot chasing their arses, with nothing to find. The thought made him feel warm

358

inside and there was no point in hanging about, now he'd made up his mind. His grandmother could rattle around in the old house on her own as much as she liked once he'd gone. He didn't give a flying fuck what she thought and it would serve her bloody right.

She was showing herself more frequently now, for some reason. Last night when he'd gone over to put Yolanda's hair in one of her little tea caddies, she had appeared on the first floor landing, peering down angrily at him over the banister as if questioning his right to be there. He had every fucking right. It was his house, not hers any longer, he had shouted. But she ignored him as usual. She was wearing her favourite navy and cream spotted silk dress, the one which she usually put on when friends came round for bridge, and he could see the bright spots of rouge on her cheeks and the hard line of crimson lipstick on her shrunken lips. Even down in the hall, he was aware of her cloying scent and she seemed so solid for a change that he was tempted to rush upstairs and try and touch her. That would give the old bag a fright and put the wind up her. But before he had the chance, she disappeared like smoke in the wind as if she had the chance, she disappeared like smoke in the wind as if she had never been there at all.

The bitch would get a shock once she realised that he had gone and he decided to look on the net for tickets that afternoon. It wouldn't take long to pack his things. But first there were some other practical issues to deal with and he took a pen from his pocket and started to make a short list on the back of an envelope.

Along with all the boring mundane items, there was that one last thing he had to take care of. In the normal course of events he wouldn't have bothered. It was also highly risky, but what the hell. He wrote down the bullet point, underlining it and marking it with a large question mark. But he knew that he had to do it. The plan had been taking shape in his mind over the last few days and it would be so, so simple, like taking candy from a baby. He saw it as his final curtain call, his swan song. It would be good to go out with a bang.

CHAPTER
TWENTY-NINE

Growing increasingly annoyed, Tartaglia paced up and down the towpath alongside the Regent's Canal, near the spot where they now knew Yolanda Garcia had been assaulted. It was past four o'clock in the afternoon and Steele and Kennedy were nearly twenty minutes late. Steele had called him earlier to say that she and Kennedy wanted to view the scene and he had no choice but to wait, although what earthly purpose it would serve was beyond him. So far, Kennedy had drawn little meaningful conclusion from the other crime scenes he had visited and Steele only echoed whatever he said. If they didn't turn up soon, it would be dark and there would be next to nothing to see.

Samples taken from Yolanda's body had been rushed through as a priority and the computer had come up with two DNA matches: Lee O'Connor and Wayne Burns, eighteen and nineteen respectively, both with form as long as your arm for a whole range of crimes, including burglary, mugging and assault. They had been arrested and questioned, each crumbling like a house of cards in the face of the overwhelming forensic evidence, each blaming the other for what had happened. Apart from that, the important details of their stories more or less matched. They explained how, high on a cocktail of alcohol and drugs, they had found Yolanda wandering along the towpath and given her what, in their view, she was looking for. However, they both vehemently denied having had anything to do with her death. At least one piece of the puzzle solved. It had never seemed psychologically probable to Tartaglia that Tom had raped Yolanda before killing her.

The spot where Tartaglia was standing was only about half a mile from where Yolanda's body had turned up. But it might have been in another city. Unlike the area around Little Venice, with its expensive houses, tall trees and glossy, colourful houseboats, this stretch of the canal was seedy and barren, surrounded by the backs of tall office buildings and dilapidated council housing. The few houseboats moored along the bank were patched and tatty, some barely habitable. A series of small bridges intersected the canal at irregular intervals and the towpath seemed to be primarily used as a local cut-through by a mixture of cyclists, dog-walkers and joggers. Even in the fading daylight it was forbidding. Wondering why anyone dared to venture along it after dark, he sighed at the thought of a young girl, on her own and new to the city, trying to get home that way.

Tartaglia was almost on the point of giving up, when he spotted Steele, walking along the towpath towards him in the gloom. She seemed to be on her own.

"Sorry I'm late," she said briskly, coming up to where he was standing. "The traffic was horrendous and I had trouble finding a place to park."

"I thought Dr Kennedy was gracing us with his presence," he said, failing to keep the sarcasm out of his voice.

"I decided to come alone," she replied curtly, offering no further explanation for the change in plan.

"Are we sure this is where she was attacked?" she asked, looking towards the area along the path where the SOCOs were working.

"According to O'Connor and Burns. They live nearby and seem to know the towpath pretty well."

She sighed heavily, as if imagining what had happened. "Pretty grim, isn't it?"

"Not where I'd choose to die, certainly."

"Are you sure we can't do the pair of them for her murder?"

He shook his head. "A lock of her hair's missing and there's GHB in her system. Who else could it be? Newlands Park have the computers from the library where she sent her emails. They're treating it as a priority and I expect they'll show she was in contact with Tom, like the others."

She nodded, as if convinced. "But we still have no idea how Tom had originally come across any of them."

"No."

"Nor how he found Yolanda?"

"No," he replied again. "Neither O'Connor nor Burns saw anybody, although given the state they had been in, they might not have noticed someone watching from afar."

"But Tom killed her along here?"

"It can't be far and it's got to be towards Maida Vale. O'Connor and Burns ran off the other way and they say they didn't see anybody."

Steele followed his eye then turned and gazed in the opposite direction. "Perhaps she was killed where her body turned up? I know that stretch with all the houseboats, it's . . ."

"Unlikely," Tartaglia interrupted before any further speculation. "This section of the towpath stops at the Maida Tunnel, further along there." He jerked his head in the general direction. "To reach the other side, you have to go up some very steep steps and walk across a series of roads. I don't see Tom risking that with her, do you?"

Steele frowned, as if irritated and didn't reply.

"We'd better get a move on, otherwise there'll be nothing to see," he said impatiently, noticing how quickly the light was dimming.

They walked together in silence towards the barrier of the inner cordon. She seemed lost in thought, perhaps regretting having come. He had no idea why she had bothered to make the journey. Maybe she just wanted an excuse to get out of the office.

"What was Tom doing down here?" she said quietly, as if talking to herself. "It doesn't make any sense. All the other crime scenes have been places he could control." She stopped and folded her arms, going through the motions of studying the scene in front of her. "So, the girl's attacked over there, O'Connor and Burns run off and leave her, and along comes Tom to murder her. It's all a bit coincidental, don't you think?" She turned to Tartaglia with a sceptical look.

"I don't believe in coincidences either," he said, a little sharply. "I'm sure he wasn't coming along here by chance. He must have known where to find her."

She nodded slowly, her eyes focusing on a distant point further down the canal as if lost in thought. "Which way's the tube?" she asked, after a moment.

"Over there." He pointed behind them. "O'Connor and Burns say she was heading that way when they met her."

She rubbed her lips thoughtfully. "So, she wasn't going to meet Tom. She was on her way home."

"That's what we think. We know that she left her employer's house between seven and a quarter to eight. If O'Connor and Burns are to be believed, it was close to ten when they came across her down here. Which gives her ample time to have met Tom."

She looked at him questioningly. "So what's your theory?"

Surprised that she actually seemed to want his opinion, Tartaglia said: "From what we know, Tom plans his killings very carefully. There's nothing opportunistic in the way he chooses his victims. So it's fair to assume that Yolanda was the intended victim, that Tom had selected her in his usual way and that the contact followed a similar pattern to the other girls."

She gave him a curt nod of agreement. "That seems logical."

"Let's say she had agreed to meet him somewhere near here. I imagine the choice of location will be his. It's a pretty seedy area and . . ."

"Low risk from his point of view," she added.

"Yes. It's pretty transient and people are unlikely to remember him, or at least that's what he was hoping. The meeting place would have to be somewhere very close to the canal for her to consider coming this way. She had a considerable amount of alcohol in her bloodstream so we're checking all the pubs and bars in the area."

She didn't say anything for a moment, as if she were thinking it all through very carefully. "But why was she coming along here without Tom? If they had met, I'm amazed he let her out of his sight."

It was the one thing that had puzzled Tartaglia too. As he gazed at the scummy, dark brown slick of water, he had a flash of inspiration and turned to Steele. "Maybe he was late. Or she got cold feet for some reason, either before they met or after."

She raised her eyebrows. "The one that got away, you mean?"

"It's the only thing that stacks up, given what we know about him."

She looked thoughtful. "That would have made him very angry indeed. Very, very angry. He would be panicking as well, worrying about failing and also worrying about leaving a trail. He would have to find her and finish her off somehow."

"If she twigged what he was up to and was trying to get away, she'd have been in a blind panic, not thinking straight. It may also explain why she was desperate enough to come along here after dark."

Steele nodded, as if that was what she was thinking too. "He has to find her. He can't let her get away . . ."

"Whatever his motivation, he must have worked out which way she went. He either found her after she had been attacked or it's possible that he even watched, waiting for his moment."

She sighed. "If he saw her being attacked, it would mean nothing to him. Someone like him has no concept of mercy. It's all just a despicable game."

He looked at her a little surprised. He could tell from the bitterness in her tone that she wasn't just thinking of Yolanda but of the emails and she seemed to be taking what had happened by the canal personally. If so, it was a brave move to come down there and try to get close to what had happened. If she wasn't careful, it would end up haunting her. Sometimes it was vital to keep a distance but after everything that had gone between them, he bit back the desire to say so.

She folded her arms and turned to him. "So where do you think he killed her?

He looked along the ribbon of water again, towards the dark entrance of the Maida Tunnel. "I don't think he'd have gotten far with her. According to the post mortem results, she had a significant amount of GHB in her system and there was very little water in her lungs. So she must have been unconscious, or almost unconscious, when she was put into the canal. My guess is that she was killed somewhere very close to where we're standing now."

Steele followed his gaze, her expression distant as if she were picturing it all in her mind. "I agree with you," she said quietly, after a moment. "He probably had something entirely different planned for her but he ran out of options and was forced to improvise."

He agreed. "I think there's a very good chance that somebody saw something. If so, we'll find them."

"You say Harry Angel was out all that Wednesday afternoon?" Donovan asked, trying to contain her excitement.

"Most definitely." Jenny Evans gave an emphatic toss of her small, round head. "I've been off sick with the flu, otherwise I'd have called you sooner."

Donovan was sitting at the small bar at the back of Wild Oats, an organic food shop immediately next door to Harry Angel's bookshop in Ealing. The shop smelled deliciously of a mixture of coffee and freshly baked bread and Jenny had just presented her with a large cappuccino on the house. With short, fluffy grey hair, Jenny looked to be in her mid-fifties. Her pink checked shirt-sleeves were rolled up and she wore a spotless white apron over a calf-length brown tweed skirt and flat slip-on shoes. Her manner was reassuringly precise and down-to-earth and she reminded Donovan of an old-fashioned school matron.

Taking a sip of rich coffee through the thick layer of froth, Donovan asked: "You are sure about this? That it was *that* Wednesday afternoon, I mean. When I came in here before, nobody remembered anything."

Jenny planted a plump, bare forearm on the slate counter and gave a sideways glance at the scrawny, scantily dressed young girl standing at the front of the shop, helping a customer to some cheese. "They wouldn't, would they? It's not their shop and half the time their mind's on other things, usually boys and pop music. All I can say is that it's a jolly good thing the till does all the adding and working out the change for them, otherwise I don't know where we'd be. At least someone had the sense not to throw away your card and to leave it on my desk for when I came back."

"Do you remember what time Mr Angel went out, Mrs Evans?"

Jenny gave her a brisk smile. "It's Miss Evans, but please call me Jenny. Everyone does. Harry came in and got a sandwich and a coffee about one o'clock and said he was popping out for a bit. He asked if we could keep an eye on things."

"What did he mean by that?"

"He gets deliveries from time to time. I was fond of his grandfather, even though he was a tricky old sod, and I don't mind signing for things and taking them in if we're not too busy. Although I draw the line at being expected to mind the shop, without even being asked, for the whole afternoon, like that Wednesday."

"So, he was gone a long time?" Donovan said, amazed that Angel had had the gall to pretend otherwise when Tartaglia had questioned him. Perhaps he thought that they wouldn't bother to check.

"Yes. I remember distinctly, he didn't come back until well after five. I was hopping mad by then. He hadn't told me he'd be gone long and I had a constant stream of his customers coming in here all afternoon, asking if we knew where he was. Naturally, thinking he'd be back soon, I told them to wait or come back later. Some of them seemed to imagine I was stringing them along on purpose, trying to con them into buying something."

"Do you know where he'd been?"

She shook her head. "He didn't even have the courtesy to let me know when he got back. He just slipped in and removed the sign. Once I found out he was there, I jolly well went round and gave him a piece of my mind. He was cool as a cucumber, even had the nerve to pretend he'd been there for quite a while. When he saw that wouldn't wash, he just thanked me for minding the shop and showed me the door in no uncertain terms."

"Did you ask where he'd been all that time?"

"I didn't bother. He wouldn't tell me. But I've a pretty good idea what he was up to."

Donovan gave her an enquiring look. "I promise to be discreet, Jenny."

"Well . . ." Jenny opened her small, round brown eyes in a conspiratorial fashion and leaned towards Donovan across the counter, speaking in a half-whisper. "It's sex, isn't it? Has to be. I'll wager he's got some lady on the go and pops round for a session of nooky in the lunch hour, only this one went on till teatime."

"You really think so?" Donovan asked, stifling a giggle and making a quick note.

"Oh, yes. Harry's always chasing after every bit of skirt that comes in his shop. His grandfather was just as bad, even in his eighties. Maybe it's genetic or perhaps it comes from living amongst all those musty old books."

"Is there any particular woman that you can think of?"

Jenny sighed as if she didn't know where to begin. "Take young Saffron over there," she jerked her head in the direction of the young girl at the front of the shop. "He was after her for a while and he was really persistent, even though she gave him absolutely no encouragement. Sadly for him, she thinks anything over twenty-five is ancient and books aren't her thing anyway. In the end, he got the message."

"He made a nuisance of himself?"

"Certainly he did. But then that new assistant of his came along and we haven't seen him for dust."

"Annie Klein, you mean? Tall, lots of red hair?" Donovan added for clarification, seeing the name meant nothing to Jenny.

Jenny wagged a stubby finger in the air. "That's the one. I didn't remember her name, although she comes in for coffee and stuff quite a lot. Yes, he seems very keen on her now, so Saffron's off the hook."

"But you think he may have someone else as well?"

"His sort always does. They can't go without."

"Does Mr Angel often leave the shop unattended?"

"Quite often, once or twice a week maybe. If he's on one of his book-buying trips, he can be gone for the whole day. At least then he puts a proper note in the window saying he's out. But if he's only out for a short while, he leaves a note that says 'Back soon' or something like that. It's a bit of a cheek, I think, making people wait around when you're actually not going to be back soon. I sometimes wonder if he's trying to cover his back for some reason."

"That's all very useful background information," Donovan said, noting the look of intense curiosity in Jenny's eye. No doubt, like everyone who fancied themselves as an amateur detective, she would be watching Angel's every move from now on, which was not a bad thing. "Would you be prepared to sign a statement saying that Mr Angel was out all that Wednesday afternoon?"

Jenny smiled. "Of course, I'd be delighted, if that's what you need. I believe in speaking the truth. Has Harry done anything wrong?" It was clear from her expression that she wouldn't be at all surprised if he had and would love to know what it was. Luckily, she seemed to have no idea just how serious the matter was.

Donovan smiled. "I'm just making routine enquiries at the moment. There's really nothing to worry about. But thank you very much for being so frank. I'll send somebody over to see you later and take down your statement."

CHAPTER
THIRTY

"This is ridiculous," Angel said, glaring at Tartaglia across the small table, arms folded. "You're just clutching at straws."

Tartaglia shrugged. "Maybe. But when I came to see you, you told me you were in your shop all that Wednesday afternoon. We now learn otherwise. As you know, we've since obtained a signed statement from a witness who says that you weren't where you said you were at the time in question."

They were sitting in a meeting room in Ealing Police Station where Angel had been brought in for questioning. Clutching at straws was an accurate description. There was as yet no hard evidence to link Angel to any crime and Steele had taken some convincing about the need to interview Angel again. However, Kelly Goodhart's body had been fished out of the Thames that morning, after the police had been alerted by the skipper of a passing barge. Her body had been taken by water to the small mortuary on the river at Wapping and a cursory examination had revealed that although she was wearing a wedding ring, there was no missing lock of hair. The ring would need to be identified by her family and a full toxicology report had been ordered to make sure that there was no GHB or similar substance in her system. But with the finding of her body, any residual suspicion that Sean Asher might be Tom had evaporated. Angel was the only suspect they had, the only one with a link, however tenuous, to both Marion Spear and, due to the location of his shop, the killing of Gemma Kramer. Once Donovan had outlined to Steele what Nicola Slade and Jenny Evans had both said, Steele had finally agreed to Tartaglia's request to bring him in.

Initially shocked and resistant when two uniformed officers had appeared at his shop to escort him to the local station, Angel had caved in once he had learned of the witness statement and agreed to cooperate. Wightman had been sent to fetch Adam Zaleski to see if he could identify Angel as the man he had seen running away from the church where Gemma Kramer had died. Separately, Donovan had gone off to North London to find Nicola Slade in the hope that she might recognise Angel as Marion Spear's mystery lover.

Angel's expression hardened. "You say you have a witness. Who is it?" He waited a moment for Tartaglia to respond before adding: "Is it Annie?" Guilt was written all over his face.

Tartaglia shook his head. "I can't tell you that at the moment, Mr Angel. But in my book, your not being where you say you were that afternoon looks suspicious. Why did you lie? According to the witness, you didn't get back until well after five. As you know, we're in the middle of a murder investigation and . . ."

374

Angel interrupted, looking outraged at the implication. "But I never even met that girl. How can you think I had anything to do with that?"

"All you need to do is explain what exactly you were doing during the time in question. It's very simple."

"I was *with* someone. Know what I mean?" Angel raised his eyebrows and leaned towards him, adopting a man-to-man tone, as if his word in such matters should be sufficient.

"What, all afternoon? I find that difficult to believe."

Angel shrugged. "Well, you know how these things are. It started off as lunch but one thing led to another . . ."

"All I'm interested in is eliminating you from our enquiries but I can't until I can prove your alibi."

Angel looked at him wearily. "See here, the lady's married. I'll give you her name but I can't have your lot wading over there with their size twelves upsetting her, not to mention what her husband would do to both of us if he finds out what's been going on. He's a really nasty piece of work."

"I appreciate all of that, Mr Angel. Really I do. But you give me no option unless you cooperate."

Angel slumped back in his chair and waved his hand in the air as if he was swatting a fly. "OK, OK. You can talk to her, but please, please tell your boys to be discreet."

"Of course we will. If the lady confirms what you say, there'll be no need for her husband to hear of it," Tartaglia said, although as far as he was concerned, lover's alibis were rarely worth the paper they were printed on.

Angel raised his eyes to the ceiling for a moment, as if he could just picture the disaster about to fall down around him, then leaned forward again, giving him a name and address in a whisper, as if he imagined that the walls had ears. "And don't go round there before nine in the morning or after six at night," he added. "That's when the rottweiler's home."

"Thank you," Tartaglia said, noting down the details and ignoring the instructions on timing. They would go when it suited them and if Angel got into trouble for his philandering, it was what he deserved. "You've been very cooperative, Mr Angel. Now, what about the identity parade?"

Angel sighed heavily. "I suppose I have no problems with that. Maybe then you'll believe me when I say I never went near that bloody church."

Just after nine o'clock that evening, Donovan arrived at Ealing Police Station with Nicola Slade. Nicola had been out having a drink with some friends in a nearby pub when Donovan reached her on her mobile and they had arranged for Donovan to pick her up outside the pub and drive her over to Ealing.

As they came into the reception area of Ealing Police Station, they met Tartaglia and Adam Zaleski emerging from the back, deep in conversation. Feeling suddenly embarrassed, Donovan turned to Nicola, explaining who Tartaglia was. Still talking, Zaleski gave her nothing more than a brief smile of recognition as he walked out the main door into the street with Tartaglia. Thank goodness Zaleski knew how to be discreet. The only person that she'd told, apart from her sister, was Yvette Dickenson. At least from past experience, she could be trusted to keep her mouth shut. Anyway, why should she tell Tartaglia? Nothing was going on between her and Zaleski and Tartaglia had hardly been forth-coming about his affair, or whatever it was, with Fiona Blake. Two could play at that game.

Donovan escorted Nicola into one of the meeting rooms where she was to wait until the line-up was ready. Nicola looked tired, dumping her bag down on the floor and sitting down heavily in a chair, not even bothering to undo her coat.

"It's strange being back in this part of town," she said with a sigh, scraping her wispy hair off her face with a hand. "It brings it all back, what happened to Marion, I mean. I still remember the way she looked that day, when I saw her with that man. She seemed really happy, positively glowing. I still can't believe she's dead."

"Let's hope we've got the right man," Donovan said.

Nicola nodded. "Me too. I've been thinking about nothing else since you came to see me."

Donovan patted her on the shoulder. "Don't torture yourself. There's nothing you could have done. Would you like a cup of coffee? I saw a vending machine in the hall."

"Please. Black with two sugars. I need something to pep me up."

The vending machine along the corridor was new and not a type Donovan was used to, offering an extraordinary array of options. As she was working out whether to go for a "double espresso" type coffee for Nicola, or to simply choose "normal with extra strength", Tartaglia appeared beside her.

"How are you getting on?" he asked.

"She's in one of the meeting rooms," Donovan said, deciding to go for the large espresso. "They'll be ready for her in a minute. What about you?" She didn't trust herself to mention Zaleski by name. "Any luck?"

He shook his head wearily. "Zaleski didn't identify Angel. There was no doubt in his mind. The man he saw running out of the church wasn't in the identity parade."

"That's a shame. What about Mrs Brooke? Do you think it's worth asking her to take a look?"

"Dave's bringing her in now but I don't hold out a great deal of hope. Zaleski got a much better view of the man and he was positive he didn't see him in the line-up. Angel's still in the frame for Marion Spear but there's nothing now to link him to Gemma Kramer."

Donovan sighed. "Well, maybe we have to face the fact that the two deaths aren't related after all."

He nodded. "Let's see what Nicola Slade comes up with first."

Sipping her coffee, Nicola gazed through the one-way glass at the ten men lined up in front of her on the other side. She walked up and down then stopped in front of Harry Angel.

"He looks familiar," she said, pushing her glasses up her small, turned-up nose and peering at him closely. "I've definitely seen him somewhere."

"Do you remember where?" Donovan said, trying not to sound too interested.

She shook her head then turned to Donovan who was standing behind her. "I just don't know. He looks familiar, as I said, but he's not the man I saw that day with Marion."

"You're sure? Please take your time."

She sighed, staring hard again at the glass, biting her lip, as if she were forcing herself to remember something. Then she added: "I'm sorry. I'm really sorry." She bowed her head and started to cry, taking a tissue out of her bag and blowing her nose loudly, dabbing at her eyes with the back of her hand. "I wanted to do this for Marion and I've failed."

"Nothing to be sorry about." Donovan put an arm around her, feeling disappointed that Nicola hadn't been more categorical about Angel. If only she could remember where she had seen him and if it was anything related to Marion Spear. But memory worked in funny ways and it was pointless putting pressure on her.

"That's the way it goes sometimes," Donovan said, steering her towards the door. "But it was worth a try. I'll take you home when you're ready. Maybe something will come back to you later."

Steele slammed the door to her flat shut and double locked it, dumping her briefcase and umbrella down in a corner, kicking off her sodden shoes and throwing her coat over the back of the sofa, where it could dry by the radiator. It had been blowing a gale outside, sheets of almost horizontal rain coming down and she had got completely soaked on the walk from her car. At least the flat was warm and welcoming but she felt ragged, barely able to hold it together any longer. The orange glow from the streetlamp outside flooded the room and she drew the curtains quickly before switching on the light. She turned on the TV, flicking through the channels until she found a news programme and let it buzz away in the background, the noise making her feel less alone.

The answer machine was showing four messages and she hit the replay button. Twice the caller hung up. Then she heard Patrick Kennedy's voice.

"Carolyn, are you there? I've tried your mobile but it's switched off. Sorry not to speak to you today but things have been a bit busy. It's about eight. If you get home soonish, give me a call and let's have a drink. I can pop over to you if you like."

The fourth message was also from Kennedy, the message recorded about half an hour before and he sounded either tired or a bit drunk or possibly both, his words a little slurred.

"It's Patrick. Give me a call when you get home. I'm at the flat. I'll be up till quite late. Gotta lot of papers to mark. It would be nice to talk."

Talk? Men never wanted to talk, at least not when you needed them to, when you actually wanted to know what was going on in their peculiar minds. Patrick was more in touch with his feminine side than most, but what did they have to talk about? If it was the case, it could wait until morning. If it was about things more personal, she had no desire to talk at all. The less said about that the better, as far as she was concerned. He was trying to get closer to her, force his way in and she wanted to knock him back, make him go away. There was something about him that unnerved her, his keenness maybe, the fact that he was so thick-skinned, so sure about things that he wouldn't take no for an answer.

Affairs at work were par for the course when you did such long hours, when you had little or no personal life. How the hell did you ever meet anyone outside, someone who would understand the pressures and put up with them? Until Patrick came along and she was taken in by his swagger and intelligence, she had never so much as allowed herself a kiss, let alone anything more, with someone she worked with. She never wanted to put herself in such a position of weakness, give anyone that power over her. The fear of wagging tongues and knowing glances stopped her in her tracks before anything ever had a chance to get started. Patrick had been the only lapse. Perhaps underneath it all, he was bitter and was looking to exact some sort of revenge. She certainly should have realised that he wouldn't let go of her that easily and she felt furious with herself for ever having brought him in on the case.

She deleted the messages and went into the kitchen. After hunting around in the fridge and cupboards, she found a pack of vegetarian moussaka in the freezer compartment and stuck it in the microwave. It was the last thing she felt like eating but there was nothing else in the flat and she felt far too tired to go out again. She looked at the half-full bottle of red wine standing on the counter. In the old days, the days before Barnes, she rarely ever had a drink in the evening. But it was becoming a habit. Sod it. She had to unwind somehow. She pulled out the stopper and poured herself a large glass, taking it with her into the bathroom, where she turned on the shower and started to undress.

If only she could get a few decent hours of sleep she'd be OK but she knew it was unlikely and she was dreading the battle ahead of her that night. Some people, who were not prone to worries, or perhaps with no conscience, seemed to fall asleep instantly. It was like a light being switched out. One minute they were talking and fully conscious, the next, they lay there completely comatose, as if they had been drugged. It was so unfair. Falling asleep had always been a struggle for her but it had got much worse since taking on this case. She'd been waking at around three in the morning, tied up in knots, thoughts spinning, unable to get back to sleep again until nearly five, when it was almost too late to bother. No wonder she felt so out of control, her emotions ebbing and flowing uncomfortably close to the surface. Just touch her and she'd bleed. It was all to do with those bloody emails. She could hear the unknown voice, imagine it whispering to her: *Do I fill your dreams? I'm the lover you've always longed for, the one who'll never leave you.* However hard she tried to block them out, the nasty little words kept wriggling their way back into her mind.

She showered quickly, put on a dressing gown and went into the kitchen, where the moussaka was steaming and bubbling in the microwave. She could smell it through the door and realised suddenly just how hungry she was. Turning it out onto a plate, burning the tips of her fingers as she did so, she topped up her wine, prepared a tray and carried it all into the sitting room, where *Sea of Love*, starring Al Pacino, was just starting on the TV. She'd seen it before but it didn't matter. Anything would do. She sank into a chair, feet up on the coffee table, gazed at the flickering screen and wolfed down the moussaka, wishing suddenly that she'd bought a larger pack. Just as she finished, the phone rang.

If it was bloody Patrick again, she'd scream. She let it ring until the answer machine kicked in. She heard her message play over the speaker, followed by the click as the person at the other end hung up. Curious, she got up and dialled 1471 but the voice said that the caller's number was withheld. It was bloody Patrick. Of course it was. It had to be. Who else would be calling her at that hour, not leaving a message, withholding their number? She knew what he was up to. He was checking up on her, trying to see if she had come home. How dare he. How fucking dare he. She put her hands to her face, biting back the tears.

Tartaglia was at home, about to get ready to go to bed, when Wightman called just before midnight.

383

"There's no sign of Kennedy, sir. I don't know what it's like with you, but it's raining cats and dogs up here. Perhaps he got put off."

"Maybe he has other plans," Tartgaglia said, listening to the sound of the rain beating against his sitting-room window, wondering why Kennedy hadn't shown. "What a shame. I was looking forward to your bringing him in. How long have you been there?"

"The best part of two hours, sir. She came home just after ten. She was on her own and nobody's been there since. Do you want us to wait a little longer?"

"Is she still up?"

"She's just switched off the lights in the front room. She's probably on her way to bed. Do you want me to go round the back and check?"

"No. You and Nick go home and get some sleep. We'll try again tomorrow."

Steele lay in bed in the dark. Ignoring instructions on the packet, she had taken two Nytol half an hour before, washed down with the last inch of wine from the bottle. But drowsiness seemed far away. She still felt tense, muscles tight, thoughts buzzing around. When would the pills start to take effect? The wind was making a terrible noise outside, rattling the old sash window in her bedroom as if some invisible hand was shaking it. She would never get to sleep with that racket going on and she got up, found some tissues in the bathroom and wedged them down the sides until there was no possible movement or sound.

As she climbed back into bed, she heard the slam of the main front door of the house, followed by the heavy tread of her neighbour who lived in the flat on the ground floor, above. She listened as his footsteps moved around and, after a few minutes, the floorboards immediately overhead creaked as he went into his bedroom. Her curtains didn't quite meet in the middle and, through the gap, she saw the light go on upstairs, illuminating the garden at the back like a floodlight. She waited for him to close his blinds and go to bed but after a moment, she heard the tramp of his feet out of the room again. After a minute, there was the distant sound of music from the front of the house.

She was never going to be able to sleep like this. She got out of bed and tried to pull the curtains shut but when she forced them together in the middle, she was left with a gap at either side, which seemed to let in even more light. They were pale cream and more decorative than practical. Her mother had made them for her as a Christmas present a couple of years before but had somehow got the measurements a little wrong. They were also thinly lined. It had never really bothered her quite as much as it did now but something would have to be done. She hadn't the heart to replace them and maybe a set of blackout blinds behind the curtains would do the trick. Perhaps she could measure the window and order them over the phone. She certainly wouldn't have a free moment to go into a shop for a while.

She climbed back into bed and stared at the light outside, willing it to go out, listening to the heavy bass beat coming from upstairs. It sounded like some sort of rap, relentlessly repetitive and she wondered how much longer she should give him before going up there and asking him to turn the bloody thing off. She was just on the point of getting out of bed when she saw a shadow cross the window. There was no mistaking it. Somebody was in the back garden.

For a moment she froze then got up and grabbed her dressing gown, which was lying across the end of her bed. Slipping it on quickly, she crept towards the window to take a look. She peered hard through the gap but saw nothing. Trembling, standing just behind the curtains, she waited in the dark listening. *Shall I come and see you? Would you like that?* Was he really out there? Would he try and break in? There were all sorts of strange noises coming from outside but it was impossible to tell what might be a footstep or what was the wind.

Her fingers felt for the window catch, checking that it was secure, that both stops were also in place. She waited for several minutes, wondering if someone was really standing out there on the other side. If she saw the shadow again, she'd dial 999. But there was nothing. Perhaps she had imagined it. Maybe her state of mind was making her jumpy. The shadow could have been cast by the trees outside, blowing in the wind. Perhaps. She went over to the bed, pulled her duvet off and wrapped it tightly around her. After checking that all of the other windows in the flat were secure, she went into the sitting room and curled up in a tight ball on the sofa, listening.

CHAPTER
THIRTY-ONE

The morning started badly. Still raining, the road was as slippery as grease and, as Tartaglia curved through the traffic around Hammersmith Broadway, a large, battered black 4×4 cut him up, accelerating and changing lanes without indicating, making him swerve and nearly come off the bike. He chased after it, swearing pointlessly into his visor, catching up with it again at the next set of lights and pulling alongside. He was about to rap his fist on the window and give the driver a piece of his mind when he saw that a young woman was at the wheel, a car-full of children in the back. As he glared at her through the streaming glass, she glanced over and gave him a sweet, fleeting smile, clearly unaware of what she'd done. As the light changed to green, she accelerated away into the distance, leaving him with a rankling sense of impotence.

He felt like that Greek who was forced to push a boulder up a hill every day only to have it fall back on him and roll down to the bottom each night. Nothing was giving, nothing going his way. With neither Zaleski nor Nicola identifying Angel, they had been forced to let Angel go and the look of smug triumph on Angel's face as he got up to leave was burned on his mind. Predictably, the lover had provided an alibi. They would keep prodding but he didn't hold out much hope of her altering her story for the moment, as she seemed quite smitten with Angel, for some inexplicable reason. As for Kennedy, it was sod's law that he had decided on an evening in for a change.

As Tartaglia crossed the bridge and passed the spot where Kelly Goodhart had jumped to her death, he slowed and said a silent prayer for her, adding one for Sean Asher. At least for him, there was still hope.

He parked his bike in the car park at the back of the office and walked up the stairs to the first floor. Shaking the rain off his helmet, he pushed open the door to find Cornish hovering awkwardly in the corridor beyond, hands in pockets.

"There you are, Mark. I was looking out of the window and saw you drive in. Do you mind coming into Carolyn's office for a minute?" He sucked in his lips, looking embarrassed for some reason.

"Sure. What's the problem?" he asked, wondering if perhaps Steele had made a complaint about him.

"There's been another email." Cornish lowered his voice to a whisper, talking out of the corner of his mouth as they walked together towards her office. "Between you and me, I think she's a bit upset. I thought you might know what to say. You know her better than I."

Tartaglia was tempted to tell him that he didn't know her at all but there wasn't much point. The subtleties of relationships were beyond Cornish.

They found Steele sitting behind her desk reading through some papers. As they entered the room, she glanced up briefly. She looked even paler than usual, her eyes bloodshot and puffy as if she hadn't slept for days.

"What do you make of this," Cornish said, picking up a piece of paper from the corner of the desk and passing it to Tartaglia.

To: Carolyn.Steele@met.police.uk
From: slwewxnsehTom98342@hotmail.com

My dearest Carolyn,
I came to you last night while you were asleep. You looked really beautiful, your dark head on the pillow, breathing deeply. You were like a child, so innocent and fragrant, I wanted to wrap myself around you and bury my face in your neck and breasts. Were you dreaming of me? I'm sure you were. I watched you for a while. I couldn't resist kissing your cheek. I just had to taste your skin, touch it with my teeth, ever so gently, I promise. You were so soft and you smelt of something sweet and heady. Is it roses? You must have felt my touch, as you stirred and gave a little moan. I didn't want to wake you, so I crept away. Our time will come very, very soon, my darling. Not much longer for us to wait now.
Your Tomxxx

Anybody, any woman receiving such vile, repellent rubbish would feel furious, if not threatened. Studying the taut lines of Steele's face, looking beyond her lack of open reaction, Tartaglia saw finally how much it had touched her and how shaken she was by it. Had Tom really gone to her flat? Surely, if he had been there, actually got inside by the sound of things, she would know. It seemed far-fetched, possibly nothing more than another wind-up. He suddenly wondered if Kennedy had had anything to do with it.

"Of course it may all be made up," Cornish said matter-of-factly, trying to make light of the matter for Steele's benefit. "But we've sent a forensic team over to Carolyn's flat to go through everything, inside and out. Perhaps you can stay with friends until this is over."

"Over?" she said, her voice hoarse as if she'd been talking a lot. "And when will that be? I have no intention of being scared out of my flat."

The muscles of her face were rigid, her mouth drawn into a hard, thin line as if it was the only way she could control it. Tartaglia wanted to tell her that nobody would think badly of her if she let herself go, everybody would understand and sympathise. But she would only misinterpret his motives, particularly with Cornish there, looking unperturbed and immaculate in his dark suit as if the stains of life never touched him.

Tartaglia glanced out the window for a moment, watching the rain run down the glass, Clarke's words coming back to him. Charm her, get her on your side. But it was far too late for that.

"There's something you both need to know," he said. There was no better time. Slowly and carefully he told them about Kennedy and what he and Wightman had witnessed outside Steele's flat. As he spoke, he saw Steele's expression harden. The colour returned to her face until she had a fierce patch of red on each cheek as though she had been slapped.

"You've been spying on me," she said, her voice catching in her throat. Her eyes swivelled to Cornish. "Did you know about this?"

"He knew nothing about it," Tartaglia said, before Cornish could reply. "I was going to tell him if it happened again."

"Happened again?"

"Dr Kennedy didn't appear last night. Dave and Nick waited for a couple of hours . . ."

She looked horrified. "You involved Dave and Nick in this?"

"Like me, they just wanted to know you were safe."

"So, that's who was round the back of my flat, in the garden last night."

"Somebody was in your back garden last night? You didn't mention this, Carolyn," Cornish said, a little accusatorily.

Steele compressed her lips tightly and didn't reply.

"Nobody went round the back," Tartglia said. "They just kept an eye from the road. You can ask them, if you want."

"Well somebody was there," she said. "I'm positive. Didn't they see anyone?"

Tartaglia shook his head. "It has to be Dr Kennedy. They must have missed him somehow."

Although clearly shocked, it was interesting that she wasn't trying to defend Kennedy or deny that he could have done such a thing.

"So, when did all this start?" she said, her voice betraying the emotion beneath.

"After the first two emails. I was concerned for your safety."

"No you bloody weren't."

"Come, come Carolyn," Cornish said, with a little embarrassed cough. "We're all under a lot of pressure at the moment. I agree it's not orthodox and Mark should have checked with me first but . . ."

Steele ignored him, eyes fixed on Tartaglia. "You were just out to spy on Patrick . . . Dr Kennedy and me. Weren't you? It's got nothing to do with the bloody emails."

Tartaglia shook his head. "As I said, I was concerned about you and it's a very good thing I did. If I hadn't, we'd have no idea what Dr Kennedy gets up to after hours. Have you considered for a moment that he might be behind the emails?"

"Patrick?" She stared at him dumbfounded then gave a small, strangled laugh. "Oh, he's Tom, is he? Is that what you really think? Dr Patrick Kennedy, a well-respected forensic psychologist, just happens to be a psycho in his spare time. That's a bloody laugh."

"Even if he isn't Tom, he could still have written the emails. Ask yourself, why are you being targeted? What are the emails designed to do? The writer wants to shake you up, make you feel vulnerable. Maybe it is Tom. But maybe it's somebody else, trying to use the situation to try and get closer to you. That's what Kennedy wants, isn't it?"

"Is that true, Carolyn?" Cornish asked.

She was shaking her head slowly in disbelief. "I can't believe he'd do such a horrible thing."

"The emails were written by somebody who knows the details of the case," Tartaglia added, meeting her eye. "Somebody who also thinks he knows you and understands how to get to you. Who better than Dr Kennedy, with all his psychological insight?"

"I still can't believe it," she said, almost gasping.

Cornish rubbed his chin thoughtfully. "I agree it sounds a little far-fetched. But Dr Kennedy's certainly familiar with the emails that Tom sent the other girls."

"Yes," Tartaglia said. "And he's more than clever enough to fake his style."

Cornish nodded. "And of course, there have been other hoaxes before. Just think of the Yorkshire Ripper."

Steele said nothing, as if she didn't trust herself to speak.

"Coming back to this morning's email," Tartaglia said. "He talks about watching you while you were asleep. The night before last, Dave saw Dr Kennedy peering through a gap in your bedroom curtains. Your light was on at the time, according to Dave. Now I don't know what Dr Kennedy might see if he did that but you can picture it. Perhaps Dr Kennedy also watched you when you were asleep."

"If it's true, I'll string him up myself," Steele said quietly. She closed her eyes momentarily and gave a deep sigh, as if it was all too much for her. Then she bent down and searched in her handbag for a tissue, blowing her nose loudly. Her eyes were red and Tartaglia could see that she was close to tears.

Tartaglia turned to Cornish. "What are we going to do, sir?"

"It's awkward. Dr Kennedy's a very well-respected academic. It's hard to believe that someone like him would have sent the emails."

"I agree. But he's definitely been peeping. Perhaps we should get him in for questioning."

"He'll deny it," Steele said, looking up at Tartaglia. "He'll just say he had my welfare at heart, just like you." Her tone was bitter. But she was right. Even if confronted with what they had seen outside Steele's flat, Kennedy would laugh it all away. They hadn't yet sufficient grounds for a warrant to search his home and take away his computer to see if he had actually sent the emails.

"But we have to do something, sir," Tartaglia said, turning to Cornish. Sensing his hesitation, Tartaglia added: "I don't believe that Kennedy is Tom. But he's definitely been up to no good and I still think he could have sent the emails. If we do nothing, it could backfire on us badly."

Cornish folded his arms and appeared to consider the matter, no doubt picturing how he might end up with egg on his face. "You're right, Mark," he said, after a moment. "We have to do something. We'd better run a background check on Dr Kennedy, see if he's done anything like this before. And I want a proper external surveillance team on Carolyn's flat for the next few nights, with cameras and a full alarm system with a panic button. After this last email, it's the only thing to do if Carolyn wants to stay there. I'll go and get it sorted right away."

As soon as Cornish had left the room, Steele stood up slowly and walked over to where Tartaglia was standing. She was trembling and her knuckles were white as she clenched her fists at her side. For a second he thought she was going to slap him.

"Why didn't you tell me what you were doing? Didn't you trust me?"

"If I'd come to you and told you what I'd seen that first night, you would never have believed me."

"But what made you go there in the first place?"

Tartaglia hesitated. How was he to explain the impulse that had led him to her flat? He had been angry and he had wanted to catch her and Kennedy out. It now seemed a nasty, shabby thing to have done, even in the light of what he had discovered. But she was right. He didn't trust her, certainly not enough to tell her the truth now. "I had a suspicion. Nothing more than that."

She raised her eyebrows. "One of your famous hunches, I suppose?"

"It's a good thing I did follow it up," he said, ignoring the sarcasm in her voice.

"Maybe, but you should have told me first."

"I needed further proof. That's why I involved Dave and Nick." He gazed at her angry, pale face for a moment then added: "There was no point in coming to you. You're blind as far as Dr Kennedy is concerned."

He saw the words hit home. "Perhaps I have been blind," she said, after a moment. "But as your superior, I find your behaviour inexcusable."

He realised that on top of everything that had happened to her, he had humiliated her and he felt deeply sorry. "I didn't mean to embarrass you and I wish that this all hadn't had to come out in front of Superintendent Cornish. But you must understand that I couldn't keep quiet after seeing that email."

She walked over to the door and held it open. "Please go now. I want to be on my own."

It was nearly two o'clock in the afternoon when Gary Jones rolled into the small office he shared with Tartaglia. He'd been out at the Old Bailey all morning, where he had been called to give evidence in an old case. Slapping down a wadge of papers in front of his computer, he sidled over to where Tartaglia was sitting, pushed aside some files and a stack of new CDs that had just arrived from Amazon in the morning post, and eased his broad girth onto a corner of the desk.

"How'd it go?" Tartaglia said, chewing on the last mouthful of avocado and bacon ciabatta sandwich he'd bought from the deli down the road and wiping his fingers on a paper napkin.

Jones stretched his short arms up in the air and yawned. "I wasn't needed after all. The arsehole's changed his plea to guilty."

"Wish they were all as easy."

"Hear you've got Cornish on the warpath about Dr Kennedy. Do you think Steele'll press charges?"

"I guess it depends what forensics and surveillance come up with. At the moment, it's only our word against his. It would be really nice to catch it all on camera."

"Yeah, but just think what a meal the press would make of it if there's a court case. My money's still on her letting it drop."

Tartaglia nodded. He wouldn't blame her if she let it go. He had seen how fragile she was underneath. Having her private life exposed in public was probably a step too far, even if it was what Kennedy deserved. "You know, Steele was furious when she found out that we had seen what was going on with Kennedy. It's amazing. You'd think she'd be pleased."

Jones shook his head. "She's a bloody woman isn't she? Logic's not their strong point."

"I don't think I'd be thinking straight either if I were in her shoes."

Jones shrugged, as if he couldn't be bothered to think about it any longer and picked up the wrapper from Tartaglia's sandwich. He examined the ingredients label. "You ought to make your own, mate," he said. "Never know what rubbish they put in them."

"Thanks. I'll remember that, when I have five seconds at home to cut up sandwiches."

"Get yourself a partner," Jones said, balling the wrapper and lobbing it into the bin. "They take care of all that business."

"More trouble than it's worth," Tartaglia said, thinking of Jones's wife, who was high maintenance, on the phone to Jones all day long, whatever they were working on in the office. Anyway, none of the women he was ever interested in seemed to have time for the domestic stuff, although it wasn't something that bothered him. Better to have an independent mind and a sense of humour than somebody who could iron and cook supper, which was something he could do himself.

Jones's eye lit on the pile of CDs sitting on the desk beside him. "Got yourself some new music? Planning an evening in, are you?"

"That OK by you?"

"You're always buying stuff. You must have quite a large collection by now."

Jones picked the top two CDs off the pile, scanned the front covers then flipped them over. "Charlie Parker and Humphrey Lyttelton? Don't tell me you're getting into jazz now."

"I'll be forty in a few years. Thought I'd give it a whirl. I like to be broad-minded."

"Broad-minded? You're certainly that, in spades from what I hear." Jones raised his pale eyebrows and gave Tartaglia what was supposed to be a knowing look, although Tartaglia had no idea what he meant by it. "You can't go wrong with 'Best of', in my book," Jones continued.

"Knowing you, that figures. You're now making me regret buying them."

"And here's Verdi's Requiem. That's a nice piece." Jones peered at the front cover and pointed a stubby finger at one of the photographs on the front. "You know, this chappie here looks just like you."

Tartaglia glanced over. "Ildebrando D'Arcangelo. He's a baritone from Pescara."

"Well, he's your dead ringer, is all I can say. It's incredible. Sure you haven't got a twin?"

"That's very flattering. Sadly, I haven't got his voice."

Jones nodded sympathetically. "I love a bit of opera myself. I've been in the choir since I was a nipper. What do you think of our boy Bryn? He's the best, isn't he?"

"I've only seen him once but he was fantastic. Wish I could afford to go more often."

Jones continued leafing slowly through the stack, examining each box as if it were some peculiar, rare specimen. "Who's Ornella Vanoni when she's at home?"

"Italian singer from the sixties."

"And Matchbox Twenty? And The Editors? Am I missing something?"

"Just stick to your Eagles cover versions and don't worry your pretty little head about it," Tartaglia said, feeling increasingly irritated and hemmed in by Jones's physical presence. He grabbed the CDs out of Jones's hands and put them on the far side of the desk. "Now piss off, Jonesey, and leave me alone. I've got work to do."

Jones shrugged and got to his feet, plodding over to his rucksack and pulling out a thermos and a wrapped pack of thick home-made sandwiches. "You sure have catholic tastes, Mark," he said, sitting down heavily in his desk chair and peeling off the foil. Within seconds of his taking his first huge bite, the usual smell of tuna fish and onion filled the air.

"I'm a Catholic, so that's not surprising." Tartaglia wheeled his chair backwards to try and avoid the smell.

Jones shook his head knowingly. "I forgot you're a left-footer. Catholic by name, catholic by nature. Does it apply to women, by any chance?" He took another bite of his sandwich, again the same mischievous look in his small brown eyes.

"Only to music . . ." Tartaglia said, with a sudden idea where this might be leading. It was amazing how even the most private of things didn't stay private for long. If Donovan had talked, he'd murder her. He was about to add something else, when a word snagged in his mind. Catholic. A shaft of light penetrated the darkness. That's what Sean Asher had said about Kelly Goodhart. She was a Catholic.

"What about female pathologists?" Jones said between mouthfuls. "Ones with red hair and . . ."

"Shut up for a minute, Gary." Tartaglia waved him away with a hand, barely hearing him, mind racing, as things started to fall into place. "I've got something. Catholic. You said Catholic."

"What about it?" Jones said, mouth full again.

Tartaglia squeezed his eyes tight shut for a moment, trying to blot out Jones. "I've just remembered. Kelly

400

Goodhart was a Catholic. So was Marion Spear. I'll bet Yolanda Garcia and Laura Benedetti were too. Maybe Gemma and Ellie were as well. We've got to check. I think it's the connection and we've fucking missed it. How can we be so fucking stupid?"

Before Jones could reply, Tartaglia had swung off his seat and rushed out of the room, running down the corridor to the open plan office, where Yvette Dickenson was at her desk, eating the remains of her lunch.

"Where's everyone?"

She shrugged. "Most of them are still down by the canal, doing the house to house. Why?"

"Call them back, whoever you can get hold of. Right away. Wait, before you do that," he said, as she reached for the phone. "Do we know if either Gemma Kramer or Ellie Best were Catholics?"

Dickenson looked at him blankly. She probably thought he'd gone mad. "I don't know about Gemma but I think Ellie was. I vaguely remember her mum saying something about it. Why, is it important?"

"I'll put money on Gemma being a Catholic too. I think I've worked out what the connection is. Tom's victims are all Catholic. Call the girls' families. Get the names of any religious associations or choirs they may have belonged to."

She looked doubtful. "But we've been through all the clubs and stuff like that, sir. There was no link."

He sighed. Perhaps it wasn't quite so simple. But he was sure he was on the right track. "If the only thing that the girls had in common was that they were all Catholic, it has to be to do with that."

"Could Tom be a priest, sir?"

He shook his head. "They lived in different parts of London. They wouldn't have had the same one." He stuffed his hands in his pockets, staring into the middle distance as he tried to work it all through. Then he turned back to Dickenson. "Look, if you're young and lonely and depressed, what do you do?"

"You have to talk to someone, or at least that's what I'd do."

"Exactly. But if you can't speak to your parents, and maybe you don't want to speak to your priest, where else do you go?"

"We checked the Samaritans and there was no connection."

Tartaglia shook his head impatiently. "I know. But maybe there's somewhere like that . . . perhaps somewhere specifically Catholic and we've missed it for some reason." He sighed heavily. It wouldn't be the first time. "Get me the names and addresses of the churches the girls went to. I'm going to talk to one of their priests."

CHAPTER
THIRTY-TWO

The familiar sweet smell of incense and candle wax greeted Tartaglia as he walked through the heavy doors of St Peter's Italian Church on Clerkenwell Road, where they had discovered that Laura Benedetti had once worshipped. Although the large original Italian community in Clerkenwell had long since dispersed, it was still one of the main focal points for Italians living in London and he knew it well. It was where his cousin Elisa had been married and Nicoletta and her husband John, living in Islington not far away, had christened both children there a few years before.

He gazed around momentarily at the ornate nineteenth century interior, with its rows of tall pillars and Roman arches. It was a riot of colour with painted panels depicting the saints, gold leaf and coloured marble everywhere and hundreds of candles burning in the small side chapels. He was struck again by how different it was to the Anglican churches where Gemma, Laura and Ellie had died. It occurred to him that maybe Tom had deliberately chosen places that were very different in feel to what the girls had been used to, places that would have no resonance of family, friends and their communities.

The next mass was not due to start for over an hour. Apart from a few elderly ladies scattered around the pews close to the altar, heads bowed in prayer, there was nobody to be seen. He had called Nicoletta before coming. Shouting over the background screams of his young nephew and niece, who were fighting as usual, she had given him the name of her priest, Father Ignazio, extracting in return a promise that he would come to lunch the following Sunday, whatever happened with "the bloody case". Given that "the bloody case" looked to be hotting up again, he bit his lip and said nothing. No point in having another row and he would worry about what excuse to make, if need be, nearer the time.

He walked out of the church and round the corner to the entrance of the parish office, which was in a small side street. An old lady showed him into a small, airless waiting room on the ground floor and told him that Father Ignazio would see him shortly. The room had a high ceiling and was painted white, with bare, dark wood floors. A massive bookcase, full of leather-bound religious works in Latin and Italian, ran the length of one wall, the only other furniture being a refectory table and a set of mahogany chairs. A large crucifix hung at one end of the room and a picture of St Vincent Pallotti, the founder of St Peter's, with two of its Fathers, decorated the other.

After a few minutes, Father Ignazio entered the room.

"I hear you want to see me," he said, gesturing for Tartaglia to sit down at the table opposite him.

404

His face was tanned and almost unlined. He looked not much older than Tartaglia, although his black hair was showing the first signs of grey at the temples. Tall and thin, he had a slight stoop and wore heavy-rimmed glasses with thick lenses that magnified his dark eyes. Tartaglia introduced himself, watching Father Ignazio's face break into a broad, warm smile when he mentioned the family connection. As Father Ignazio spoke of Nicoletta and her family, whom he seemed to know well, he switched to his native Italian, talking in a heavy Neopolitan accent, which Tartaglia found difficult to follow at first.

"Unfortunately, I'm here on police business," Tartaglia said, reverting to English, once Father Ignazio had finished. As Tartaglia explained what he was after and the connection with Laura Benedetti, Father Ignazio frowned and, sighing heavily, crossed himself.

"Of course, I read about the case in the papers. You really think there's a connection to our church somehow?"

"Indirectly, possibly. It's the only thing we can find that all the victims have in common." He gave a brief background profile of the three young girls, leaving out Marion Spear and Kelly Goodhart. There seemed no point in complicating the picture.

"You think the murderer is a Catholic?" Father Ignazio said, after Tartaglia had outlined the situation.

"Probably, or at least working for some sort of Catholic organisation. As the girls lived in different parts of London, my feeling is that it isn't at a local level."

Father Ignazio nodded, apparently reassured by this.

"They were all depressed, possibly suicidal, although they were coerced in that direction," Tartaglia continued. "At some point they may have sought counselling. Given that, for some reason, they may not have wanted to talk to their priests, I wondered . . ."

Father Ignazio nodded again. "Yes, I understand. They were very young. It's natural. You're wondering if there may be some other place where they would go."

"Exactly, either by phone or in person, where they could be anonymous, where there would be no chance of their family finding out."

"The Samaritans perhaps?"

"We've looked at that. I was thinking of something specifically Catholic which the girls could find out about, possibly through their local churches or communities."

Father Ignazio stroked his chin thoughtfully. "Well, there are several small organisations that I know of, all run on a voluntary basis, of course. Come with me. I think there are some leaflets that may interest you, at the front of the church."

He got to his feet and Tartaglia followed him out into the hall and through a small door, which led directly into the church. They walked down the aisle and across to the main entrance doors where Father Ignazio stopped in front of a wooden rack filled with a variety of information pamphlets.

"There are a quite a few here," he said, gathering together a handful of leaflets from the rack. He studied them carefully, then put several back before handing one to Tartaglia. "Maybe this is what you're looking for. It's the only one that really fits what you've told me. They're like the Samaritans, only Catholic."

Tartaglia looked at the leaflet. The organisation called themselves "CHA: the Catholic Help Association". "We treat your calls in total confidence," the blurb said. There was no office address, only a phone number. He had never heard of the organisation but reading quickly through the blurb, it seemed genuine and, as Father Ignazio had said, very similar in vein to the Samaritans in what they were offering. He could just picture it now, the girls calling in, feeling depressed, Tom answering the phone at the other end. It all made sense. They had gone through the girls' home phone records very carefully and had checked for any contact with well-known organisations like the Samaritans. But perhaps out of ignorance or human error they had missed the significance of any calls to "CHA". It was equally possible that the girls had gone somewhere else to phone, like a friend's house or a public call box.

"This looks like it," he said, turning to Father Igazio. "Thank you. Do you have any idea where they're based?"

Father Ignazio shook his head. "All I know is they're in London. I've seen their leaflets in other churches too. I'm not sure if they have a presence elsewhere." He walked with Tartaglia out of the main door and down the steps to the street. "It's a terrible, terrible thing to contemplate, somebody abusing such a position of trust, such a . . ." Father Ignazio's voice trailed off. He gazed down at the pavement for a moment, shaking his head slowly, and then looked back at Tartaglia with a heavy sigh. "Of course, there are evil people in all walks of life. No doubt you see more of them than I do."

Tartaglia nodded. "I imagine so. Thank you very much for your help. I'll let you know if we find anything."

Father Ignazio smiled, took Tartaglia's hand in both of his and gave it a hearty shake, clasping it warmly as he met his eye. "It would be nice too to see you here one day, Inspector, come along and join the rest of your family."

Tartaglia smiled back, thinking it was probably something long overdue. "I promise you I will, Father. Very soon."

After leaving the church Tartaglia called the office and found Yvette Dickenson still at her desk. No doubt, with her impending maternity leave, she was grateful for all the extra overtime, although, in his view, she should have been at home long ago, putting her feet up. He gave her the details from the pamphlet to check.

"Call this number and find out where they're based. Then get someone over there right away. If they're not cooperative, tell them we'll get a warrant. I want a list of anyone who's worked for them over the last couple of years, in any capacity. But I'm particularly interested in anyone who's been manning the phones. We'll need access to their phone records. While we're at it, we'd also better check the other churches and see if they have the same or anything similar. Then call me back."

"I've had Nicola Slade on the phone, sir. She's rung several times to speak to Sam. She's quite insistent."

"Why can't Sam deal with it?"

There was a pause at the other end. "She went home a little early." He could tell that Dickenson was being evasive.

"What did Nicola Slade want?"

"She wouldn't say. Just said she had to speak to Sam."

"Well, where is Sam?"

There was another pause before Dickenson spoke. "She's got a date." There was another second's hesitation before she added, as if in justification: "She's allowed a personal life, isn't she?"

A date? This was the first he knew of Donovan having anybody around. Last thing he'd heard was her moaning about a total absence of attractive men. "Of course she's allowed a personal life, but what a time to pick. We're in the middle of a bloody investigation." He wasn't sure whether he felt angrier from a professional point of view or from a personal one. Now was hardly the time to go out on hot dates. Also, Donovan usually let slip most things about her private life, such as it was, even asking for his advice sometimes. Why hadn't she told him about this? There had been ample opportunity.

"It's just tonight," Dickenson said a little sharply, as if trying to excuse her.

"OK, OK. Point taken," he replied irritably. There was no gain in antagonising Dickenson and getting the sisterhood in the office up in arms against him for trying to stop one of their tribe from having a bit of fun. He would have words with Donovan in the morning. "Give me Nicola Slade's number and I'll ring her now." He took down the details and hung up. He was about to call Nicola when his mobile buzzed, Wightman at the other end.

"Sir, we've got something," he said. "I'm over at the canal and we've found a pub where Yolanda went the night she was attacked. There's a bloke here who recognises her picture. He says she was in here drinking with a man and it sounds like Tom."

He paused for a moment, trying to calm himself and collect his thoughts. Things were starting to happen. He could feel it. What was that old saying about buses? You're standing there in the cold but nothing comes along. You're almost on the point of giving up and then suddenly three of the damned things appear. Life was often like that and investigations were no different. This was what he had been waiting for.

"Give me the address," he said, trying to contain his excitement. "I'll be over there right away."

The Dog and Bone was perched on the corner of a bridge over-looking the Regent's Canal, close to the stretch of water where Tartaglia had met Steele the other day. The bar was full, the air thick with smoke and sweat, loud music pumping through ceiling speakers above. The majority of the clientele seemed to be tourists, with a large, loud contingent of Australians or New Zealanders gathered close around the bar,

410

although he couldn't tell which they were from the accents. Judging by the merriment and the general look of things, they'd been in there a while and had already put away several beers.

He found Wightman perched on a stool in a corner at the far end, talking to a burly man in his mid-thirties, with a shaved head and tattoos covering every inch of what could be seen of his arms. Pint in hand, legs stretched out in front of him, he lounged against some cushions in the middle of a large velvet sofa with the air of someone who owned the place.

Tartaglia pulled up a stool from another table and sat down next to Wightman, opposite the man.

"Mr Stansfield was here the other day," Wightman said, turning to Tartaglia. "He remembers seeing Yolanda in here with a man."

"That's right," Stansfield said, taking a large gulp of bitter and wiping his mouth with the back of his hand. "They was sat right here. Where I am now. And I was standing over there where Paul and Mick are." Stansfield jerked his head towards a couple of men who looked like clones of himself, grouped around a cigarette machine, on the opposite side of the room.

"Do you remember if they came in together?" Wightman asked.

"She was here on her own for a bit then he appeared, this poncey git."

"Poncey? What do you mean?" Tartaglia asked.

"Fancied himself, didn't he? Right flash so-and-so, he was."

"Early to mid-thirties, short dark hair, medium height and build . . ." Wightman read from his notes. "Sounds like our man, all right."

"Yeah? Well he spoke real proper."

"You spoke to him?" Wightman asked, looking up surprised.

"I was just getting round to telling you that when the Inspector arrived," Stansfield said, taking a slurp of beer. "They was talking for a while, him and the young girl."

"Was the pub full?" Tartaglia asked.

"Yeah, more or less."

"If you were standing over there with your mates, how come you noticed what they were doing?"

Stansfield jabbed his thumb at the table. "This 'ere's my place, see. It's where me and me mates sit. We're working over the road and we're in most nights. When I come in and see the young lady sat here, I thinks to myself, OK, not a problem. She doesn't know. But I keeps an eye on it, see. She don't look much of a drinker to me, she'll be on her way soon, I thinks. But then this bloke turns up and they sit here having a right old chinwag, at least he's doing most of the wagging. And he keeps nipping off to the bar to buy her drinks, trying to get her pissed, know what I mean? Next minute I look over and see her hop it, out that door there." Stansfield jerked his head in the direction of one of the exits. He raised his almost non-existent eyebrows. "Can't blame her, can you, poor girl."

412

"So, she left the pub without him? On her own?"

"Yeah, picks up her jacket and bag and legs it while he's at the bar. I thought it was dead funny."

"Nobody else followed her out?"

Stansfield shook his head. "Then the plonker comes back and sits here waiting for her, twiddling his thumbs. Made me laugh again, it did. Well, she's not coming back is she? So I move over here and I sits down in her place. 'Someone's sitting there' he says, all hoity toity." Stansfield screwed up his face and mimicked the voice. "Told him he needs flamin' glasses. Nobody's sat here, are they? Takes a minute for him to work it out and he doesn't look best pleased when the penny drops and he sees she's gone and buggered off."

"Did he say anything else?"

Stansfield thought hard for a minute, draining his pint and putting down his empty glass with a loud clunk as if making a point. He cleared his throat as if something was catching in it.

"Another pint, Mr Stansfield?" Wightman said, smiling.

Stansfield nodded. "Don't mind if I do, particularly if you're buying, mate. Sure is nice to take one off the old Bill for a change."

"So, what did he say, Mr Stansfield?" Tartaglia asked, as Wightman got up to go to the bar.

Stansfield stretched his short muscular arms out wide along the back of the sofa as if he was settling in. "Well, he comes up with some cock and bull story about her being sick, or something. But it was clear as bleedin' daylight what'd happened. She don't fancy the poncey toad, does she?"

"What happened next?"

"He fucks off, he does. Out of here like greased lightning."

"Which way did he go?"

Stansfield shook his head. "Dunno. Tanya'd come over, hadn't she? She's my bird. I don't remember nothing after that." He gave Tartaglia a wide, toothy grin, showing several large gaps.

"We'll need you to make a formal statement, Mr Stansfield, and we'll also need your help putting together an e-fit of the man. It sounds like you got a very good look at him."

"No problem." The smile suddenly disappeared and Stansfield frowned. "You telling me this is the bird what was killed down by the canal a few days ago?" he said. "The one who was sat right here?"

Tartaglia nodded.

"Bleedin' hell. You think this bloke I saw did it?"

"We're at an early stage of the investigation, Mr Stansfield."

Stansfield gave him a knowing look and shook his head. "Yeah, yeah. Pull the other one. It's got bells." He gave a heavy sigh, examining a food stain on his T-shirt as if he'd only just noticed it. "The minute I clapped eyes on him, I knew he was a wrong 'un. Poor, bleedin' girl, that's what I say. Poor little thing." He met Tartaglia's eye. "I hope you string him up right and proper when you find him. Prison's too good for his sort."

"I agree," Tartaglia said, getting to his feet. Stansfield didn't know the half of it.

CHAPTER
THIRTY-THREE

"Have you lived all your life in this country? Donovan asked.

Adam Zaleski nodded. "London born and bred, although I've never felt at all English. Never really felt I belong here, or anywhere else for that matter."

They were sitting at a table in the window of a little French restaurant in Ealing, near where Adam Zaleski lived. They had eaten oysters, followed by turbot with hollandaise sauce, Zaleski choosing the same things as Donovan, something that she found strangely reassuring. It was nice to know they had the same taste in food, at least. She thought she had never had anything quite so delicious, but perhaps it was his company making everything seem gilded and amazingly heady. He was so easy to talk to, so relaxed and interesting. There was nothing that grated or felt awkward and he seemed genuinely interested in her, not like some men who only wanted to talk about themselves. Her course of hypnosis being finished, Zaleski had bought a bottle of champagne to celebrate and it tasted wonderful. And the incredible thing was, she didn't crave a cigarette at all. When someone at the table behind them lit up, she felt almost sick.

The waiter appeared at the table and they ordered dessert: sorbet made with fruit and some sort of plum brandy for Donovan, Zaleski preferring the cheese.

"Are both your parents Polish?" she asked, taking a sip of champagne once the waiter had moved away.

"My mother was, but she's dead. Died when I was very young and I was brought up by her parents. Zaleski's their name. I've never known my father. He dumped her when he found out she was pregnant."

"Oh." The word sounded stupid but she didn't know what else to say.

"She was only seventeen and they weren't married," he continued, appearing not to mind.

He spoke matter-of-factly but she wondered how he really felt inside. "Have you never wanted to get in touch with him?"

His face hardened and he shook his head, pausing momentarily before answering. "I never want to see him. Ever. From what I know, he was a right sod. I'd scrub his genes away, if only I could. Apparently I look just like him, which is ironic, given how I feel about him."

She gazed at him inquiringly, wondering if she should change the subject. But curiosity got the better of her. "You said your mother died?"

He nodded slowly, swirling his champagne around in the glass until little bubbles fizzed angrily around the edge.

"She killed herself. It's the ultimate abandonment, isn't it? I was only three, luckily too young to remember her, although I've got photographs."

"I'm sorry."

He sighed. "It's OK. I'm old enough now to feel detached, or at least have some perspective. Most of the time I try not to think about it. I mean, what's the point? What's done is done. Luckily, someone was there to look after me."

He took off his glasses, dropping them on the table, and rubbed his face with his hands. Then he looked up at her and she noticed for the first time what nice eyes he had. They were hazel, neither green nor brown but somewhere in between. He reached across and took her hand, his face creasing into a smile. "Let's talk about more cheerful things. Tell me about you. Where do you come from?"

Her hand felt so small in his and although the touch was lovely, she felt awkward and suddenly shy. "Like you, I'm a Londoner, born and bred. I was brought up in Twickenham. My parents are both teachers, although they're now retired."

"Do you have any brothers and sisters?"

"One sister, Claire. She's two years older than me. She's a solicitor for one of the big City firms."

"Are you close?"

She nodded, pulling her hand gently away on the pretext of reaching for her glass of champagne. "We're very different, very, very different but we get on most of the time. We share a house together."

"Hammersmith, you said?"

"That's right. It's Claire's house but I contribute to the mortgage."

"Does she look at all like you?"

Donovan laughed. "Not at all. Nobody would even guess we're sisters. She's tall, nearly five nine, with dark, curly hair. Takes after my father. And, as for me, well . . ." She shrugged.

"I think you're lovely," he said, looking her in the eye and taking her hand again, stroking it gently with his fingers. "Really lovely. Your skin feels so smooth and soft."

She could feel the colour rising to her cheeks but before she had time to say anything silly, the waiter appeared with her sorbet and Zaleski's cheese.

Tartaglia was on his way out of The Dog and Bone when his phone rang. He heard a woman's voice saying something faintly at the other end.

"Who's that?"

"Is that DI Mark Tartaglia?" the voice repeated, louder this time.

"Hang on a minute," he said. "Can't hear anything in here." He went outside, sheltering in the doorway from the rain, the phone cradled tightly against his ear.

Speaking quickly, in a breathy voice, the woman announced herself as Nicola Slade and he realised he had forgotten to call her back.

"I spoke to the lady at your office and she said you'd be calling me," she continued. "When you didn't, she gave me your number. I hope it's OK."

"Of course it's OK. I'm sorry. I would have got back to you sooner but I've just been interviewing someone."

"I really wouldn't have bothered you but this is important and I can't get hold of DS Donovan. You know the man I said I saw with Marion? The one she was keen on? Well, he was at Ealing Police Station. I didn't realise it was him until afterwards," she said, almost chatty, not knowing the impact of her words. "I had a dream last night about Marion and . . . well, it only hit me late this afternoon. He looks so different now, you see. He's changed his appearance and things."

"You mean the man in the line-up?"

"No. I told you it wasn't him. It was the bloke you were with, when I was standing at reception with DS Donovan. You and the man went outside together. Do you remember?"

As she spoke, he felt as though a wave of freezing air had blown over him and he shuddered. The answer had been lying in front of them all of the time. Everything clicked into place now. Horribly so, and they'd been so stupid. So bloody stupid. Marion Spear. Laura Benedetti. Ellie Best. Gemma Kramer. Yolanda Garcia. It all made sense. Perhaps there were others that they knew nothing about.

"You are absolutely sure that it's the same man, Miss Slade? It's easy to make mistakes."

"He really looks different," she added, trying to justify why she hadn't recognised the man before. "But I'm sure it's him now. I'm positive. I wouldn't have called you otherwise."

When they got outside the restaurant, Zaleski took Donovan by the hand again, looking down at her smiling. "If you're tired, I could take you home." He paused. "Otherwise, I've got some very good Polish

420

vodka in the freezer at my place, if you fancy a night-cap."

"That would be lovely," she said, with a giggle. "I don't feel in the least bit tired."

"Good. It's only about five minutes away." He kissed her lightly on the cheek and they walked hand in hand down the road.

Even the frosty night air couldn't bring her down. She felt elated, on a high. It was as if she were playing hookey, mobile switched off, pager at home, and all the cares of the job left behind for a while. She damn well deserved some fun for a change and Adam was so nice. Tartaglia would be furious if he found out, but she didn't care. He wasn't her keeper.

The route took them past the parade with Angel's bookshop. As they walked past, she glanced in through the window. The shop was in darkness, but looking up she saw lights blazing on the first floor, curtains wide open, and she saw what looked like Angel and some blonde-haired woman moving around in the room. She stopped, listening to the distant strains of opera that drifted down, wondering who the woman was and what Angel was up to.

"You OK?" Zaleski said.

"Fine," she replied, still distracted, wondering if perhaps she should give Nicola Slade another call now and see if anything had come back to her. Maybe she should tell Zaleski that she'd skip the vodka this evening. He was sure to understand and if he was interested, he'd call her again.

"Come on then," he said, pulling her gently by the hand. "We'll catch our death standing around out here."

She hesitated, not knowing what to do. Something was telling her to call Nicola Slade.

"What's the matter?" he said, his tone a little impatient. He followed her gaze to the window above. "Is that someone you know?"

She looked back at him and smiled. "No, not really . . . it's just that, well, we've got so much on at the moment, I'm a bit preoccupied. Perhaps I should be getting home."

He took both her hands in his, looking at her quite seriously, almost offended. "Are you having second thoughts?"

"Of course not." She was being stupid. Why ruin the evening with Zaleski because of the bloody case? It was late and Nicola would probably be in bed by now.

"Let's go, then," he said, taking her firmly by the arm.

With a last lingering look up at Angel's window, she allowed herself to be steered away. There was no point worrying about all of that stuff now. It could wait until the morning, when she got into work, hopefully not too late or hung-over. She'd give Nicola a bell then.

They crossed the main road, walking for a minute along the green.

"That's Pitshanger Manor," he said, as they passed a large eighteenth century house, set back from the road behind wrought iron railings and a wide drive. "It used to belong to the architect Sir John Soane. Sadly, it's now owned by the council and there's nothing worth seeing."

She nodded, the name meaning nothing to her, other than the connection with Angel's bookshop. Angel. Why couldn't she stop thinking about him? She felt suddenly tired and it occurred to her that she really ought to go home. Even if it was too late to call Nicola Slade, it might be a good idea to get some sleep. She also felt that in her state of mind, she'd be better off on her own.

She stopped walking and turned to him. "Look, Adam, would you mind very much if I went home?"

"What's troubling you?"

"Work, that's all. I'm sorry. I just can't seem to switch off."

"You're sure that's all?"

She saw the disappointment in his eyes and suddenly felt guilty for having mentioned anything. Bloody work. It was always getting in the way. "I promise. I've had a lovely evening. Thank you."

"If you want to go home, that's fine," he said. "But I haven't said anything wrong, have I?"

She smiled, hoping to reassure him. "Not at all. Really, it's just the case. I'm just a bit preoccupied, that's all."

He nodded slowly. "I understand. Your work's obviously very important to you and it must be difficult to put it aside for the evening."

Important? It was important. But she felt so silly letting it intrude like this.

"What about just a quick one?" he said, before she had time to reply. "My house really isn't far from here and then I'll call you a cab."

She hesitated, seeing the anxious look on his face, and nodded. "OK. Just one would be lovely."

He took her by the hand again and they walked along the side wall of what looked like a large garden attached to Pitshanger Manor, threading their way through a series of residential streets beyond, with rows of low-built Edwardian redbrick houses, some terraced, some semi-detached in neat, matching mirrored pairs.

The area was strangely deserted and the only person they saw was a stout, middle-aged woman, bundled up in a bulky anorak, out walking a small brown and white Jack Russell. As they passed her, the little dog ran up to Zaleski, running in circles around his feet, jumping and yapping as if it wanted to play. They were forced to stop.

"Can't you keep your dog under control?" Zaleski shouted at the woman, who had walked on, stabbing at the dog with his foot, trying to keep it at bay. "It should be on a lead."

"Sorry," the woman said, rushing back to where they were standing. She picked up the wriggling dog in her arms. "Fred's not usually like this." She sounded affronted, clearly thinking that it was Zaleski's fault. She turned on her heel and strode away, the dog, still fighting for freedom, tucked tightly under her arm.

"I hate dogs," he said, vehemently, once the woman had gone, brushing the legs of his trousers as if to remove any trace, before taking Donovan's hand again and walking on.

"That one's certainly very energetic," she said, wanting to diffuse the tension.

It was interesting how both dogs and cats could sense people who didn't like them. Donovan loved dogs, all animals in fact, and she found Zaleski's reaction a little extreme and off-putting. But there was no point in getting into an argument about it. Perhaps he hadn't been brought up with any animals.

Zaleski gave her a tight smile in reply and they walked on together in silence. Two minutes later, Zaleski stopped outside a low-built semi-detached house, that looked like all the others, and pushed open a small white wooden gate, holding it open for her. The woodwork looked as thought it could do with several licks of paint but the small strip of garden was neat and tidy, bins tucked under a shelter, a high, clipped hedge at the front, separating it from the road.

"Here we are," he said, leading her by the hand up the short path to the front door. "This is my house."

As soon as Tartaglia had hung up on Nicola Slade, he called Dickenson's mobile.

He could hear the sound of traffic as she answered.

"I need you to check a name for me," Tartaglia said.

"I'm just crossing Hammersmith Bridge. I'm on my way home."

It was late and, in her condition, he couldn't blame her. But now was not the time to be going home. "Is anyone else in the office?"

"Dave and Nick just got back. They're following up on the info you gave me. I'm sorry, I thought it was OK to go."

"Look, this is urgent. I think Tom is Adam Zaleski. Call them and get them to check if he works at the CHA in some capacity."

There was a second's silence at the other end. "Zaleski! You mean the witness? The hypnotist?"

"Of course," he said sharply, no time to explain.

"Shit! Sam's having dinner with him now."

He felt his heart miss a beat. "She's having dinner with Adam Zaleski? How the hell . . . Where?"

"I don't know. Oh my God!"

"Get onto Dave and Nick immediately. I need Zaleski's address. NOW. It's somewhere in Ealing. Should be in the file. And get a team over there with a warrant. We've got to find him before . . ." His voice trailed off as he thought about what might happen. Thank Christ he had his bike. He could be in Ealing in twenty minutes. Fifteen if he was lucky.

CHAPTER
THIRTY-FOUR

Donovan watched as Zaleski unlocked the door and followed him inside, waiting while he switched on the hall lights. The interior smelt of damp and something musty but it was pleasantly warm after the cold night air. The first thing she noticed was a large oil painting of a man, wearing a beret, in military uniform, hanging in the hallway by the door. It looked like the ones she'd seen in the Polish Club.

"That's my grandfather," he said, just behind her. "He was quite a hero in his day."

She turned around. "He doesn't look at all like you. In fact, he looks very fierce."

He smiled grimly. "He certainly was. But he's dead now, thank God. So's my grandmother. This was their house. It's where I grew up."

He took her coat and hung it up on a rack nailed high on the wall, made of dark varnished wood and what looked like some sort of small animal horns for hooks. It had a brass plaque in the middle with an inscription, which she was too far away to read.

He led her into a small sitting room at the front. "Make yourself at home. I'll be back in a minute with the vodka."

She sat down on the sofa feeling suddenly uncomfortable. Her family house in Twickenham, where she had lived all her life until going to university, was similar to Zaleski's architecturally. But the atmosphere was so completely different: noisy, chaotic and cheerful, full of animals, people coming and going, with all the resultant mess and the feel of things permanently in a state of flux. Here everything was so formal, from the hard back and curved arms of the sofa, covered in what appeared to be some sort of expensive-looking red damask, which wouldn't last a second in her home, to the faded chintz curtains with the tight pelmet and the ornate gilt mirror hanging over the mantelpiece, way too large for the small room, as if it was meant for a much bigger house. A clock ticked quietly from a mahogany card table in the corner and, in the dim light, she felt as though she had stepped back in time, into another world that wasn't entirely English. The house was like a museum, a place for show, not for use, and she couldn't picture Zaleski, either as a small boy or as a man, living there.

After a few minutes, he reappeared with a small wooden tray. A bottle of vodka, with a bright yellow label, nestled in a silver ice bucket, two shot glasses beside it, already full, the sides misted from the cold liquid inside. He put down the tray on a long, low wooden stool. The seat was covered in needlework, faint shades of blue and red the predominant colours, the design some sort of crest, possibly belonging to his family. He passed her a glass and sat down beside her, resting his arm lightly on the back of the sofa behind her. She felt suddenly excited by his closeness, wondering when, if, he would kiss her.

"*Na zdrowie*," he said, raising his glass and clinking hers. "Here's to you, Sam Donovan."

She smiled, managing to knock back half the glass, this time prepared for the burning sensation, actually beginning to enjoy it. She sipped the rest slowly, waiting for the wave of warmth that would follow.

"I know I shouldn't ask, but I was wondering how the case is going?" he said in an off-hand manner. "That man you wanted me to identify, is he the one you're after?"

He was looking at her inquiringly, waiting for her reply.

"Yes," she replied, after a second's hesitation. "Or, at least, we think so."

She knew she shouldn't have said anything but he'd never asked before and he was so nice to be with. Good-looking too. Afraid that he could read her thoughts, she tried to focus on something else. She was beginning to feel a little giddy, must try to keep a check on things, just give him the bare minimum and change the subject.

She drained the final drop of vodka and put the glass down on the tray.

"Unfortunately, we haven't got anything so far to put him at the crime scene. It's all a bit disappointing."

"I'm sorry I couldn't help," he said, shrugging. "I just didn't recognise the man, I'm afraid."

"That's fine. You can only say what you saw. It's just that . . . well, we think we can link him to two of the murders." She found herself saying it without meaning to.

"What about the latest one? I read in the papers about a murder down by one of the canals. Are they linked?"

"Yes. Yes, they are." She took a deep breath, surprised that he'd made the connection. As far as she was aware, the press hadn't yet. Stop there. Don't say anymore. Change the subject, but she couldn't think of what to say next. Her mind was feeling a little hazy.

He took the small bottle of vodka from the ice bucket. "One more for the road?"

She hesitated, then passed him her glass. "Why not?"

"You're getting a taste for it, aren't you? That's good," he laughed, topping up both glasses and passing one over to her. He clinked her glass. "Now, down in one this time."

She did as she was told, although she was suddenly beginning to feel quite drunk. As she stretched forward to put her empty glass back on the tray, she missed and knocked it over. "Sorry."

He righted the glass for her. "Don't worry about it."

For some reason it was affecting her far more than usual. Had she really had a lot to drink? She didn't think so. Vodka on top of champagne. That was it. Silly thing to do. No more vodka. Perhaps she should ask him to call a taxi now. But she felt such a fool. He'd think she was no better than a schoolgirl who was unable to hold her drink. Perhaps if she waited a minute, she'd feel better, maybe ask for some coffee or water.

430

She could feel his fingers gently stroking her shoulder.

"So, if you can't find anything, what do you do?" he said. "Do you just keep an eye on him?"

She nodded, concentrating on keeping her eyes open and the muscles of her face under control. He was studying her closely. Perhaps he had guessed she was drunk. She hoped he wouldn't think badly of her. What was strange was he'd had roughly the same amount to drink. Although he was a man. Much bigger. It was all about body mass.

"What evidence do you have on him?" he asked.

She answered automatically. "That's the problem. Well . . . we haven't got much to go on." She could hear herself slurring.

He shook his head slowly and took off his glasses, folding them carefully, and putting them down next to him on the sofa. "No, I suppose you haven't."

Gazing down at her toes, she giggled. Somehow, even though there wasn't anything funny, she couldn't help herself. "No, we've got fuck all, sweet FA."

He stared at her for a moment then said: "You lot haven't got a clue, have you?"

It wasn't just the words that penetrated, making her raise her eyes again slowly to look at him. It was the change in his voice. His tone was cold and unfamiliar and she frowned, struggling to focus. She saw a different person in front of her. A stranger. Somehow his face had transformed, morphed into something unrecognisable. What she saw frightened her.

"A clue?"

"Yeah. The answer was staring you in the face all the time and you haven't got a fucking clue."

Through the thickening fog in her mind, she realised what was happening.

"It's you . . . isn't it?" she said, barely able to get the words out. "You're Tom." She tried to get up but her arms and legs wouldn't work properly.

She felt him grip her wrists and push her down in her seat. "Save your energy. You're not going anywhere."

She knew she couldn't fight him. She felt as though she'd been anaesthetised, no control over her body, eyelids heavy as lead. Somehow she had to stay awake. She had to. He was going to kill her. Mustn't let him. Try and work something out. "How come you're not . . ."

He smiled. "Drunk or drugged, like you? You're feeling it now, aren't you? We've both had two glasses but I'm still sober. What a riddle. To be nice, I'll tell you the answer, as I can see you'd have problems working it out on your own and you won't be conscious for much longer."

His words sounded distant. Echoing. Her head lolled back heavy on his arm; she couldn't help it. The room was spinning. She wanted to be sick. "Drug . . ."

He grabbed her face with his hand and forced her to look at him, digging his fingers into her cheeks. Although she was aware of what he was doing, it felt as though it was happening to someone else.

"Yes, GHB, what a lovely little substance it is. Once in the system, particularly taken with alcohol, it takes

432

no time to work. It was in your first glass. There's some in the bottle too, for good measure. You're so far gone, you didn't notice that I didn't drink mine. Look, here it is." He held the full glass in front of her eyes, moving it slowly from side to side like a pendulum. "Can you still hear me?"

"Why?" She mouthed the word, not even sure if any sound came out. Keep awake. Try and keep awake. "Why . . ."

He pushed her face away and she slid off the sofa onto the floor, head knocking against the stool.

"Why? Why did I kill all those sad little girls?" He got up and came and stood over her. His face looked so far away, distant, staring down at her from high above. "There is no 'why'. Things just are the way they are."

It was the last thing she heard.

Tartaglia was nearly in Ealing when he felt the vibration of his phone in his inside breast pocket. He pulled over to the side of the road, looked at the caller ID and rang Dickenson straight back.

"The address is in South Ken, sir," she said, her voice high-pitched and full of alarm. "I called you before to tell you but you were probably on the road."

"South Ken?"

"Yes. Gary and the team are over there now but there's no sign of Zaleski. No sign of anyone, in fact. It looks like it's some sort of office building and everyone's gone home."

"Check the file again. Zaleski definitely lives in Ealing."

"I have, sir. But this is the address he gave."

Heart pounding, he tried to calm himself, think clearly, remember back to what Zaleski had said when he had first interviewed him. He distinctly remembered him saying he lived in Ealing, which was why he was there when Gemma Kramer had died. Think. Think. For fuck's sake try and remember. What had Zaleski been doing? Why was he there? What had he said? He was on his way home. Yes, on his way home and he was dropping his car at a garage . . . no, collecting it, that was it, when . . .

"I've got it!" he shouted. "Zaleski was collecting his car from a garage. I know we checked it out to corroborate the timing. The licence number should be on file. Run it through the system and call me back immediately with Zaleski's address."

CHAPTER
THIRTY-FIVE

Tartaglia stood outside the gate of number 89 Beckford Avenue. Upstairs the house was dark but a light was on in the ground floor front room, just visible behind the curtains. For a moment, he wondered what to do. Maybe they were still out at dinner. Maybe Sam was safely at home in bed by now. But if not . . . Should he ring the bell, see what would happen? If Sam was in there, Zaleski might do something desperate. Surprise was his only advantage, coupled with the fact that Zaleski didn't know that he knew.

The house was semi-detached with a tall gate at the side leading, he assumed, to the back garden. He tried the gate but it was locked. He took off his helmet, heavy jacket and gloves, dumping them out of sight under the hedge, then jumped, catching hold of the top of the frame of the gate and hauling himself up and over it, landing almost silently on the other side. Shadowed from the light coming from the street, the narrow sidepassage was almost black and he could barely see in front of him. He felt his way along the brick wall of the house, no lights showing through any of the side windows, and into the back garden where visibility was a little better, a general dull light reflected from the sky above. He could just make out a small stretch of lawn, flowerbeds and a paved area by the house, a few shrubs in large tubs lined up along the edge. There were no lights on except in a room at the very top of the house and there was no sound or movement coming from inside. Watching for a moment, he saw a shadow cross the top floor window, which he hoped was Zaleski, although he had no idea whether Zaleski lived there on his own or not.

Two doors gave out onto the garden, one a pair of French windows, the other half-glazed, leading out from a small side extension. He tried the French windows first but they were locked, the curtains drawn tightly against them. The other door was also locked and, pressing his face to the glass, he peered into the dim interior, just making out a table or desk with a computer, the screensaver giving off a flickering glimmer of light. Maybe someone had left a key in the lock. If not, he wasn't sure what he would do.

Looking round for something hard to use, he found a sturdy-looking trowel sticking out of the earth in one of the pots near the door. He took off his pullover and, wrapping it around the handle of the trowel to deaden any noise, he aimed the handle at the glass. It took several blows before the corner of the glass shattered with a muffled tinkle. He chipped away at the small hole with the edge of the trowel until it was big enough to put his hand through and, hand now wrapped in the pullover, reached inside, feeling for the key, praying that it would be there.

He felt its cold edge. Thank God. He turned the lock, opened the door and stepped gingerly through, over the glass, into the dark study. A door led into the hall and he opened it carefully, listening. Apart from the distant buzz of traffic several roads away, everything was silent. Light filtered in from the street outside through the stained glass panels which framed the front door. Beside it sat a plastic petrol can and a small suitcase. Was Zaleski going away somewhere? Was he even there? Was Sam? The house was so quiet.

Two doors led off the hall, one he presumed going into the room with the French windows on the garden side, the other, at the front, had a strip of light showing through the crack at the bottom. Perhaps they were in there, although he couldn't hear the sound of anyone talking. As he crept towards the door, trying to deaden the sound of his boots on the tiled floor, he heard a step behind him and felt the edge of something cold and hard pressed like a finger against the back of his neck.

"Don't turn around. This is a gun."

Tartaglia recognised Zaleski's voice instantly. A light was switched on, illuminating the hall.

"Oh, I see it's you, Inspector," Zaleski said from behind. "What are you doing breaking into my house?" He kept the gun pinned to Tartaglia's neck.

"Where's Sam? She's here, isn't she?"

"She's upstairs powdering her nose. Why, are you doing the jealous lover bit? Is she your girlfriend?" Zaleski prodded Tartaglia's neck with the nose of the gun. "I'd have thought you'd go for something a bit more raunchy."

"Sam's my friend."

"What, you'd risk your life for a friend?"

Risk his life? It struck him for the first time that that was what he was doing but he felt strangely calm. "Yes. Yes I would."

"There's no accounting for taste. I'm surprised that you care about her that much. She seems quite an ordinary little tart to me. Really nothing special."

"Is she OK?" Tartaglia said levelly, refusing to give Zaleski the satisfaction of a reaction. Was the gun real or a replica? Not worth taking a punt on it, though, given what he knew of Zaleski.

"Depends what you mean by OK. She got a bit out of control, so I had to calm her down, get her into the right state of mind. That's what it's all about, with women."

"You mean drug them so you can do what you want?"

"Stop trying to be provocative, Inspector. It doesn't suit you. Do you like guns? I'll bet you're a good shot, aren't you?" he said, when Tartaglia didn't respond. "This one's a Luger and it's got a nice history to it. My grandfather took it off a dead German in the Second World War. That's after he killed him, of course. He used to love telling me about it when I was a child. Apparently, it was quite gruesome, the killing, I mean. I don't have the stomach for blood and gore, myself. But guns give you a real sense of power, don't they?"

"I wouldn't know," Tartaglia said, firmly, wondering what the hell he was going to do, wondering also if it explained why Zaleski had thrown the girls to their

438

deaths rather than killing them outright. He hadn't wanted to get his hands dirty. He wanted to distance himself from the mess and physical foulness of death. A gun was arm's length too . . .

"Yeah, a real sense of power," Zaleski continued. "It goes like this. I'm the one with the gun, so you're going to do what I want. You're going to jump when I tell you to jump. Have you got that? Now open that door in front of you . . . push it wide open, that's right . . . now, put your hands on your head, walk in slowly, and go and sit down on the sofa. Don't try anything silly," he added, seeing Tartaglia hesitate in the doorway, as he wondered if he had time to slam it shut in Zaleski's face and barricade himself in until help arrived.

"The Luger may be an antique but it still works and I'm a bloody good shot."

Tartaglia turned the handle and walked inside, his eyes flicking around the room, looking for a means of defence or escape. But there was none. It was a peculiar place, full of horrible old-fashioned, brown furniture and knick-knacks, a strange, dusty smell hanging in the air as if the room wasn't often used or aired. As he turned round and sat down, he saw Zaleski for the first time, standing by the fireplace, gun in hand pointed straight at Tartaglia's heart.

Zaleski was wearing a dark overcoat, scarf and leather gloves. He looked as if he was on his way out. The bag by the door. The petrol. What was Zaleski going to do with the petrol, if that's what it was? He had removed his glasses and he looked different, a lot tougher and much more confident, his face hard and drawn, lines more pronounced. He was a little shorter than Tartaglia, possibly not as fast or as fit. In the normal course of events, Tartaglia wouldn't baulk at taking him on. But there was the gun. And Sam.

Where was Sam? Why had she allowed herself to be drawn in by Zaleski? Single women with too much imagination and too much time to think about things were a danger to themselves and other people. If only she'd said something. If only. But what would he have done? Reprimand her? Tell her not to see Zaleski? It wouldn't have worked. Sam had a mind of her own and would have told him to get lost. At least, if Zaleski was here, hopefully she was still alive. Maybe upstairs somewhere.

"It's a shame you've butted in and tried to spoil my plans like this." Zaleski's manner was suddenly more urgent. "Just when Sam and I were getting down to business."

"She's alive?"

"Don't waste your time worrying about her." Zaleski smacked his lips, studying Tartaglia, gun still pointed at his chest. "Now, what the fuck am I going to do with you? It's very inconvenient, you see, your turning up like this. I'm going to be late . . . late for a very important date. Miss Donovan's waiting and I don't want to disappoint her."

It was a pointless question but Tartaglia wanted to string things out, keep Zaleski there as long as possible. "You work for CHA, don't you? That's how you found them all, isn't it? You're one of their helpline volunteers." He noted the surprise in Zaleski's eyes.

440

"My, my. We have been a busy little bee. Well done for finding the connection. You're more on the ball than I thought."

"They came to you needing help and support and you killed them. Why?"

"Why does everyone want to know why? It's like nature. When you're hungry, you have to eat."

"That's shit and you know it."

"They wanted to die with me. They were begging me, gagging for it. I just helped ease things along."

"You'll be put away for life for this."

"Can't hang a bloke for being helpful. Anyway, what evidence do you have? If you bother to read the emails the girls sent me, they all wanted to die."

"Not Sam."

"Tarts like that are accidents waiting to happen. They only have themselves to blame and I'm doing her a favour."

"Marion Spear didn't want to die."

Again there was a flicker of surprise on Zaleski's face. "Christ, Inspector. I'm really impressed. I'll admit little Marion was a bit different but let's not get pedantic. She was one of those foul clingy types who won't leave a bloke alone. She made me feel claustrophobic. I had to do something."

"You killed her straight out. None of this fake suicide crap."

"Like the others she wanted to die, I can assure you. If she couldn't have me, she wanted to end it all. That's what she said. The whining cunt's better off where she is."

"You're sick."

"Enough chitchat. I haven't got time. Stay right where you are and don't move."

Zaleski walked quickly over to a small table in the corner, eyes fixed on Tartaglia, unblinking. A tray with an ice bucket stood on the table and Tartaglia watched as Zaleski took a bottle of clear liquid out of the bucket and filled a shot glass to the brim. Gun still pointed at Tartaglia, he put the glass down on a stool in front of the sofa, pushing it gently towards Tartaglia with his foot.

"Drink it," he said. "NOW," he shouted when Tartaglia didn't move.

What on earth was he to do? No doubt the drink was drugged. If only Zaleski would come a little closer, maybe he'd have a chance. But Zaleski had moved away again, standing with his back to the fireplace, his head reflected in the mirror behind. Play for time; that was the only thing left. Play for time. Hopefully, the team would be there soon.

Tartaglia leaned forward slowly and picked up the glass. It was cold and wet to the touch. As he held it up, he saw a trace of lipstick on the edge and wondered if it was Sam's.

"Fucking drink it," Zaleski shouted again. "I haven't got time to waste watching you pussy around."

Tartaglia put the glass to his lips and tasted the ice-cold liquid with the tip of his tongue. Some sort of vodka, with a slightly aromatic smell. GHB was tasteless. No point in speculating how much was in it.

442

"Now, knock it back. In one," Zaleski said. "That's how we Poles do it, you know."

Should he throw it in Zaleski's face, aim for the eyes and blind him momentarily while he lunged and took the gun? But Zaleski didn't look away, not for a second and there was nothing to distract him with. If the gun really was loaded and in working order, Tartaglia knew he wouldn't stand a chance. But if he didn't do something, if he drank the vodka and passed out, what would become of Sam? Zaleski would kill her for sure. Kill both of them. Stall. Play for time. It was the only option.

"What were the emails about, the ones to Carolyn Steele?"

"You mean the policewoman? The one on *Crimewatch*?"

"Yeah. You emailed her."

Zaleski shook his head, looking genuinely surprised. "Not me. Why would I? She's not my type."

If it wasn't Zaleski, then it had to be Kennedy, although whether he would ever live to make sure Kennedy got his come-uppance, was another matter. "Sam's not your type either. Let her go."

Zaleski laughed. "My type? That's an interesting question. I hadn't really thought about it before. But I don't actually think I have a type, you know."

"Yeah, you do. You like them weak and vulnerable, so lonely and depressed they'll do whatever you want. It's a bit like the gun. Makes you feel in control, doesn't it? More like a real man."

Zaleski's face hardened and he stabbed the air with the Luger. "Shut up about the fucking girls and drink."

"You're just a coward. A fucking, spineless, dickless wimp who . . ."

"Fucking shut up and drink." Zaleski shouted, his voice rising to a shriek.

"If you want me to drink it, you'll have to come and make me."

"Oh, tough guy, are you now? Been watching too many cop films. But we're not in the movies. This is real life and you are going to die."

Zaleski watched him for a moment, as if deciding what to do next, then kicked the stool away from in front of him.

"Put the glass down and get on your knees, hands on your head." He pointed at the floor in front of him. Hands on head, kneeling. Execution style. Tartaglia realised he had nothing left to lose.

"GET DOWN ON THE FLOOR," Zaleski screamed.

Now. Now was the moment. Head bowed, eyes locked on Zaleski's legs, he sighed and slowly made as if to kneel down. Then he lunged, hurling himself in mid-air across the small room. Zaleski fell back, crashing hard against something behind and the gun went off. Tartaglia felt a sharp pain on the side of his head and everything went black.

CHAPTER
THIRTY-SIX

"Well, you two've certainly been having a lively time without me," Clarke said light-heartedly from his horizontal position in the hospital bed.

"Yeah, life was getting dull without you so we thought we'd liven things up a bit," Tartaglia replied.

It was Sunday morning, two weeks later, and Tartaglia and Donovan had dropped in to see Clarke on their way to Nicoletta's for lunch. He was looking a lot better than the last time Tartaglia had seen him, over two weeks before. The colour had come back to his face and he seemed to have more energy and interest in life, even though he was still barely able to move his head. Tartaglia had borrowed two rickety chairs from another ward and he and Donovan sat by Clarke's bedside, Tartaglia recounting everything that had happened, Donovan listening quietly, head bowed, barely adding anything to the flow.

"It's nice you can both make light of it," Donovan said, sharply. "Particularly you, Mark. I'm surprised at you."

"Sorry," Tartaglia said, reaching over and patting her hand gently. He could kick himself for being so insensitive. She gave him a tight, grudging smile and stared back at the floor, her fingers tightly clenched in her lap.

Make light of what had happened? What else could they do? It had been a complete balls-up from start to finish. He . . . they . . . were both lucky to be alive. And Zaleski had got away, no trace anywhere. When the team arrived at Zaleski's house in Ealing, they found the house on fire, filled with smoke and petrol fumes, flames licking the front door. If they had got there even fifteen minutes later, it would have been too late for Tartaglia and Donovan.

Discovering Tartaglia's motorbike parked outside and his jacket and helmet by the hedge in the front garden, Gary Jones had insisted on going in, refusing to wait for the fire brigade to come. He and Nick Minderedes had kicked in the front door, jackets wrapped around their faces, and had found Tartaglia and Donovan lying together side by side on the floor in the front living room, seemingly lifeless.

Still comatose, Tartaglia and Donovan had been taken to hospital. Apart from smoke inhalation and a deep gash to the side of Tartaglia's head, which had been caused by the ricochet of the bullet when Zaleski's gun had gone off, there was no serious, lasting physical damage to either of them. Although, when Donovan came round six hours later, she complained of the worst hangover of her life. They were both kept in for a couple of days for observation and then released.

But that wasn't the end of it. He found himself replaying in his mind over and over again what had happened, picturing Zaleski standing there, smiling, gun pointed at his chest, remembering Zaleski's words so clearly. "It's like nature. If you're hungry, you have to eat." It was probably the best explanation they would ever get, if they needed one. If only the bullet hadn't grazed his head, he would have had Zaleski, no question about it. He would have overpowered him, smashed his face in and held him there until help came. But there was no point in torturing himself about what might have been. Things hadn't happened that way. If nothing else, attacking Zaleski had bought them a little time and saved his and Donovan's life. It was probably the best rugby tackle he'd ever made, although that was small consolation for the fact that Zaleski had got away.

For Donovan, too, the nightmare was still going on. It was as though a dark cloud had enveloped her, letting in no light or air. She had turned down all offers of professional counselling for the moment and seemed to have retreated inside herself, uncharacteristically subdued. Under pressure from Claire and her colleagues, she had taken a week off work but had insisted on coming back after only three days, even though everybody could see she wasn't ready. But it was worse being at home, she said, particularly when there was nothing physically wrong with her. In a quiet moment she had confided in Tartaglia how she dreaded being on her own, dreaded going to sleep, fearful of the dreams that she knew would come. Although it was painful watching her go through the bare motions of life, coming to work, going home, lost in her own world, he understood why she preferred to keep going. Illogically, she blamed herself for everything that had

447

happened, even for Zaleski's getting away, and nothing that he, or anyone else, could say made it any better. All he could do was to try and keep her occupied, keep her mind off things and hope that, in time, she would heal.

At least the idea of seeing Clarke had brought some light to her face. Nor did she mind coming along with Tartaglia to Nicoletta's, as protection from whatever Machiavellian match-making scheme Nicoletta had up her sleeve. The idea actually seemed to amuse her and she seemed curious to meet Nicoletta. For the first time since the night at Zaleski's, she seemed to have made an effort with her appearance, putting on some make-up, dressed in a tight black polo-neck, short skirt, feet encased in impossibly high, purple suede wedge shoes that were held on by what appeared to be little more than a couple of straps. He'd never seen her in a skirt before and realised she had good legs. He wanted to tell her how nice she looked but something so trivial and superficial was probably the last thing she needed to hear.

"So, there's no trace of Zaleski," Clarke said with a grunt.

"No," Tartaglia replied. "His name was on the passenger list of an Air France flight to Paris that night but he could be anywhere by now." He glanced over at Donovan. She was still staring fixedly at the floor, mind far away.

"Once the fire was put out, we searched the house in Ealing, as well as another small flat which we discovered he was renting nearby," he continued. "We also searched his office in South Ken. But we found nothing. Whatever computer he used to send the emails was gone and there were no trophies, no locks of hair or rings or anything to directly link him to any of the girls' murders, other than the fact that he did voluntary part-time work as a counsellor for CHA. Although it's clearly how he came across them, we've been through the girls' phone records again and there's no direct evidence that any of the girls called or even spoke to him there. We assume they must have used a public phone, or someone else's phone, to call. Kelly Goodhart is the only one who we know called the helpline and as she used her office line, it took us a while to trace."

"So, you've got nothing on him?" Clarke said, sighing heavily.

"We're just scratching the tip of the iceberg. There are probably other girls we don't know about and I suspect he probably killed his grandparents too. But there's no proof. I'm afraid that attempted murder of two police officers is the best we can do."

Before Clarke could say anything else, a well-built, middle-aged nurse bustled into the room and came over to the bed.

"Won't be a minute, will we, Mr Clarke?" she said, briskly drawing the curtains around Clarke, without any further explanation. She had a thick Irish brogue and something about her manner and general physique, as well as the unforgiving glint in her eyes, instantly reminded Tartaglia of a nun who had once taught him his catechism, rapping his knuckles with a ruler every time he made a mistake.

"Time for my morning ablutions," Clarke groaned from behind the screen of green. "It's the high spot of my day."

Donovan excused herself to find the ladies and Tartaglia waited patiently by the side of Clarke's bed, listening to all sorts of strange rustling and slapping sounds, accompanied by further groans and sighs from Clarke.

"Have you made your peace with your new DCI?" Clarke asked, after a few moments.

"Sort of," Tartaglia replied, thinking back to the previous Friday when Cornish had paid a flying visit to Barnes and announced to the assembled team that Steele would be taking over permanently from Clarke. It came as no surprise to anybody but it was clear from the hushed silence that greeted the announcement that few were pleased. "Thinking of what you said, I took her some flowers when I heard the news. I thought it might help build a bridge or two."

"There you go, you're learning, mate. They love flowers."

"She had the decency to thank me for them and she didn't gloat. I don't know what I was expecting but at least she was polite. I said I hoped we could put everything behind us and she said she did, too, in that clipped tone of voice she uses when she's not interested and wants to hurry you along."

"So, that's that, then. Everything in the garden's rosy."

"Funny you should mention roses. When I went into her office later to talk to her about something else, they were stuffed in the bin, still in their wrapping. Cost me a fortune, they did."

Clarke gave a wheezing laugh from behind the curtain. "There's bloody women for you. Ungrateful cows, the lot of them. The nicer you are, the worse they behave. At least you made the effort."

"I guess she's still upset about the emails and everything that happened with Kennedy. Even though she wouldn't press charges for the peeping, he's looking at a jail sentence for sending the hoax emails."

"She's a strange one."

"Yeah, she knew I'd seen what she'd done with the flowers but she said nothing. When I went into her office the next morning, there were the flowers sitting in a vase on her desk as if nothing had happened."

"You see? I told you Carolyn's got a sensitive side to her."

"Possibly," Tartaglia said, nodding slowly. He hadn't realised quite how badly everything had affected her, how personally she took it. He was never very good at working out what went on in women's minds and he found Steele's impenetrable. Not for the first time he wondered if maybe he had misunderstood her all along and that maybe he was more than half to blame for all the problems that had gone on between them. "I think the cleaners took pity on my poor roses and fished them out and Steele hadn't the guts to throw them away again."

"No, Mark. My money's on Carolyn having second thoughts. Like all women, she's just bloody complicated and tricky and she knows how to yank your chain.

Ouch," he shouted suddenly. "That hurts. Can't you be more bleeding careful, Nurse Mary?"

Outside, it was a dazzling winter day, the sky a piercing blue with barely a cloud, the air cold, a slight breeze ruffling the bare branches of the trees. Tartaglia got out of Donovan's car along the street from Nicoletta's house in Islington and stood on the pavement waiting for her, warming his face in the weak sunshine. She was busy scrabbling around in the back of the car trying to pick up the contents of her handbag, which had fallen off the seat onto the floor when she took a corner too fast.

His phone rang. Thinking it might be Nicoletta, wondering where they were, he took it out of his pocket and saw from the caller ID that it was Fiona Blake. He let it ring, waiting for voice-mail to pick up. Donovan was now busy checking her face in the mirror, applying some lipstick or something. Wary, wondering what Blake wanted, he dialled 121 and listened to her message.

"Mark, it's Fiona. I probably shouldn't call. Just wanted you to know I've broken up with Murray." The tone was hesitant, voice soft. After a long pause she added: "Maybe we could meet for a drink. Give me a call. If you want to, that is. I hope you do."

The last time he'd seen her or spoken to her was in the forensic tent beside the canal, standing beside Yolanda's body. Assuming that it really was all over between them, he had come round to thinking that it was probably better that way. She was no good for him, not what he needed, whatever that was. But knowing it didn't make it any better. Hearing her message reawakened the longing and, not for the first time, he felt powerless to stop himself doing what he knew he shouldn't. Inevitably he would call her.

For the moment, he switched off his phone and turned to Donovan, who was climbing out of the car, bag in hand. She locked the doors and he walked her to the small wrought iron gate of Nicoletta's house.

"I apologise in advance for the mess," he said, holding the gate open.

"What on earth for?"

"You'll see. Carlo and Anna are three and five and the house is usually in chaos. Nicoletta doesn't seem to care and my brother-in-law, John, just turns a blind eye. Anything for the sake of peace, as far as he's concerned."

"You know me," she said quietly. "I'm used to a bit of chaos on the home front."

"Oh yes, I was forgetting. But you won't have seen anything like this. Just watch where you sit. There's bound to be something sticky or sharp on the seat."

Just before he pressed the bell, she touched his arm lightly, and he turned to her.

"You know, you're asking a lot," she said.

"Look, we don't have to go, if you don't want to. I can easily tell Nicoletta that you feel ill or something. After everything that's happened, she'll understand."

She shook her head, her expression serious. "I didn't mean that. I'm happy to come with you to the lunch. It's good to keep my mind off things and it's kind of you to ask me. It's just . . . well . . . I've never had to *play* at being somebody's girlfriend before."

He looked at her and smiled. "Thanks. I appreciate the effort. But then it's not everyone who gets to save your life. I must be special to you." There he was making light of things again but it was what came naturally.

She shrugged, as if none of it mattered and he looped an arm around her, pulling her into him and giving her shoulder an affectionate squeeze. "I'm very fond of you, Sam. I hope you know that."

She looked up at him and smiled back for the first time in a while. "Yes, I do and it means a lot."

"Thought I'd lost you there for a moment."

"You very nearly did."

He bent down and kissed the top of her head. "Are you ready? Are you sure you're OK with this?" She nodded and he took her by the hand. "Right, let's go."

CHAPTER
THIRTY-SEVEN

Adam Zaleski climbed out of the small plane onto the tarmac and was greeted by a wave of searing heat and humidity. Even through his dark glasses, the sky was an electric blue, not a cloud to be seen. Bag in hand, he waved goodbye to the pilot and followed behind the two other passengers towards the airport buildings at the end of the short, dusty runway. They were no better than a collection of shabby, prefabricated huts, a herd of strange-looking, scrawny cattle plucking at the scrub in front, everything reassuringly far removed from the Western world. Even the air smelt different. He felt like skipping for joy, jumping up and down for the sheer fucking fun of it. He was free. Totally free. He had got away with everything.

He had picked up an English paper along the way and read about how Donovan and Tartaglia had been rescued in the nick of time. It was the only thing that grated and it made him angry just to think about it. He should have poured the petrol over their fucking bodies. But no point in crying over spilt milk. He was long gone and the photograph of him, printed in the paper, was a dud. Nobody would recognise him as he was now, tanned, with short, dyed blonde hair and a light beard. If anything, he looked a bit like David Beckham, although his eyes were the wrong colour. Anyway, he was now well out of reach of English newspapers.

Sam Donovan's small face swam into his thoughts again, all lipsticked, rouged and perfumed, ready for death and cradled in his arms as he carried her back downstairs before dumping her beside the other policeman. He had dressed her in one of his grandmother's favourite silk numbers but she was such a scrawny little thing, it kept gaping open and he'd had to tie the belt around her twice to make her decent. Sam. The dirty stain on an otherwise glorious chapter. He thought of her as she was before, sitting on the sofa beside him, eyes half closed, mumbling, struggling to keep her mind together, failing dismally. "Why?" she had asked. Why? Why? Why? The question still hung in the air, nagging at him, screaming at him just like his fucking grandmother. Even though he hadn't actually seen *her* for a while, her voice was still there, whining and wailing in his ear like a fucking banshee. He'd thought about it a lot since, tried to come up with an answer to silence the witch once and for all, make the old whore go back to her grave along with all the rest of them. Why does anybody do anything? Why? Because they want to. That's why, stupid cow, stupid fucking bitch. *Because they can.* It's that fucking simple.

Little Sam. The one who had wriggled away. The only one. He didn't care about the other stupid wanker of a policeman. He was nothing. But Sam mattered, she mattered all right and the thought was eating away at him until he had no peace. He'd been greedy to go for her, plain greedy and he deserved a ticking off, a firm, hard rap over the knuckles. He should have called it quits after Yolanda. But along came the little whore, gagging for it, offering herself to him on a plate, poor fucking, pathetic tart. It would have been churlish to refuse, although it had cost him dear. At least they had nothing on him to link him to any of the others. No forensic trail. Sweet fuck all, in fact. Still, it was a pity she had lived to tell the tale. She was unfinished business. He couldn't rid himself of her, her face, her voice, her smell. That awful smell of gardenias from his grandmother's old scent bottle. Sam was taunting him, laughing at him. The one that got away. But not for long. As he crossed the short stretch of tarmac, he promised himself that he'd find her again. One day soon. Then he'd make the little bitch rue the day she first tasted Polish vodka.

Also available in ISIS Large Print:

Dead Cold

Louise Penny

Winter in Three Pines, and the sleepy village is carpeted in snow. While children play on the ice, sensible folk curl up indoors. It's a time of peace and goodwill — until a scream pierces the biting air. There's been a murder.

The local police are baffled. A spectator at the annual Boxing Day curling match has somehow been fatally electrocuted. Despite the large crowd, there are no witnesses and — apparently — no clues.

Called in to head the investigation, Chief Inspector Armand Gamache unravels the dead woman's past and discovers a history of secrets and enemies. But Gamache has enemies of his own. Aware of being frozen out of decision-making at the highest level of the Sûreté du Quebec, Gamache finds there are few he can trust. As a bitter wind blows into Three Pines, something even more chilling is sneaking up behind him . . .

ISBN 978-0-7531-7780-8 (hb)
ISBN 978-0-7531-7781-5 (pb)

The Endings Man

Frederic Lindsay

"Why is it," Barclay Curle grumbles to his agent Jonah, "that all the regional Edinburgh detectives have monosyllabic first names like Jack and Bob?"

Then Curle publishes his newest book — about an Edinburgh detective called Doug — which incites a letter from an anonymous admirer accusing him of stealing the murders she has committed.

Fact and fiction become increasingly inseparable when a woman discovered dead in a Newtown flat is found to have been murdered by the method favoured by the serial killer in Curle's novel. For Detective Inspector Meldrum — first name Jim — Curle seems the most obvious suspect.

Faced with a second murder and a darkening cloud of suspicion, Curle decides the time has come to take action. After all, he asks himself, who has more experience of solving murder mysteries than a crime novelist?

ISBN 978-0-7531-7800-3 (hb)
ISBN 978-0-7531-7801-0 (pb)

The Wrong Kind of Blood

Declan Hughes

Ed Loy hasn't been back to Dublin for 20 years. Now is mother is dead and he has returned home to bury her. He soon realises that the world waiting for him is very different from the one he left behind all those years ago.

An old classmate, Linda Dawson, pleads with him to find her missing husband, Peter. She doesn't want the police involved. As if a worried wife with a seductive persona weren't enough to keep Loy occupied, his childhood pal turned small-time criminal, Tommy Owens, shows up on Loy's doorstep with a hard-luck story and a recently fired gun.

When Loy finds an old photograph of his long missing father on Peter Dawson's boat, and a corpse is discovered in the foundations of the local town hall, things begin to get personal. Suddenly, in this place where he grew up, he finds himself thrown into a world of organised crime, long hidden secrets, corruption, violence and murder.

ISBN 978-0-7531-7664-1 (hb)
ISBN 978-0-7531-7665-8 (pb)

The Chemistry of Death

Simon Beckett

A human body starts to decompose four minutes after death. The body, once the encapsulation of life, now undergoes its final metamorphosis. It begins to digest itself. Cells dissolve from the inside out. Tissue turns to liquid, then to gas. No longer animate, the body becomes an immoveable feast for other organisms.

Young Neil and Sam learn this disturbing information first hand when they come across a maggot trail on the edge of Farnley Wood. They might have anticipated the discovery of a dead animal — but not the naked, unrecognisable body of Sally Palmer.

And Dr David Hunter never anticipated being revisited by his troubled past. When he escaped to the village of Manham, Norfolk he thought he'd closed that chapter of his life forever. Instead he finds himself assisting the police in an investigation that will shatter the tranquillity of the insular community forever.

ISBN 978-0-7531-7602-3 (hb)
ISBN 978-0-7531-7603-0 (pb)

Now You See Me

Margaret Murphy

When Megan Ward goes missing, suspicion falls on the stalker seen outside her house. The police would love it to be so simple, but the closer they look the more mysterious Megan herself becomes. They find no photos, no passport, no family or friends from an earlier life, only the corrupted computer files in Megan's strangely impersonal room.

Meanwhile Patrick Doran, owner of Safe Hands Security, is living his own nightmare. A hacker has breached his computer network, where he thought he had safely buried his past.

Then Megan's landlady is murdered — and the shadowy Megan re-emerges. The woman who doesn't exist becomes very real, very elusive and very dangerous . . .

ISBN 978-0-7531-7561-3 (hb)
ISBN 978-0-7531-7562-0 (pb)

ISIS publish a wide range of books in large print, from fiction to biography. Any suggestions for books you would like to see in large print or audio are always welcome. Please send to the Editorial Department at:

ISIS Publishing Limited
7 Centremead
Osney Mead
Oxford OX2 0ES

A full list of titles is available free of charge from:

Ulverscroft Large Print Books Limited

(UK)
The Green
Bradgate Road, Anstey
Leicester LE7 7FU
Tel: (0116) 236 4325

(Australia)
P.O. Box 314
St Leonards
NSW 1590
Tel: (02) 9436 2622

(USA)
P.O. Box 1230
West Seneca
N.Y. 14224-1230
Tel: (716) 674 4270

(Canada)
P.O. Box 80038
Burlington
Ontario L7L 6B1
Tel: (905) 637 8734

(New Zealand)
P.O. Box 456
Feilding
Tel: (06) 323 6828

Details of ISIS complete and unabridged audio books are also available from these offices. Alternatively, contact your local library for details of their collection of ISIS large print and unabridged audio books.